Blown Red

Susan Philpott

Published by Simon & Schuster Canada
New York London Toronto Sydney New Delhi

Simon & Schuster Canada
A Division of Simon & Schuster, Inc.
166 King Street East, Suite 300
Toronto, Ontario M5A 1J3

This book is a work of fiction. Any references to historical events, real people, or real places are used fictitiously. Other names, characters, places, and events are products of the author's imagination, and any resemblance to actual events or places or persons, living or dead, is entirely coincidental.

This Simon & Schuster Canada edition January 2015

SIMON & SCHUSTER CANADA and colophon are registered trademarks of Simon & Schuster, Inc.

For information about special discounts for bulk purchases, please contact Simon & Schuster Special Sales at 1-800-268-3216 or CustomerService@simonandschuster.ca.

Interior design by Aline C. Pace
Jacket design by TK
Jacket art by TK

Manufactured in the United States of America

10 9 8 7 6 5 4 3 2 1

ISBN 978-1-4767-6529-7
ISBN 978-1-4767-6530-3 (ebook)

For Steve

In the United States when a train disobeys a stop signal, it is sometimes called a "blown red."

The Night Before

Elena gaped at the body, the percussive pop of displaced cervical vertebrae echoing in her ears. The man, who moments before had held her at gunpoint, lay in a heap, a marionette with its strings cut. His head, twisted at an unnatural angle, rested on its right cheek, his familiar blue eyes cloudy, as though an unseen hand had drizzled thick cream into the corneas.

With a flatulent eruption the corpse released the contents of its bowel and bladder. Gasping, Elena shot to her feet, the effluvial stench like a vial of ammonia under her nose.

She gave her head a rough shake, and as her brain rebooted, she became aware of the incongruent sound of rat-a-tat chatter. Swivelling her head in the direction of the voice, she shrank back when she saw the killer lounging on her battered leather couch, one leg crossed over the other, looking more like a genial grandfather than a seventy-year-old who had just snapped a man's neck. He was speaking into a cellphone in what she now recognized as rapid-fire Cantonese.

Registering Elena's shocked gaze, the killer concluded his conversation, then slipped the cellphone back into his pocket. With one eye on her, he plucked the dead man's trench coat from the floor and laid it over the still form like a tweed shroud. He stepped toward her.

She skittered backwards.

The killer held his hands out, palms up, murmuring soft words. "Everything will be okay, honey. You're safe now. Everything is fine. Try to take some deep breaths."

Elena stared at him, uncomprehending, even though he had switched back to English.

The killer inhaled a lungful of air in an exaggerated fashion, his cheeks puffed out like a blowfish. When he blew out, Elena remembered her father pressing a seashell to her ear, the sound of the ocean roaring in her head.

"What?" Elena tested out her voice. Her lips felt rubbery, as though she'd just endured a root canal.

"Don't try to talk. Just breathe." The killer repeated his comical chest expansions and Elena felt a giggle form deep in the pit of her stomach. The ripple grew, becoming a rumble, then a shaking, then a visceral earthquake. She slapped a hand over her face but it was no match for the volcanic laughter that erupted from her mouth.

Turning her back on the killer, she bent at the waist, allowing the howls to sweep through her body until her eyes streamed with tears and her rib muscles threatened to tear. When at last the mirthless laughter ceased, she allowed the killer to take her by the hand and guide her to the couch.

2

Sinking into the soft leather, she clasped her knees to her chest, folding her body into a protective ball. With the grotesque figure stiffening a few feet away, she focused her attention on the killer as he stepped into the kitchen.

Realizing that he was clad only in a set of cotton pyjamas, she felt tears prick behind her eyes, and as she watched him stand on tiptoe, searching her shelves for the special tea he knew she loved, she felt her heart flip inside her chest.

The piercing whistle of the teakettle announced the entrance of the man's wife. Without bothering to glance at the dead man on the floor, Mrs. Zhang hurried across the room, the soles of her leather slippers sliding across the linoleum like skates over ice, her blue silk robe swirling around her ankles. Strands of thinning black hair, streaked with grey and stiff with sleep, clung to the side of her cheek. Not usually given to displays of emotion, Mrs. Zhang wrapped her arms around Elena in a fierce embrace.

Elena pressed her face into the woman's narrow chest.

"You okay now?" the woman asked, a few minutes later, as she gently patted Elena's cheek with bony fingers.

Elena forced a weak smile and another when Mr. Zhang placed a mug of sweet tea into her shaking hands.

"What happened?" said the woman, her eyes darting over to the body.

Elena glanced at the broken remains of the framed photograph the intruder had been examining just before he died. Staring at the smiling faces of her mother and father, frozen in time behind the fractured glass, she shook her head. She had no answer.

Chapter

1

Not seeing the warning sign until it was too late, Signy Shepherd slammed on the brakes, her battered Saturn fishtailing through freshly laid gravel. The car jolted over the rusting train tracks with a bone-rattling crunch before sliding to a halt. Searing dust billowed in through the open windows. Ahead, a bulldozed mound of rocks marked the end of the road.

With a flick of her wrist she turned off the ignition and climbed out, the high-pitched whine of cicadas piercing the sudden silence. The oily reek of creosote assailed her nostrils, making her stomach flip. What genius had decided to drop a rail line in the middle of nowhere? And where the hell was the damn house?

"This is your fault," she said, slapping her hand on the trunk of the car. She'd purchased the vehicle well past its prime, charmed by its chili-pepper red exterior. "Why do you always take me places I shouldn't go?" As usual, the weary car, having faded over the years to a stale paprika, refused to accept the blame.

Strands of long blond hair lashed the spray of freckles that dusted her sunburned nose. Turning into the hot wind, she braided her unruly mane into a loose plait, fastening it with an elastic tie she'd slipped onto her wrist that morning.

Shading her eyes, she surveyed her surroundings. Seeing nothing but parched fields in all directions, she hummed a few bars of the singsong mantra that sometimes helped her focus.

Oh dear, what can the matter be?
Oh dear, what can the matter be?
Oh dear—

Perched in the branches of a dead cedar, a murder of crows mocked her with raucous cackles. Whirling to glare at them, she spotted a set of ruts that led north before disappearing over a small knoll in the distance.

Seconds later she was steering the car up the faint track. Cresting the hill, she could see the house in the distance, a tired-looking bungalow plunked down in the middle of a sea of weeds, its neglected wood siding cracked and rotting.

Pulling to a stop in front of the house, she considered her situation. When a new client requested a home visit, there were several cautionary procedures to follow. Signy mentally checked off all the protocols she had broken: *Always conduct a risk assessment before going out on a home visit*—ignored. *If the situation is of moderate or high risk, never go alone*—overlooked. *No situation is so urgent as to compromise staff safety*—discounted.

What could she do? She'd been alone in the office when the call had come in on the help line, everyone but she had been invited to some birthday lunch, or whatever. She could have waited around for someone to show up, but by then it might have been too late.

Glancing up at the sketchy house, she took a deep breath and hoped her impulsiveness didn't come back to bite her in the ass, again. She kind of liked this job.

She picked her way over a minefield of broken patio stones that led to the house. Sharp weeds stabbed at her sandal-clad feet, and her short, yellow sundress offered little protection from the brambles that lined the path.

Her cellphone rang. Shit. She checked the number. *Zef.* Her mouth twisted downward. Things were going well. It was time she grew up and listened to her head for a change instead of her damn hormones. Zef was the last thing she needed. She stabbed the off button.

She climbed a set of punky wooden steps up to the porch. Before she had a chance to knock, the door swung open and a young woman hauled her inside.

"I thought you was gonna get here sooner," said the woman.

Signy shrugged. "You weren't kidding when you said this place was hard to find."

"It's a fucking nightmare," said the woman, her voice high-pitched and shaky. She sounded more like a ten-year-old girl than a young woman. Five feet tall and rail thin, she wore mousy brown hair in two stringy pigtails. She had on a pair of short shorts and a tight T-shirt festooned with small red fruits and the logo *Cherry Juice Is Sweeter!* Under one eye the fading remnant of a black eye stained the delicate flesh a jaundiced yellow.

The woman plucked at Signy's arm, dragging her down a dark hallway and into a cramped living room. The acrid bite of nicotine seared Signy's nostrils and she made an effort not to cover her nose with her fingers.

The only adornment on the washed-out grey walls was a calendar that swung on a push-pin, the well-endowed blonde draped across the hood of a red Mustang convertible sporting a crudely drawn moustache.

In one corner, a soft leather La-Z-Boy chair sat facing a gleaming fifty-two-inch flat-screen television, a heavy glass ashtray overflowing with butts perched on one arm. The only other furniture was an old school-bus seat, foam bursting from several jagged tears.

The woman motioned Signy to the La-Z-Boy, then walked over to the front window and peered outside, chewing on a fingernail. Signy could feel the tiny woman vibrating like a bumblebee trapped inside a glass jar. She had a sinking feeling that this visit was not going to be run-of-the-mill—not by a long shot.

"Did you see anyone else coming this way?"

Signy shook her head. "When you called the help line, you hung up before I could get your name."

"Thank God. When he goes on a booze run, he's almost always gone all afternoon."

Signy leaned forward. "Tell me how I can help."

"Jenny Dalton."

"Excuse me?"

"Jenny Dalton. That's my name."

Signy smiled. "Jenny, how can I help?"

"It's my husband. Daryl. He's mean and he's crazy. Me and the kids haven't been out of this hellhole since he moved us here three months ago and that was bad enough." Wrapping stick-like arms around her chest, she continued, "But now he's starting to freak out on the girls."

Signy frowned. "Like what?"

"Like, Halo, she's the youngest. She's only two. So, last week she crawled up onto his 'Don't Touch My Fucking La-Z-Boy' and fell asleep. It was my fault. I didn't notice. Jesus Christ, he got so mad I thought he was going to take her arm right outta the socket."

Taking a deep breath, Signy uncurled her fingers, allowing her hands to rest gently on her thighs. She was aching to smash something. Or someone.

"It's Angel he really goes after. He wants her out of the way and quiet when he's home. I try to make her shut up, but how do you keep a four-year-old quiet, twenty-four fucking seven?"

Signy attempted to smother the heat flaring in her chest by mentally running through a list of practical follow-up calls—police, Children's Aid Society, doctor?

Jenny's eyes shot to the window.

"What about you?" Signy asked. Jenny glanced at her, and Signy pointed a finger at the fading bruise under her eye.

Jenny shrugged.

"Have you called the police?"

"Not a fucking chance. Daryl's dad is a cop. I call those bastards and it's game over."

9

"Is he on the Linden Valley force?" Signy asked.

Jenny nodded. "His name is Richard Dalton but everyone calls him Big Dick." She flashed a humourless smile. "I'm surprised you haven't heard of him. Are you new in town?"

Signy nodded and made a mental note to find out more about Officer Richard Dalton once she had his daughter-in-law and grandchildren safely stowed.

Jenny shivered. "Be real careful around that asshole. If anyone can out-crazy Daryl it's his old man." Tears stood out in her eyes. "He's the one bought this dump for me and Daryl." Jenny swallowed heavily. "He comes out here sometimes when Daryl's not around."

Signy watched Jenny's eyes slide away and down to the floor. Was something going on with the father-in-law?

"I don't know how I ever let this happen. I shoulda gotten me and the girls outta here long ago. I suck as a mother." Jenny lifted up her shirt, using it to wipe at her nose. "Jesus Christ, can we please just get the hell outta here? Can you take me and the girls to that shelter?"

Standing, Signy said, "Let's go."

"Girls!" hollered Jenny. She grabbed a plastic grocery bag sitting on a counter in the small galley kitchen, opened a cupboard, and began stuffing the bag with boxes of cookies, cans of soup, and other small items.

"Never mind, we've got all that," said Signy. "Just make sure you have identification for everyone. So long as we have ID, we'll be able to get you everything you need."

Jenny smacked her forehead with her hand, then tossed the half-full bag into the sink, where it landed with a clatter.

"Birth certificates would be best," said Signy, placing a soft hand on the young woman's quivering arm.

Jenny nodded and hustled over to a brown wooden door. Yanking it open, she said, "Come on, girls, we're going for a drive with this nice lady," before disappearing inside.

Signy could hear Jenny opening and closing drawers as two small girls crept out from the bedroom. In the lead the oldest, dressed in faded blue overalls, glared at her. Signy recognized the look. Many of her foster brothers and sisters had arrived at the Shepherds' front door, that same defiant expression on their faces.

Angel planted herself protectively in front of her sister, small hands balled into fists. Dropping to one knee, Signy addressed the little fighter eye to eye. "Angel, my name is Signy. Would you like to come and stay at a big house in town? We have fun toys and other kids to play with."

Angel eyed her, speculatively. "You gots Barbies?"

"Yup, lots of Barbies. And we've got colouring books and building blocks and videos. We even have a model train with tracks that run all over the house. You can watch the train go through tunnels and up hills. It's really cool."

"Like Thomas the Tank Engine?"

"Yup, just like Thomas." Signy smiled. "So, what do you say? You want to come with me?"

Angel examined her fingernails, eyebrows furrowed. "Only if Halo gets to come too." She turned and clutched the hand of her younger sister, pulling her forward.

Clad only in a soggy diaper, the younger child toddled on legs that lacked the usual chubbiness Signy associated with two-year-olds. With tangled masses of baby blond hair framing her thin face, Halo peered up at Signy through huge blue eyes devoid of emotion. Mesmerized, Signy had the uncanny sensation she had fallen through time and was standing in front of a mirror.

Jenny ran from the bedroom, her wallet and two birth certificates clutched in one hand, barely pausing to scoop Halo into her arms as she hurried toward the front door. Leaning down, Signy offered Angel her hand. Without further hesitation the little girl allowed Signy to walk her toward the front door.

As she hustled the little family toward the door, Signy glanced one last time through the front window. She felt her heart miss a beat as she caught sight of an ominous cloud of dust trailing an approaching vehicle.

"What kind of a truck does your husband drive?"

"A black Dodge Ram." Jenny turned to face Signy, clutching Halo closer to her chest. "How'd you know he drives a truck?"

"Damn," said Signy, letting go of Angel's hand.

Daryl Dalton was less than one minute away.

Chapter

2

Elena Morozov sat on the edge of a bed in a windowless room. Beside her, an untouched grilled cheese sandwich congealed on a paper plate. At her feet, a small plastic suitcase lay on its side.

The last time she'd used it, she'd been on an overnight to Vancouver Island. She'd taken the ferry over and done some sightseeing in Victoria. The gardens had been breathtaking and the boat trip spectacular. It seemed like a lifetime ago.

Picking up the suitcase, she snapped open the two metal latches. She couldn't remember what she'd thrown inside. It had been such a blur: old Mr. Zhang; the piercing whistle of the teakettle; Mrs. Zhang shouting at her to hurry; the dead man crumpled on the floor. She shuddered.

Digging through a jumble of mismatched clothing, she found the picture of her father and mother she'd retrieved from the shattered frame. She tucked the photo into a side pocket, then resumed her inspection.

Shaking her head, she picked up her introductory physiology textbook. It weighed about a hundred pounds, and she doubted that studying would be at the top of her agenda. Still, the book had cost about twice what it weighed. She left it in the case.

Rounding out the contents was a bottle of shampoo (no conditioner), a bulky photo album (the only record she had left of life with her parents), and her round hairbrush (thank God).

She checked the interior pockets and ran her hand around every inch of the lining, then mentally kicked herself. She'd thought to bring a useless textbook but had forgotten a toothbrush. Her mouth felt like the inside of a birdcage.

She considered climbing the stairs to ask for a toothbrush, but her instructions had been clear. Stay in her room until they called her. She slammed the lid of the case shut. This couldn't be happening. She felt like a prisoner. They'd taken away her cellphone, her ID, her credit cards, even her library card. It was all so unfair.

She remembered Mrs. Zhang's words when she'd made the same complaint the night before. "Life isn't fair, Elena. Sometimes the cards are against you, but you have to play anyway. Do you understand?"

She hadn't understood at all, but shell-shocked, and with nowhere else to turn, she'd allowed Mrs. Zhang to lead the way. After a crazy drive through the dark streets of the city, they'd ended up at Mrs. Zhang's office at the Vancouver Community College. She remembered sitting collapsed in a visitor's chair while Mrs. Zhang sat behind her desk, fingers skipping through her Rolodex.

"Are you calling the police?" Elena said.

Mrs. Zhang looked up at Elena and shook her head.

"Why not? There's a dead man in my apartment, for God's sake."

"Exactly," Mrs. Zhang replied. She sat back, tenting her fingers together. "You know better than most, Leonid Volkov is a very powerful man in this city. He's already caused you so much trouble, and now his bodyguard has been killed. By my husband." Mrs. Zhang sat back, struggling to keep her voice level. "What do you think will happen if we call the police?"

Elena stared at her for several moments, then her eyes slid down to the floor.

Mrs. Zhang reached out and patted Elena's hand. "The good news is there are people willing to help. They'll bring in the police once they figure out what is really going on." She leaned forward. "What do you know about the Underground Railroad?"

"You mean the slaves?" A crease formed between Elena's brows as she struggled to see where Mrs. Zhang was going with this.

Mrs. Zhang nodded her head and assumed a professorial tone. "The Underground Railroad was a network of secret routes and safe houses set up to help American slaves escape to the North, where all people, regardless of colour, were considered free. The conductors"—Mrs. Zhang paused to draw air quotes around the word—"included freeborn blacks, former slaves, white abolitionists, and Native Americans."

"I know about the Underground Railroad, Mrs. Zhang," Elena interjected, her voice rising.

"Hear me out. There is a similar underground route operating today. They call it the Line. It assists women for whom the usual legal channels have failed."

Elena ran her hands through her hair. "I can't believe this is happening."

"Sadly, your situation is not all that rare. It's frightening how easily the system can be manipulated by money and influence." Mrs. Zhang shook her head. "Unfortunately, Leonid Volkov has plenty of both."

"I don't care who he is, this shouldn't be happening to me. It's just plain wrong."

"I agree," Mrs. Zhang continued. "The fact that Volkov is able to twist the law in his favour is a terrible injustice, but that is, unfortunately, the way of the world, and for now we must deal with your reality, as it is."

Elena shot the older woman an outraged look, then slouched down in her chair.

"The positive thing is that you are not alone, my dear. The Line helps these women disappear in very much the same way as the original Underground Railroad helped the slaves. A variety of people will guide you. Each will move you a little farther along until they are able to set you up in a safe place."

"Disappear?" Elena frowned. She hadn't heard anything after Mrs. Zhang had uttered that word.

Mrs. Zhang nodded. "Unfortunately, there is the rare occasion when going underground is the only option. At least until the situation can be resolved."

"But I'm starting school next week."

"Your studies may have to wait, I'm afraid."

"No." Elena shot to her feet. "I've paid my fees. They're expecting me."

"Most regrettable," said Mrs. Zhang firmly, "but with everything that's happened, your safety is paramount."

Ignoring Elena's sputtered protestations, Mrs. Zhang picked up the phone. It was clear she had awakened the person on the other end.

Slack-jawed, Elena watched Mrs. Zhang's lips move but couldn't make out her words. The only sound she could hear was the pulsing of her own blood as it squeezed through her veins.

Finally, Mrs. Zhang hung up the phone with a decisive click, then glanced up at Elena. "It is arranged. You will leave tomorrow." She consulted her watch. "Today actually."

"Leave?" Elena covered her face with her hands. "What are you talking about?"

Mrs. Zhang shrugged. "We're both going away. I am heading to Vancouver Island to stay with my friend's sister. You are going to the Surrey women's shelter. From there you will be shuttled east."

Elena let her hands drop into her lap. "Oh, Mrs. Zhang, I'm sorry. I didn't think—"

Mrs. Zhang waved a hand. "I'll be fine, I'm just being cautious."

"What about Mr. Zhang?"

"He's taking care of the body, and after that, he'll do what he can to help the Line figure out why Volkov sent that man to pick you up." Mrs. Zhang waved a hand in dismissal. "Don't worry about him; he was Chinese State Police for almost thirty years. He knows what he's doing."

Mrs. Zhang leaned forward. "When you get to Calgary, there will be a young woman there to meet you. Her name is Signy Shepherd. My contact assures me she's tip-top." Mrs. Zhang smiled. "She will take you to Toronto, where you will be met by another conductor. What happens then, I don't know, although I'm sure they will do their best to keep you safe until this mess is sorted."

Mrs. Zhang had looked at her watch then and ushered Elena out of the office. As the two women hurried through the silent halls back out to the parking lot where the first conductor waited, Mrs. Zhang had said, firmly, "Listen carefully, and do whatever this lady tells you. I will see you soon."

Now, alone in the women's shelter in Surrey, and remembering Mrs. Zhang's weak promise, Elena toppled back onto the bed, exhaustion finally catching up with her. She lay down on her side and curled into a ball. Her experience with the Line so far had been less than stellar. The first conductor had been a taciturn woman, with long, stringy hair, who hadn't said two words during the drive to Surrey.

Elena hoped the woman picking her up in Calgary would be easier. Signy was an unusual name. She'd only heard it once before, during a mythology course she'd taken in high school. That Signy had avenged the death of her family in spectacular fashion. A bloodbath, if she remembered correctly.

As she drifted off to sleep, she hoped this modern-day Signy would prove a little more conventional. She wasn't sure she could take any more excitement.

Chapter

3

The Dodge Ram rolled up the driveway trailing a funnel cloud of dust. The truck slid to a halt beside Signy's Saturn and a broad figure stepped out into the haze.

Over Signy's shoulder, Jenny Dalton gasped.

Without taking her eyes off the man, Signy said, "Take the girls into the bedroom. If I don't come for you in the next five minutes, call the police."

Nodding, Jenny grabbed Angel by the hand and fled, slamming the door behind them.

Signy watched Daryl Dalton checking the licence plate on the Saturn, his hands balled into fists, his thick features the dull red of raw beef. She stood, framed in the window, as he looked up and caught sight of her.

Damn. She really liked this job.

She called up the mantra her elementary-school psychologist had taught her. When you find yourself getting angry, he'd told her, distracting the mind helps curb impulsive behaviour. He'd suggested deep breathing, snapping a band around her wrist, or reciting nonsense in her head, the ABCs or the like.

Eyes narrowed, she examined the ignorant asshole as he thudded up the path, trying not to let the fact that he was an overblown, child-abusing, wife-beating moron hamper her reason.

Oh dear, what can the matter be?
Johnny's so long at the—

She didn't notice her hands clenched into fists.

She strode back up the dark hallway, arranging her features into a pleasant smile before flinging open the front door and leaping off the stoop, bypassing the rickety stairs.

"Hi," she said, raising her hand in a cheery greeting.

He stared at her, his brows bunching together over the bridge of his nose.

"Daryl, isn't it?"

"Do I know you?"

She held out her hand. "I'm Signy Shepherd."

Confused, he gave her fingers a cursory shake. "I ain't interested in buying nothin'."

"No worries," she said, "I'm not selling."

He took a step back and eyed her suspiciously, "You one of them religious nuts? 'Cause I don't believe in that shit."

She shook her head dramatically.

"So what then? You a cop, or something?"

She laughed. "Hardly."

Daryl stared at her, then turned and spat into the dust. "Enough with the twenty questions. What the hell are you doing on my property?"

"Your property?" said Signy, pressing forward, pushing into his personal space.

Daryl took a step back.

"I was under the impression your father owned this charming home."

"What the fuck does my father—?"

"Daryl? Do you mind if I call you Daryl?" Her grin widened to a hundred-watt smile. "I didn't mean to bring up your father issues."

"Father—what?"

"I understand how hard it must have been to have a bully as a father. You're left feeling so inadequate. Like a loser, really." Signy reached way up and placed a comforting hand on his massive shoulder.

Daryl batted the hand away and took another step back. "What the fuck you talking about?"

"Having Richard Dalton as a father? No one would expect you to turn out to be a normal person." She shook her head sadly, then observed with satisfaction as his face changed from the dull hue of raw beef to the bright red of a boiled beet.

"Well of course you're not normal, silly"—rapping him playfully on the side of his arm. "Only cowardly assholes bully women and children."

Without warning, Daryl roared, lunging at her like a crazed bull. With the grace of a matador she sidestepped him, smacking him on the rump, counting coup as he lurched past.

"No need to get bent out of shape, Daryl," Signy said, her back pressed against the Saturn. "You're probably just trying to come to terms with your latent homosexual feelings."

Daryl dove at her, pile-driving his clenched fists toward her head. At the last moment she dropped to one knee and the thunderous blow exploded harmlessly off the roof of her car. Springing up, she flung herself sideways as he swiped at her again.

Just beyond his reach she called out, "You know what they say about protesting too much," then watched with genuine amusement as he tried to collect his thoughts. She thought it must be like chasing confetti.

"Bitch!"

"It's over, Daryl. You're done hurting your family. I'm getting them out of here."

He shook his head from side to side, a grizzly in that split second before a charge.

She held his eyes with hers.

"Fuck you, lady."

She pointed her chin at his face. "Give it your best shot, dickhead."

The grizzly attacked, faster than she could have imagined. Grabbing her by the throat with a massive hand, he squeezed, digging into the muscles on the side of her neck with his fingers. Bending her backwards over the roof of the car, he brought his mouth close to her ear. He had a weeping cyst on his neck and she could smell the fetid odour of rot along with a rank blend of unwashed skin and testosterone.

"Get the fuck out of here, you crazy bitch," he said, spittle

22

spraying her face. Peeling his fingers off her neck, he turned toward the house. "I'm calling the cops."

Wiping her cheek with the back of her hand, Signy watched him turn away. She could let him go. He'd assaulted her in broad daylight, the bruising on her neck all the proof she needed. More than enough to get him charged.

But then what? With his father the cop and the law as toothless as it was, he'd be likely to spend no more than one night in jail. And Jenny and those innocent little girls were almost certain to bear the brunt of his wrath. She needed more. She turned, reached through the open passenger window and snapped open the glove compartment. She palmed a cylindrical canister, not much larger than a tube of lipstick.

"Hey, asshole," Signy called.

He spun to face her, shouting with exasperation.

Signy raised a hand to her neck. "I'm pretty sure they can get fingerprints off human skin these days. You're a failure as a husband and you're the worst kind of father. Say goodbye to your wife and kids."

She knew before she finished her sentence that he'd made up his mind. Time slowed as she watched him cock his arm back, his fist the size of a sledgehammer. Leg muscles bunched, he pulled the trigger, aiming at her face.

Signy sprang forward and into the blow. She'd learned the manoeuvre not from her karate master but from Zef, a particularly adept street fighter. If she was lucky, the punch would impact her with only half the force, and if she was very lucky, she'd be able to duck under it.

She heard his fist slice through the air just millimetres from her ear. Staying close, she could feel him hauling his arm back again. Eyes closed, she drove her knee up into his crotch with everything she had.

As he doubled over, eyes wide and mouth agape, Signy brought the canister in her hand up to his face. Flicking the safety latch off, she pulled the trigger. Noxious capsaicin pepper spray, concentrated enough to fend off even the most determined pit bull, streamed into his eyes.

Daryl screamed and reeled backwards, his feet tangling beneath him. Signy followed him all the way down, never wavering, keeping the nozzle fully depressed.

He rolled in the dirt, his eyes swollen and streaming, the delicate tissues of his nose, throat, and lungs inflamed and burning. She kept it up for the full twenty-five seconds of life the canister promised.

As the Mace sputtered to a halt, Signy leaped backwards. Her own eyes were streaming with tears even though she'd avoided most of the gas. When she found a patch of fresh air, she doubled over gasping for breath. She hacked and coughed and only slowly became aware of the sound of screaming.

Jenny Dalton teetered on the wooden stoop, wailing at the top of her lungs, Halo still wrapped in her arms. Angel stood beside them, eyes wide with shock, watching her father's desperate struggle for air.

Standing up, Signy managed to get her lips to move. "Jenny, bring the kids and let's go."

Jenny showed no signs of winding down, so Signy stumbled forward, slowing her breath, willing her muscles to relax. She placed a hand on Jenny's shoulder, then ran it slowly down her arm as though gentling a skittish horse. She held the young woman's eyes with her own. "Are you with me? We have to go now."

Jenny shot a quick glance at her husband, took a few halting breaths, then nodded. With Jenny covering Halo's eyes, the trio made their way past Daryl, writhing on the ground, suffocating in his own tears.

Hustling the group into the car, Signy slammed the doors. She fired up the Saturn and floored the accelerator, unconcerned with the spray of gravel that pelted Daryl as he attempted to rise to his hands and knees. Tearing down the dirt road, she flew over the aging train tracks, wincing as the car bottomed out.

She didn't notice the brilliant headlamp of an oncoming train in the distance.

Chapter

4

Leonid Volkov pushed his chair back from the massive oak desk that commanded centre stage in his home office. Pavel was not answering his phone. He should have been back hours ago. Volkov stood and walked over to the window. Across the sparkling waters of English Bay he could see the Vancouver skyline and the gleaming office tower that bore his name.

He slipped a rich Cuban cigar from his shirt pocket. He was never far from a good smoke. He didn't believe in that lung cancer bullshit. Seventy-six years old and he was still as strong as an ox.

Inserting the cigar into the ring of the clipper, he snipped off the end. He loved this part, the way the earthy smell of the tobacco cleared his head. He needed his wits about him. Something had obviously gone wrong.

Standing at the window, he watched the gardener wave a pair of pruning shears around one of the obscenely expensive bushes Marisha had insisted on having planted last year. He frowned. The damned thing didn't need a trim. Volkov jabbed the tip of the cigar at the window and glared.

On days like this, he felt nostalgic for the old Soviet Union. In those days workingmen knew their place and didn't demand an arm and a leg to piss around in a garden all day like fairies.

He sucked in a mouthful of pungent smoke. Hell, in the good old days, he could have marched into the girl's apartment in the middle of the day and taken what he wanted, and anyone who dared to complain would earn themselves a one-way ticket to Siberia, or worse.

He banged on the glass with his fist until the gardener looked up, confusion evident on his weathered face. When the hapless man caught sight of Volkov, he scuttled across the lawn and out of sight, not stopping to retrieve his tools.

Volkov breathed in another mouthful of the rich smoke and thought about Pavel Ivanovitch. Unlike the pilfering gardener, Pavel was a hard worker and loyal employee, had been for almost fifty years. They'd met when Leonid was eighteen and Pavel a year younger, as recruits in the Soviet Red Army.

Hazing rituals in those days could be brutal, and Leonid and Pavel had had the misfortune to be assigned to a unit where newcomers were treated to a particularly vile form of welcome that involved unspeakable treatment with broomsticks.

On the evening of their second day at boot camp, Leonid and Pavel were cornered in the shower room by a half-drunk sergeant and a couple of his henchmen. They were ordered to assume the position, backs to their tormentors, hands spread against the slimy concrete wall.

Even at eighteen Leonid presented an imposing figure. He had filled out early, with powerful shoulders and arms and a broad chest that tapered down to an iron belly and slim hips. He had a thick head of copper hair that he tended with an almost religious intensity, and flashing black eyes that never failed to charm the ladies.

Nor was that muscle just for show. Since being dumped at Children's Orphanage Number Three in Stalingrad as a young boy, he'd had to fight for his supper on a daily basis, and he had never gone hungry. He'd acquired a formidable reputation, and even the staff had learned not to mess with Leo the Lion.

With one glance, Leonid took the measure of the younger man standing naked beside him. The boy was short and slight, although with sinewy muscles poised for battle. The boy knew how to fight.

The sergeant repeated his order, his words slurred. The two boys glanced at each other and grinned. In that moment Leonid knew he had found a kindred spirit. Dripping wet, they complied, offering their unprotected buttocks to the leering soldiers.

Perhaps if the sergeant had imbibed less of his homegrown vodka, or perhaps if his men had had at least one complete brain between them, they might have realized that in choosing Pavel and Leonid as victims, they had made a fatal error.

Within less than a minute it was over. One of the hapless thugs scrabbled on the slippery shower floor, howling, both knees crushed, while another lay where he had fallen, pulpy grey matter oozing from a ragged crater in his skull. The sergeant sat crumpled against the dank concrete wall, his useless fingers still clutching the broken broomstick that protruded from his throat.

That might have been the end for Leonid and Pavel had it not been for a higher-ranking officer who decided that the Soviet Army needed more men with the initiative shown by the two young recruits. He'd had them transferred to an elite special operations unit.

They'd been a high-functioning team ever since. Not once over the course of almost a half century had Pavel failed to check in after a job. Volkov bit down on the cigar. Something was definitely wrong.

Turning with surprising grace for a man of his age, Volkov strode over to the Kandinsky that hung above the fireplace. Lifting the canvas from the wall, he opened a concealed safe, then extracted a small leather satchel.

It had been several years since he'd needed to utilize the tools of his former trade, but his instincts were telling him he had little time to spare. He had sent his oldest friend on what should have been a simple job and now the man was missing. And until that girl was brought in, the sword of Damocles would continue to swing over his head. He had to move now.

He picked up the phone and barked into the receiver, demanding that a car be brought round immediately. He felt instantly better. He was never more alive than when he was on the hunt.

He thrilled to the surge of hot blood as it coursed through his body, the large muscles in his arms and legs seeming to grow in size and power as he took the elevator down to the main floor, then strode with authority to where his car waited, its German engine rumbling.

Grinding the cigar into the concrete driveway with his heel, he smiled. Despite his gnawing concern, it felt marvellous to be back in the game.

Chapter

5

Finally back on a main road, Signy pulled the Saturn onto the gravel shoulder and shoved the gearshift into park. She waited for a line of traffic to whiz past before rolling down her window. The after-effects of the adrenaline explosion were making her feel slightly nauseous. She leaned out the window and breathed in a few drafts of air.

Despite the heat, the fresh air helped, and she sat back in her seat feeling a little steadier. She glanced in the rear-view mirror. Angel was examining her with that mixture of horror and irresistible curiosity usually reserved for a monster under the bed.

Halo was stretched out across the back seat, her blond head nestled in her sister's lap, one tiny thumb plugged into her mouth. Her eyes were wide open, although she appeared to be staring at nothing.

Signy opened the car door and stepped out of the vehicle. Watching for traffic, she leaned down and opened the back door, then popped her head inside. Both girls drew back.

"Hey, it's okay," said Signy, trying to smile. "We just need to get your seat belts on." She glanced into the front seat. Jenny Dalton sat, staring out the front window. "Right, Mom?"

The young woman had yet to open her mouth, although they'd been driving for almost twenty minutes. Signy had no idea how much of the altercation Jenny and Angel had witnessed. How long had they been standing on the porch? She touched a finger to the tender flesh around her throat. It was getting achier by the second.

When Jenny didn't respond, Signy turned back to the girls. Angel was sliding her fingers down Signy's long braid, apparently fascinated by the silky texture.

Signy grinned, lifted up the tufted end of her plait, and dabbed it like a paintbrush on Angel's nose. She was rewarded when Angel poked a tongue into her cheek, trying to suppress a smile. She snapped Angel's seat belt into place.

She then lifted the inert form of Halo into an upright position and buckled her in, tucking the shoulder strap under one armpit. Surveying the result, she clicked her tongue. Not great, but better than nothing. She made a mental note to always carry a car seat in the trunk from now on.

"Are you a-scared?" asked Angel, in a piping voice.

Signy didn't say anything for a second. Finally, she smiled at the little girl and shook her head. "I was, but not anymore," she said. "Are you?"

Angel stared up at her for a second, then said, "Your eyes are all red."

Signy touched the corner of one eye with the tip of her finger. "Yup," she said, "I need to give them a bath."

Angel giggled. "You can't give eyes a bath."

Jenny twisted in her seat. "Angel, leave the lady alone. We have to go."

Angel's face drooped. She glared at her mother, then crossed her arms over her chest.

Signy gave her one last dot on her nose with the tip of the braid, then climbed back into the driver's seat. She glanced at Jenny. "Are you okay?"

"Can we just go?" said Jenny.

"If you're worried about your husband, I don't think he's going anywhere for a while." She slipped her cellphone out of her purse. "I have to call nine-one-one and let them know what happened. Then we'll go."

"No," shouted Jenny, placing a restraining hand on Signy's forearm. "I told you. You can't call the cops."

Squeezing the young woman's hand, Signy said, "I have to. It's my job. You'll be okay. I promise."

Jenny searched Signy's eyes for several moments before offering a reluctant nod.

Signy flashed a reassuring smile. She scrolled through her inbox on her phone, relieved to see that no one from the office had been trying to reach her, although she stifled a hiss of irritation when she saw that Zef had left another message. *Hey Babe, I'm heading your way. Wanna hook up?* With a stab of her finger she deleted the message.

When the 911 operator picked up, she identified herself as a worker at the Women's Centre, said she needed police response, then relayed a watered-down account of the altercation with Daryl Dalton. At the conclusion of the call, the dispatcher asked Signy to stay close to the phone, that an officer would need a statement from her after they talked with Mr. Dalton.

Signy felt her heart sink as she hung up the phone. This was really happening. She plastered a bright smile on her face. "Okay," she said, "are we ready to roll?" She put the car in gear and waited for a break in the traffic.

"Can my dad see Thomas the Tank Engine too?" asked Angel.

Signy shot a look at Jenny.

Jenny sighed then turned to look over her shoulder. "Daddy can't come with us, chicken."

Angel regarded her for several moments before saying, "Is he in trouble?"

"I dunno, honey, maybe."

Angel gnawed at her thumb for several moments, then looked back up at her mother. "Good," she said.

Signy felt a tug in her heart and thought Jenny must have felt the same way, because they exchanged a brief glance. Signy wondered if that might be an encouraging sign. She wished she could just explain herself, make Jenny understand that sometimes you just had to take the bull by the horns. If she could find out just what Jenny intended to say to the police, she'd know how to respond.

She sighed. No matter how she spun it, she didn't feel right trying to save her own skin when Jenny's entire world was imploding. She would just have to hope that she made it out of this mess, job and reputation intact.

Eyes back on the road, she noted with some relief they

were entering the outskirts of Linden Valley. Situated an hour and a half north of Toronto on the southern edge of cottage country, Linden Valley was a mid-size Ontario town with a population of ten thousand. Those ranks swelled in the summer when local cottagers poured into town to shop for groceries and to poke around a glut of quaint shops searching for handmade chocolates, scented candles, maple syrup, and the like.

With the Labour Day long weekend fast approaching, and everyone desperate to cram as much fun as possible into the last few days before the responsibilities of school and work resumed in earnest, the road was jammed with cars.

Signy sighed and joined the steady stream of traffic inching into town. In the rear-view mirror she watched Angel staring in fascination at the rows of strip malls, the new Walmart superstore, and the ubiquitous fast-food joints.

Maybe she'd stop at McDonald's. If Angel had seen the entire fight, maybe a Happy Meal and an ice cream cone would make her more amenable to Signy's side of things. At this point, she could use all the help she could get.

She shifted uncomfortably in her seat. She was contemplating bribing a couple of infants. How low was she going to have to go before she learned to use her head instead of her fists?

She squeezed the wheel until her knuckles turned white. She'd been amazed when Grace Holder had agreed to hire her last year, even more so when she'd been invited to join the Line. She'd tried hard to stay on the straight and narrow and had managed surprisingly well, although she supposed that depended on one's strict definition of *straight and narrow*.

She loved the work. Her heart raced every time Grace handed her a red file, indicating a new passenger on the Line.

A low-slung Mustang, rap music booming, cut in front of her, and she consciously resisted flipping the driver the bird. She took a deep breath.

Oh dear, what can the matter be?
Johnny's so long at the fair.

Although the air conditioner had kicked in a while ago and was pumping out a weak stream of chilled air, she felt sweat bloom on her forehead. She swallowed hard. If her impulsive actions with Daryl Dalton had screwed up her job with the Line, she didn't know what she'd do.

Just ahead, she saw the familiar golden arches. "What do you say, guys?" she asked, peeling her lips back in the semblance of a smile. "Anybody want an ice cream?" She was gratified to see a wide grin split Angel's face.

If blackmail was what it took to ensure her place in the good books of the tiny witnesses in the back seat, then so be it. She was not above debasing herself when push came to shove.

Chapter

6

Watching Angel periscope up and down in a pool of brightly coloured plastic balls, Signy wondered at the resiliency of children. Less than an hour before, she'd seen her father struggling for breath on his hands and knees. It was amazing what a Happy Meal and an ice cream cone could accomplish.

Unfortunately, she couldn't say the same for the young woman sitting next to her. Watching her kids play, Jenny sat, slack-jawed, her pigtails lank on her shoulders. She was twirling a plastic stir stick in a half-empty cup of coffee. Calling on every ounce of her training, Signy had tried to open up a line of communication more than once but had been repeatedly shut down with monosyllabic replies.

She tried again. "You must be feeling overwhelmed."

Jenny shot her a sidelong glance, then shrugged.

Okay, Signy thought, how about this: "Did you grow up in Linden Valley?"

Wiping her nose on her sleeve, Jenny shook her head.

"Me neither." She sat back and gave Jenny an appraising look. "How old are you, nineteen? Twenty?"

Jenny rolled her eyes. "I still get asked for ID when I buy smokes for Daryl but I'm twenty-five."

"No way," said Signy. "You're only a year younger than me? Where did you grow up?"

"New Brunswick."

"Wow," said Signy, taking another long sip, "you're a long way from home."

Jenny sniffed, then glanced over at the kids.

"Are your parents still alive?"

Jenny nodded, slowly. "I haven't seen them in ages."

Signy offered her a napkin. "I don't know about you, but I miss my mom." This was not technically true as Signy did not know her biological mother, but she did occasionally remember her foster mother with some fondness.

"My parents couldn't stand Daryl," Jenny continued. "I married him just to piss them off, you know what I mean?"

Signy snorted. "Totally, I can't even tell you how many times I went out of my way to screw around with my mom. If she said the sky was blue, I said it was red; if she said up, I said down. If she said it was cold outside, I'd put on a miniskirt and give her the finger."

Jenny looked straight at her for the first time, "Really?"

Signy pointed at her own chest. "Number one badass," she said with a grin. "Ran away from home, smoked a little too much weed, hung with losers, you name it, caused that woman no end of grief." Again, not technically true, but she'd learned that building common ground was an effective tool when interviewing clients.

Jenny looked at her quizzically. "So what happened? I mean look at you. You're pretty. You got a car and a job. And the way you beat the shit outta Daryl? That was awesome. Like, how did you do that?"

Signy winced. "When I was in high school, they said I needed to 'channel my anger.'" She drew quotation marks in the air with her fingers. "They hooked me up with a martial arts instructor."

"Awesome."

"Look, Jenny. Knowing how to fight when you have to is a good thing." Signy tapped her temple with an index finger. "But using your head is always better."

A quizzical look crossed Jenny's face.

"Look at me," Signy said, doing a biceps curl until her muscle popped. "How does that compare to Daryl's arm?"

Jenny shrugged. "Ya, but Daryl lifts weights."

"It doesn't matter how good I am, most guys could take me out in a heartbeat. The smartest thing to do is to avoid a fight altogether. But if a fight comes to me, I do whatever it takes to disable the attacker." She flashed a crooked grin. "And then I run like hell."

One corner of Jenny's mouth crooked upward. "What was that stuff anyway? Pepper spray?"

"I don't think you're hearing me. Getting involved in a physical altercation is not only dangerous, it can make things very complicated"—Signy caught Jenny's eye and held it—"if you know what I mean."

Jenny peered into Signy's eyes for several seconds, then nodded. "Sure, I get it."

Signy gave Jenny's hand a light squeeze. "You know what really made a difference for me? I got to where you are right now. So low I wasn't sure I knew how to drag myself back up." Her grin was rueful. "You might not like this, but I swallowed my pride and I called my parents. I moved back to the farm for a couple of months and got my head on straight. Best move I ever made."

Jenny glanced over at the girls. Angel was holding Halo's hand as the younger child inched her way down a yellow slide. She shook her head. "I dunno. I'm probably the last person they'd wanna hear from."

"Really?" Signy pointed at the two little giggling girls. "What about those two? Is there anything they could ever do that would make you turn your back on them forever?"

Jenny watched the girls for almost a minute before a faint smile crossed her face.

"Exactly," said Signy. "Sometimes you have to put yourself in the other guy's shoes. You're a mom. You know what it's like. You'd go to hell and back for those kids." She frowned. "Let's face it, you've already been to hell."

Snapping her plastic stir stick in two, Jenny nodded.

"So, maybe it's time to come back. You did awesome calling us today. What do you say?"

Jenny opened her mouth to speak.

Signy's cellphone rang.

Jenny sighed and looked back at the kids.

"Dammit," said Signy. She raised the phone to her ear. "What?"

"Where are you?"

Despite the urgent whisper, Signy recognized the voice of the shelter supervisor, Carmen Calzonetti. "McDonald's," she answered.

"McDonald's?" Carmen said, her voice rising. "What the hell are you doing there? And why didn't you give me the heads-up? There are cops crawling all over the place and they want to talk to you. Are you all right?"

"Crap," said Signy.

"That about sums it up," said Carmen. "It's a veritable shit-storm here. Grace is on her way. Might I suggest that you get your butt over here asap?"

"Look," Signy said, feeling a familiar heat rise in her cheeks, "I've got a couple of hungry kids with me. They've been through hell. Tell the cops we'll be there when we get there."

"Signy," said Carmen, her tone dangerously low, "I'll tell them you'll be here in five minutes."

Gritting her teeth, Signy forced an affirmative response from between her lips.

"Move it," said Carmen, before disconnecting the line.

"Cops are at the shelter," Signy said. "We have to go."

As they cleared away the detritus of their meal and retrieved the girls, Signy warned Jenny that things were about to get wild. Besides the cops there would be an intake interview for Jenny, a children's worker to see to the girls, assignment of clothes and toilet articles and whatever else they might need, and a hundred other things. "It's gonna be nuts, but you'll get through it no problem," said Signy.

Jenny smiled, weakly.

As they walked through the parking lot, Jenny put a hand on Signy's arm. "Promise me, you'll watch your back, okay? Daryl's a shit but Richard Dalton is one mean dude."

"Don't worry about me." Signy narrowed her eyes. "I'm sure I can handle it."

"Right," said Jenny, lifting Halo onto her hip, "that's exactly what I thought."

Chapter

7

Strolling the private beach in front of his home, Leonid Volkov breathed in the salty air and watched the antics of a flock of seagulls as they hunted for fish. He admired the stronger birds, the way they harassed the weak, dive-bombing their hapless kin until the targets were forced to give up whatever morsel they'd managed to catch. Survival of the fittest, he thought, scraping his bristly chin with one hand. The cycle of life.

Puffing on a cigar, he reflected on the strange events of the last twenty-four hours. His chat with Elena's landlord had proved enlightening. He'd caught the man unawares, cleaning blood from Elena's floor. After a quick jab with a hypodermic into the man's neck, he'd taken him back to his studio, where it hadn't taken long to get the man to open up. He smiled. It had been like riding a bike.

Volkov blew a stream of smoke at the ceiling. Things had not gone as well for poor Pavel. A single lapse of judgment, one stroke of bad luck, and his friend of fifty years was gone. He wished he could have given Pavel a suitable send-off. He chomped down on the end of the cigar.

It was shocking, really, how suddenly everything could change. Since the moment that girl had walked into his hotel, he'd known that she was a ticking time bomb. He'd hoped the matter would have been cleared up quickly and cleanly. But now, because of Pavel's blunder, the girl was missing and his world was teetering on the edge.

He whipped the cigar butt high over the waves, watching as one of the larger birds caught it in mid-air. If he didn't find the girl soon, he had no doubt that everything he had worked for would come crashing down around his ears.

He pulled out his phone and punched in a familiar number. If the Tracker couldn't find the girl, then no one could.

• • •

Concealed behind a line of hanging tapestries depicting Navajo legends in indigo and scarlet, the Tracker watched her move, appraising the sway of her hips, the line of her neck, and the determined set of her jaw. He felt his heart flip inside his chest as she spun toward him, her golden hair flashing in the sun. There was no doubt in his mind. She could be a candidate.

He'd been shadowing the girl for almost an hour as she'd meandered through the sun-drenched stalls of the Plaza, and now he held his breath as she fingered the very tapestry behind which he stood. He calculated her position from the almost imperceptible disturbance she created in the atmosphere as she breathed in and out. Tiny knots at the back of the hanging fabric brushed his face as she traced the design with her hands. He stood motionless listening for the faint click of her heels as she strolled on.

It was unusual for him to pursue a candidate so close to home and without the due diligence he normally afforded such a hunt. Still, something about this girl had piqued his interest and he couldn't let her just walk away. He felt his palms itch with the compulsion to play this little game of his out to its conclusion.

Slipping from his hiding place, he manoeuvred past a trio of Tilley-clad tourists gushing over the quality of the embroidered wall hangings. He glanced into the eyes of the copper-skinned Navajo who was hoping to make the sale. The old man blinked, then looked away before returning his attention to his customers.

The girl had crossed the square, and he eyed the curve of her back as she bent over to examine an array of handcrafted jewellery laid out on the ground in front of an apple-cheeked old woman who was knitting a pair of socks with multicoloured yarn.

"What's this design?" She pointed at a pair of silver drop earrings festooned with geometric slivers of turquoise.

The old woman glanced up from her knitting. "Twenty-nine dollars for one pair, and forty-five for two."

"Sorry," said the girl, "I was just wondering if this design has any special significance."

The old woman returned to her knitting, the click of the needles sharp in the lazy afternoon.

He was behind her now, so close he could have clipped a lock of her hair had he been so inclined. But the day was warm and he had nowhere else to be. He could afford to take his time.

"Never mind," he said into the back of her neck.

"Oh." The girl whirled to face him. "You startled me."

He smiled. "I don't think Mrs. Chee has cracked a smile in twenty years."

The old lady regarded him with a gimlet eye, wrinkling her nose.

The girl covered a smile with her fingers.

Closing his eyes for a second, he inhaled the sound of her voice. Melodious and rich, it rang with good humour. He took a step back.

"Are you at the university?" she asked, eyeing his backpack.

"Philosophy," he lied.

"Anthropology," she said, pointing at her chest.

"Ah. Hence the interest in symbolism?"

"I'll be starting my freshman year in a few weeks and I wanted to get a head start."

He sighed. Everything about her was wrong. From the pretty voice to the guileless blue eyes, everything about her screamed well-adjusted, wholesome, and happy. She'd have people at home who loved her, who were in all likelihood waiting for her next phone call with eager anticipation.

"I'm Olivia."

He checked his watch and shrugged. He had created so many identities over the years, he barely remembered the name his mother had given him, and he wasn't about to share that with this little piece of fluff. The few people who were privy to his business knew him as the Tracker and he preferred it that way.

He smiled. "I'm Hunter."

"Nice to meet you, Hunter." She waggled her fingers. "I'm from Ohio and I totally love down here. It's so sunny and gorgeous and, well, dripping with history. Don't you think?"

He allowed his eyes to roam over her body and was pleased when her cheeks flushed warm and rosy. There's no way she would ever be a candidate, but there was no need for the afternoon to have been a complete waste of time. He linked his arm through hers. "If we're to be schoolmates," he said, "we should get to know each other a little better."

She returned his gaze with a frank appraisal of her own, a wicked smile playing around her spectacular lips.

In the back pocket of his jeans his phone vibrated. Only one person knew this number and she never bothered him unless it was urgent. He dropped the girl's arm and waved her away. "I have to take this."

The girl shot him a pouty look.

"Helen, you just lost me the catch of the day. I hope what you have is worth it," he said, as he watched the girl retreat back across the square.

"Would I call if it wasn't?" Helen said, her words clipped and irritated.

"Sorry, what have you got?" He sometimes forgot that he'd hired Helen not for her conversational skills but because she had a sixth sense as to what he might need, she was resourceful, and best of all, she was available 24-7. As an added bonus, she wasn't fazed by the fact that she'd never laid eyes on her demanding employer.

"Volkov," she said simply, knowing she needn't say more.

The Tracker made a noise in the back of his throat.

"I know, I know," said Helen, "but he pays well, very well."

The Tracker turned his thoughts to the new telescope he'd been coveting for some time now. The timing was perfect. The P/Levy comet he'd missed during its last flyby in 2006 was due to return and might even reach ninth magnitude by the end of the year. With the new Meade twelve-inch telescope, he'd have the best seat in the house.

"Alex? Are you still there?"

The Tracker sighed. "I'm on my way home now. Email me the details and get me on the first flight to Vancouver."

"Will do."

He grinned at the phone. She sounded happier and he knew why. A Leonid Volkov payout meant a hefty bonus to her bank account as well.

"And Alex?"

"Hmm?"

"Be careful."

"As always." He ended the call before she could sputter any number of angry retorts.

Chapter

8

The Linden Valley women's shelter, known as Vicky's Place in memory of a local woman killed by her husband, sat on a quiet side street just off the main drag, far enough from the hustle and bustle to provide a semblance of normality for the residents but close enough that urgent services like fire, police, and hospital were within shouting distance. The welfare office was nearby, as was a medical arts building, and for any other places the residents might need to visit, the bus stopped at the corner.

A former doctor's residence, the house stood as a testament to an era when building had been considered an art form. Originally constructed in the classic Ontario style, a solid red brick two-storey box with a central gable situated over the main entrance, it had a later addition of white gingerbread trim that lent a more whimsical air and served to remind new residents that they were entering a home, not an institution.

An ancient red maple tree graced the rolling front lawn. Unfortunately, the backyard had not fared as well. The space that hadn't been eaten up by a two-storey addition was used as parking for staff and residents. Blue recycling and garbage containers lined the side fence, while a squat garden shed housed a lawn mower, a snow blower, and other odds and ends.

Staff was reminded on a regular basis not to let the exterior of the house fall into disarray. The NIMBY crowd had almost prevented the shelter from opening years ago, and there was always some disgruntled neighbour on the lookout for a chance to stir the pot. Because it operated like a family home, staff and residents, when they were willing and able, took turns mowing the lawn, shovelling snow, and tending the gardens.

Pulling her Saturn to a halt beside a sleek, unmarked cruiser, Signy was relieved that Grace Holder's silver Prius was nowhere in sight. Maybe she'd be able to smooth the waters before her boss arrived.

While Jenny hauled the kids from the car, Signy did a quick survey of her appearance. Wrinkled and dusty, her yellow sundress was smeared with grease at the back where Daryl had shoved her against the car, and there were browning blood spots staining the right shoulder.

She held a hand to her ear and winced. Daryl must have brushed her ear with his fist when he let loose with that roundhouse punch. It was a credit to her adrenaline surge that she hadn't noticed the scrape that ran up the side of her neck and the slight tear in her earlobe.

Her feet were filthy, one sandal torn almost in half. But it was her throat that garnered the most attention. Bending over the side mirror, she tilted her head to one side and checked out the vivid indigo bruises that circled her neck like an obscene string of pearls.

She ran her hand down her long, blond braid. Stray hairs protruded willy-nilly. She looked like a porcupine that had been run over by a car. Standing tall, she glanced over at the security camera, then squared her shoulders, wondering how she could spin her appearance in the best light possible.

Guiding the small family toward the side entrance, she was relieved when the door opened the minute the little group clomped up the stairs and onto the porch. She was even more relieved that the person standing there was Laurel, the children's worker. Almost as tiny as some of her charges and with energy to burn, Laurel provided a happy air of welcome to the traumatized kids that shuffled through the front door.

Laurel made the requisite oohs and aahs, exclaiming in delight when Angel announced that they had just had lunch at McDonald's. When Signy mentioned that the girls were dying to see the little train that steamed from room to room, Laurel scooped Halo into her arms, then clutched Angel by the hand. It was a tribute to Laurel's skill at putting children at ease that neither girl exhibited a moment's hesitation at being separated from their mother.

Unfortunately, the exit of Laurel was followed by an audible jingling coming from down the hall. Carmen Calzonetti's trademark was the dozens of bangles that dangled from both her wrists, and if the overabundance of glittery jewellery charmed many of the residents, for the staff it functioned primarily as an early warning system. As the jangling grew in volume, Signy knew that Carmen was just around the corner and approaching fast.

She took the opportunity to give Jenny a hug. "Show the bastards," she said quickly into the younger woman's ear. "Call your parents and get the hell out of here."

Then Jenny was swept away by an intake worker and Signy didn't see her again.

• • •

His mind on Leonid Volkov, the Tracker swerved west onto the Red Rock Highway, desert sand the colour of ochre billowing out behind him like a giant rooster tail.

His last job for Volkov had been relatively straightforward, locate a missing employee who'd been reckless enough to abscond with a significant amount of cash. It had been an easy matter for the Tracker to locate the unfortunate woman hiding out in a motel in the outskirts of Chicago.

A quick phone call and Volkov and his money had been reunited. The Tracker hadn't wasted a second thought on the fate of the hapless thief. It was not his fault if these fools wouldn't learn that there was no substitute for careful preparation and constant vigilance.

It was another half hour before he'd negotiated the unpaved tracks that led to his modest home. It wasn't much to look at, a trim double-wide trailer perched on a small knoll surrounded by boundless desert, white paint cracking under the relentless sun.

He could have had his pick of the monster homes springing up in Santa Fe or Albuquerque, but he preferred the anonymity of being just one among the many mobile homes that dotted the lands of the Navajo Nation.

Much of the surrounding territory was communal and could be neither bought nor sold, but a section in the northwest of New Mexico known as the checkerboard still had some public land for sale.

After his mother's death, the Tracker had abandoned their hogan, a traditional Navajo dwelling, and had purchased this property not far from where he'd grown up in Arizona.

The property had several critical advantages. Under the wide-open skies of one of the sunniest states in America, he'd been able to install a solar array that provided all his electricity. With no close neighbours, his comings and goings were unobserved and he was able to see for miles in any direction, a significant advantage should an unwanted visitor come calling.

By far, the most desirable feature of the property was the abandoned test pit he'd discovered when he'd first walked the land.

New Mexico was dotted with over fifteen thousand abandoned mine sites. Some, like the one the Tracker found on his property, were relatively harmless, shallow depressions where a mining company had tapped the soil in the hopes of striking coal, uranium, or perhaps even gold. Others were old working mines up to five hundred feet deep, uncovered and treacherous.

The shallow pit he found on his property consisted of a wood-shored four-by-four entrance shaft that dead-ended no more than ten feet below the surface. At the bottom of the shaft a sixteen-by-sixteen pit, the size of a large room, had been carved from the rocky soil and reinforced, perfect for his needs.

It had taken a few months and a ton of elbow grease before the pit was transformed into a climate-controlled underground bunker. It was directly over this bunker that the Tracker had placed his mobile home.

Parking on a dirt pad just outside the front door, he sat for a moment, enjoying the silence. He was relieved to hear nothing more than the sigh of the wind over the hills in the distance and the ticking of the engine as it cooled.

As he exited the truck and climbed the wooden steps that led to the front door, he smiled at the cry of an eagle soaring high overhead.

Slipping his key into the lock, he stepped inside and called out, "I'm home." Instantly, recessed incandescent lights powered up, an air conditioner cranked over with a soft hum, and a series of clicks and buzzes indicated other essential functions had whirred back to life.

The floor was laid in a honey blond hardwood, waxed and shining. Arranged in front of a picture window, a matching couch and love seat of crisp white leather formed a perfect L shape. Sleek black end tables completed the arrangement in dramatic fashion.

In the kitchen he heard a Jura Capresso coffee centre whir softly, grinding a dark roast coffee bean mix he'd preloaded before leaving home. He walked over to the machine, the heady odour of the crushed beans soothing his disappointment that his latest candidate had proved such a letdown.

"Report," he said, as he reached into a cupboard for a ceramic mug.

"All systems within normal limits, zero probability of incursion." A mechanical voice issued from speakers located at strategic points throughout the trailer.

He'd installed the voice recognition technology as a means of efficient communication with the computer mainframe that controlled many of the functions of his home. With simple commands the system monitored power, water, and ambient light levels, regulated all appliance usage, monitored internal and exterior security, and even watered his plants.

"How was your trip, sir?"

He smiled. He'd chosen an upper-class British accent for the computer, as he'd always thought the posh phrasing lent an air of sagacity to any conversation, no matter how trivial.

"Frustrating. I am going to take a shower. Please warm the water, then boot up the control centre."

"Very good, sir."

After decanting the rich brew into his cup, he strolled toward the rear of the trailer and opened the door to his sleeping quarters. A king-sized bed dominated the space, the six-hundred-thread-count Egyptian cotton sheets tucked so tightly they would have easily passed the most stringent hospital inspection.

The walls were bare, with the exception of a dramatic turquoise and gold Navajo rug that hung over the bed. Ingenious cupboards recessed into the walls provided plenty of storage. He slid one open with the touch of his hand.

Removing his T-shirt and pants, he carefully folded them before placing them into the bin of clothes he would take to have laundered in town. After showering, he dressed in a pair of fresh shorts and a crisp T-shirt before walking back into the kitchen and placing his empty coffee cup into an ultrasonic wave technology dishwasher. The thing had cost an arm and a leg but he believed its reduced environmental footprint more than justified the extravagant expense. The telescope he was hoping to acquire, well that was a different matter.

"Computer on," he said. Sitting atop a glass and stainless steel table, surrounded by an array of complex electronic equipment, a twenty-seven-inch Apple monitor glowed to life. He tapped a few keys, and a shiny image of the Meade twelve-inch telescope filled the screen. Scanning the specs that accompanied the photo, he felt like a kid in a candy shop ready to blow his allowance on one great big fabulous treat.

He sighed. His uncle had taught him well. Work must always come before pleasure. Minimizing the enticing picture of the telescope, he opened his email. A message from Helen gave him details of his flight to Vancouver. There had been no direct flight available and she'd booked him on a circuitous route that was going to take all night. Still, he didn't need to be at the airport for a while yet. He could afford to spend some time with his girls.

Entering his bedroom, he walked over to the bed and pressed his hand to a section of the headboard. The entire bed rolled on heavy casters several feet to one side, exposing the hardwood floor below.

Strolling into the en suite bathroom, he opened the mirrored medicine chest that hung over the sink and removed a can of shaving cream and box of Band-Aids, revealing a screen about the size of a pack of playing cards. Leaning forward, he brought his right eye in close.

With a quick flash of light the retinal scanner confirmed his identity and automatically sprang the lock on an almost-invisible trap door built into the hardwood floor beneath his bed.

Sliding the door open, the Tracker climbed down a metal ladder that led into the old mining pit, allowing the familiar feeling of anticipation to wash over him. No sounds penetrated the thick walls, and the temperature hovered at a steady sixty-five degrees Fahrenheit. The floor space was bare, with the exception of a basic office swivel chair.

Stepping over to the chair, he took a seat, the padded cushion having moulded to his shape over the years. Using one foot, he sent the chair spinning, and the dizzying display of pictures that adorned the walls flashed past his eyes in a kaleidoscope of colour.

Covering three of the walls were photographs of women, more than two hundred in all, each of them in their early to mid-twenties. Precisely one inch below each photograph an index card provided identifying information.

At first glance the women looked very different. Hair colour varied from platinum blond to brunette, from auburn to jet black, including a scattering of Lucille Ball–type redheads. The shape of the faces staring out at him had no discernible pattern. Some were round, others heart-shaped or square-jawed.

Some of the women had been caught in natural poses, laughing, chatting in a bar with friends, running on the street. Others stared out from driver's licence photos, workplace ID cards, and one or two depicted grim-faced mug shots.

On closer examination, however, it became clear that there

was a commonality among the photos. Each woman had the same startling blue eyes.

On the fourth wall was a smaller display, only twenty-seven photos, each with the same index cards hanging underneath. Slashed across each pretty face was a blood red *X*. He sighed. It was unfortunate he had not been able to add the pretty girl from the plaza to his collection.

Whirling in lazy circles, he let his mind wander, fantasizing about which enticing candidate he would visit next.

Chapter

9

After Jenny was led away, Signy turned her attention to Carmen Calzonetti, who was quickly bearing down on her, trailed by a woman that Signy figured must be the cop. The woman towered over Carmen, thanks in large part to the four-inch heels she was wearing. Signy sneered inwardly. She'd figured only TV cops wore such impractical footwear on the job. She'd pay money to see the woman chase after a crook in those ridiculous shoes.

Dragging her attention away from the flashing red soles, she ran her eyes over the female detective, older, maybe mid-forties? Café-au-lait skin, black hair straightened professionally and pulled back in an elaborate slide, cream silk blouse hanging loose over tailored black slacks. A real looker, as her foster father had been fond of saying when confronted by such an elegant specimen.

"Signy Shepherd?" The woman did not offer her hand.

"Guilty," said Signy, not surprised when her weak attempt to lighten the situation imploded with an almost audible thunk.

"Detective Sergeant Winnifred Lavalle, Linden Valley Police Services." Detective Lavalle's voice was level and steady, with a mellifluous French accent Signy recognized as Haitian. Wiping a hand on her torn sundress, Signy resisted the urge to curtsy.

Detective Lavalle peered at Signy's face, taking in the ragged scrape and wounded ear. "We're going to need pictures of these injuries." Her eyes flicked downward. "And I'd like to take the dress, as well."

Furrowing her brow, Signy glanced over at Carmen Calzonetti.

Carmen stared back at her, looking distinctly cross. "Grace will be here shortly. Meanwhile, she said to give Detective Lavalle our full cooperation."

Detective Lavalle inclined her head toward the shelter supervisor.

"I just want you to be aware that this intrusion is highly unorthodox," Carmen said to Detective Lavalle. "As you can imagine, police presence inside the shelter can be quite disruptive to the residents, especially the children."

"I understand," agreed Detective Lavalle. "We shall try to finish up as quickly as possible." She gestured toward the office Grace kept at the shelter. "You'll find a change of clothes in there," she said, handing Signy a standard evidence bag. "When you're dressed, Constable Tran will take a few pictures."

"Is all this really necessary?" said Signy.

"I'll take your statement shortly," replied Detective Lavalle, holding Signy's eyes with her own.

Signy considered arguing, then thought better of it.

"The faster you go, the quicker we'll be done here," said Detective Lavalle.

Signy nodded and stepped past her. Detective Lavalle was proving to be a formidable presence, although whether she was foe or ally, Signy could not yet determine. She touched Carmen on the arm. "May I have a quick word?"

Carmen threw up her arms as if to say, What next? Then she followed Signy into Grace's office.

Signy shut the door with a quiet click.

"What were you thinking going out to the Dalton house alone?" Carmen whispered. "Are you out of your mind?"

Signy took a step back. "What?"

Carmen looked at her aghast. "Everyone knows about Constable Dalton and his nasty son."

Signy crossed her arms over her chest. "I must have missed that meeting."

Carmen narrowed her eyes. "Do you really think that now is the time to get smart with me?"

Signy threw up her hands. "I really don't know anything about them."

Carmen regarded her suspiciously for several seconds, then said, "You've been with the agency for how long now, a year?"

"Almost."

"And how many times have I invited you to do a shift or two over here?"

"I know, it's just that—"

"Sometimes I think that you people over at the Women's Centre think you're too good for us here at the shelter."

Signy opened her mouth to protest, then hesitated, wondering if what Carmen was charging didn't hold an element of truth. Although Vicky's Place and the Women's Centre were two halves of the same agency, of which Grace Holder was the executive director, their functions were quite different.

At the Women's Centre, located in a nondescript office complex across town, social workers and therapists worked a nine-to-five schedule, assisting women who had been impacted by various forms of abuse.

Signy thrived at the Women's Centre. Despite the endless paperwork, she enjoyed the fact that something different was always going on. On any given day, she might help a battered woman navigate the complex legal system, educate a class full of raucous teens about domestic abuse, or take a crisis call as she had today. Whether it was helping to develop safety plans, teaching budgeting, or assisting a homeless family to find housing, she loved the wide variety of tasks her job entailed.

Conversely, workers at Vicky's Place were on duty 24-7. One or two manned the crisis lines in a stuffy basement office, while two or three others toiled in the close quarters of the upper floors, shoulder to shoulder with each other and with the women and children who found safety within its solid walls.

Signy had always thought it took a special kind of person to be able to tolerate the inevitable drama that erupted from time to time. As an introvert, she'd learned that it was essential that she take regular breaks from others in order to function effectively, and she knew she couldn't tolerate the close confines of the shelter for very long. Working at the Women's Centre afforded her the necessary freedom to come and go as she pleased.

Looking at Carmen, she tipped her head in agreement. "You're right. I have been avoiding coming over here."

Carmen heaved a dramatic sigh, then leaned in. "What you should have known is that we've had complaints about both Daltons come in on the anonymous crisis line, especially the elder. He gets off on wielding his power. He's good at it too. So far, no one has had the courage to go public." She shook her head. "We've tipped off the powers that be, of course, but without a formal complaint, there's nothing the force can do."

"Honestly, Carmen, if I'd known, I'd have waited for backup," Signy said, feeling on firmer ground now that the shelter supervisor had provided her with a tailor-made excuse.

"Really?" Carmen said, her eyebrows disappearing up under her wild hair.

Signy opened her mouth to protest.

"Just listen," said Carmen, bangles jangling as she jabbed a finger in the air. "This work is hard. It requires a team effort."

"I know that."

"I'm not sure you do, Signy." Carmen frowned. "This isn't the first time you've gone off half cocked."

Signy winced, recalling, as Carmen had likely intended, her confrontation with a gang of teens a few months ago. She'd been standing at a window in the office, sipping coffee, when she spied a group of boys accosting a young woman out on the street. She'd run from the building without thinking, placing her body between the menacing bullies and the terrified girl.

Her mouth twisted as she remembered the sickening thrill that coursed through her body as she'd imagined smashing their jeering faces into the pavement, stomping their moronic heads into a bloody pulp, and the almost-overwhelming degree of self-control she'd brought to bear in order to hold back. For once, she'd been glad to see the cops arrive, lights flashing, sirens blaring.

Signy forced her face to relax. "That was different."

"Look, honey, you're of no use to anyone if you end up in the hospital, or worse." Carmen peered intently at Signy. "You must learn to think first, act later."

Signy looked down at her feet, the nearly identical admonition she'd passed on to Jenny Dalton a few minutes ago ringing in her ears.

Carmen gave Signy the once-over with a cynical eye but must have concluded she'd tried her best because she left it at that.

Signy waited for a couple of seconds, then continued, "The reason I called you in here was to tell you that I think something might be going on between Jenny Dalton and her father-in-law."

Carmen leaned in. "Did she say something?"

"Not in so many words," Signy said. "It was something about her body language, or maybe something she left out when she was telling her story. Whatever, I'm positive he's doing something to her. She's terrified."

Carmen nodded. "I'll see what I can find out."

"One other thing," continued Signy. "I'm hoping she might call her parents. She's originally from New Brunswick and I think she wants to go home. Can you help with that?"

"If she's ready to get out from under that dreadful husband of hers, then it will be my distinct pleasure to help her in any way I can."

"Thanks," said Signy.

Carmen nodded, then turned to go.

"And Carmen?"

One hand on the door, Carmen glanced over her shoulder at Signy.

"I'm sorry about all this."

Carmen sighed, then held up her hands up like a priest offering a benediction. *"Cosi è la vita."*

A few minutes later, Signy popped her head out into the hallway, as instructed. She'd thrown on the grey track suit that Carmen had provided from the donations pile. It was threadbare, had lost the elastic around the waist, and was at least two sizes too large. She had to keep her fingers curled around the waistband to keep the pants up.

Clicking past Signy, Detective Lavalle picked up the evidence bag. She held it up to the light, peered at it closely, then set it back down on Grace's desk. She handed a similar bag to Signy and asked if she would please remove her shoes.

"Why on earth would you want my shoes?"

Detective Lavalle must have presumed the question to be rhetorical, because she did not answer.

After Signy had reluctantly slipped her sandals into the bag and zipped it shut, she handed it over, muttering, "I just bought those."

Detective Lavalle smiled. "We appreciate your cooperation."

Standing in her bare feet, Signy was forced to look up. The height difference and the tolerant expression on the detective's placid face made her feel more and more like a recalcitrant child.

Oh dear, what can the matter be?
Oh dear, what can the matter be?

"I believe that's everything," said Detective Lavalle. "Of course, the officers who attended the scene at the Dalton residence have collected the canister of Mace."

Signy smiled sweetly. At least she hoped it was a pleasant smile. Without a mirror handy she could well be sneering like an angry teen being forced to hand over the half-empty bottle of hooch. That's how guilty this holier-than-thou cop was making her feel.

Detective Lavalle narrowed her eyes. "Were you aware that the use of pepper spray as a weapon is illegal in Ontario?"

"Hey," said Signy, through clenched teeth, "Were you aware that—"

"Signy?" Grace Holder had finally appeared and was standing in the doorway with her arms crossed firmly over her chest. She was studying Signy with the same impassive gaze as Detective Lavalle, although Signy could see the warning in her eyes.

"Grace," said Detective Lavalle, with a smile.

"Winnie," said Grace, tossing an arm full of files she'd been clutching onto her desk before enveloping the detective in a warm hug.

Great, thought Signy, they know each other.

"How are Dexter and the boys?" asked Grace, sliding over a chair and inviting Detective Lavalle to sit before taking her place behind her desk.

"Growing like weeds, all three of them." Detective Lavalle

said, with a laugh that sounded like wind chimes in a soft breeze. "And Kim?"

While the two women caught up on their respective families, Signy dragged another chair over and sat, wondering if Grace had orchestrated the entire "let's all sit and relax" manoeuvre. If it had been an artful ploy, Signy was grateful. She felt far more at ease now that she was eye level with her interrogators.

"Well," said Winnie, finally, "perhaps we can ask Signy to tell us what happened."

Both women shifted in their chairs and looked at Signy.

Feeling a hot blush creep up her neck, Signy dug her nails into the arms of the chair. She had done nothing technically wrong and she wasn't about to allow these two women to make her feel like she was a criminal.

Oh dear, what can the matter be?
Johnny's so long at the fair.

What followed was a watered-down version of the events out at the Dalton house: the desperate phone call, the urgency of Jenny Dalton's request, the frightened woman and her traumatized children, the raging bull in the yard. Sprinkling a liberal amount of verbal detergent into the mix, she hoped her sanitized version of events was passing muster.

She talked and talked until she heard herself starting to babble. She wrapped up quickly with the image of the poor little girls making their first visit to McDonald's. Anything more and she risked contradicting herself, or worse. She smiled, shut her jaw with a clack, and sat back in her chair.

"I think that all makes perfect sense," said Grace, sliding her chair back. She made as if to rise. "Will you need Signy to dictate her statement to Constable Tran?"

Signy shot a grateful glance at her mentor, but Grace did not acknowledge her. In fact, Grace wasn't looking at Signy at all, which did not seem a particularly good sign.

Detective Lavalle nodded. "I quite agree, Grace. Ms. Shepherd's version of events appears to make perfect sense."

"Well, then," said Grace, rising to her feet.

Detective Lavalle motioned her back down. "The problem, you see," she continued, "is that Mr. Dalton has a quite different version of events."

Grace reluctantly resumed her seat.

"He's lying," cried Signy, unable to help herself.

"Signy," Grace cautioned, "I'm asking you to say nothing further."

Signy opened her mouth to argue but hesitated when she saw Grace piling her curly wad of Marge Simpson hair high over her head. Signy had learned that for Grace, fiddling with her hair was a nervous tic, and the gesture meant Grace was worried. Signy clammed up.

"The question remains as to whether Ms. Shepherd overstepped her bounds," said Detective Lavalle quietly.

"This is ridiculous," said Grace, jabbing a finger toward the ring of bruises on Signy's neck. "Look what that . . . that . . . so-called man did to her."

"Indeed," agreed Detective Lavalle, "and I have no doubt that he will be charged to the full extent of the law."

"I'm glad to hear you finally making some sense, Winnie," Grace interjected.

Detective Lavalle held up a finger. "Presuming Ms. Shepherd's story proves accurate."

Signy snorted derisively but choked it off when both women glared at her.

"Unfortunately, Grace," Detective Lavalle continued, "Mr. Dalton claims that Ms. Shepherd attacked him first, that he put his hands on her throat in an attempt to hold her at bay as she sprayed an entire canister of Mace into his face." Detective Lavalle shot Grace a grim look.

"I see," said Grace, assuming a blank expression. She stood and, crooking a finger, motioned for Signy to do the same.

Signy scrambled to her feet, remembering only at the last second to haul up the waistband of her sagging sweatpants.

"Grace," said Detective Lavalle, "it is most important that I stick to procedure in this case like a fly sticks to honey. You understand?"

Grace sighed. "I do."

Detective Lavalle nodded. "Thank you, Grace." She looked at Signy. "I will see if Constable Tran is finished with Mrs. Dalton. Please remain here and he will be in shortly to take the necessary pictures, and Ms. Shepherd?"

Signy looked at her.

Detective Lavalle raked her dark eyes over Signy's face. "The Dalton men, both senior and junior, are not to be trifled with, especially the elder. He is as slippery as an eel and about as pleasant. Your actions today may have helped the young woman and her children in the short term, but with a little forethought you could have employed more expedient methods that may have resulted in a longer-term solution. It is a long-term solution that I am after, Ms. Shepherd, and unfortunately your rash actions have not helped me."

Holding Signy's eyes with her own, Detective Lavalle said, "Please think about that the next time you decide to play chicken with a speeding train. Do I make myself clear?"

Signy bobbed her head and mumbled, "Yes, ma'am."

Detective Lavalle produced a business card from a pocket of her black slacks and handed it to Signy. "If you think of anything else, or if you need anything, please don't hesitate to call."

Signy clutched the card tightly in her hand. "Yes, ma'am," she repeated, unable to think of anything else to say.

Chapter

10

After Detective Lavalle left in search of her colleague, Grace shut the office door. Turning to Signy, she placed her hands on the girl's shoulders, holding her at arm's length. She ran her eyes over the scraped cheek, the torn ear, and the nasty array of bruises. "My God," she said finally, before engulfing Signy in a fierce hug.

Crushed against Grace's prodigious bosom, Signy resisted the urge to wiggle free. Uninvited physical contact did not sit well with her and it had taken some effort to become even semi-comfortable with the public displays of affection her colleagues employed with liberal abandon.

Finally, Grace stepped back. "Are you okay?"

Signy touched the bruises with a fingertip. "I'll live."

Grace searched Signy's eyes, opened her mouth to say something, then shut it again. Muttering to herself, she stepped toward the mini-fridge she kept in the corner of her office.

Sliding the sagging track pants back up over her hips, Signy wracked her brain for something to say. Should she thank Grace for defending her in front of Detective Lavalle even if Grace had only done it to protect the agency's reputation? Maybe she should go over her story again, pump up the urgency of Jenny's phone call. Better still, maybe she could claim that a lack of communication between the shelter and the Women's Centre staff had been to blame. She glanced over at Grace.

Hunched over the mini-fridge, Grace was peering inside, her eyes unfocused. Signy was reminded of her foster mother, who had sometimes stood the same way in front of an open refrigerator door, blank-eyed and confused, as though not sure what she was looking for. Even as a child Signy had understood that Sarah Shepherd had orchestrated these cooling respites as a way of tapping into her often-dwindling reserve of patience. More importantly, she had learned that at such moments it was best to hold her tongue.

Signy bit her lip and studied her employer. Grace Holder had probably always been the tall kid in school pictures, standing dead centre in the back row. In those days she'd likely been all gangling arms and legs. These days, on the down side of forty, she exhibited a soft roundness that spoke of a love affair with her own legendary baking.

She wore an open-necked linen blouse over a voluminous paisley skirt. Curly brown hair, streaked with grey, clung to her head like a squirrel's nest and jiggled when she walked, a sight that resulted in no end of hilarity among the shelter's younger residents. A handsome woman, Signy's foster father would have said.

Eventually, Grace rose back up, her skirt swirling about her knees like a matador's cape. She turned and offered Signy a Coke.

Accepting the sweating can with a wary smile, Signy took the same seat that Detective Lavalle had recently vacated. She thought about the detective's silly shoes and glanced down at Grace's solid size tens. Signy had always admired the fact that Grace never wore anything but plain, brown Birkenstocks, with socks in the winter, feet bare in warmer weather.

Despite their being ridiculed as the footwear of choice for lesbians and social workers, both groups to which she proudly claimed membership, Grace steadfastly refused to give up the comfort of the form-fitting sandals. Whenever someone poked fun at her, she would throw back her head and laugh. "If you try to march to the tune of a different drummer in Jimmy Choos, you won't get far," Signy had heard Grace say on more than one occasion.

Grace popped open her Coke and leaned forward. Anchored to the front edge of her desk was a brass plaque with an inscription running across it in black cursive letters: "Never Regret, Never Explain, Never Apologize."

"Words to live by?" Signy asked, indicating the plaque with a flick of her eyes, "I hope?"

Grace slammed her Coke onto the desk. "We have procedures and protocols for a reason. They not only keep you and your clients safe but they also help people like Winnie Lavalle do their job. And in the long run that is what we want, right? Trash like Daryl and Richard Dalton off the street?"

"But—"

"But what? You think stooping to bully tactics helps anybody?"

"That's not fair."

"Grow up. You of all people should know that meeting violence with violence gets you nothing but more violence."

Feeling the pulse at her neck jump, Signy scraped her chair back and flew to her feet.

"Not to mention," said Grace, "that your unorthodox methods will keep me up to my eyeballs in red tape and paperwork, and just when we have work to do." She fanned out the stack of files on her desk.

Signy saw a flash of red hidden in the pile and glanced up at Grace.

Grace stared back at her, unblinking.

A quiet knock at the door sounded, and Constable Benjamin Tran poked his head inside. "Am I interrupting?"

"Not at all," replied Grace, opening a drawer and sliding the files inside. She stood and smiled at the young officer. "I was just heading back to the office." She turned to Signy. "When you're done here, give me a call on my cell."

Once Grace had swept from the room, Signy turned her attention to the young cop, who returned her gaze with a frank appraisal of his own. Conscious that her baggy sweats had slipped far too low on her hips, she hauled them up with both hands.

One corner of Constable Tran's mouth twitched upward.

"Very funny," she said, but his grin was infectious and she struggled to hold back her own smile.

"Sorry," he said, extending his hand. "I'm Benjamin Tran, but my friends call me Ben."

She accepted a hand that felt surprisingly pleasant in her own and gave him the once-over. Definitely a cut above the cowboys, jocks, and gangster wannabes that constituted much of Linden Valley's male under-thirty crowd. No more than a few inches taller than she was, he cut a very attractive figure in his blue uniform. A cute smile that crinkled the corners of his kind, dark eyes suggested that it was no accident that he'd been the officer assigned to take photos at the women's shelter. His black hair stood in stiff spikes, and she wondered if his liberal use of gel complied with regulations.

Ben flicked his eyes at the door. "Your boss?"

She rolled her eyes, then flashed him a grin. "Apparently, I really stepped in it."

"Big Dick Dalton?" He frowned. "You sure did."

"People really call him that?"

"I've never met a bigger one," replied Ben, "not that you heard that from me."

Signy laughed. "I thought you cops stuck together, the thin blue line and all that."

Ben lifted a digital camera from its case hanging around his neck. Looking down, he adjusted the settings. Without raising his eyes, he said, "More like the thin white line."

Signy shook her head.

He pointed the camera in her direction, then peered down at the digital display. He touched a couple of buttons, watching the readout. "Are you from around here?" he asked.

"Linden Valley? Nope. I grew up outside of Richmond Hill."

"Almost a city girl."

"Almost," she said, watching him fool with the camera. "You from Toronto?"

"Born and bred." Lifting the camera, he peered through the lens at her.

"Do you miss it?"

"What, the big TO?" He snapped a few shots.

"Hey, I wasn't ready." She smiled.

"No worries, you look great."

Signy pretended not to notice the way the tips of his ears glowed scarlet.

He moved closer and asked her to pull back the collar of her sweatshirt.

She heard the sharp intake of breath when he caught sight of the purple bruises.

"I do miss the city," he said, slowly moving around her in a circle, snapping shots every few seconds, "especially when I have to deal with douche bags like Dalton."

Signy didn't say anything, surprised the young cop was being so open with her. Was he playing some kind of good cop to Detective Lavalle's bad cop?

"I've only been here for a month. Special task force. That hate crime investigation."

"The nip tipping?" Signy regretted the horrible words the second they left her mouth. The rivers and lakes that surrounded Linden Valley were a haven for fishermen, and Asian people often drove up from the city to try their luck in the evenings.

Local thugs, with few brains and even less humanity, had

taken it upon themselves to send a message to the unwelcome newcomers. Seeking out unwary Asian fisherman, gangs of young men would attack, throwing the unfortunate victims into the water, usually after inflicting a nasty beating. Nip tipping, they called it. Hate crimes, local prosecutors had rightly labelled it.

Ben Tran didn't seem to flinch at the offensive term. He nodded. "I've discovered quite a few things about myself, not the least of which is that I hate fishing."

Signy laughed.

He moved round behind her.

She could hear the click of the camera and felt the touch of his breath on the back of her neck like a feather. He smelled good, sweet and spicy.

"But I've also learned that I can't stand small-minded bullies like Dalton. It wouldn't surprise me in the least if I catch him in my net one of these nights."

Signy whirled to face him. "Why are you telling me this?"

"Look," he said, glancing at the closed door and lowering his voice enough that she felt compelled to lean in to him, "that guy is bad news. I heard what you did to his son, and frankly, I don't care what went down out there. You did the right thing."

For a brief moment Signy wondered if he was wearing a wire. Yet despite her paranoia, she felt warmth spread in her belly.

"Look," he continued, "Daryl Dalton is a big bully in a small pond. A jerk to be sure, but he hasn't the stones to go all the way. But Constable Richard Dalton? Now there is a bona fide psychopath, the real deal."

Signy remembered her passing thought that maybe she'd rattled the wrong cage. She stared at Ben.

He slipped the camera back into its case and snapped it closed. "I'm sorry if I've scared you."

"I can handle myself," she said.

Ben grinned. "I'll bet you can. It's just that after this is all over, I intend to ask you out for dinner."

"What?"

He opened the door, then turned back to her. "So until then, make sure you stay in one piece, all right?"

Her mouth dropped open but he'd left the room before she could think of a pithy reply.

Chapter

11

It was after seven before Signy climbed the stairs to her apartment. She rented the top floor of an old Victorian house, and though the hot water wasn't always reliable, she was grateful she hadn't been forced to share the space with a roommate.

Her steps felt heavy, a hangover more from the turmoil of the afternoon than from the bumps and bruises of the physical altercation. She slipped the key into the door and stepped inside, grateful for the cooling drone of the air conditioner.

God, she wished it would rain. Dark thunderclouds had been building all afternoon, and with them came a humidity so cloying she felt as if she could hardly breathe.

She threw her keys and purse onto a wobbly Ikea kitchen table, then peeled off the ridiculous track suit she'd been given at the shelter. Stepping into the bedroom, she removed her underwear. The bra reeked of sweat and cigarette smoke; she shoved it into a laundry basket in the closet. She'd have to remember to get the laundry done soon or the entire room would stink. She pulled out a fresh towel and, wrapping it around her body, headed for the shower.

She barely had room to turn around in the bathroom, but at least it was easy to keep clean. A medicine chest with a mirrored door hung above a chipped aquamarine pedestal sink. A half-empty tube of toothpaste and other grooming essentials perched on a flimsy shelf she'd screwed into the wall herself.

Sliding a new bottle of shampoo from the centre of the row, she held her breath. If the shelf picked this moment to collapse, there was no way she was cleaning up the mess. Luckily, the shelf held, and drawing back the cheap white shower curtain, she turned on the water.

Stepping into the tub, she backed under the flowing stream, allowing hot needles to drive onto her head and shoulders, wincing as the water poured over the scrape on her face. Scrubbing away the remnants of her fight with Dalton, she stood under the soothing stream until the hot water ran out.

After towelling dry, she donned a pair of shorts and a sports bra. Despite her sore face and distant rumbles of thunder, she was looking forward to a run. It helped quiet her mind, and with negative thoughts building as furiously as the storm clouds outside, she needed a good run more than ever.

Her routine rarely varied. She would choose one of two routes. On a good day, she would leave her house, turn right, and head out toward North Street, pounding down the sidewalk until she reached the roundabout that marked the centre of town. The traffic circle was an unusual feature in small-town Ontario and as far as Signy knew was unique to Linden Valley.

She'd jog through a quarter of the circle, passing a gift shop, a café offering fair trade coffee, and an adult lingerie outlet before turning up the unimaginatively named West Street. A few kilometres later she'd arrive at the community park. She'd make a loop around the stately band shell that hosted Sunday concerts in the summer and visits from Santa in the winter before heading back toward home.

On a bad day, like today, she would run in the opposite direction, only as far as the park and back. Not much of a workout, but enough to leave her feeling virtuous if not relaxed.

She'd just laced up her runners and had a hand on the door when her cellphone rang. She considered letting it go to voice mail, but decided she'd pushed her luck far enough.

She looked at the number. Zef, again. She remembered he'd tried to call when she was sitting outside the Dalton house. It seemed like days ago. Whatever he wanted, she'd be much better off not knowing. She punched the off button, tossed the cellphone on the table, and took off into the gathering storm.

Starting off at a light jog, she let her mind wander. After Detective Lavalle and Constable Tran had wrapped up their investigation that afternoon, Signy had called Grace Holder, as instructed. Grace had given her a brief rundown on the contents of the latest red file. A young woman named Elena Morozov was on the run. Grace had said she'd fill in the details later, but meanwhile, Signy's attendance was required at a debriefing session back at the office.

She'd had to bite her lip in order to stifle a groan of protest. Debriefing sessions were required practice whenever a staff member had been impacted by a critical incident: an altercation with an abusive husband, breaking up a fist fight at the shelter, a client suicide. Any type of frightening situation that might cause emotional turmoil demanded a prompt debrief in an effort to curtail post–traumatic stress symptoms.

Signy loathed these sessions. Having to watch poor sods bare their soul in a public therapy session was bad enough; being the subject of that well-intentioned compassion was torture.

Sitting at the head of the boardroom table that afternoon, she'd squirmed in her seat as her colleagues insisted she tell and retell the story in an effort to purge any emotional demons. When one of the ladies had burst into tears, triggered by a painful memory from her own childhood, Signy briefly considered faking an epileptic seizure or even a small heart attack.

Instead, she brought a tissue to her eyes, listened and nodded, and wondered if anyone realized that she deserved an Academy Award for her angst-filled performance. When it was finally over, she declared herself thoroughly debriefed, thanked the crowd for their comfort and encouragement, and even managed to initiate a few hugs.

Stumbling over a broken bit of sidewalk, she determined to change the subject in her head. She wondered what the story was with her new passenger, Elena Morozov. How did a young, seemingly normal girl find herself with no option but to be placed on the Line? Most of the women she'd worked with were older, victims of powerful, well-connected spouses or employers. Perhaps the perpetrator was her father, or maybe she'd chosen the wrong young man to date.

She reviewed the schedule. In the morning she was to drive with Grace to Toronto, where they'd meet with Maitland McGuinness for a briefing. Then Signy would fly out to Calgary in the afternoon, pick up the girl, and shuttle her back to Ontario.

Grace had cleared the trip with Detective Lavalle, who had agreed to the special assignment with the caveat that Signy be available by phone for any follow-up questions. With any luck she'd be back in three days.

Evening shadows were closing in as she thumped across the grassy park toward the ornate wooden band shell just visible in the gathering gloom. Dusk had brought little relief from the soaring temperatures and sweat dripped down her face, stinging her scraped cheek. Her breath came harder than usual as her lungs struggled to process the soggy air. She needed a break.

Stumbling up the steps of the band shell, she flopped down on one of the wooden benches that lined the perimeter. Soft purple flowers fringed the round building, lending an intoxicating fragrance to the night air. Her stomach grumbled and she remembered she hadn't eaten anything since breakfast, not counting the milkshake at McDonald's.

Wiping her brow, she glanced around. The park was deserted, unusual for this time of evening but not surprising. Most sane people were taking refuge inside, air conditioners blowing full blast. She watched a Linden Valley police cruiser slide to a halt out on West Street and a uniformed officer exit the vehicle.

She felt the hairs on the back of her neck tingle. Keeping a wary eye on him as he made the rounds of the park, she thought about the cute cop from that afternoon, Ben Tran. As helpful as he'd been to her, it didn't bode well for his career to be spreading dirt about a fellow officer.

She remembered reading about a young cop who'd had the audacity to charge an off-duty detective with a DUI. Despite the fact that the older cop blew way over the legal limit, the young cop's career was ruined. Blackballed, he'd been relegated to pushing paper when he wasn't getting his butt kicked in the change room.

Signy wiped her face with her T-shirt. Ben Tran had warned her that Richard Dalton was the real deal, a true psychopath. She peered out into the murky darkness. She'd lost sight of the cop. Opening her eyes wide, she scanned the hidden corners of the park until she spotted a shadow ambling around the closed-up hot dog stand.

She followed his progress as he strolled toward the soccer fields. He poked around the aluminum bleachers and a few minutes later she heard him rattle the chain that secured the shed where the town stored soccer nets, bats, and balls.

Bending down, she tightened the laces on her running shoes. Watching fat plops of sweat drip from her forehead onto the wooden deck, she grinned to herself. Maybe she would take Ben Tran up on his dinner offer. Not that she was looking for any more complications in her life right now. God knew she had enough of those to last a lifetime.

Still, she thought about his sweet smile and the sparkle in his eye when he'd pointed the camera at her. She felt a shiver in her belly, then shook her head. Before she could even contemplate a future in Linden Valley, she had to survive Detective Lavalle's investigation.

She sighed and sat up, noticing with relief that the uniformed cop had re-entered his cruiser and was pulling away from the curb. She climbed to her feet and did a couple of squats before turning back to the stairs that led out of the band shell. She stopped dead.

Blocking the stairs, a second uniformed cop regarded her with flat eyes.

She took an involuntary step backwards. The cop tipped his hat back on his head. She was struck by the hardness of his jaw, the prominent mastoid muscle speckled with a grey grizzle that matched his military buzz cut.

Ripped biceps bulged from beneath his short-sleeved uniform shirt, and his gun belt bristled with the weapons of his trade. Signy flinched at the clack of his steel-toed shoes as he crowded her backwards.

"Signy Shepherd," he said.

He spoke her name in a slow hiss, and the image of a coiled rattler flashed in her head. She felt for the canister of Mace she kept tucked alongside her water bottle, then remembered she'd left her fanny pack at home.

"I was watching you run." His eyes slid down the length of her body, then flicked back to her face. "I'm impressed."

Signy's eyes darted left and right but the grassy fields remained deserted.

Following her eyes, the cop said, "I thought I should warn you about running at night. It's not safe for a pretty young lady to be out here on her own."

Ignoring the pounding in her chest, Signy took a step forward and grinned. "Big Dick Dalton, I presume?"

Chapter

12

Dalton threw back his head and laughed, then swiping his hat from his head, used it to whack the side of his leg.

Signy glared up at him, hoping he couldn't see the pulse jumping wildly in her neck.

In a flash, he jerked forward, lashing out his hand as though he meant to grab her ass.

Unable to help herself, she yelped and jumped backwards.

He laughed again, then took a seat on the bench. "See what I mean? You never know what could happen out here. You're lucky that I'm an officer of the law." With a wave of his hand he invited her to sit beside him.

She stayed where she was, her fingers unconsciously probing for the missing canister of Mace.

"Suit yourself, Signy Shepherd." He rolled the words around his tongue. "Uncommon name you have there. Didn't take long to find you in the system." He picked his nose, absently. "Your file certainly made for some interesting reading."

"You can read?" She opened her eyes wide in mock surprise.

He chuckled. "The boy was right. You do have a smart mouth."

She made a move toward the stairs. "We're done here."

He jumped to his feet, blocking her path.

She stared up at him. "You must know that talking to me is a conflict of interest."

"Conflict of interest? Aren't you the smart one." He snorted. "Although, I guess with a record like yours, you've picked up a legal trick or two."

"What record?"

"No formal charges yet," he said, conceding the point with a nod of his head, "but you do skate dangerously close to the line."

"You know what they say? Close only counts in horseshoes."

He narrowed his eyes. "Don't forget hand grenades."

"What?"

"If you're going to shoot off your mouth, at least get it right." He leaned toward her. "Close only counts in horseshoes *and* hand grenades."

"I'm out of here."

"You'll leave when I tell you to."

She glared at him. "I figured your subnormal jackass of a son didn't fall far from the tree." Watching Dalton's sunburned face turn an even deeper shade of red, she risked a quick glance over her shoulder, praying that someone had decided on a late evening stroll. No good. They might as well have been on the moon.

When she turned back, his face was inches away. She could smell onions and beer and something fetid, gum disease, or bilious fumes from an abused liver?

Digging meaty fingers into her upper arm, he pulled her close. With his other hand he grabbed her buttocks, grinding her pelvis against his. He brought his lips to her ear. "I like you, Signy Shepherd. You got guts."

She sprang off one foot trying to ram her knee into his groin, but he blocked her with an iron thigh.

"Simmer down," he said, holding her tight, "unless you finally want that assault charge you've been jonesing for."

"Go to hell."

Quicker that she could have ever imagined, Dalton's hands flashed up, clamping her head in a viselike grip. Using his thumbs at the hinges of her jaws, he forced open her mouth, then jammed his tongue into her mouth, grinding his lips against hers.

Unable to bite down, she squirmed against him, raining useless punches against his rock-hard torso. After what seemed like hours, he reached around and yanked her ponytail, wrenching her head backwards. He glared down at her.

Hunger, dehydration, and fear were working against her. Black spots floated in her field of vision and she willed herself not to faint.

Staring into her eyes for several seconds, Dalton bared his teeth, "Now that's what I like to see." Letting go of his grip on her hair, he chucked her under the chin as though she were a child, then shoved her away.

Signy stumbled backwards.

"Cunts like you think you own the world." He jabbed two fingers into her chest. "You think that you can waltz into a man's home and steal his kids? What about his rights?"

Signy stared at him, incredulous. "Your son beat the shit out of Jenny. He lost his rights."

"She's a liar."

"Bullshit."

"What do you know? Sluts like her cry rape all the time."

Signy chomped down on her lip. Arguing with this moron was pointless. Worse, she was aching to wipe that smug look off his face.

Oh dear, what can the matter be?
Oh dear, what can the matter be?

"Daryl is not going to lose his girls because some bitch lied through her teeth." He narrowed his eyes. "And you're going to get them back."

"Sounds like you have some experience with losing kids."

He stared at her, impassive. "Go shrink someone else's head, sweetheart. All I need from you is them girls back."

"What does that have to do with me?" she said, crossing her arms over her chest. "Jenny wants nothing more to do with your freak of a son."

He reached for the hat he'd left on the bench, then snugged it on his head. He walked over to the steps, then turned to look at her. "You're the smartass, I'm sure you'll think of something."

Signy glared at him.

He rested a thick hand on the butt of his holstered gun. "If my grandbabies aren't back where they belong by tomorrow night, then you and me are going to have ourselves a party." He walked over to the steps, then paused. "By the way, if you mention this to any of them dyke friends of yours or that voodoo detective . . ." He held her eyes with his. "I think you get the picture."

Signy stood motionless as he clumped down the steps. Just before he melted away into the darkness, he slammed his palm down twice onto the wood siding of the band shell, the double tap of an assassin's bullet.

Chapter

13

"Mr. Tracker!" said Leonid Volkov, the word sounding more like *Meeister* in his heavily accented English. "Good of you to come on such short notice."

The Tracker held out a hand.

"Forgive me," Volkov said, wiping his hands on a thick white towel. He was wearing a white lab coat over a pair of soft, brown corduroy pants and a tight cotton pullover that showed off his powerful chest. "I've been in the darkroom, developing some prints. I had a very exciting session this morning. The model was perfect, very animated."

He shook the Tracker's hand. "Join me in a drink?"

Following Volkov to the bar, the Tracker admired the big man's exquisite taste. Glass and brushed steel furniture accentuated the contemporary white-on-white decor.

One interior wall glowed with an artful display of Volkov's own photographs. The Tracker peered closely at a stark black and white of a homeless woman camped out on a street corner, staring defiantly into the dark sky. In the bottom right hand corner was the stylized rendition of a lion's head that Volkov used to sign all his work.

"I attended your exhibit in Los Angeles last month," the Tracker said, accepting a crystal glass containing two fingers of icy Stolichnaya vodka. "Your exploration of shadows is fascinating."

"Did you?" Volkov tossed the contents of his glass down his throat without swallowing. "Every man needs a little creative outlet, don't you agree?" He poured himself another shot.

The Tracker smiled thinly over the rim of his glass. The shock of white hair and road map of burst blood vessels that covered his bulbous nose aside, the man was as sturdy as a locomotive, and equally imposing.

"It's a lovely evening," said Volkov. "Why don't we talk on the balcony."

The two men stepped onto one of three terraces that opened off Volkov's penthouse office suite. Located on the west side of the forty-storey headquarters of Volkov Developments, it afforded a spectacular view of the city of Vancouver far below and the surrounding mountains.

Leaning over the railing, the Tracker gave a low whistle. Hosting the 2010 Winter Olympics had obviously done wonders for the old girl. The city sparkled like a jewel on the shores of an azure sea.

"Beautiful, is it not?" inquired Volkov.

"Most impressive."

Swirling the contents of his glass, Volkov looked down over his adopted city. "And yet, I find myself unable to enjoy my good fortune."

The Tracker glanced at Volkov. Something was different since the last time he'd worked for the old man. He couldn't pinpoint what had changed. A bit more flesh around the jowls, a falter in his step?

"I lost a dear friend last night." Volkov extracted a linen handkerchief from his suit pocket and dabbed at his eyes. "I've known Pavel since we were boys."

Murmuring a meaningless condolence, the Tracker looked away.

"You Americans," said Volkov, blowing his nose into the handkerchief, "so afraid to show a little emotion."

Raising an eyebrow, the Tracker took a sip of vodka.

Volkov mopped his streaming eyes, then barked with laughter.

The Tracker gritted his teeth. "You said the matter was urgent?"

Ignoring the Tracker's impatience, Volkov downed the rest of his vodka and asked with a chuckle in his voice, "You are wondering if perhaps I have slipped down the rabbit hole?"

The Tracker glanced sideways at the big man. That was exactly what he'd been thinking.

Volkov sighed, then stepped over to a long glass table. Gripping the back of one of the wrought iron chairs, he leaned forward as though taking a strain off his back.

He shook his head. "Not to worry, Mr. Tracker. I am in my right mind. It is just that I have had a bit of a shock." He glanced over at the younger man. "When you have lived as many years as I, you will learn that sometimes life conspires to reach out, grab you by the throat, and give you a good shake."

He sat down heavily, then with a wave of his hand invited the Tracker to join him.

Volkov slipped a photograph from his pocket and slid it across the table.

Under the soft glow of pot lights the Tracker examined the picture without touching it.

"Beautiful, isn't she?" Volkov stated.

"Quite," replied the Tracker. The girl was a green-eyed redhead, close to six feet tall judging by the length of thigh flowing out from beneath a smoky grey skirt. The white blouse and black money belt strapped to her waist pegged her as a waitress. She was smiling at the camera, although the two spots of colour that bloomed on the pale contours of her cheeks suggested a certain level of discomfort.

Volkov leaned over and ran a finger over the girl's face. "Her name is Elena Morozov. I found her this summer working in one of my hotels. Isn't she unique?"

With some effort the Tracker maintained a neutral expression. The way the old man was fingering the photograph turned his stomach.

"We got off on the wrong foot, you see, a little misunderstanding. You know how it goes."

The Tracker dipped his head in false acknowledgement.

"I sent a friend to her apartment to extend an invitation. She misinterpreted his intentions and ran." Volkov replaced the photo in his pocket. "I need you to find her."

The Tracker nodded. "Do you have any indication of where she's gone?"

Volkov tented his fingers together. "I had a nice chat with her landlord this morning and he agreed that she would be better off under my protection. Mr. Zhang was most helpful. He informed me that after the disagreement last night, Elena was driven away by his wife. He did not know the girl's ultimate destination but did mention that his wife works at Vancouver Community College as a lecturer. He understood his wife was taking the girl there, possibly to enlist further assistance."

The Tracker nodded, then set his glass down on the table.

"Not very much to go on, and unfortunately Mr. Zhang has left the building." Volkov chuckled. "Just like your Mr. Presley."

Keeping his expression a perfect blank, the Tracker rose to his feet. "You've given me more than enough to get started, sir."

Volkov gripped the Tracker's hand with an iron fist. "I sent for you, Mr. Tracker, because you are the best. I am insisting that you not let me down."

Trying not to flinch at having the bones in his hand ground into chalk, the Tracker said, "I will find her. You have my word."

Volkov showed his teeth. "Screw this up, young man, and I will have more than that."

The Tracker returned the grin, clasping the back of Volkov's hand with his free hand. With his index finger he applied a precise amount of force to a particularly painful pressure point in the webbing between Volkov's thumb and forefinger.

Volkov jerked his hand free and took a step back.

"Leo," said the Tracker, the smile disappearing from his face, "are you suggesting I could be defeated by a mere girl?"

Rubbing the sore spot with the other thumb, Volkov let out a harsh laugh. He shook his head. "My apologies, Mr. Tracker, no offence intended."

"Of course not," replied the Tracker. He held the big Russian's dangerous blue eyes with his own. "Nothing has changed in my world, Volkov. I locate the girl, you pay me. That is as complicated as it gets."

Volkov rubbed his knuckles along the side of his jaw, then shrugged. "Perhaps you are correct, Mr. Tracker. But I have learned that it is always prudent to prepare for the unexpected." He stepped in and clapped a huge hand on the Tracker's shoulder, knocking the smaller man slightly off-kilter. "Hubris goes before a fall, Mr. Tracker. Did you learn nothing from the folly of your predecessor?"

Regaining his footing, the Tracker stared up at Volkov. "I'll be in touch."

"I have no doubt," said Volkov, before turning away and walking back to the bar.

Chapter

14

Signy hunkered down in the dark band shell even though she knew that Dalton was long gone. Stomach roiling, she could still feel the foul taste of him like bitter poison inside her mouth. He'd said his piece and she'd received the message loud and clear. Figure out a way to fix the situation or face the consequences. Unfortunately, she had exactly zero ideas on how she was going to manage that.

When she felt like her legs might finally support her weight, she crept down the wooden steps and loped across the grassy expanse back out to West Street, her mind racing. Reaching the relative safety of West Street, she slowed to a walk. Her legs felt like rubber. The local cinema had just let out and she was relieved at the number of people milling about. She remembered the card Detective Lavalle had given her at the shelter that afternoon. What would happen if she told the detective about Dalton's threats?

She aimed a half-hearted kick at an empty paper cup littering the sidewalk. She had no doubt Big Dick would deny the whole thing. Worse, if Dalton had been able to access her juvenile records, then Lavalle would be equally aware of her checkered past. Lavalle already suspected she'd deliberately incited the violent confrontation with Daryl Dalton; why would she believe Signy's account of the incident at the band shell?

As she rounded the corner onto her own street, she considered another possibility. Should she come clean with Grace? Her mouth twitched. She could almost hear her boss's angry proclamation: "Dalton has been allowed to run the show in Linden Valley for far too long. It's time to draw a line in the sand."

Signy collapsed onto a bench at a lighted bus stop and rested her head in her hands. A steady throb was building behind her left eye. Perhaps she and Grace could work together to come up with another way of taking down Dalton. As Carmen Calzonetti had reminded her that afternoon, she needed to be more of a team player, reach out for help, accept the fact that she couldn't do everything on her own.

Stretching her back, she looked up. The quarter moon, a dim sliver in the night sky, offered little guidance, and the smattering of stars that shone through the light pollution of Linden Valley seemed cold and distant.

She shook her head. She wouldn't tell Grace. She had no idea how her mentor would react once Dalton started spewing her past indiscretions far and wide. She couldn't risk it. She had too much to lose.

Hauling herself off the bench, Signy checked up and down the road for the ominous sight of a Linden Valley police cruiser.

Satisfied that she was alone, she turned for home. Dalton had given her until tomorrow night. She'd just have to stall him until she figured out a way to settle the matter on her own.

As she passed the house two doors down from her own, she caught sight of a beat-up Ducati motorcycle parked across the street. Her eyes darted left and right until she could just make out the shape of a figure leaning against the fence beside her property. She stopped in her tracks.

She hadn't thought this day could get any worse, but apparently the gods were not yet done playing with her. Taking a deep breath, she marched the last few steps, rounding the corner onto her driveway. She stalked up to the figure leaning casually against the wooden fence.

He was wearing a worn black leather jacket and a pair of faded blue jeans slung low on his hips. On his feet, a shiny new pair of black and white Nike Yeezy running shoes. His face was smooth and she could tell he'd washed his hair. It fell in soft brown curls over his eyes. She could smell a sweet mix of marijuana and apples. She watched his teeth flash white in the darkness.

"Hey, babe," he said, in the distinctive drawl that never failed to hit her deep in the belly. "Miss me?"

Chapter

15

The world was a different place than it was even ten years ago. Unless a person made their home in a mud hut in sub-Saharan Africa, it was the rare individual who could make a move on this planet without leaving bread crumbs for someone else to follow. Almost everyone trailed electronic signatures behind them like waving flags.

It was this new reality on which the Tracker relied. The girl had been on the run less than twenty-four hours, and according to Volkov her only assistance came from a geriatric community college teacher. He predicted that he'd have the location of the girl within the hour and be back in his New Mexico home before the skittish Vancouver weather had a chance to turn on him.

His hunch would prove accurate on only one count.

He began with an immediate search of her phone, Internet,

and credit card records. Her most recent expenditures might give him a clue as to her location. Unfortunately, her most recent cellphone usage was over twenty-four hours old and a quick check proved she did not have a land line.

A search of her Internet usage proved equally frustrating. No Facebook page, no Twitter account, and the sites that she surfed were almost all related to her upcoming studies at university. With the exception of the odd YouTube video of the adorable kitty variety, she visited very few frivolous sites.

She did have a Visa card but it hadn't been used in months. The girl was really off the grid for a young woman her age. He'd have to take advantage of Volkov's intel and pay a visit to the community college office of the landlord's wife.

Mrs. Zhang's office proved a snap to invade. The only minor impediment came in the form of a middle-aged Australian security guard with a frizzy perm and an enormous gap between her front teeth. She seemed to be under the impression that allowing visitors into the main administration building without subjecting them to a full interrogation, if not a strip search, would be tantamount to a national security breach.

He didn't mind the distraction. He appreciated her diligent attention to duty. As usual, it required no more than a boyish toss of his dirty-blond hair, a few scorching glances, and some whispered entreaties to make his way past the troll at the gate.

He wasn't sure why he had this effect on women—and on more than a few men. He'd been told more than once that he'd won the lottery in the looks department. He had a thick head of blond hair and pleasing blue eyes, and he worked hard to keep himself in shape, but there was something else, some innate quality that seemed to attract people. He chalked it up to the biological luck of the draw. He must have had good genes.

He found it curious that in spite of the Australian pit bull, the college fell woefully short when it came to decent security hardware. The lock on Mrs. Zhang's office door was a joke. He was inside within seconds.

The office was tiny, not much more than a large utility closet. He barely had room to turn around, hemmed in as he was by the desk at one end and a pair of flimsy shelves that lined both sides of the room. Cheap wood planks groaned under the pressure of an eclectic variety of feminist literature.

A quick look around proved his theory. There were bread crumbs scattered everywhere. A battered Dell laptop, cover closed, power off, sat in the middle of the desk. He slid a scratched student-chair to one side and squeezed in behind the desk. Flipping open the lid, he pressed the power button.

As the screen glowed to life, he noted that the conscientious Mrs. Zhang had been savvy enough to protect her data. A prompt in the middle of the screen was demanding a password. Breaking a password that consisted of a combination of more than eight letters and numbers would take more time than he was willing to waste.

Most people used something mundane, a birthdate or phone number, the name of a pet or a grandmother. If he'd been privy to anything about the private life of Mrs. Zhang, he would have enjoyed unlocking her secrets, but he did not have that information, nor did he have the inclination. He wanted to find this girl and get out of there. He was itching to move on to his next candidate, the familiar need growing stronger by the hour.

He turned his attention to the phone. It was an older model, a basic office phone system, he noted with satisfaction, a breeze to crack. Bending down, he followed the cable that led from the phone to the wall jack and squeezed the clear plastic plug, releasing the cable.

He grabbed his knapsack and burrowed into the main compartment, extracting an electronic device about the size of a small DVD player. He plugged the cable he'd just removed from the wall jack into an identical jack on the small device. He then unwound a similar cable from the back of the device and, bending down, inserted that end directly into the wall. He pushed the power button and waited.

A few seconds later, the LCD screen on the device lit up. He tapped out a series of commands and before long nodded with satisfaction as a list of phone numbers flashed on the screen. He had successfully hacked into the college communication system, and all that was needed was to locate this office extension and determine what calls had been made, and to whom, right about the time the girl went missing.

It took him less than five minutes to determine that Mrs. Zhang had put through two calls from this office at 3:30 a.m. and 3:36 a.m. The first had been to an unlisted, secure number. Tapping in a few more commands, the Tracker was rewarded when the three-digit area code of the call was revealed. It was a simple matter to determine that the 416 prefix originated in Toronto, Ontario.

The second call was even easier. The name of the party was

listed directly beside the ten-digit number, Fraser Valley Women's Shelter, Surrey, British Columbia. A quick check of the Rolodex that Mrs. Zhang kept on her desk revealed the address of the shelter in the suburbs of Vancouver.

He stared at the screen. A women's shelter would be a perfect place to hide a girl on the run. The thought set off a faint buzz at the edges of his consciousness. What was it? After several seconds of fruitless mental effort he shook his head. It would come to him. He'd let it go for now.

He returned his attention to the screen. Given that the first call had been to the 416 area code, he guessed that someone in Toronto was orchestrating the girl's flight. Maybe she had ties there? Unfortunately, there was no indication of when the operation was going down. He hoped he wasn't too late. It would be much more difficult to pick up the trail again.

Shutting off his device and replacing it in the knapsack, he snapped the phone cable back into its jack in the wall. He arranged the Dell laptop exactly as he'd found it, replaced the desk and visitor chairs, then took a last look around.

Satisfied, he slipped out the door, leaving behind only his gratitude that Mrs. Zhang had left so many crumbs for him to follow and it would not be necessary to subject her to a nice chat with Leo the Lion.

Chapter

16

"What are you doing here, Zef?" Signy glared at him, her hand on her hip.

"You haven't been returning my calls."

She shoved past him and assumed a blocking position between him and her front door. Crossing her arms over her chest, she glared at him. "And what does that tell you?"

"Hey, if I recall you paid me a midnight visit a few weeks ago."

She narrowed her eyes. "That wasn't my fault."

"Oh, right," he said, laughing. "Your old shit box drove itself." He grinned. "When are you going to stop blaming the car and admit you can't resist me?"

She opened her mouth to spit out a snide retort, then shut it again. "Look, this really is a bad time. I've had a brutal day."

Taking a step closer, he peered at the bruises on her neck. "Been up to your old tricks again?"

"Go to hell," she said, turning away.

He grabbed her by the arm and spun her toward him. Reaching out, he traced a finger down her neck where the dark bruises pulsed.

She felt the fine hairs on the back of her arm stand to attention. She slapped his hand away.

"Why don't you let me come inside and explain?" He took a step back. "Hands off, I promise. It's just that I have a *situation* here, Sig."

A situation? That had been their 911 code for as long as she could remember. It was the one thing Zef didn't take lightly. If he was invoking the emergency code, then things must be pretty bad. "All right, you have ten minutes." Heading for the door, she called over her shoulder, "And don't call me Sig."

Laughing, he glanced over at his motorcycle. "Mind if I park the bike behind the house?"

She looked at the Ducati, then him, then out onto the street again. "What shit are you bringing down on me, Zef?"

He put his hands up in mock surrender. "Just taking the usual precautions."

She waved a hand in the direction of the parking area out back. "Put it beside my car, then come on up. I need to have a shower."

"Do you want me to scrub your back?" His voice dripped honey.

She stopped in her tracks. "Do you want to come up or not?"

Jamming his hands into the front pockets of his jeans, he chuckled. "Hands off, I swear."

While Zef parked the bike, Signy raced up the stairs to her apartment and called the shelter. She asked the night worker if Jenny and the girls had been safely processed and was relieved when she was told that the little family had been put on a plane a couple of hours ago. They were on their way to Jenny's parents' place in New Brunswick.

"That was fast," said Signy, smiling with relief.

The worker made an affirmative noise. "Grace wanted to be on the safe side."

"Thank God for that," she replied.

"Are you okay, Signy? I heard about what happened. That was a hell of an afternoon."

"Me? Sure. Everything is good here." After promising to call if she felt the need to talk, Signy hung up. Jenny and the kids were safe. She had some breathing room, time to figure out just how she was going to deal with Big Dick Dalton.

She grabbed a cold bottle of water from the fridge, popped a couple of Tylenol, then turned on the shower. She took a quick shower, then brushed and rebrushed her teeth, trying to erase the memory of Dalton's tongue in her mouth.

After she'd donned a pair of shorts and a clean T-shirt and twisted her hair into a wet braid, she felt human enough to face Zef. She walked out of the bedroom and was hit by the heavenly aroma of frying bacon and eggs. She heard the pop of the toaster and watched Zef snap up two pieces of golden bread and apply a thick spread of jam to each.

"Hope you don't mind," he said over his shoulder. "You looked starved."

Unable to help herself, she smiled weakly, then sagged down onto one of her wobbly kitchen chairs. The table was set with two placemats he'd concocted from clean tea towels. He'd folded paper towels into neat triangles and tucked them under the forks. A wineglass sat at each setting. A half-melted candle he must have scrounged from under the sink twinkled from the centre of the table. For one horrible instant she felt tears prick behind her eyes.

As she watched him cook, she remembered the day he'd been dropped off at the Shepherd foster home, one eye swollen shut and spoiling for a fight.

Mrs. Entwhistle, the social worker, had practically shoved him into the house, announcing that he liked to be called Zef, before exchanging a long look with David Shepherd.

Signy, at fourteen, maybe a year or two younger than the new boy, watched the scene covertly from the top of the stairs. She liked to spy on the new arrivals. She could tell a lot from the way they stood in the front hallway with Mrs. Entwhistle.

Some of them stared glumly at the floor, shoulders hunched, refusing to speak. Others offered an appeasing smile and open hands, as if to say, "Please don't hurt me." It was only the first-timers who let tears flow. The veterans knew that if you showed any signs of distress, you might as well stick a Kick Me sign on your back.

Others, like this new boy, entered the Shepherd house bristling with fury. Signy had learned to interpret the silent communication between Mrs. Entwhistle and her foster parents. This boy must be a real shit disturber judging by the fact that Mrs.

Entwhistle's eyebrows were arched up so high Signy thought they might disappear into her helmet of salt and pepper hair.

The boy ignored David's outstretched hand before casually extracting a pack of cigarettes from his jacket pocket and tapping one into his palm.

"Gotta light?" The boy grinned at David, and Signy thought her heart might stop. He was without a doubt the most beautiful human being she had ever seen in her entire life.

David sighed and opened his palm, staring at the boy without blinking until the kid finally relinquished the pack of smokes with a snort of disgust.

Watching the scene from above, Signy was hardly able to breathe. With his shining hair the colour of dark honey hanging in glossy waves over his eyes, and his tight black T-shirt on which a picture of Tupac glowered, she decided he rated a twelve out of ten on the coolness scale. And where did he get a name like Zef? She'd never heard anything like it before.

As David and Zef continued the opening salvos of what would prove to be a year-long sparring match, Signy chewed on the end of her long braid. She sent a fervent prayer out into the universe that David would put Zef in the room beside hers, empty since the Baxter twins had been sent out west to live with their aunt.

David reached down to pick up the garbage bag that held all of Zef's worldly possessions.

"Hey man," said Zef, grabbing the bag and hefting it in one hand, "that's my stuff."

David sighed, then nodded and led the way up the stairs.

Signy melted back down the hallway and into her bedroom, leaving the door open a crack so she could get a closer look. As he sauntered by her hiding spot, she noticed with a stab in her chest that his knuckles were white where he clutched his bag.

David opened the door of the room beside hers and stepped inside. She could hear him extolling the virtues of the large bedroom the boy would have all to himself. Zef paused at the threshold, then leaned against the door jamb. He tossed the garbage bag inside the room.

"Can I have my smokes back, man?"

David did not respond, and Signy could imagine him regarding the boy with that look of unruffled patience he often assumed when starting off with a new kid.

Zef stared at David for several long moments before he blinked and pushed himself away from the door jamb.

"Whatever," he said, jamming his hands into the front pockets of his jeans. "It's your house." He took one step into his new bedroom before popping his head out into the hallway and looking directly into Signy's eyes.

"Hey, kid," he said, with a long, slow smile. "Catch ya later."

Signy's mouth had dropped open and the braid she'd been chewing fell from her fingers.

He'd winked, then followed David into his new room.

Twelve years later and the big jerk still had the same effect on her. Despite the fact that he'd been the cause of so much trouble in her life—hell, he'd been the reason she'd been fired from her last job—and despite the fact that she'd vowed never to see him again, she still couldn't stop herself from opening the door and inviting him into her life.

Chapter

17

Hunkered down in the front seat of the rental, the Tracker watched a dust devil swirl to life outside his window. Black thunderheads like plumes of smoke churned high into the eastern sky and he could smell a hint of ozone in the air. He hoped the rain would hold off.

He was parked in a twenty-four-hour Safeway market located directly across the street from the Fraser Valley Women's Shelter. His nondescript Nissan Sentra attracted no unwanted attention alongside Toyotas and Fords, and he had a clear view of the shelter's front entrance.

The shelter was an imposing Victorian structure, and he could imagine the days when the stately homes that graced this main thoroughfare proclaimed their owners' high status. Unfortunately, those days seemed long gone.

The old beauty was in a terrible state of disrepair. A kid could ski down the sloping veranda, and a shoddy addition tacked onto one side was beginning to show signs of separating from the main building. Peeling paint completed the picture of a grande dame left to moulder by ungrateful children.

A cursory examination with a tiny but powerful set of binoculars proved that what the shelter lacked in structural soundness it more than compensated for in security. Closed-circuit cameras were visible on all sides of the building, and the main entrance, located on the north side, appeared state-of-the-art.

He smiled. Not that he would ever go near the place. He would use only his ears to enter the aging fortress. Using one's head rather than brute strength almost always resulted in a successful outcome with fewer complications.

Opening a steel case on the passenger seat, he removed a parabolic listening device. He placed the dish, no larger than a small apple, on his dashboard and pointed it toward the shelter.

Inserting an earbud, he settled down to listen. In less than five minutes he had his confirmation. Heaving a sigh of relief, he made the call.

"I found her," the Tracker said into the headpiece he'd plugged into his ear. "She's in a shelter in Surrey."

"Quick work," said Leonid Volkov.

He didn't answer. He'd already wasted too much of his valuable time.

"Wait a minute, what do you mean, a shelter? They've stashed her in a bomb shelter?"

"Not a bomb shelter, a women's shelter, a safe place for women."

"Ah, yes, the Sapphic tradition is alive and well."

The Tracker shook his head and raised his eyes to heaven. On occasions like this it rankled when he considered the people with whom he was forced to do business. If he never had to have another ridiculous conversation like this again it would be too soon.

"Be that as it may, I have found her."

"Are you positive?"

"Quite. I heard one of the staff speaking to her just a few minutes ago. They are planning on moving her this evening." The Tracker waited but there was no response. "Mr. Volkov?"

"I'm thinking."

The Tracker didn't like the sound of that.

"Where are they taking her?" asked Volkov, his tone suddenly brisk.

"She's being driven to Calgary tonight and then to Toronto soon after."

"Toronto?"

The Tracker could hear Volkov sucking on one of his foul cigars.

When Volkov did not speak after several seconds, the Tracker said, "If you wish to have her picked up, you'll need to send someone quickly."

"No," said Volkov with an air of finality, "I want you to follow her. See where she goes, with whom she meets."

"With respect, you don't need me. Any one of your staff could have located the girl. She doesn't know what she's doing and the people helping her are amateurs. Why don't you save yourself a lot of money and send one of your own men?"

"This situation is delicate. I want it treated as such. Keep her under surveillance at all times. Tell me who she meets, where she goes. When I am ready, I will send someone to pick her up."

"It will cost you," he said into the Bluetooth.

Volkov sighed. "What does one ever get from this life for free? Do it."

The Tracker severed the connection and examined the shelter with renewed interest. The stakes in this game had just changed. He watched another dust devil, more powerful than before, churn up debris in front of his car. He grinned as it danced eastward before vanishing as mysteriously as it had appeared.

• • •

"I found your stash," Zef said, filling her glass with a Chardonnay she'd hidden near the back of the fridge.

She took a grateful slurp, then tucked into the all-day breakfast he slapped down in front of her. She didn't come up for air until she'd used the last crust of toast to scrape the plate clean. When she finally looked up, she found him smiling at her. "What?" she asked, touching her sore face in a self-conscious gesture.

"I forgot how beautiful you are."

"Hey," she warned, narrowing her eyes.

"No hands," he said, raising his hands in the air. "I'm a man of my word."

She smiled back at him. "Since when?"

He raised his glass in a mock salute and then appeared to notice the scrape on her cheek for the first time. His smile died.

"Seriously, Sig." He tipped the rim of the glass toward her face. "Is everything okay?"

"I'm fine."

"If someone did this to you, I'll personally kick his ass."

She sighed. "That ship has already sailed."

He grinned. "That's my girl."

Pushing her chair back, she gathered her plate and tossed it into the sink. "So what's so critical? After what happened, I thought I made it perfectly clear that you and I were done."

"You know I'm sorry about that; it was my fault entirely."

"Understatement of the century," she mumbled under her breath. "You got me fired."

"How is she?" he asked quietly.

"Skyler?" She knew he was referring to the fifteen-year-old client that Signy had been charged with taking to the Eaton Centre in Toronto for a celebratory lunch over a year ago. Signy had been working then at a group home for at-risk youth, and one of her favourite clients, a prickly young woman named Skyler, had managed six months of good behaviour. The trip to the Eaton Centre was to be her reward.

Signy loved working at the group home. She had a way with the girls, probably because she'd been where they were. She knew what it was like to feel things more acutely than other people, to react to even the most minor slight with nothing short of a nuclear meltdown. It had taken years of therapy, but she'd clawed her way back, learning to think first, act later. At least most of the time.

When she and Skyler had run into Zef that afternoon, he'd immediately charmed the younger girl and invited himself to lunch. Signy had reluctantly agreed. Skyler was having such a good time, she hadn't wanted to throw rain on her parade. At least that's what she told herself.

After lunch, just as they were about to part ways, the trio had been confronted by a couple of thugs who were seriously pissed off with Zef for some infraction or another. The gangsters had listened to no more than twenty seconds of Zef's whining excuses before they attacked.

What they hadn't counted on was the out-of-control banshee who had launched herself onto the back of the smaller one, clamping onto his ear with her teeth and, quite literally, ripping it off. When the goon finally shook her off, Skyler had fallen to the concrete floor and hit her head. She'd been unconscious when the medics had taken her away.

Signy had been summoned to the head office the next morning and fired on the spot. She'd also been barred from any further contact with any of the residents of the group home. She'd accepted the punishment without question. She knew Zef wasn't really to blame. The responsibility for Skyler's injury lay entirely with her. She was the one who had allowed Zef near the vulnerable youngster.

She bit her lip. "They wouldn't let me visit her in the hospital. I don't know what happened to her."

Zef covered her hand with his. "I'm sorry, Sig."

She felt a flutter in her lower belly. "Don't call me Sig." She slipped her hand away.

"Ah, babe," he said, "I wish things could have been different." He grabbed her hand again and brought the fingertips to his lips.

She stared at his mouth, remembering the exquisite touch of his lips on hers. "Me too," she said, snatching her hand back. She rose abruptly and walked over to the counter, where she poured another glass of wine. Leaning against the counter, out of his reach, she said, "All right. Give it to me. What's going on?"

He glanced over at her and shrugged. "It's tricky, I won't lie to you."

"You better not," she said.

One corner of his mouth crooked up. "I've been doing some work for a guy up in Cornwall."

"Cornwall? Are you running illegal cigarettes again?"

He shrugged. "It was either that or meth and that stuff scares the shit out of me."

Signy sighed, then waved her hand in a "go on" gesture.

"We had a communication breakdown somewhere along the line and now he's claiming I owe him thirty large." He stood, shoving his chair back with a loud scrape. "I told him I can get the cash but he'll have to wait until next week. One week. Is that too much to ask?"

Signy looked at him from beneath hooded eyes. "I take it he isn't the understanding type?"

"This is one serious dude, Sig. But listen, the good thing is I have another deal closing in a couple of days. I just need a place to crash until then." He flashed the grin that she knew from bitter experience never failed him. He held his hands together in front of him in an attitude of prayer. "I swear this is the last time, Sig. Never again, I promise."

She stared at him for almost a minute. She recalled the words of one of her better therapists. *In a moment of crisis, Signy, give yourself the time and space to think. Take a few deep breaths. Is what you are planning to do likely to make the situation worse? What is that wise voice in your head trying to tell you?*

Signy inhaled, then exhaled. The wise voice inside her head couldn't have been more clear had it been shouting at her through a megaphone. She needed to shove Zef out the door and let him clean up his own mess.

She raked her eyes over his body, unable to resist the play of the candlelight on his golden skin, the shine of his freshly washed hair, and the curve of his tight jeans. For a brief instant, an image of cute Constable Benjamin Tran popped into her mind, but she pushed it away. Dragging her eyes away from him, she looked up at the ceiling. "I know I'm going to regret this."

He beamed at her. "You won't, I promise. Three days, four at the most, then I'll be out of your hair."

"And you won't come back?"

He held two fingers aloft in the universal salute. "Scout's honour."

Signy laughed despite herself and then, setting her wine-glass down on the table, she stood. The anger and dread that had plagued her all day had vanished. Her heart was pounding, sending a delicious heat throughout her body. She felt a tug as though every cell in her body had shifted, was standing to attention, polarized in his direction.

He watched her approach, a smile playing around his lips. "I thought you said hands off?"

"New rule," she said, then stepped into his arms.

•　•　•

A half a block away, Dalton slouched in his cruiser, watching the action in the Shepherd apartment. He'd let out a long, slow whistle when he saw the leather-clad man grab the girl. By the way they were going at it, he wouldn't have been surprised if they fucked right in front of the window.

When the show was over and the lights winked out, he jogged around the back of her house and took down the licence plate of the Ducati Streetfighter. No way a leather-bound asswipe like that could afford such a sweet ride. Drug money? Pimp? That last thought made him smile.

He'd run the plates on the Ducati later. Right now, he was content to wait and watch. Like a circling shark.

Chapter

18

Tucking the sheets tight around her chin, Grace Holder watched as her partner, Kim Blackwater, searched through the bedside table drawer. A late-evening breeze from the open window battled with the lingering heat of the day. Unsettling, thought Grace, like the clash of opposing weather fronts before a storm.

"Do you have to smoke?" Grace asked.

Kim pulled a half-empty pack of cigarettes from the drawer before leaping back into bed.

Grace never tired of looking at Kim's naked body. Her bronze skin glowed as if lit by some mysterious internal fire. Her choppy lengths of unruly dark hair, accented by chunky streaks of pink and blue, only added to the impression that she was an indomitable force of nature.

Sliding beneath the sheets, Kim flopped one long leg over Grace's plump thigh.

"For the love of God! You're boiling," Grace said, giving Kim's leg a half-hearted shove.

Snagging a pack of matches from the nightstand, Kim lit a cigarette. She inhaled deeply, then blew the smoke up high toward the ceiling. Chuckling, she threw her other leg over Grace, trapping her beneath a tangle of fiery limbs.

Grace tried to wiggle away, but Kim leaned over and kissed her mouth, putting a stop to any further protestations. Grace felt the sweet heat invade her body. They lingered this way, tasting the salty remains of their recent intimacy.

Kim was the first to break away. She took another deep drag on her cigarette. She blew perfect smoke rings, watching them float up to the ceiling.

"Why so late tonight?" asked Kim.

"Sorry about that. We had an incident this afternoon."

"I wondered about that. I treated that Dalton asshole."

Grace propped herself on one elbow and grinned. "I hope his eyes burned like hell."

Kim chuckled. "From the amount of blubbering, you'd think he'd been doused in gasoline and set on fire."

Grace frowned. "Were the cops there?"

Kim nodded.

"What did you say?"

"Just the facts, ma'am."

Grace flopped onto her back. "Thanks."

Kim popped a few smoke rings into the air. "So, how is the blond bombshell?"

Grace sighed. "Do you have to start?"

"You can't tell me you haven't looked."

"Of course I've looked. I'd be dead if I hadn't." Grace glanced at Kim. "I don't think she has any idea how pretty she is."

"Oh, she's a real showstopper, all right," replied Kim, dryly.

Grace gave her a gentle poke in the ribs. "You can't tell me you haven't checked her out."

Kim chuckled. "Maybe. Still, why do you spend so much time and energy on her? Today proves it. She's like a bomb waiting to explode."

Grace grinned up at the ceiling. "You're worried about me."

"I'm serious, Grace," Kim said, rolling over and running her palm over an angry raised scar that bisected Grace's upper arm. "If I hadn't been there, you'd have bled out on the living room floor."

"That was different."

"How?" asked Kim, sitting up and stubbing out her cigarette. "Nobody else seems to attract shit like you do."

In the distance, the whistle of the midnight freight train announced the witching hour was upon them.

Watching Kim's thin back, Grace frowned. "That's not fair."

"That bastard almost killed you, Grace. Inside our own home. And before that it was the nut job who almost took you out trying to get to that American woman, and before that, it was that creepy actor, and before that—"

"Enough, I get it," said Grace.

"I feel like I'm always waiting for the next shoe to drop. How are we supposed to start a family if we can't be safe in our own home?"

Grace reached out and ran her fingertips down Kim's back, tracing the bony processes of her spine. "I promised you I'd cut back and I am. You'll be happy to know that we have a new passenger and I'm sending Signy on her own."

Kim twisted around and peered at Grace. "Really? That's a first."

"I think she's ready."

"In spite of what happened today?"

Grace shrugged. "I don't know, maybe because of what happened today."

Kim pulled her legs back up on the bed and lay back down, propping her head on one elbow and staring into Grace's eyes. "She reminds you of yourself at that age, doesn't she?"

Taking the question at face value, Grace pondered for several seconds before answering. Finally, she said, "There's no doubt she's volatile, but I like the way she thinks on her feet."

Kim scoffed. "Whenever I've talked to her, she looks at me like I'm about to shove a knife in her back."

"Maybe she thinks the same thing about you?" Grace chuckled. "She does read people well."

Kim rolled her eyes.

"She came highly recommended, you know."

"Even after what happened at her last job?"

"It surprised me too. Just after I received her resume, I had a call from a Children's Aid worker I knew. Marion Entwhistle gave Signy a glowing report. She said she'd known Signy since she was a kid and that she'd had a rough go of it. Do you remember the story of the Dumpster Baby?"

Kim paused for a moment, then shook her head.

"You remember. That toddler they found stuffed in a Dumpster near the Eaton Centre?"

"Maybe." Kim frowned. "Was it around Christmastime?"

Grace nodded. "Tossed like so much garbage in a back alley."

"That was Signy?"

Grace nodded again.

"Christ," said Kim, "what a terrible story."

"It's weird the way things happen. I always remembered that little girl. Who knew she'd work for me one day."

Kim stared at the ceiling a few moments. "You know, there was one detail that really stuck with me."

"Let me guess," said Grace. "Was it the red ribbon they found tied to one of her wrists?"

Kim nodded.

"That was very creepy," Grace confirmed. "The media made a big deal about it but the cops never did find out what it meant."

"I can't believe that was Signy," Kim said, frowning. "I often wondered what happened to that kid."

Grace leaned in. "This is strictly confidential."

Kim lifted her eyebrows, in an "obviously" gesture.

"She never was adopted. They tried a few times, but apparently there were behavioural issues." She shot a warning glance at Kim. "Don't say it."

Kim shrugged, innocently.

Grace shook her head, then continued, "She spent her whole childhood in foster care."

"A foster kid?" said Kim. "That definitely explains a few things." Kim glanced over. "No offence intended."

"None taken. Marion practically begged me to take a chance on her."

Kim sighed. "You've always been a sucker for a sob story." She leaned over and brushed Grace's lips with her own.

Grace kissed her back and for the next several minutes they didn't think about Signy Shepherd or the Line or anything at all. They were interrupted by the click of nails on the hardwood floor. Grace shrieked as a cold nose touched her exposed thigh.

"What are you doing up here, Chivas?" said Kim, rolling over and pulling on one of the dog's floppy ears. Kim had inherited the giant mutt from a dying patient a few years ago and he'd quickly become an indispensable fixture in their home. "Do you have to go outside?"

"I'll take him," said Grace, throwing off the sheets.

"You sleep," said Kim. "I'll do it."

Grace mumbled her thanks and snuggled down under the covers.

Kim pulled on a pair of shorts and a T-shirt, then called for the dog. At the door, she turned. "Do you remember the story you told me, about how you and your brother used to race the train across the trestle out behind your house when you were kids?"

Grace cracked open one eye.

"I think you're still trying to beat that train, Grace. Still pushing the envelope, seeing just how far you can go."

Grace watched her, the sheets tucked protectively around her chin.

"I'm not like you, sweetie." Kim buried her fingers in the big dog's ruff. "I don't need any more craziness in my life. I spend my days in a state of constant crisis. When I come home, all I want is normal, boring stability."

"I want that too," said Grace quietly.

"I'm not sure you know what you want." Kim flashed a sad smile. "You're a champion, Grace, and I love that about you. But if you're serious about starting a family, you have to give this shit up."

"I've already told you—"

"I know what you've said, Grace," said Kim. "It's what you do that's the problem. Seriously, hon, I don't know how much longer I can continue to pick up the pieces." She turned and walked down the stairs.

Gnawing on her thumbnail, Grace watched Kim disappear down the hallway. When she noticed a single drop of blood fall onto Kim's white pillowcase and stain it a bright scarlet, she hurriedly stripped the pillow, then tossed the incriminating evidence down the laundry chute out in the hallway.

She was back in bed and feigning sleep by the time Kim returned.

Chapter

19

Waiting was the hardest part. Over the years he'd learned to keep himself occupied during the long hours spent huddled in cars, hanging out on street corners, or skulking in shadows. Sometimes he'd play mind games. Name every bone in the human body, recite pi to the one thousandth decimal place, or list all 118 elements on the periodic table—backwards.

More often, he'd contemplate which of his candidates he'd focus on next. Would it be the blue-eyed wonder he'd come across in San Francisco, or the graduate student at NYU he'd spotted at a presentation on string theory? He thought about where they lived, how accessible they'd be, how he'd make his approach.

Mostly, he thought about their eyes. The colour had to be the perfect marriage of azure blue and slate grey, soft and hard at the same time, yin and yang, fully seasoned and forever young.

Today, however, as he waited for Elena Morozov to be spirited away from the shelter, he thought he would spend some time researching the city of Toronto. He'd never done business in Canada's largest urban centre and it would be useful to have a sense of the place.

Firing up his MacBook Pro laptop, he connected to wireless Internet using a Turbo Stick. Googling Toronto, Ontario, he was confronted by over a half billion hits. The first was the city's official website, which seemed a good place to start. He clicked on the link and was met by another array of choices.

Choosing a general overview, he skimmed the touristy stuff, peaceful city, highly diverse, CN Tower, blah, blah, blah. He paused, however, at the description of the main drag. Apparently, Yonge Street, at 1,178 miles long, was the world's longest street. He got a kick out of towns that promoted the biggest this and the most awesome that, so he clicked on the link.

A somewhat-dated image popped up of an urban thoroughfare that could have easily been a main drag in Boston or Chicago or Atlanta. There was absolutely nothing special about it. And yet, sitting in this rented Nissan, doing nothing more than wasting time, his heart began to race, galloping in choppy bursts like a spooked horse.

His eyes raked the parking lot, the nearby vehicles, and the road out front. Had his cover been blown? All was quiet at the shelter across the street. He could pick out no one observing him.

Was he having a heart attack? He placed a hand over his thumping chest. He was only twenty-nine, fit, and had been for a physical not two months previous. Blood pressure normal, cholesterol levels excellent.

His mind raced. It was not impossible that one of his biological parents had been a ticking time bomb of cardiovascular disease. His heart thumped faster, his breathing accelerating.

He rarely suffered from feelings of nervousness. He eschewed the self-indulgent habit of sifting through the detritus of one's life deliberately searching for painful memories to re-experience over and over, like some kind of masochistic cluster-fuck. So why did his heart feel like it was about to explode?

Tapping a few keys, he zoomed in on the laptop's streetscape image. He leaned into the screen and tried to determine what about this particular image might be responsible.

His attention was drawn to a commercial sign that dominated the field of view, a rectangular sign, maybe forty feet wide by fifteen feet high with a cherry red background and two prominent long-playing records sitting side by side.

Above and below each huge LP was the word SAM followed by letters too tiny to read. Zooming in further, he read the words out loud, "Sam the Record Man." The black discs pulsed before his eyes and his heart danced a tarantella in his chest.

SAM—THE—RECORD—MAN.

He doubled over as an inexplicable odour of greasy french fries and malt vinegar assaulted his nostrils, and he struggled to catch his breath.

Slamming the laptop shut, he barely managed to get the car door open before vomiting. A steaming pool of airline snacks and the turkey on rye he'd eaten for dinner splattered onto the tarmac. He retched over and over until nothing was left but strings of yellow bile. Ribs aching, he crawled back into the car.

What the—? The thought was cut short as a tinny, off-key

tune warbled to life inside his head. It felt as though someone had cranked up a wobbly turntable. Jesus H. Christ. The jingling tune seemed familiar, as if it might have been the soundtrack for a half-remembered dream. And though he wasn't a religious man, he was willing to call on anything or anyone to make this stop.

"Elena . . ."

The sound of the girl's name sliced through the fractured tones and images and he remembered, with a start, that the bud was still plugged into his ear. He reached up and, after adjusting the earpiece, realized with relief that the horror story playing in his head had been silenced. He tried to focus on the conversation.

"When does she arrive?"

"She said she was five minutes out."

"Bring her upstairs. We need the transfer to go as quickly as possible."

The laptop felt hot on his thighs and he had the irrational thought that it might burst into flames. He whipped out the Internet stick and tossed the MacBook onto the back seat.

Jesus Christ. What was this? Hallucination? Bad turkey? Whatever it was, it would most definitely need to be addressed. Right now, however, he had more pressing concerns. He needed to get his head back in the game.

Sheet lightning sparked in waves across the leaden sky. He invoked Tonenili, asking the Navajo god of water to crack open the skies with thunder and allow a cleansing rain to wash him clean.

Unfortunately, it seemed Tonenili was up to his usual tricks.

All he could hear was the snickering of gravel as it rattled against the side of his car. On the wind, a hint of sulphur sent a shiver up his spine.

He slammed his fists against the dashboard. "Three," he said, "point one, four, one, five, nine, two, six—" He continued to recite the value of pi until the soothing properties of the infinite number eased his irrational fears.

•   •   •

Signy swept her eyes over Zef's battered body, her heart sinking as she took in the new scar on his chest, a ragged semicircle of raised tissue running just over his left pectoral muscle. She reached out a finger.

Zef's hand snapped shut over hers.

His eyes remained closed but she watched a smile play around his mouth. She jerked her hand in an effort to release it, but he held her fast. He pushed her hand lower, sliding it over his belly and down toward his groin. He rolled toward her, eyes smiling. "Good morning, Sig."

Glaring, she gave up the struggle for her trapped hand.

"I'm happy to oblige, but I may need coffee first," he said, letting her hand go. "You almost did me in."

Rolling her eyes, she pushed back the sheet and sat up on the edge of the bed. Her hair fell in golden, tangled masses, bright against the nut-brown glow of her skin. A fine spray of freckles across the bridge of her nose sparkled in the early morning sun. "Grace is picking me up in an hour," she said, shivering, as his hand traced the curved line of her backbone.

"Well, look at that," he whispered, pulling her down on top of him. "It seems I don't need that coffee, after all."

Damn.

A half hour later, she asked, "So what happened?" She traced the scar on his chest with her finger.

"A minor disagreement."

Narrowing her eyes, she said, "What did you do?"

"Why do you always assume that I'm to blame for everything?"

She snorted, then leaped out of bed and went into the bathroom to take a shower. By the time she had dressed and packed a small bag for her trip to Calgary, he was sitting at her kitchen table, drinking her coffee and eating her toast.

"This," she said, twirling her hand in a gesture that encompassed the two of them, "was a mistake."

He shoved a piece of toast into his mouth and mumbled, "So you say."

"You know what I mean."

"No, I don't know. Look at you," pointing a triangle of toast at her.

She was wearing a sleeveless sundress, cut low at the neck. As she leaned against the counter, the soft pink fabric stretched tight across her breasts.

Leering, he gulped down the rest of his coffee, then rose to his feet and took a step toward her.

"Sit down, Zef."

Grinning, he did as he was told, holding out his cup for a refill. She brought the pot over, keeping a wary eye out, but he only smiled sweetly. Replacing the carafe in the unit, she kept her back to him and asked, "When are you leaving?"

"Don't be like that, Sig."

She inserted the plug into the kitchen sink and, as the sink filled with warm water, added a squirt of dish soap, swirling her hand in the foamy bubbles. Without turning, she said through her teeth, "I have a good life here."

"I'm glad for you, Sig."

"Quit calling me that."

"Last night," he said, in an amused tone, "you practically begged me to stay."

The dishes clinked together in the sink as she applied her cloth more roughly than necessary.

"Ah, come on," he said, standing up, a goofy smile on his face, "I'm only messing with you."

"That's all you ever do, isn't it? Mess with people?"

Watching his smile die, she faltered.

He looked genuinely contrite as he brushed a tuft of hair away from his eyes. He moved in close behind her. Twining her braid around his fist, he reeled her in, brushing his lips against hers. "I never meant to hurt you."

She felt light-headed as his free hand gripped the small of her back, pressing her to him.

"You know I love you," he whispered.

She pushed him violently away. "You must think I'm a total idiot."

He shook his head. "Why do you always have to fuck every-thing up?"

She took a step back, crossing her arms over her chest. "Because I'm sick of being at your beck and call like some kind of pathetic loser. Because I'm tired of cleaning up after you every time you fuck up."

His mouth twisted. "Hey, don't hold back on my account."

She glared at him. "All right. The fact is I don't want you anywhere near me. You ruin everything and everybody you touch." Even as they spilled from her mouth, she choked on the words. This stupid, hopeless, beautiful man had shown her everything she knew about love.

He'd taught her how to fight, quick and dirty. He was the one who fixed her up that night in the barn when she could not tell anyone what had happened to her, not even him. He was the only one who showed up at her dorm room the day her foster mother died, standing at her door with a wilting bouquet of posies he'd likely picked on the side of the road. He'd held her and stroked her hair until she was able to sleep.

She stepped toward him, "Zef, I—"

The phone rang.

Turning away from him, she grabbed the receiver, hanging onto Grace's voice like a lifeline.

By the time she hung up the phone, he'd left the kitchen. Hearing the water running in the shower, she took the opportunity to run downstairs and wait for Grace. With any luck, when she returned from her trip, Zef would be out of her life, this time for good.

Chapter

20

Hunkered down in the back seat of a minivan, the blackout windows obscuring her from curious onlookers, Elena stared at the driver. A skeletal woman in her mid-forties with a smoker's cough, she'd barely said a word since picking Elena up at the shelter in Surrey.

Morticia, as Elena came to think of her, was about as chatty as a patio stone and wouldn't even allow the radio. She knew she should feel grateful for the risk these women were taking on her behalf, but she couldn't. She was well aware she was feeling selfish and childish, but she didn't care. She wanted her life back. To have finding her classrooms and worrying about the workload be her only concerns.

She felt as though she were perched at the precipice of a roller coaster, staring down into the abyss, knowing she had no choice but to hang on and try to survive the ride.

They arrived in Calgary just after dawn. After winding through one suburban neighbourhood after another, Morticia pulled into the driveway of a house that looked the same as all the others—two storeys, tan vinyl siding, garage in front.

Picking up her small suitcase, Elena crawled out of the minivan feeling stiff and out of sorts. Morticia backed down the drive and was gone before Elena had a chance to say thank you. She turned away just as the front door to the house opened.

"Welcome!"

Hustling toward her was a plump, middle-aged woman with burgundy hair.

"Come on inside, luv. You must be starving. How was the trip? Did you get any sleep? Probably not! You'll have to nap later. Do you like bacon and eggs?"

Elena allowed herself to be dragged along, overwhelmed by the verbal barrage. Once inside, the woman, who had introduced herself as Thelma, interrupted her stream of consciousness to take a critical look at Elena. Shaking her head, she said, sadly, "Sorry, luv, but the hair has to go. Any fool with one good eye could spot you a mile away."

And that was how Elena came to be standing in front of a mirror in Thelma's basement salon, bemoaning her new appearance.

Thelma had cut off almost twelve inches and styled the remaining locks into a feathered bob that just brushed Elena's chin. She swallowed hard when the towel was removed after the dye had set. Parted on the side, her new chocolate bangs swung over one eye, giving her face a rounder, softer appearance.

"There you go! You look just like Katie Holmes," said Thelma, fluffing Elena's hair with her fingers.

Elena smiled weakly. "Thanks, I guess."

"You're more than welcome, luv. Now, let's get you upstairs and get you set up with some new clothes."

Following Thelma up the narrow stairs into a small room off the living room, Elena was almost able to tune out the older woman's incessant chatter. The den was set up as a sewing room, with a professional-looking Singer machine dominating the space. A set of wooden shelves held a wide variety of seamstress paraphernalia, and a full-length mirror sat on a stand in the corner.

Thelma opened the folding closet doors, exposing a rack full of women's clothing. She clicked through the metal hangers, selecting a pair of white golf pants, a coordinating sky blue shirt, and a pair of white flat shoes from the wide selection that lined the bottom of the closet.

Once Elena had donned the new outfit, Thelma exclaimed in delight. "Look at that. Your own mother wouldn't recognize you."

Examining herself in the mirror, Elena had to agree. With her bouncy new haircut and designer clothing, she looked more like an affluent young mother on her way to the country club for lunch with the girls than a young university student.

"Well? What do you think?"

Elena smiled, weakly. "Call me Katie."

"I'm the best, if I do say so myself," said Thelma, reaching out to place a pair of large round sunglasses on Elena's head.

"See the way the glasses seem to change the bone structure of your face?"

Elena nodded, truly surprised at how a few small changes could impact her appearance in such a profound way.

Thelma returned to the closet and pulled out more clothing—jeans, sweaters, T-shirts, and a wide-brimmed straw hat. "Take these as well. These are a larger size than you normally wear and will make you look heavier."

Elena crammed the extra clothing into her small suitcase, squeezing the lighter T-shirts into the space around the physiology textbook. Still, she had to turn the photo album sideways in order to fit everything inside.

"Good Lord," cried Thelma, glancing at her watch, "tea time."

Elena sat at the kitchen table and watched Thelma brew a pot of tea. The two Advil she'd popped earlier that morning had eased the headache that had been plaguing her ever since she'd left Vancouver, but she still felt exhausted. "Do you have any idea what happens next?"

Setting a steaming mug in front of Elena, Thelma took a seat opposite, pouring a generous dollop of milk into her own cup. "You've been told that a young woman will pick you up here this afternoon and she'll take you on to Toronto?"

Elena nodded.

Thelma chuckled. "I'm sure you'll be glad to have the company of someone your own age."

She waved away Elena's feeble protestations. "After that, I'm not sure. What I do know is that the powers that be are working overtime trying to figure out a solution to this mess."

Elena swiped at her eyes.

Thelma set her mug down on the table. "Drink up, luv. You're exhausted. I'm putting you to bed. I want you to get some rest before young Signy arrives."

Allowing herself to be pushed down a long hallway toward the guest bedroom, Elena felt the ground slip from under her feet. The roller coaster was racing downhill and there seemed to be nothing she could do to stop it.

Chapter

21

"Why me?" asked Signy, frowning. "Why now?"

"Maitland's wanted to meet you for a while now." Hands loose on the wheel, Grace checked the rear-view mirror. They were heading west on Highway 401, the main east/west thoroughfare across the top of Toronto. "But after the Dalton incident, she insisted."

"Oh, great." Signy twisted in her seat.

"Don't worry," said Grace. "She also wants to update us both on the Morozov case."

"Do you think she's upset about the Dalton thing?"

Grace glanced over, with a faint smile. "Only one way to find out." She touched the gas pedal and the car leapt forward, slipping into the fast lane.

As they barrelled toward Pearson International Airport and their meeting with the storied engineer of the Line, Signy wondered about the old lady. When she'd been recruited, Grace had given her the basics on the origin of the Line but not much more. Maitland's daughter, Catherine, had been nine months pregnant with her first child when she'd been shot to death by her husband, Jeffrey. Catherine had been staying with her parents at the time, having fled the beatings that started soon after she'd announced her pregnancy.

Maitland and her husband had exhausted all legal avenues to keep their daughter safe. But other than reluctantly issuing what proved to be a useless restraining order, the legal system had failed to take their concerns seriously, a fact Maitland blamed on the old boys' network.

Apparently, Jeffrey's father, a prominent investment banker, and the city's mayor had been so far up each other's asses, it was amazing either one was able to breathe. So when Jeffrey's father asked the mayor to fix things for his son, the mayor obliged with one phone call to the budget-conscious chief of police. The investigation, and any consequences Jeffrey might have faced, had been conveniently swept under the carpet.

Signy remembered Grace tearing up when she described how responsible Maitland felt for her daughter's death. "No one can convince her any different," Grace had said. "Maitland feels she put her faith in a corrupt legal system, then sat idly by as a madman walked into her home and took the lives of her daughter and her unborn grandson. She's never been able to forgive herself. The only way she could make any sense of it all was to 'get up off my complacent, silly ass,' as she put it, and make sure no one else ever again has to suffer through such a terrible nightmare."

A tricked-out pickup truck forced its way in front of them. "Jerk," Grace said, crowding the Prius into the guy's rear bumper until she apparently thought the better of it and eased off.

Signy watched a 747 take off from Pearson, trailing a shimmering line of superheated exhaust. She wiped a sheen of sweat from her upper lip. Despite the air conditioning, the temperature inside was still uncomfortably warm. Only ten a.m. and the mercury was already pushing thirty-two degrees Celsius, with a humidex of almost forty.

Grace had CBC radio playing in the background. As a prelude to a segment on global warming, a meteorologist was discussing the rarity of this type of late-summer heat wave. Not since 1949 had the temperatures soared to these levels so late in the summer. Today would be the fifth straight day of an extreme heat alert in the city and there was no sign of it letting up anytime soon.

Signy glanced over at her boss. She should have guessed something was up when Grace arrived wearing the grey business suit and jacket she typically reserved for her monthly meetings with the Ministry uppity-ups. Signy hoped she'd be able to keep her wits about her. She figured she'd managed about twenty minutes of real sleep, but she desperately wanted to make a good impression on the Engineer.

"Did you sleep okay?" Grace asked.

"What?" Signy jumped in her seat. Grace's freaky ability to read minds was starting to creep her out.

"You look sore." Grace pointed at the scrape on Signy's cheek.

Signy relaxed, probing the ring of bruises around her neck. "I'm okay. Any updates on the Dalton investigation?"

Grace smiled. "You mean did Jenny Dalton corroborate your story?"

"It's not a *story*," Signy said. "It's the truth."

"Uh-huh. Unfortunately, while Jenny Dalton said she believed your version of events, she had to admit she hadn't witnessed the entire confrontation. She said that by the time she ran out onto the porch, all she saw was you standing over Daryl, emptying the can of Mace into his eyes."

Signy made a hissing noise in her teeth, then slouched back in her seat.

Grace leaned over and gave her a reassuring squeeze. "Winnie is still waiting on the results of evidence analysis, and if it comes down to a 'he said, she said' situation, you'll win hands down in the credibility department."

"I understand Jenny and the girls are in the wind?" Signy asked, hoping to change the subject to anything other than a discussion of the state of her own credibility.

Grace didn't respond. She was intent on crossing several lanes of traffic. The exit to Pearson International was almost upon them. Finally she said, "They're safe for now. The bad news is that the cops released Daryl right after he was booked, on a promise to appear. I'm glad you'll be out of town for a few days. Perhaps it will allow time for some tempers to cool."

Signy nodded but doubted that Grace's theory had legs. Contrary to his son, who was, as Ben Tran had said, not much more than a big fish in a small pond, Richard Dalton was a shark.

Signy had seen the cold calculation in his eyes. Unlike his son, Dalton was in control of his rage. She had no doubt he'd come up with some way of getting payback with minimal risk. If that meant waiting for the right time and the right place, she was sure he'd be up to the challenge. As Jenny said, she was going to have to watch her back.

So far, her response had been weak, at best. In an effort to buy some time, she'd called the Linden Valley police station and left a message on Dalton's voice mail telling him that she was being sent out of town for a few days, that the trip had been planned for weeks. She assured him that she had said nothing to anyone and that she promised to fix the situation upon her return. She had no idea if her stalling tactic would be effective, but it was the only thing she could come up with at the moment.

"In any event, I think we need to focus on one thing at a time," said Grace. "Let's get Ms. Morozov back to Ontario and then we can deal with the Dalton problem."

"Sure," said Signy, liking the sound of "we" but knowing that she was going to have to manage Dalton on her own.

"This is it," said Grace, sliding in behind a gleaming Lincoln limousine that was parked in a short-term stopping zone. She turned off the ignition, then smiled at Signy. "Prepare to be amazed."

Signy grabbed her carry-on bag from the back seat, then followed Grace up to the limo. The smell of jet fuel was heavy in the humid air, the rumble of the limo engine inaudible over the roar of an incoming plane. Signy swallowed heavily, not sure what to expect.

Then the rear window slid down, a snowy head popped out, and Grace was right.

Signy was amazed.

Chapter

22

Maitland McGuinness Spencer, aka the Engineer, popped her head out the window, releasing a cloud of jasmine and lavender. Snowy hair was gathered at the back of her head in a precisely coiffed chignon, held in place with a sparkling, diamond-studded comb.

"Darlings, hop in. We have a lot of ground to cover." Her voice was low and sultry. Signy would not have been surprised if Humphrey Bogart were keeping Maitland company, drinking a mint julep and practising his whistle.

Her driver, a lean black man with salt-and-pepper hair and wearing the ubiquitous black suit favoured by security types, exited the car. He pulled open the back door, ushering the two women inside.

Signy sank into the leather seat across from the Engineer. For a moment she was struck dumb, convinced she had entered a well-appointed drawing-room and not the interior of a motor vehicle. She didn't think she'd ever sat on such a comfortable chair in her entire life. A table covered with a crisp white cloth, freshly squeezed orange juice, a selection of breakfast pastries, and fresh berries made her mouth water.

"Signy Shepherd, at last." Maitland beamed. "And Grace, dear, how wonderful to see you."

Plastering what she hoped was a professional smile on her face, Signy examined the Engineer and tried not to gawk. The old gal had to be at least eighty years old. She wore an ecru linen skirt that came just to her knees, showing off a set of gams that would have made Betty Grable envious. Under a matching linen jacket, she wore a creamy silk shirt pinned at the throat with an emerald brooch. Her shoes were practical patent-leather flats, twinkling gold buckles lending an air of sauciness to the ensemble.

"I'm sorry about the unorthodox meeting space, ladies, but I'm trying to kill two birds with one stone. My son, Daniel, is flying in from Tokyo, and since he rarely has time to spare for his old mother, I decided to lie in wait."

As she talked, she began to put together two plates of food, one for Grace and one for Signy. "Please help yourself to tea or coffee." She indicated a silver set on a side table.

"Marshall?"

The driver turned in his seat.

"Could you manage a plate?"

Smiling, he shook his head. He glanced at Signy, then patted his stomach. "Watch out for this one, she'll have you busting at the seams."

Signy grinned, taking an instant shine to him. Marshall exuded a poised confidence, his voice was low and measured, and he had kind eyes.

"Don't listen to him, dear," Maitland said, handing Signy a plate towering with goodies. "You have a long flight ahead of you. You need to keep up your strength."

Nibbling at a delicious raspberry pastry, Signy glanced at Grace, who seemed to have no worries about bursting at the seams and was stuffing a chocolate croissant, slathered with butter, into her mouth.

Maitland clapped her hands together. "No time to waste. First things first. Ms. Shepherd, I must say I am impressed with how you handled that thug yesterday." Maitland glanced at Grace. "And I have no doubt that our wonderful Ms. Holder will keep the legal hounds at bay, won't you, dear?"

"Doing my best," mumbled Grace, her cheeks stuffed with pastry.

Maitland leaned in, her eyes glittering. "There are times when the ends do justify the means. I believe that unequivocally. The trick is knowing when to push past the limits, and how far. You achieved that fine balance yesterday, Ms. Shepherd. Good for you."

Signy's eyes widened and she risked a quick glance at Grace, but whether her mentor had anything contrary to add, her mouth was currently too full to speak.

Maitland raised a china teacup in a bold salute. "Still, there is no rest for the wicked." She picked up a red folder. Fitting a pair of pince-nez on her nose, she opened the file. "Elena Morozov," she began, with no further preamble. "Age twenty-one. Lives in Vancouver, where she rents a basement apartment from a Mr. Jianguo Zhang, former Chinese State Police, and his wife, Mai-Li Zhang.

"She is starting medical studies at the University of British Columbia this fall. She was born in Russia and immigrated to Canada with her parents when she was four years old. She was raised in Mississauga. Her parents are deceased, killed together in a car crash when Elena was seventeen. She was taken in by her employer, a Mr. Fang Chan, who happens to be the brother of Mrs. Zhang."

Maitland peered over her glasses as if to ask, Any questions? When neither Grace nor Signy indicated affirmatively, she resumed her recitation. "This past July, Ms. Morozov relocated to Vancouver. She obtained a part-time serving position in the piano bar of a downtown hotel which is where her story came to intersect with one Leonid Volkov."

"Leonid Volkov?" Signy asked, holding up a finger. "Where have I heard that name before?"

"It would be hard to have missed it. He practically owns Vancouver."

"That's right," said Signy, snapping her fingers, "I saw a documentary on him last year. That CBC show where they profile successful new Canadians? If I recall correctly, Volkov bought up as much useless property as he could and reclaimed the land. From what I remember, he's cornered the market on condo development throughout the lower mainland."

"Give the girl a gold star," said Maitland. She flipped a page over and adjusted her glasses. "Not only is he one of Canada's foremost entrepreneurs, he's also a world-renowned photographer." She glanced up at the two women. "I've actually been to one of his shows. A couple of years ago, I was in Boston on business. The city was abuzz about the opening of the latest Volkov exhibit. I must say, his work is exquisite."

Grace nodded. "I saw a spread on him in the *New York Times* a couple of years ago. He takes pictures of the city at night?"

"Indeed," Maitland confirmed, "he has an ingenious way of using shadows to invoke all the emotions one associates with the dark: apprehension, vigilance, terror. One gets the sense that something evil is lurking, just beyond the frame, watching and waiting." Maitland slid the glasses off her nose and chuckled. "Listen to me, I sound like a frightened schoolgirl."

"He obviously makes an impression," said Grace.

"That he does," said Maitland, "and he certainly made an impression on young Elena. What little I've been able to glean so far is that Volkov frequented the establishment where Elena worked. She is quite distinctive-looking." Maitland handed a photograph of the girl to Signy and a copy to Grace. "Apparently, Volkov took one look at her and was smitten."

Signy grimaced.

Maitland nodded. "I'm sure Ms. Morozov would agree with your sentiments." She shrugged. "At first, she tried to be polite. The man was a fellow countryman, decades her senior, and she thought he was probably lonely. She felt he just wanted someone to talk to, someone who shared the same language, and someone to whom he could reminisce about Moscow and life on the Black Sea, two of his favourite topics, apparently."

Signy peered down at the photo. Willowy, with flowing red hair and exotic, almond-shaped eyes, the girl had the ephemeral loveliness that she'd always associated with Eastern European women. "So, what happened?"

"The usual," Maitland replied. "He monopolized her time, became more and more persistent in his efforts to win her over, and eventually invited her to his home in North Vancouver, ostensibly to show her some photographs."

Maitland adjusted her glasses. "She'd twigged, by this time, that his attentions were not merely those of a lonely old man, and she asked him to leave her alone. He didn't, of course, and eventually she was forced to complain to her employer, although that avenue proved to be a dead end."

"Let me guess," said Grace. "Her employer turned out to be old Leonid himself."

"I'll be running out of gold stars if you two keep this up," said Maitland. "Yes, indeed. Volkov owned the hotel where Elena worked. When her complaints to her immediate superior went unanswered, she tried moving up the chain of command. Apparently Volkov had, by this time, received her message loud and clear and did not take the news well. He claimed that *she'd* been stalking *him*, that she was nothing more than a predatory female after a poor old man's money."

Signy shook her head.

"Just playing devil's advocate," said Grace, "but I have to ask."

"Is there any chance that we are dealing with a clever girl angling for a windfall?" Maitland asked for her.

Grace nodded.

"It's happened before," Maitland agreed. "But if that were the case, why wouldn't she have accepted Volkov's advances in the first place? And how do we explain the man Volkov sent to abduct her from her apartment? It was sheer luck that her landlord was able to intervene."

Grace nodded in acknowledgement.

"Attempted abduction?" said Signy.

Maitland flashed a questioning glance at Grace.

"I thought it best that Signy hear the story directly from you," said Grace.

Maitland nodded, then turned to Signy. "Two nights ago, Ms. Morozov came home to find a man in her apartment. He demanded that she accompany him to meet with Volkov. When she refused, he put a gun to her head."

"A gun?" said Signy, her head swivelling back and forth between Maitland and Grace.

"Luckily, the landlord is a former cop and he was able to subdue the intruder." Maitland peered over her pince-nez at Signy. "To be perfectly accurate, he killed the man."

"Killed?" Signy inhaled sharply. "Seriously? Why aren't the police involved? You know better than me, but isn't this out of our league?"

"Unfortunately, the situation is even more complicated," Maitland said. "Mr. Zhang made the decision not to involve the authorities. Volkov worked closely with the Chinese during the Soviet era and, as a member of the state police, Zhang had heard rumours about the man."

"Like what?" Signy asked.

"Mrs. Zhang told me her husband never mentioned specifics but said that Volkov would have no trouble convincing the authorities that Elena was responsible for the murder of the man in her apartment."

"What about the forensic evidence? Wouldn't that explain what happened?"

"Evidence can be manipulated and, from what we have learned, Volkov is a master of deception," said Maitland. "I think Zhang made the right call. He's given us some breathing room. Hopefully, we'll be able to figure out why Volkov is after the girl and how to stop him." She nodded at Signy. "Meanwhile, we must keep her safe."

"To that end," Grace interjected, "what have you been able to find out about Volkov? What are we up against?"

Maitland glanced at the file folder in her lap. "Before he made his millions in Canada, Volkov was a general in the Soviet Army. He was a career soldier, in fact, leaving the military only when the Soviet Union fell apart in 1991. First wife deceased in 1993; he married Marisha Andropov, a year later."

She turned the page. "He and his first wife had one child, a girl named Lilia. She married and does not appear to have maintained contact with her father. He remained in Russia for several years, although his history is murky during that period. He immigrated to Canada in 2000 and seems to have been an exemplary citizen ever since."

"Elena and Volkov are both from Moscow," Grace said. "Any connection there?"

Maitland nodded. "I wondered that as well, but if there is some relationship between the two, I've found nothing. Elena was born to Alexei and Maria Morozov, no relation to Leonid Volkov. Alexei worked as a maintenance engineer at the University of Toronto, and Maria worked as a clerk at the store owned by Mr. Fang Chan, and then as a baker."

"And Mr. Chan is the brother of Mrs. Zhang, Elena's landlord?" Signy asked.

"The same," Maitland confirmed. "When her parents died, Mr. Chan took Elena in. Again, not an unusual circumstance. She was alone with no other family and Mr. Chan took it upon himself to look after her." She turned to Grace. "I'd like you to pay Mr. Chan a visit. See if there is anything else you can dig up."

Nodding, Grace scribbled Maitland's instructions on a pad she had on her lap. "I'd also like to know his take on the car accident that took Elena's parents."

"Meanwhile, we have another unrelated avenue of pursuit that looks promising. We weren't able to hack into the old Soviet records, so we know nothing of Volkov's service record. When we trolled through the Russian press, however, we did come across an interesting story. It seems that just prior to the fall of the Soviet Union, a series of vicious sexual assaults dating back years had been determined to be the work of a single perpetrator. There were whispers in the press at the time that one of the persons of interest was a respected general in the Soviet Army."

"Volkov?" Signy asked.

"His name was bandied about," Maitland said, "and the women involved were all young, pretty, and living on their own."

"Just like Elena," Signy said.

"Just like Elena," Maitland agreed, "but the story was quickly suppressed. In fact, the reporter who broke the story was found in his apartment with the back of his head blown off."

Signy shifted uncomfortably in her seat. "Not to belabour the point, but should I be worried?"

Maitland allowed her glasses to slip from her nose onto her chest. "Unfortunately, our work on the Line is not without risk, although I do my best to mitigate the hazards. In this case, I am feeling confident. The conductor who shuttled Elena to Calgary is one of my best, and she insists she was not followed. Elena has had her appearance changed so much that I doubt even Mrs. Zhang would recognize her." Maitland inhaled deeply and leaned forward. "I'm confident that by sending you I am further minimizing the chance of exposure. Volkov will be looking for a young woman on her own, not two girls travelling east by car."

Maitland clutched Signy's hand. "Be that as it may, dear, should anything happen that sets your antennae buzzing, anything at all, you call Grace and we'll send reinforcements."

Signy nodded.

Maitland checked her watch. "Good heavens, look at the time." She smiled at Signy. "You have a flight to catch, dear." She handed Signy a stuffed manila envelope. "Inside you'll find more than enough cash for the next few days, a prepaid burner phone, and a complete set of false identity papers. I assume you left your own papers at home? Including driver's licence?"

Signy nodded.

"Very good. From now on, you're Carol White."

Signy set her plate aside, mostly untouched, and accepted the envelope from Maitland. She smiled. "It was good to meet you."

"A pleasure, my dear." She reached out and gave Signy's fingers another squeeze. "Please remember, we are all on the same team. If you need help, don't hesitate to ask. We'll be there."

The leering face of Big Dick Dalton flashed in her head and she almost opened her mouth to say something, but Maitland was right. She did have a plane to catch. Instead, she allowed Grace to give her a brief hug, then climbed out of the limo and hurried into the terminal without a backward glance.

Chapter

23

Richard Dalton let himself into his son's house, wrinkling his nose against the reek of boozy vomit and cigarette.

"Boy?" When there was no answer, he walked into the living room. Daryl was passed out on the La-Z-Boy, an empty bottle of Jack Daniels beside him.

Dalton sighed. Whatever semblance of order Jenny had brought to the place had been turned upside down in a matter of hours. Every cupboard door in the kitchen was standing wide open. Empty liquor bottles lay scattered about and a soggy wad of cigarette butts was disintegrating inside a half-empty glass.

Striding over to where his son lay snoring, he looked down and examined the boy. Stubble sprouted in patches over his meaty neck. His mouth hung open and a bubble of spit expanded and shrank with each ragged breath. Not for the first time he thought about how much better life would be if his ex-wife had aborted this piece of shit like he'd demanded.

Dalton knocked the boy on the forehead with his knuckles.

Daryl groaned, trying with little success to force open crusted eyelids.

"Wake up, asshole."

Daryl rolled off the La-Z-Boy, landing on his hands and knees before hauling himself to his feet. He glared at his father. "What the fuck?"

Dalton slipped a hand into his shirt pocket and removed an airplane ticket. He snapped it in front of Daryl's face until he was certain the boy had managed to focus.

Daryl reached for a bottle of vodka that still held a finger or two of liquid.

Dalton kicked the bottle away before Daryl could wrap his fingers around the neck.

"Ah, fuck," said Daryl, his knees threatening to buckle beneath him. He wiped spittle from his mouth with the back of his hand. "What?"

"You're leaving for New Brunswick tonight."

"What?" Daryl shook his head, then scratched at the stubble on his chin.

Dalton stared at his son until the younger man dropped his eyes.

"I had a chat with Signy Shepherd last night."

Daryl rubbed at his eyes, still inflamed from the effects of the pepper spray. "Bitch."

Dalton snorted. "That bitch wiped your ass and handed it to you on a platter." Stuffing the ticket in his son's shirt pocket, he leaned in. "You got whipped by a hundred and twenty pound cunt."

Daryl glared at his father, then looked away.

"I told her to fix the situation with Jenny and the girls, but it seems the foolish Ms. Shepherd doesn't listen too good. Looks like she took off." He bent over and picked up the empty mickey of Jack Daniels and tossed it into the garbage. "That can mean one of two things. Either Jenny and the girls are still in the shelter, in which case we have some time, or Shepherd is hiding them."

"Can't you just call the shelter and find out where they are?"

"Shelters have rules, dumb-ass. Unless you have a court order, they don't have to tell nobody who's inside."

"Fuckin' dykes." Daryl scraped his fingernails over the stubble on his neck. "So you think maybe she's heading to her parents' place?"

Dalton regarded his son, impressed that he'd been able to string more than two words together to make a sentence. He shrugged. "Can you think of anywhere else?"

Daryl looked up at the ceiling, his tongue waggling inside his cheek as he plumbed the depths of his memory bank. "Nope," Daryl said, finally. "Jenny ain't got no one else. That's where she'd go."

Dalton tapped the airline ticket inside Daryl's pocket. "Check it out."

Daryl nodded, punching one fist into the other palm.

"I don't want you to *do* anything. Just watch the house. See if the girls are there and report back. You got that?"

Daryl shook his head. "I'm her husband. Those are my kids. They'll do what I say."

Dalton examined the fruit of his loins, taking in the swollen red eyes, the crusted drool, and the dried urine stains at his crotch. "Think they'd come with you, looking like that?" He shook his head. "We're gonna need to handle the situation more quiet-like, with a little finesse."

Daryl's eyebrows drew close together as he puzzled over his father's words.

Dalton shook his head. "I'll deal with Ms. Shepherd."

Daryl grinned. "I'd like in on that."

"You just concentrate on getting yourself out east. See what you can find." Dalton turned on his heel and, picking his way through the detritus, called over his shoulder, "Take a shower. You stink like shit."

Chapter

24

Grace was lucky to find a parking spot on the road almost directly in front of Chan's corner market. As she exited her Prius, she was forced to sidestep a couple of young boys no older than ten or eleven, racing each other down the busy thoroughfare on a pair of tricked-out skateboards. Neither one was wearing a helmet. She considered shouting after them, then shook her head. Given some of the wild things she and her brother had gotten into, it was a wonder they'd both made it out of their childhood alive and kicking.

She smiled sadly at the memory of her big brother high on the roof of the Holder mansion, his intense eyes shining, a homemade cape wrapped around his shoulders. The last time she'd seen Ethan, he'd been pacing the hallway of the psych ward, mumbling about frightening creatures she could not see, his ears tuned to voices that hectored him twenty-four hours a day, without respite.

Approaching the front entrance of the tiny shop, the sad memories drifted away as she admired a display of freshly cut flowers and a cart brimming with baskets of fresh Ontario peaches. She turned and pulled open the shop door. As she stepped inside, a tinkling bell announced her arrival.

Behind the counter a balding Chinese man, wearing a neatly pressed, white Oxford shirt over wrinkle-free khaki slacks, acknowledged her presence with a nod of his head.

"Mr. Chan?" she asked, reaching out her hand.

"You must be Ms. Holder," he said.

Grace detected a hint of British public school in his accented English.

He gave her hand a warm shake before offering her a cool drink.

"Thank you," said Grace, watching as Chan selected two bottles of lemon iced tea from a cooler beside the counter.

He twisted the lids and handed Grace the bottle.

She held the sweating glass to her forehead, then smiled ruefully. "Who said global warming was a myth?"

Mr. Chan nodded his head in agreement. "I grew up in Beijing. When I returned for a visit with my sister a few years ago, we were both shocked." He shook his head. "The smog was almost unbearable, the weather much hotter than I remembered. It is shameful the way we treat this planet."

"Thank you for agreeing to see me," she said, with a smile. She'd taken an instant liking to the man.

He frowned. "I would do anything to help Elena."

"You've heard what's happened?"

"I spoke with my sister on the phone this morning. She filled me in on the details." He reached under the counter and brought forth a clean, white handkerchief that he used to mop his forehead. "I don't know what to say. I can't understand it. Elena is a good girl."

"I don't think there is any question on that front, Mr. Chan." Grace watched the slight man's shoulders settle a little more comfortably in their sockets. "What I am trying to determine is why this Leonid Volkov person might be targeting her."

Chan frowned. "I simply cannot understand it."

"What do you know of the car crash that killed Elena's parents?"

"Most unfortunate. Elena was only seventeen."

"Police reports claim it was an accident. Did you ever have any reason to suspect otherwise?"

Chan paused for several moments, his eyes cast upward. Finally, he said, "Alexei and Maria Morozov were a lovely couple, hard workers. Good parents." He shrugged. "Were they secretive? Yes. Paranoid even? Perhaps."

He took a sip of his tea. "You must understand what it is like to live in a Communist country. Every move you make is scrutinized. Employers monitor attitudes and actions, neighbours are encouraged to inform on neighbours, even friends will turn on each other if offered the right incentive. In a society where even the most minor infraction can result in heinous punishments, everyone has secrets."

"Are you saying the Morozovs had secrets?" Grace asked.

Chan shrugged, then tapped a clipped fingernail on the glass countertop. "People who live in such a society trust no one, not even their own children." He leaned forward over the counter. "So, if you are asking if this Russian brute is after Elena because of something her mother and father did, I'm not sure what to tell you. All I know is that they kept that little girl on a very tight leash."

He took a sip of his drink, then smiled widely. "She's done so well. She's going to be a doctor, did you know that?"

"Thanks in no small part to you, I understand," said Grace.

"I stepped in after her parents died. Anyone would have done the same."

Grace smiled. "I don't know about that, Mr. Chan."

Apparently embarrassed by her praise, Chan began organizing a stack of flyers into a neat pile on the counter. After a moment he looked up. "What I do know," he said, "is that Alexei was one of the worst drivers I've ever seen." He smiled sadly. "Poor Maria, she was always trying to get him to let her behind the wheel, but he never would. Male pride, I imagine."

"So you believe it was just that, an accident?"

He shrugged. "I wasn't surprised when it happened. I'm just grateful Elena was in school that day."

Grace nodded. "You must have been fairly close to the family."

Chan shrugged. "Maria worked for me when they first arrived. She moved on to work at the bakery down the block." He smiled. "She made the most amazing cakes."

"Perhaps her employer at the bakery might know something?"

Chan shook his head. "They sold the shop to a young couple and retired to Florida soon after the accident." Seeing Grace's eyes widen, Chan continued, "Their move to Florida had been planned for some time."

Grace sighed. "I seem to be hitting one dead end after another. There doesn't seem to be any connection between Elena and this Volkov character other than the fact that she was a pretty young girl he met at a bar."

Chan's eyes narrowed. "Unfortunately, that is often more than enough."

Grace tipped her head in acknowledgement. "Volkov will claim that Elena is a disgruntled former employee, and until we can determine his true motivation, he holds all the cards."

Chan tipped his empty bottle into a blue recycling bin. "I wish I could be of more help."

As she handed him her empty, Grace reassured Chan that he had been very helpful, that they could cross off the idea that Volkov was somehow tied up in Alexei and Maria's deaths. She headed to the door, pausing to peer at a framed photograph hanging on the wall. "Is this Elena?"

He smiled proudly. "That was taken soon after she started working here." Chan walked over and straightened the frame. "If you are talking to her, please let her know I am praying for her."

"Thanks again, Mr. Chan. I'll let you know if we find anything," Grace said. She turned to go.

"Wait a minute," said Mr. Chan. "It's probably nothing." His eyes sparkled with excitement. "But there was a box."

"Yes?" Grace said, when Mr. Chan sputtered to a halt.

"Sorry," he said, "I was trying to remember. I keep a set of lockers in the back in which staff can store their belongings while they are at work."

Grace nodded encouragingly.

"Shortly after she started working for me, Maria asked if she could store something personal in her locker. It was a package wrapped in brown paper." He held his hands up and outlined a rectangular shape, roughly the size of a large cake box. "I told her it was her locker and she could keep whatever she wanted in there. When she left to work at Berkovitz's Bakery, she asked if she could leave it with me."

"That seems a bit odd."

"I thought the same thing. Why would she want to leave a personal item with me?" He leaned in. "I admit I wondered about it. Was there something in there she didn't want anyone else to see?"

"Or something she needed to keep safe?"

"Indeed," Mr. Chan agreed. "After she died, I gave the package back to Elena. I told her that I'd found it in a back cupboard, that her mother must have left it by accident. I didn't want her to speculate on why her mother had been so secretive."

"Did she open it?"

He shook his head. "Not in front of me, at least. I never found out what was in it."

Grace reached into her purse and withdrew a card and handed it to Chan. "If you think of anything else, anything at all, please don't hesitate to give me a call." She smiled. "You've been a huge help. Thanks, Mr. Chan."

Grace was just pulling on her seat belt when she saw Mr. Chan exit his shop and hustle over. She slid down the window.

"One other thing," he said, popping his head inside the passenger seat window. "She's not too concerned yet, but my sister says that she hasn't heard from her husband since the scene in Elena's apartment."

Grace frowned, then thanked the man again and pulled away from the curb. She filed that last disturbing bit of information away. She hoped that by the time she updated Maitland, Mr. Zhang would have turned up, safe and sound.

As she headed down the busy street, she saw Chan waving in her rear-view mirror. A secret package? He was probably right; in all likelihood it meant nothing, but she was glad to have even a tenuous lead to follow.

She'd call Signy later to have her ask Elena about the package; meanwhile she was headed to the University of Toronto, where Alexei Morozov had worked as a maintenance engineer. Perhaps his colleagues there could shed some light on his life, and his tragic death.

Chapter

25

Catching sight of the brass number plate hanging over the garage door, Signy heaved a sigh of relief before steering into the driveway. She was running behind schedule. The lineup at the rental desk at the airport had snaked on for miles, and it had taken over an hour to pick up the green Ford Focus she'd rented under the name of Carol White.

Despite the delay, she'd taken the time, after leaving the airport, to pick up a few essentials at a local hunting and camping supply store. Then, having finally found her way into the Calgary suburb where Elena was holed up with a conductor named Thelma, she'd felt like a rat running circles in an unsolvable maze.

Streets with names like Harmony Way and Tranquility Crescent seemed to run together, coiling back on themselves like a writhing mass of mating snakes. The GPS app on her phone and the tiny map they'd handed her at the car rental at the airport had both proved next to useless.

As she hurried up the walkway, she did a quick inventory of her appearance. The soft pink cotton fabric of her sundress was stained a dusky rose beneath her arms and her hair was one massive tangle.

As she twisted her hair into a ponytail, she chanced a surreptitious sniff under one armpit, then wrinkled her nose. Gross. What kind of an impression was she going to make on the traumatized young woman waiting for her inside? She needed the girl to be strong, not turned off by a stinking, dishevelled, tardy conductor. Luckily, the door opened before she had a chance to worry about it further.

A beaming woman sporting burgundy hair ushered her inside. Before Signy had a chance to reach out her hand, Thelma gathered her into a bear hug. "We're so glad to see you, luv. I have a little gal here who can't wait to get on the road. How was your trip? Was the flight smooth?"

Signy struggled to extricate herself from Thelma's embrace. What was it with all this hugging? Why couldn't these women shake hands like normal people?

Thelma released Signy and held her at arm's length. "Good Lord, that looks sore!"

Signy touched the scrape on her cheek, then shook her head. "I'm sorry I'm late," she said. "I got turned around."

"Ha!" Thelma laughed. "One of the builders thought the plans looked like a Buddhist maze, and he was right if you ask me, so they came up with names like Serenity Lane and advertised it as a 'little slice of heaven.' The houses sold out in record time. Just goes to show you that with some inventive spin, you can sell anything to anybody."

Thelma stood back and gave Signy an appraising look. "Although I hear I don't have to tell you that."

Signy furrowed her brows. What was that supposed to mean? She opened her mouth to speak.

Clapping her hands together in front of her, Thelma exclaimed, "I digress. It's not me you've come to see." She drew back and waved a hand at a brunette just coming down the stairs.

Signy could not conceal her surprise. The statuesque redhead from the picture had been radically transformed, and from the way the girl was hanging her head, she wasn't happy with her new appearance.

"Your eyes aren't lying, luv. This is Elena." She reached out and fiddled with Elena's new bob, sweeping the bangs to one side. "It was tragic about the hair, but it will do some good. I'm sending it to a woman who—"

As Thelma prattled on, Signy made a quick appraisal of her new passenger. Her eyes were red-rimmed. She was either exhausted or she'd been crying or both, and the way she was plucking at the unfamiliar clothes, Signy could tell she wanted nothing more than to rip them off her body.

"You look great," Signy lied.

"They make the most amazing wigs. Of course the hair has to be dye-free, which I am amazed to say—"

Elena shook her head.

"Hey, I'm serious," Signy whispered, "you look like you've stepped right off the pages of *Chatelaine* magazine."

"With that much hair, they'll be able to make several wigs. It's a crime more young women don't donate their hair. Why, I remember when—"

"Super. Exactly the look I've always wanted."

Signy's eyes widened in surprise and a smile played around the corner of her mouth. The girl still had a sense of humour. That was an encouraging sign.

"Isn't that amazing?" exclaimed Thelma.

Signy forced her attention back to the older woman. What was she yammering about? Unsure of the appropriate answer to Thelma's question, Signy bobbed her head in the combination affirmative nod and negative shake that she employed on occasions such as these.

Thelma eyed both girls suspiciously, then grinned. "You girls don't fool me. I know a conspiracy when I see one."

"Thelma, I can't thank you enough," Elena cut her off, "for the hair, the clothes, everything."

Signy reached behind her, groping blindly for the front door handle, relieved when she felt the cold metal under her hand. She pulled the door open.

"It was my pleasure, luv." Thelma clutched Elena to her bosom, then eyeballed Signy. "No heroics, you hear me?"

Signy frowned. What had Grace told this woman? She covered her discomfiture by bending over to pick up Elena's small suitcase, which proved heavier than she expected.

Shouldering past her, Thelma opened the door wider and scanned up and down the curving lengths of Serenity Lane.

"I wasn't followed," said Signy, "if that's what you're thinking." Frowning, she hefted the case in front of her like a shield.

"I'm sure you weren't, dear," replied Thelma, allowing Signy and Elena to move past her onto the front stoop, "but two heads are better than one." She leaned forward and gave Elena a hug, then turned to Signy. "This little gal is a sweetheart. We're all counting on you to keep her safe. Make sure you call in if you need anything. You have a team behind you, don't forget."

Signy suppressed a sharp retort. She didn't need Grace using this chatterbox to tell her how to do her job. She forced a smile, then turned and marched toward the car.

Appearing as desperate as Signy to escape this little slice of heaven, Elena rushed toward the car, lost her balance, and pitched over onto the black tarmac of the driveway. She came down hard on hands and knees.

Waving Thelma off, Signy said, "Come on, Miss Chatelaine, let's get out of here."

Elena responded with a sniff of laughter.

Signy smiled. It looked as if Elena Morozov was made of stern stuff. It was a relief to know that her passenger would be up to a challenge, should push come to shove.

Caught up in her thoughts, she didn't spot the Nissan Sentra parked at the curb a block behind them, a blond man sitting casually behind the wheel.

• • •

They might as well be riding in an ice cream truck, thought the Tracker. Elena Morozov and her new driver had just rolled past him, as oblivious as a couple of twelve-year-olds on their way to the mall. *This* is what I'm facing? He sat up straight, stretched his cramped back, then drummed his fingers on the dashboard. If Volkov wasn't overpaying in such an extravagant fashion, there was no way he'd be wasting his time babysitting these novices.

It had been child's play to pursue Elena to Calgary. Sitting in his car in the parking lot, he'd watched as the minivan had collected her from the women's shelter. The transfer had been smooth and quick. He'd caught a brief glimpse of the driver, middle-aged with salt and pepper hair hanging in greasy strings to her shoulder and thin lips that curled down at the corners. She wouldn't win any beauty contests but she seemed to know her business.

Nevertheless, after a quick calculation involving the capacity of the minivan's gas tank, the likelihood that she would not allow the tank to fall below half full as she made a midnight dash on the lone route through the Rocky Mountains, and a quick perusal of available service stations along the route, he'd been able to correctly predict where and when she would stop for refuelling.

He'd been waiting at the station when she pulled in and, as she edged the minivan up to a pump, had nosed in behind her. As his car filled with gas, he'd made a show of cleaning his windshield. The woman was shrewd. She took note of his presence and he could almost hear the wheels turning in her head as she evaluated his threat level.

Ignoring her, he'd finished scrubbing the passenger side of the windshield, then moved around the front of his car to work on the other side. Slipping sideways between his car and her rear bumper, he'd stumbled, dropping the squeegee. Bending to pick it up he'd slipped a tracking device the size of a dime out of his pocket and attached it to the underside of the minivan's bumper. The entire process had taken less than two seconds.

After that he'd been able to follow Elena to this Calgary suburb without ever having to make visual contact with the minivan. A relief, as he was almost positive the driver would have picked up his tail no matter how careful he'd been. She had an air of experience about her and might have proved formidable.

The burgundy-helmet head at this address also seemed competent. She'd done a decent job changing Elena's appearance. Gone were the long tresses of gorgeous red hair. Gone also were the ubiquitous shorts and T-shirt of a young student. Instead, Elena had been outfitted in the standard uniform of suburban affluence. He'd snapped off a few photos of the girl with a telephoto lens as she'd tripped down the driveway.

As he thought about the tag team that was working to move the girl across the country, the bell that had been chiming softly all night in the back of his mind suddenly rang out like Big Ben. He'd heard rumours about a shadowy group modelled after the Underground Railroad, but he'd never encountered it before now—remarkable really, considering the inherent overlap of their respective clientele.

The word was that an elderly woman in Canada used the shelter system throughout North America to ferry runners away from troublesome situations. A formidable organization, it had stymied many a seasoned tracker.

He'd been curious about the scope of their operation. He'd anticipated a stimulating thrust and parry, but so far, he was unimpressed. Pitting children against an opponent of his calibre seemed desperate and pathetic.

He allowed the girls to get only a block ahead before firing up the Sentra and pulling out to follow. He'd have to keep them within visual range, especially in this suburban maze. One wrong turn and he'd lose them. He'd been unable to attach a tracking device on the blonde's car as it sat in the driveway. He couldn't take the chance that they had a lookout posted at the front window. That's what he'd have done.

Not to mention that everywhere he looked, people were out and about, tending their properties like an army of suburban slaves. Clad in Crayola-hued plastic shoes, men and women scurried about, clipping and chopping and slashing at metastatic vegetation. Frankly, the entire scene turned his stomach. How people lived like this he had no idea.

Riding their wake, he thought about the two women. He hadn't had a close look yet at the little blonde with the long ponytail, but he knew she'd be inconsequential fluff to a man like Leonid Volkov. And Elena? He was certain that there wasn't a single scenario that didn't end badly for her.

He frowned. For some inexplicable reason, the image of these two young women lying side by side in a shallow grave didn't sit well. A tinny echo of the tune that had been plaguing him since yesterday rang in his ears.

He punched on the radio, relieved when the frantic chatter of an afternoon talk show erased the haunting strains of that godawful tune. As the ditty slowly faded, he reminded himself that he could not be held responsible for the actions of his clients. They paid him to find people and that's what he did. Whatever happened after that was simply none of his business.

Chapter

26

"Carl," said Richard Dalton, peering through the window that opened into the evidence locker.

"Dick," said Carl Becker, barely glancing up from his computer screen. "Are you about to ruin my day?"

Dalton hefted a large cardboard box onto the counter. "Just got this load back from the crime scene techs. It's various and sundry from that dope bust last month."

Carl nodded, his eyes still glued to the computer screen.

Dalton tossed the property control inventory report on top of the box.

Carl eyeballed the box suspiciously. "How much is in there?"

Dalton scanned the report. "A shit load of small crap, bullet casings, fingernail clippings, nose hairs, what the hell do I care?"

Carl glanced up, scowling.

Dalton sighed. "I can lock it up for you, Carl."

Carl studied the box for a moment, then glanced at his screen, then back up at Dalton. "Fuck it," he said, tossing Dalton a locker key. Dalton caught it deftly in one hand. "Go on back. The shit from that dope bust is in two forty-five. Just shove in the box. I'll process it later."

"Sure, man," said Dalton. As he threaded his way through the tunnel of evidence lockers, Dalton could not suppress a grin. What Carl lacked in common sense, he more than made up for in his ability to ignore policy. Allowing evidence out of his sight at any time was grounds for instant dismissal, but Carl Becker had never allowed threats from the jackwads upstairs to interrupt his online gaming, and so far, he'd been right in his assessment of the suits. The "Don't ask, don't tell" policy applied to more than just fags. As long as the evidence was still there when it came time for the lawyers to shove their noses in, nobody gave a damn what happened to it in between.

Dalton slipped the key into locker 245 and cracked open the door, then removed a plastic box about the size of a small microwave oven. Dalton snapped open the lid, then paused for a moment, his ears pricked. Nothing but the pops and whistles from World of Warcraft, or Grand Theft Auto, or whatever the hell Carl jacked off to while the rest of the department was out catching bad guys.

Inside the plastic box were thirty-two Baggies, each containing five hundred grams of crystal meth. He knew because he'd been the one to count them. Extracting one of the small bags, he slipped it into his coat pocket, then replaced the lid. After returning the plastic box, he shoved in the cardboard container. He slammed shut the locker door, then gave the lock a series of hard tugs, making sure it was secured. At least someone was doing their job around here.

When he let himself out, he didn't bother to acknowledge Carl. Not that the asshole would notice. He was still staring at his screen, his fingers dancing over the keyboard, the rat-a-tat of gunfire like corn kernels dancing in a hot fire.

· · ·

Before leaving Calgary, Signy had stopped once to load up on cold drinks and snacks. She'd seen no further sign of the Nissan Sentra and had concluded that it had probably been just another disoriented driver trapped in that ridiculous suburban maze.

Still, she felt much better once they were barrelling down the Trans-Canada. It was a divided highway, and out on the flat prairie she was able to see for miles.

The view was astonishing. Under a cloudless blue sky, the wind blew across expansive fields of amber grain, rippling the golden surface like waves over the ocean. In stubbly fields that had already been cut, huge round bales of hay stood like toy soldiers massing for battle. Now and then, the weathered ghost of a wooden grain elevator, standing forlornly amid the ruins of an abandoned town, spoke of a simpler time.

Where the fields were too bare for crops, cattle, horses, and even the odd herd of domestic bison roamed free, grazing on hardy grasses. Signy was impressed. In Ontario, livestock spent their short lives penned in small pastures if they were lucky, or housed in sterile barns if they weren't. She was most excited to see a herd of pronghorn antelope dancing up the side of a sandy hill and, for a moment, could imagine she was visiting the African savannah rather than the Canadian prairie.

But it was the trains that were truly amazing. At any given time, she might see one or even two trains chugging across the wide expanse. Carrying wheat, oats, barley, and canola to market, the trains could reach over a mile in length, requiring several powerful engines at both the front and the back. Yet even though she was able to see them from end to end, they looked no larger than the model train that steamed through the shelter in Linden Valley, so vast was the landscape.

She drove at fluctuating speeds. On a long, flat highway, most vehicles tend to arrange themselves into discrete clusters with stretches of empty road in between. Any vehicles that stayed with her despite her erratic driving would be suspect.

So far, there had been nothing to suggest they were being followed; still, she did not let down her guard. For the past ten minutes, a charcoal grey Lincoln Continental had been dogging their steps, the driver invisible behind tinted glass.

Elena had been nattering almost nonstop, filling Signy in on her plans for medical school, her apartment at the Zhangs' place, the awesome beach just minutes from her house. In fact, she'd been chatting about everything but the nightmare in her apartment and the shocking aftermath. Signy had been waiting for her to wind down. Finally, the girl sputtered to a halt.

Signy glanced over at her. "I can't even imagine what you've been through. How are you holding up?"

Elena picked at a fingernail but didn't look up. "Have you ever been to Algonquin Park?" she asked.

Signy shook her head.

"My parents used to take me up there in the summer. We'd camp by the lake, do some canoeing. We went up one winter. Stayed in a motel and did some snowshoeing. The snow was piled high as far as the eye could see. It was magical. And quiet—you know?"

Signy watched in her side mirror as the invisible driver in the Lincoln Continental decided to make a move. The big old boat of a car was so wide it took up the entire passing lane, and she was careful to ease her car a bit to the right to leave enough room. She'd noticed that the driver had a tendency to let the Lincoln drift over the lane marker now and then.

"I remember one particular winter day. The sun was brilliant, but man, it was cold. We'd just gotten out of the car and were getting our heavy jackets on when a tree exploded just off the trailhead. Have you ever heard a tree explode under the pressure of frost?"

Signy shook her head.

"That's what it sounded like."

Signy waited, saying eventually, "That's what *what* sounded like?"

Elena stared out the window. "His neck. That's what his neck sounded like when it snapped."

Signy shifted in her seat.

Elena's lips twisted downward. "I know there's probably no way it was as loud as that exploding tree, but that's what it seemed like to me. Like a shotgun blast."

Signy winced.

"You know what the weirdest thing is?" Elena swivelled in her seat. "I could tell he was trying to be nice to me."

Signy frowned. "By putting a gun to your head?"

"I know, but when I got home from the movie, I walked over to the sink and poured myself a glass of water. The next thing I know this big hairy hand is clamped over my mouth. I almost had a heart attack. I dropped the glass and it shattered. I didn't have any shoes on, and he picked me up and carried me away from the shards." She stared at Signy. "It was as though he didn't want me to cut my feet."

"Maybe he was worried you'd start screaming or something?" Signy tucked in behind one of the transports, drafting in its wake.

"All I know is that he was trying hard not to be too scary. He spoke in Russian and kept trying to convince me everything would be okay if I just came with him quietly." Elena sighed. "Maybe I should have just gone with him. Everyone would be better off."

"Back up a second," Signy said, refusing to rise to the bait. The girl couldn't afford to wallow in self-pity. "Tell me about Volkov."

"What about him?"

"I don't know. Whatever comes to mind. What does he look like?"

Elena answered immediately. "When he walks in the room, everyone turns to look. He seems bigger than life. He's gotta be over six feet, with thick white hair and twinkling eyes." She glanced at Signy, a ghost of a smile playing around her eyes. "And he's always buying drinks for people or bringing in little gifts to the servers, that kind of thing."

"Sounds like Santa Claus."

Elena chuckled without humour. "I have to admit, I thought

of him that way, a big, benevolent Santa Claus." She shook her head. "Stupid me."

"Don't beat yourself up. Men like him work hard at perfecting the nice-guy persona. How many times have you heard people describe a serial killer as one of the nicest guys they ever met?"

Elena jumped in her seat. "Do you think Volkov is that bad?"

"I don't know anything about him," Signy said, "except maybe that he's the kind of person who needs protection. You told Maitland that the guy who came to your apartment was often in the company of Volkov. Do you think he was a bodyguard?"

"Maybe. I don't know for sure. It just seemed that whenever Volkov came into the bar, the other guy was always around, watching him. I remember the guy had the bluest eyes." Elena frowned. "It just doesn't make any sense. What could Volkov possibly want with me?"

"Sex?" Signy asked bluntly.

Elena shook her head. "I never got that vibe off of him, although God knows I don't have a ton of experience in that department." She smiled. "Strict parents."

"What about your parents?"

"They're dead," she said.

Signy nodded. "That must have been tough. You were what, seventeen?"

Elena sighed. "It was the worst thing that ever happened to me, but it's been over four years. I've done okay."

"That's the understatement of the century. Medical school? Wow."

"Like I said, I had strict parents. Not to mention going to Catholic school." Elena ran a hand through her clipped hair. "We had a very normal life. At least I think we did. My parents may have been a little more isolated than most. They were adamant that I get home right after school, no hanging around, that sort of thing. But a lot of kids from immigrant families will say the same thing."

"Let's assume that, in your case, it was something more than overprotective parents. Did they ever give you any indication that they might be shielding you from something worse?"

"Never, just the usual parental stuff, and I was a good kid. Never got into trouble, never gave them much to worry about anyway."

"What about your friends?" Signy asked. "Did your parents have any concerns about them?"

Elena looked down and picked at the damaged fabric on the knee of her white slacks, torn during her fall on Thelma's driveway. The subject of friends apparently rankled. A failing they had in common, Signy thought ruefully. "I didn't have any heavy-duty friends, no BFFs, if that's what you mean. My life was going to school, studying every night after school, and working on the weekends."

"Sounds harsh."

Elena smiled. "I didn't mind, really. I was an only child and I always seemed to get along better with adults than with kids my own age. I enjoyed hanging out with my parents, as weird as that may seem, and after they were gone, Mr. Chan really stepped up."

"He was the guy you worked for?"

Elena nodded. "He owns the variety store just down the block from the apartment where I lived with my parents. I know it sounds lame, but I liked working there. I liked chatting with people from the neighbourhood, and Mr. Chan is great. He kind of reminds me of my dad."

"I understand he's Mrs. Zhang's brother?"

"Uh-huh, that's how I got my apartment in Vancouver. Mr. Chan set it up for me." Elena smiled. "The Zhangs have been great, especially Mrs. Zhang. She's a hoot." She patted her head, self-consciously. "I've always been sensitive about my height. I don't know how she does it, but Mrs. Zhang pokes fun at me in a way that makes me feel good about myself." Elena's voice cracked. "I miss her already."

Signy reached over and touched Elena's leg with her fingers. "I'm sorry this is happening to you."

"I don't understand," said Elena, jerking in her seat. "All I did was try to be nice to an old man and the next thing I know I'm on the run like some criminal."

Signy looked over at her. "On the plus side, you've got a lot of people working overtime trying to answer that question. I know they'll figure it out sooner or later and your life will go back to normal. Meanwhile, you have to try and hang in there a little longer."

Elena hung her head. "It's just so unfair."

Signy glanced in the rear-view mirror, then pulled into the fast lane. The Lincoln chose the same moment to make another move, zooming up behind her until it hovered just inches from her tailpipe. "We're going to be teaching you a lot about how to disappear and stay hidden. Lesson number one, it is what it is.

You're going to have to deal with whatever comes and make the best of it. I know that sounds trite, but you really don't have any other choice."

She touched the gas, luring the Lincoln on. Ahead, a transport truck had pulled out to pass a slower-moving tanker truck. She yanked the wheel, jerking her car into the slow lane, then zooming up alongside the truck that was attempting the pass. With inches to spare, she shot in front of the passing truck, earning herself an angry squawk from the trucker's air horn. She smiled. She may have pissed off the trucker, but she'd also managed to leave the old Lincoln in her dust, boxed in and going nowhere.

Elena squeezed her eyes shut and leaned her head against the window, and for a long while they didn't speak at all.

Chapter

27

Less than a half hour behind the two women, the Tracker tapped the accelerator. He was irked that the driver had obviously glimpsed him hanging too close as they'd negotiated the twists and turns in the Calgary subdivision, although he was certain she hadn't seen him attach a tracking device to her right rear wheel-well when she'd stopped for drinks at a corner store.

Still, being detected by his prey was a rarity, and if he were a superstitious man, he'd be having his Tarot cards thrown or watching the alignment of the stars for portents of disaster. As it was, this atypical blunder had incurred no long-term consequences. He'd already planned on dumping the silver Sentra and, after leaving the variety store, had driven the car directly back to the airport, where he'd exchanged it for a black Honda

CR-V, the most common SUV in North America. In his experience it was more effective to hide in plain sight.

Now, with the windows down, he was enjoying the hot prairie wind in his hair as he surged along the Trans-Canada Highway exactly sixty-one kilometres behind his prey. He was keeping track of their position on the MacBook Pro standing open on the passenger seat beside him, the Ford Focus a flashing red blip that he glanced at now and then as it moved ahead of him into the east. A window in the right upper corner of the screen spelled out their exact location.

Glancing at the screen, he saw they were no longer moving. He reached over and, keeping one eye on the road, tapped a few keys. The map upon which he'd been tracking the two women was suddenly superimposed on a much more detailed illustration of the road ahead. He could see where they had stopped.

Less than twenty minutes later he exited the Trans-Canada and parked at a roadside rest area. He'd given the SUV free rein, burning up the miles that separated him from his prey, and he was now less than five kilometres from the truck stop where the two women were apparently taking a long lunch.

He reached into the back seat and extracted one of the burner cellphones he'd purchased back in Vancouver. Many of the next-generation communication devices such as smart phones or PDAs had built-in global positioning, making it a simple matter for any party to track your position, a state of affairs he avoided at all costs. He punched in an eleven-digit number and waited.

The call was answered on the second ring by the big man himself.

"Reporting in," said the Tracker.

"Where is she?"

"Middle of nowhere, Saskatchewan, heading east in a green Ford Focus." He relayed the Alberta licence plate number. "They're burning up the miles. At this rate, they'll be in Toronto in a couple of days."

"Has she stopped anywhere? Talked to anybody?"

"In addition to the shelter people in Surrey, there was the woman who drove her to Calgary. She spent another few hours in Calgary with a second woman who modified her appearance. I'm emailing you a picture right now." The Tracker tapped a few keys, and a picture of Elena with her brunette bob was transferred into Volkov's inbox. "She's with a new driver now."

"Is that going to be a problem?"

The Tracker knew that an affirmative answer would have only one outcome, so for now he hedged. "She doesn't look experienced enough to be anything but a driver, but I'll let you know."

"Fine, meanwhile do whatever it is you do, and for Christ's sake, don't lose her." Volkov's breath was heavy through the phone lines. "Call immediately if anything changes." Volkov severed the connection, leaving only the soft hum of the dial tone in his wake.

The Tracker removed the battery and the SIM card, then snapped the cheap phone in two and deposited the pieces in two separate garbage receptacles. Volkov hadn't given him the chance to mention the Underground Railroad connection. He shrugged. He'd fill him in next time.

Meanwhile, he was starved. He wondered if he might be able to find a roadside restaurant that served a nice light salad. Since his strange attack outside the shelter in Surrey where the hallucinatory smell of french fries had nearly brought him to his knees, even the idea of greasy fast food was enough to set his nerves on edge.

Fingers trembling slightly, he reached out and switched on the stereo system, grateful as the soaring tones of Measha Brueggergosman singing "Rêve Infini" drowned out the memory of that strange attack.

Glancing at the computer screen, he noticed that the flashing blip was once again on the move. The girls had finished their lunch and were back on the road. He put the SUV into first gear and hit the gas, delighting in the feeling of power as the car leapt forward.

Peeling back onto the freeway, he threw back his head and provided Ms. Brueggergosman with a confident, if not totally harmonious, tenor accompaniment. Within minutes his mind had regained its tranquil state and he was once again on the hunt.

• • •

Poking through Signy's fridge, Zef grumbled. He'd used up almost everything edible when he'd cooked for her last night, and now the shelves were almost bare. All he had found were a couple of suspicious lumps wrapped in foil, a small tub of margarine, and an unwrapped package of hot dogs, so dried out they'd bowed in on themselves.

On the door was a crusted squeeze bottle of yellow mustard, a jar of strawberry jam, and a chunk of mouldy cheese. He picked up the cheese and gave it an experimental sniff before setting it back in its container. If he put that anywhere near his mouth, Signy would probably find his putrefying corpse curled over the toilet when she got back.

He yanked open the vegetable crisper and peered inside. Other than a wilted cabbage and a tumbleweed of feathery onion skins hugging one corner, the drawer was empty. Grumbling with disgust, he sat back on his haunches.

He stood up, stalked over to the television, and snapped it off. He'd been staring at the damn thing all day, and the urge to throw it out the window was overpowering. "Chill, man. Order a pizza," he muttered.

Tucked in the holster on his belt, his phone beeped. He clicked on the text icon, read the message, and felt his toes curl. The hot brunette from a couple of nights ago had just sent him a half-naked picture and an invite to a party at her place.

Glancing around the tiny apartment, he felt the walls closing in on him. How could Sig stand living like this? Stuck in Bumfuck, Ontario, with nothing to do, nothing to eat, and most importantly, nothing to take the edge off?

He used his phone to look up a local pizza joint, but when the young dipshit that answered the phone told him they didn't offer delivery service, he uttered an expletive and punched the off button.

"Fuck this shit," he said, grabbing his leather jacket from the back of a chair. He used the back of an unopened envelope he found on the kitchen table to scribble Signy a brief explanation, then signed it with his signature, "Z."

As he locked her front door and deposited the keys in her mailbox, he grinned. Signy was going to be seriously pissed. He'd promised her he'd stay on the straight and narrow at least until she got back. Screw it. His only priority now was to get the hell out of this skanky, two-bit hick town and back to the real world. He skipped down the steps and rounded the corner of the house, heading down the dark driveway toward the small back lot where he'd left his bike.

Bent over his phone, he whistled tunelessly as he tapped out a reply to the gorgeous brunette. He had just pressed send when he plowed head-on into a blue wall of muscle.

He skittered backwards, his hands balled up in front of him. A huge cop was lounging against the Ducati, one hand hovering over his pistol.

"What the fuck, man?" Zef said, shoving his phone into his leather jacket.

The cop tossed a half-smoked cigarette onto the pavement and ground it out with the heel of his heavy shoe. "Hello, Mark."

Zef took a step back, his mind whirling. The pig must have run his plates.

The cop grinned, a flash of white in the dark. "Mark Saunders, aka—Zephyr? Must have been an ill wind that blew you into my town." The cop chuckled at his own joke, then jabbed a thumb toward the Ducati. "It seems a bike just like this one was seen earlier tonight tearing up the turf over at the soccer field."

"You got to be kidding," Zef said.

"Nothing funny about it, Mark," Dalton said. "Imagine my surprise when I inspected your bike and found this." He held up a Baggie, the bottom corner stuffed with a crystalline powder.

Zef peered at the contents, then reeled back. "Fuck you, man. That ain't mine."

Before Zef could react, the big cop grabbed him by the neck, his beefy fingers digging deep into the muscle layer. "You're in deep trouble here, Mark." He dug his fingers in deeper and leaned his body weight forward, forcing Zef to his knees.

"This is crazy, man. I don't go near crystal," Zef pleaded, his eyes watering.

Dalton forced Zef's head down to the ground until his cheek scraped the pavement. He yanked the smaller man's arms behind his back and cuffed his wrists together, then hauled him to his feet and bulldozed him toward a cruiser parked down the block. He thrust him roughly into the back seat.

Zef sat hunched forward as the huge cop got into the driver's seat and cranked the engine. The Interceptor roared to life with a bone-rattling rumble.

"Yo, man, why you doing this?" Zef's outrage was betrayed by the rasp of fear in his voice.

"You have a rap sheet as long as my arm. Add another trafficking charge and by the time you get out, that girlfriend of yours won't even remember you."

"Signy? What the hell does she have to do with this?"

Dalton caught Zef's eye in the mirror and smiled.

Zef opened his mouth to retort, then eyes wide, scuttled sideways across the seat, pushing into the far corner. "You're that asshole cop she told me about."

Dalton made a clucking noise with his tongue. "And I thought me and her were friends."

"What the fuck do you want with me?"

"Didn't she tell you? Your girlfriend made me a promise, then she went and skipped town." Dalton grinned in the rear-view mirror. "I think she needs a little reminder regarding the urgency of the situation."

Dalton slammed on the brakes and Zef jolted forward, cracking his head off the metal grille that divided the front and back seats. Blood gushed from his nose, splattering down the front of his shirt.

Dalton called over his shoulder, "Buckle up, asshole. It's the law."

Chapter

28

Wadding up her paper napkin, Signy tossed it onto her empty plate, patted her bulging stomach, and sighed. She'd hoped an all-day breakfast would have provided a much-needed boost but it had only served to make her feel even sleepier.

She and Elena sat on opposite sides of a booth in an all-night diner. When they'd shuffled in almost an hour ago, a career waitress with calf muscles like elongated yams had warned them the air conditioner was on the fritz. Too tired to care, they'd shuffled over to a booth, oblivious to the ceiling fan that threatened to rip free with each precarious rotation of its blades.

Peeling her bare legs off the faux leather seat, Signy rose up and peered through the bank of windows that looked out over the parking lot. Other than a couple of local teens shoving each other in a half-hearted sparring match, the lot was deserted.

Catching the waitress's eye, Signy twirled a finger over the rim of her empty coffee. The first cup had jolted her back to life; she hoped a second would provide the stamina to manage the final six hours of hard driving that lay ahead.

The waitress shuffled over and poured a steaming stream into Signy's cup, then looked at Elena and raised a brow. Elena shook her head. She was picking at a slice of cherry pie with her fork. She cracked her jaws open in a wide yawn before returning her attention to the television screen hanging in the corner just behind Signy.

The stark overhead fluorescents were casting shadows like dark bruises under the girl's eyes. Signy wondered how much longer she'd be able to manage this blistering pace. It would have been much simpler had they been able to put Elena on a flight to Toronto, but Volkov's long reach had precluded that option.

Volkov would have ordered watchers posted at the Vancouver International as well as bus and train stations as soon as he realized Elena was missing. After that, a snatch and grab in a crowded terminal building would require little more than the administration of a fast-acting drug and the solicitous removal of an "ill" relative.

Conversely, college kids were everywhere as the dog days of August bled into September. For even the best tracker, pinpointing Signy and Elena's exact location would be like getting jabbed by the proverbial needle in a haystack.

She glanced out the window again, raking her eyes over the parking area. The jousting boys had departed and the lot was deserted with the exception of her car, a red Camry, and a black

SUV. The only other patrons in the diner were two men sitting together at a table, deep in conversation, and she presumed the two vehicles belonged to them.

She ripped open two pink packets of sweetener, tapping the contents into her cup, then smiled wanly at Elena.

Propping her head on her elbows, Elena said, "Mrs. Zhang had to go stay with a friend. I hope she's okay."

"I'm sure she's fine."

"I don't know," said Elena, impaling a blood red cherry on the end of her fork, "maybe I should give her a call?"

Signy set her cup down and stared at Elena. She leaned forward. "Don't tell me you have a cellphone on you?"

Elena shook her head. "They took it from me at the shelter along with my MasterCard and my bank card. They kept everything else as well."

"Good," said Signy, relaxing back into her seat. "Lesson number two: you have to stay completely off the grid. Service providers may talk up a storm about privacy, but it's child's play to use your phone to access your location, incoming and outgoing calls, the sites you've surfed on the web, everything."

"I know. They told me. It's just that I'm worried about the Zhangs."

"I know and I'm sorry, but there is no way you can contact Mrs. Zhang, or anyone else for that matter. You might as well pull the trigger yourself." Signy knew she was being harsh, but it was essential that Elena understood her new reality.

Elena shuddered, then laid her napkin over the remnants of her cherry pie, splashes of scarlet bleeding through the thin white paper; it looked like a shrouded corpse at an accident scene. She swiped at her eyes. "I can't tell you on how many levels this entire situation sucks."

"The powers that be," said Signy, with a slight smile, "have definitely decided to set up a latrine in your backyard."

Linking her fingers over her head, Elena hooked one corner of her mouth upward. "Is that your way of telling me that shit happens? I can handle the truth, you know."

Signy chuckled, then gestured at the waitress for the cheque. She drained her cup, then put her elbows on the table and leaned in toward Elena. "You know, everyone thinks it's the terror that gets to you, but it's not. It's the loneliness. I worked with a woman once: we'd placed her in Toronto and she did well for about six months until she just couldn't resist calling her mother. She thought that after all that time her ex-husband would have stopped looking for her."

Signy reached for her purse and extracted her wallet. "She was wrong, of course. He'd bugged her mother's phone and was able to determine her position in Toronto within minutes. It was sheer luck that she spotted that goon he sent to pick her up and called us."

"Six months? If this is supposed to make me feel better, it's not working," Elena said.

Signy shook her head. "The reality is you're not going to feel better until this nightmare is over."

Elena bit her lip.

"Listen to me. Your only job right now is to lay low until our team figures out a way to bring Leonid Volkov down. No phone calls, no Facebook, no Twitter, nothing. I'll get you to Toronto and then the big guns will take over. They'll set you up with a new identity."

"I don't want a new identity."

"You'll get a new driver's licence, credit cards, passport, the works," Signy continued, as if she hadn't heard the complaint. "They'll set you up in a nice apartment and someone will stay with you for a few weeks to teach you what you'll need to know to stay under the radar."

Elena opened her mouth to reply but was stymied by the appearance of the sinewy waitress, who wished them both a good evening before dropping a handwritten chit on the table.

Signy surveyed the damage, then opened her wallet. As she counted out the bills, she hoped her speech had gotten through to Elena, although she knew that realistically she would likely have to repeat it over and over before the message finally sank in.

Grace had told her that no matter how often the rules were explained, the chances were still only fifty-fifty that a passenger would remain compliant. The urge to reconnect with loved ones was too strong. That, coupled with an overwhelming desire to deny the reality of the situation, caused far too many passengers to derail the efforts to keep them safe.

She placed the bills on the table and added a generous tip. There was no telling how long it would take to resolve Elena's situation. Sometimes Maitland dug up enough dirt on the perpetrator to have the runner back home within days. Other times it was not so easy.

She tucked her wallet back into her purse. With a man as powerful and well connected as Leonid Volkov, Signy had the sinking feeling that Elena's ordeal was going to be more of a marathon than a sprint. If the young woman hoped to make it to the finish line, she was going to have to start by accepting her new reality.

Signy started to slide out of the booth but stopped when she noticed Elena staring up at the TV, her eyes brimming with tears.

Craning her neck, Signy looked over her shoulder at the TV, just in time to catch the end of the news segment that had caught Elena's attention. The picture of an older Asian man filled the screen. Below the image a caption scrolled slowly. "The body of Zhang Jianguo found dumped in Stanley Park exhibited obvious signs of trauma. Vancouver police report Zhang's wife, Zhang Mai-Li, is missing. Indications point to a violent struggle in their basement apartment. Police are searching for Elena Morozov, age twenty-one, in connection with the case."

The picture of Mr. Zhang was replaced with a smiling photo of Elena, her glorious tresses of red hair spilling in waves over her shoulders. "Police ask that if you see Ms. Morozov, do not approach her. Call nine-one-one immediately."

Elena clapped a hand over her mouth in an effort to stifle a shocked scream. Tears ran down her cheeks as the news reader shook his head in simulated sorrow at the tragic news from Vancouver. Brightening, he promised the first pictures of a brand new baby elephant born to Iris and Thunder at the Calgary Zoo, after the break.

As the screen filled with manic commercial images, Signy stood, slid into the booth beside Elena, and grabbed her by the elbow. "Come on," she said. "We have to go." She glanced over her shoulder at the waitress, who was looking at them curiously.

"Now," Signy said, pinching the tender flesh at the back of Elena's arm. Her action had the desired result.

Elena winced, her eyes slowly coming back into focus.

"We're going to get up and walk out of here, right now. Do you understand?"

Elena dipped her chin further onto her chest, a gesture Signy took as assent. Clutching Elena by the elbow, she hauled the girl upright, then edged both of them out of the booth. With her arm firmly around Elena's waist, she guided her past the lunch counter and toward the exit.

"Everything okay?" asked the geriatric waitress who was standing behind the counter refilling a tray of glass salt shakers. She cast her eyes over the two women, her gaze settling on Elena.

"Fine," said Signy, stepping between Elena and the inquisitive server, "my friend just needs a little fresh air."

The waitress nodded, her eyes flicking over to the TV screen, then back to Elena.

Signy smiled, then hustled Elena out into the parking lot. When she looked back, she could see the waitress watching their retreat. Frowning, Signy watched the waitress bend over and reach for something behind the counter.

Was she going for a phone? The idea that the waitress had identified Elena from that old photo seemed unlikely, but Signy wasn't willing to take any chances. Cursing under her breath, Signy redoubled her pace.

As they reached the car, Elena turned suddenly. "Look," she said, "I think we should just call the police."

"Not gonna happen," said Signy, firmly.

"No, you have to listen to me. Mr. Zhang is dead." Her voice caught. "He was murdered, because of me." Her words spilled out in a hiccupped torrent. "The police think I had something to do with it. I've seen enough TV to know that you could be charged with aiding and abetting." She grabbed Signy's hands. "I have to give up."

Signy shook her hands free. "What you have to do is keep it together. You have an army working for you."

Elena's mouth twisted downward. "Sure, and one of the most powerful businessmen in the country working against me. Who do you think they are going to believe?"

Signy nodded her head violently. "Exactly my point. You need to give the Line a chance to get to the bottom of this." She leaned in, her face inches from Elena's. "I know you feel responsible, but you have to listen to me. Volkov is the culprit here, not you."

"But—"

"But nothing," Signy said. "Until we find out why Volkov is doing this to you, you're going to lay low. The sooner you're safe in Toronto, the sooner we can bring Volkov to justice."

"I—"

"Until then," Signy continued, "you need to trust me. Just do what I say and we will be in Toronto in a couple of days."

Elena stared at Signy for several moments before deflating. She looked like a tired balloon that had been punched one too many times. Her shoulders slumped.

"Good," said Signy, placing a gentle hand on Elena's back and guiding her to the passenger door. "We'll be fine, I promise. All you need to do is hang in there a little bit longer. Can you do that for me?"

Elena opened the door, then paused. "All right," she said, nodding at Signy, "but if anything happens, I'm going to say you picked me up hitchhiking on the side of the road."

Signy smiled. "It won't come to that. Trust me." She eyed Elena from the corner of her eye as she peeled out of the parking lot. The murder of her landlord had pushed Elena that much closer to the edge, and Signy didn't know how much longer she was going to be able to hold the girl together.

She sent a silent prayer out to the powers that be, asking that if they were done dumping on Elena Morozov, it might be time to cut the poor kid a break. If she'd known what the next few days would bring, she would have saved herself the effort.

• • •

Slouched down in the back seat of the SUV, the Tracker watched the little blond driver hustle an obviously upset Elena out the door of the diner. He wasn't surprised that the young woman was losing it. Even the most hardened runner eventually cracked under the pressure, and this girl was hardly more than a kid.

Keeping his head down, he followed the progress of the two women, wondering with some curiosity how the driver would handle the situation. Trying to contain a panicked runner was like trying to plug cracks in a dike with your hands. Sooner or later you run out of fingers.

Their car was parked directly under a light standard, so he was afforded a clear view as the duo paused for a moment in front of their car and engaged in an intense conversation. When they broke apart a minute later, Elena scuttled around the front of the car to the passenger seat while the driver paused for a few seconds. He imagined her taking a deep breath, trying to maintain her equanimity in the face of the agitated runner.

As the driver turned toward him, her blond ponytail draped over her shoulder, he felt his breath catch in his throat. Under the glow of the overhead lamp, she was lit up like a soloist on a dark stage and he had an unobstructed view of her for the first time. He gasped out loud.

There was something about her. The blond hair, the confident posture, the grit that it took to shuttle runners cross-country. The dreaded tune jangled to life inside his head and he felt adrenaline burst in his chest, hot and intensely exciting. He squeezed his eyes shut in a vain attempt to block the noxious melody as the image of the blond driver danced behind his eyelids.

In her little pink sundress and strappy sandals she might project a picture of youthful femininity, but there was something about the sharp angle of her jaw and the long, proud nose that belied that image. She seemed more Nordic princess than sweet English rose. And he was almost positive her eyes would be blue.

There was no doubt about it. She could be a candidate.

The song played on inside his head louder and more discordant than ever. With a Herculean effort of will, he resisted the urge to cover his ears, certain that even the slightest movement would draw the attention of the disconcerting driver. He huddled in the back seat, gritting his teeth against a desperate desire to shout out loud.

A squeal of tires announced their hurried departure, and as he watched their tail lights trail off into the distance, the melody began to fade, as though an unseen hand had reached inside his head and turned down the volume. Panting, he opened the door and stepped out into the evening air. He inhaled deeply, but the foul odour of cooking oil wafting from the diner did nothing to calm the wild beating of his heart.

After several long moments, he snatched open the driver's door, climbed inside, and rested his head on the wheel. Twin discs advertising the Toronto music store, the rancid smell of fried potatoes, and now the discovery of a new candidate. What was it about these seemingly unconnected details that fired up the disconcerting hurdy-gurdy tune inside his head?

He banged his forehead lightly off the steering wheel. There was no connection. They were nothing more than random events, no more sinister than the classical station he'd tuned in on the radio, the spinach salad he'd eaten for lunch, or the cerulean blue of the Vancouver sky.

He felt his bowels clench. It was as if he were clinging to the edge of a cliff by his fingertips with the nightmarish tune dragging him down. He needed to dig in and climb up if he was going to save himself. He needed to take back control.

He flipped open the MacBook and watched the little red blip moving off into the east. Putting the car in gear, he charged after them. His heart was pounding, his teeth on edge.

He tried to focus on the blonde. Nothing brought him peace like the pursuit of a new candidate. If he wanted to get his head back in the game, then he needed to get the blonde alone and unlock her secrets. He could think of only one way to do that. He had to make Volkov believe that if he was going to snatch Elena Morozov, he had to do it now or risk losing her for good.

He smiled, feeling instantly better. He knew exactly what he needed to do to make that happen.

Chapter

29

After leaving the restaurant, Signy drove only a couple of blocks back toward the highway before pulling into a twenty-four-hour grocery store. She parked near the back of the lot, careful to tuck into a line of other vehicles. She watched a young woman bundle a sleeping toddler into a nearby car, then drive away.

Despite her initial misgivings she thought it unlikely that the nosy waitress had recognized Elena from the brief image of a glorious redhead on a TV screen halfway across the room. And even if she had been suspicious, the woman certainly wouldn't have been able to determine the make and colour of the Focus in the dark parking lot. Signy took a breath. They were safe for the moment.

She turned to Elena. "I'm so sorry about Mr. Zhang."

Elena gulped back a sob, her hands twisting in her lap.

"As for you being a person of interest? That must be Volkov's work."

Elena dug her fingers into her thighs. "I lied back there when I said I could handle the truth. This is insane. I can't deal with any of this."

Signy nodded. "Look. I won't sugar-coat this for you. The only other person that knows what went down in your apartment is in hiding and, if I know the Engineer, Mrs. Zhang is going to stay under the radar until this is sorted out."

"Good," said Elena, in a fierce tone. "If I have to go to jail, then fine, but I won't let Mrs. Zhang suffer anymore."

"You're not going to jail," said Signy, risking a weak smile.

Elena shook off Signy's hand. She hiccupped, then buried her face in her hands.

As she waited for the storm to pass, Signy tracked a black SUV rolling down the aisle toward their car and sat up straighter as it pulled into an empty spot directly in front of them. Across the dark aisle, she eyed a young guy with blond, maybe light brown hair, wearing jeans and a plain white T-shirt, exit the vehicle and move around to the back.

She dropped her eyes for an instant and grabbed the bag of supplies she'd purchased at the camping store near the Calgary airport. When she looked up, she saw that he had opened the hatch and was fiddling with something inside the back. Keeping her eyes on him, she fumbled inside the bag with one hand.

She relaxed when she saw the man emerge with nothing more sinister than a reusable shopping bag. He shut the hatch with a loud clunk, then walked off toward the grocery store, a cellphone plastered to his ear. She could hear the slap of his sandals against the pavement and then a loud chuckle as he reacted with amusement to whatever was being said on the other end of the line.

"I'm going to call in," Signy said, tossing the camping supply bag onto the floor of the back seat.

Elena pinched the bridge of her nose with her fingers and looked out her window.

Signy dialed Grace.

"I was just about to call you," said Grace. "Have you heard the news?"

"We just saw it on TV." She glanced over at Elena. "How much trouble are we in?"

"Has anyone spotted the girl?"

"I'm not sure. I don't think so. Thelma did an amazing job." The fact that Grace had evaded her question was not lost on her, but she decided not to push the issue.

"Where are you now?"

"An hour outside Regina. I'm hoping to make Winnipeg before we stop."

"Good. Listen, we don't have much time. Change of plans. How fast do you think you can get here?"

Signy, who had been thinking about little else, answered almost before Grace finished the question. "With luck, we'll be in Linden Valley by early afternoon the day after tomorrow."

Grace drew in a loud breath. "Are you sure you can manage that?" she asked.

"Absolutely," Signy said, with a smile in her voice, "no problem."

"We could send Marshall."

Signy remembered Maitland's driver and wasn't surprised to

hear that he had other talents besides chauffeuring an old lady around town. "Forget it. By the time he gets out here, we'll be halfway home. Besides, I think the original idea of two under-grads on the road is still a good one. We're not attracting any attention. If you send in the big guns, all hell might break loose."

"I agree, at least for now," Grace replied. "It would be better if we don't give the men an opportunity to play with their toys."

"Meanwhile, do you have any news?" Signy said, smiling at the hint of humour in Grace's tone.

"Not much. Maitland is pursuing the sexual predator angle but she doesn't have much to report yet. Trying to piece together a cold case on another continent in a country where secrecy is the norm is almost impossible. At the same time, she's looking into a couple of vague rumours about money laundering. Canada is a haven for the Russian mafia, and Volkov's business interests would be a perfect front for washing money."

Signy glanced over at Elena. The girl was watching her intently. She smiled brightly.

"Speaking of secrets," Grace continued, "I need you to ask Elena about a box that Mr. Chan returned to her after her mother's death. It probably doesn't mean anything, but her mother had asked Chan to store it for her."

"Okay," Signy said.

"I learned nothing from her father's side. His colleagues at the U of T hardly remember him, said he kept to himself for the most part."

"Excellent," said Signy. She gave Elena a thumbs-up, gratified when the girl responded with a hint of a smile.

"Is she listening?" asked Grace.

"Oh ya," Signy said.

"Is she falling apart?"

"I'm working on it," Signy said, flashing another brilliant smile at Elena.

"Hang in there," said Grace.

"Will do," said Signy.

"One more thing," said Grace. "I'd like to stay radio silent for the duration. I don't want to take any chances. Volkov has a very long reach. Are you okay with that?"

"Brilliant," said Signy, grinning at Elena.

"You could remove the battery, but since you're on the move, I think it'll be okay to leave it in. Check in when you can. If I have news, I'll leave you a text. And vice versa, okay?"

"Sounds perfect," said Signy.

"Okay. See you the day after tomorrow. Drive safe." Grace hung up.

"I'll tell her," said Signy, speaking into dead air.

"Tell me what?" asked Elena.

"The wheels are turning," said Signy, with a bright smile. "It's only a matter of time."

Elena relaxed into her seat, the hitch in her chest slowing.

Signy fired up the car and eased out of the parking spot. She didn't think a little white lie at this juncture was going to make a whole lot of difference. Besides, it was only for a couple of days. Just long enough for her to safely deliver the girl to the next conductor. She had no idea of how very wrong that assumption would prove.

• • •

The Tracker watched the girls exit the grocery store parking lot in a squeal of tires. He smiled. It had been a calculated risk to pull in directly across from the two women, but he'd needed to get close enough to utilize a new piece of tech.

He'd purchased the remote listening device a few months ago and was pleased he'd finally had a chance to use it. Within a certain distance, the gadget allowed him to activate the microphone in the target's cellphone, enabling him to hear both sides of any conversation they might have.

The manoeuvre had afforded him full access to both sides of the exchange between the blonde and her boss, even though he could see she'd taken the precaution of using an untraceable burner phone.

He walked back to his SUV, the bud still plugged into his ear. He had the information he needed but, even better, he had the blonde's first name and her final destination. She was the strongest candidate he'd encountered since that tough little waitress in San Antonio. He'd had high hopes for that one but it had ended badly, such a waste. He hoped this one would prove more worthy.

He'd felt her eyes on him as he'd dug around in the back of the SUV, playing out the innocent shopper routine, and the sensation had been thrilling. In spite of her scrutiny, he doubted that Signy from Linden Valley had been able to get a good look at him. Not that it mattered; they'd be meeting face to face soon enough.

He climbed into the SUV and started it up. He was back in the driver's seat. He could take what he wanted, and what he wanted now was to relieve his new candidate of the distracting need to save the girl. For that, he needed Leo the Lion to play his part.

He thought about the old man. It was serendipitous that he hadn't mentioned the Underground Railroad connection to Volkov before now. Volkov had gone to great lengths to establish himself as a legitimate real estate tycoon in Canada, and he'd move heaven and earth before he'd allow an underground group of meddlesome women to take him down.

The Tracker dialed Volkov and passed on the disturbing information about the involvement of the Underground Railroad. Volkov's over-the-top reaction was gratifying and he hung up a few minutes later, satisfied that he'd set the wheels in motion.

Interestingly, his information had turned out to be somewhat redundant. Apparently, Volkov had left the disposal of Zhang's body to an underling, and instead of disappearing forever, the body had turned up in a local park. Volkov was apoplectic. Because of his earlier efforts to incriminate the girl, she was now considered a person of interest in the murder and he was frantic to get his hands on Elena before she disappeared into the system. The old man had been clear. He wanted the girl picked up, now.

The Tracker flicked on the radio, filling the car with the romantic strains of a Tchaikovsky violin concerto. His head nodding in time to the music, he smiled. By this time tomorrow, Elena Morozov would be history, he would be free of the discordant tune that had taken up residence in his mind, and most importantly, he would have the undivided attention of the candidate with the Nordic-sounding name.

Chapter

30

Signy turned off the ignition, then rested her head on the wheel. After almost fourteen straight hours of driving, and too many cups of coffee to count, her ears were buzzing like crickets on a hot August night. She pressed a middle finger to the outside of each ear and tried an experimental wiggle, although she knew from experience that nothing quieted the irritating tinnitus except a few hours of unconsciousness.

She could hardly remember when she'd last slept. Had it really only been last night that Zef had shown up? She sighed. He was like chewing gum, sweet for a minute, then quickly losing its flavour. For the hundredth time, she hoped he'd be gone by the time she got back. Then, for the hundred and first time, she hoped he would still be there.

She raised her head and examined the quiet parking lot with satisfaction. Situated a few kilometres off the highway, the motel was small and quiet, fewer than sixteen rooms, half of which opened onto a back parking lot, affording a modicum of privacy from casual passersby out on the road.

She glanced over at the passenger seat. Elena was half sitting, half lying, her head thrown back, her mouth wide open. A thin stream of drool had crusted at the corner of her mouth. Her feet pumped against the floor as though she were running, and she made hooting noises in the back of her throat.

Signy grinned, reminded of her old dog, Jazz. She'd always imagined he was chasing bunnies through the fields when he got like this. She doubted Elena's dream was as pastoral.

She reached over and gave Elena's arm a gentle shake. "Hey, wake up," she said.

"What?" shrieked Elena, scrambling upright.

"It's okay," said Signy, "it's just me."

"What?" Elena repeated, staring at Signy through sleep-crusted eyes.

"We're here," said Signy.

"Where?" Elena asked. She touched a spot of crusty drool on her cheek. "Gross," she said, moistening a finger and wiping her face.

"Winnipeg." Signy smiled. "Right on time. Wait here. I'll go check in."

She had to push a buzzer several times before a plump young woman stuffed into an undersized pair of Harry Potter pyjamas appeared from behind a curtain in the back. The girl shoved a registration card across the desk, mumbled a surly welcome, then rubbed at her face, smearing thick, black mascara under her eyes.

Her face covered by a ball cap, Signy filled in the registration card using the name Carol White, glad that Maitland took great pains to ensure that the conductors' true identities not be compromised. It was essential that a conductor's life on the Line stay separate from her private life, not only to ensure her safety and the safety of her family, but to maintain a boundary between the excitement of the Line and the realities of real life.

Grace had emphasized that if a conductor allowed that line to blur, then everyone suffered. At the time, Signy had guessed that Grace was passing on more than just a perfunctory warning. For a brief second, she'd contemplated asking Grace if her work on the Line had impacted her relationship with the awful Kim Blackwater but had quickly thought the better of that idea. Grace's personal life was none of her business. She felt her cheeks flush at the thought of Grace weighing in on her complicated relationship with Zef.

"Checkout time is eleven a.m.," the girl said, handing Signy an old-fashioned room key, the number nine embossed on the plastic fob. She hadn't waited for a response before she turned and slipped back behind the curtain.

As she walked back out to the car, Signy guessed that the clerk was probably high. Her pupils had been the size of quarters. Her concern about why a stoned young woman was being sent out to confront strangers in the middle of the night aside, Signy was relieved. It was doubtful that the reluctant desk clerk would remember her own name in the morning, let alone the random woman she'd checked in the night before.

Signy pulled the car around back, and although the other rooms were dark, the two women hustled inside with their heads down. Their room was small but relatively clean, and there were two beds and a shower. It would do, Signy thought, tossing her bag onto one of the beds. She walked over and gave the plasticized window curtains a tug, making sure that they were completely closed while Elena opened her own bag.

"Do you want to take a shower?" she asked Elena.

Elena answered by rummaging in her bag and pulling out a bottle of shampoo and another of conditioner.

"Okay," said Signy, "but when you get out, we need to go through your stuff."

"Why?" Elena asked over her shoulder, as she shuffled toward the bathroom.

Signy opened her mouth to answer but yawned instead, a great jaw-cracking affair. She lay down on the bed, meaning to rest her eyes for a few seconds.

She didn't hear Elena turn on the water or climb into her own bed a few minutes later, nor anything else until the sound of shrieking kids thumping up and down the walkway outside jolted her awake the following morning.

•   •   •

Signy jerked upright, her heart pounding, her eyes wild, as she clawed her way out of the recurrent nightmare that often shattered her sleep. The bad dream always started the same way. A black-haired man, with eyes like raisins and skin the colour of the desert, bursts into her bedroom, grabs her around the waist, and hauls her into the air, his hand over her mouth. She claws at him but he is like a monster from a fairy tale, with fists like anvils and forearms rippling with raw power.

In the dream, she hears the sound of a child screaming from somewhere behind her and she knows she should feel compassion, but the childish cawing only enrages her further and she attacks the monster with the only weapon she has, her teeth.

She bites her assailant's arm over and over but cannot penetrate the leathery skin, and eventually she gives up, as helpless as a kitten in the jaws of a lion. It is in that moment that she feels the rumbling laughter inside the monster's chest and realizes with a sickening finality that she is going to die.

It is that horrible realization that wakes her at the same moment every time. This morning was no different. Signy sat up. Tiny footsteps thundered along the wooden walkway outside the motel room and a child shrieked with laughter. She scrubbed at her eyes, then glanced over at Elena. The girl was curled on her side, one fist tucked under her chin, her breathing slow and steady. Signy got up slowly and tiptoed to the bathroom.

Turning on the tap, she stepped into the shower, letting the warm water wash away the gnawing sense of impending doom. The dream always ended the same way, with her being borne away into the dark by the black-eyed monster. She unwrapped a waxy sliver of soap and lifted it to her nose. It smelled harsh, a potent mix of lye and rancid oils.

She'd been having the nightmare for as long as she could remember. She looked at the foul piece of soap and wondered, if she were ever given the opportunity to unwrap the dream, to follow it through to its conclusion, would she dare?

The soap squirted from her hand, and as she bent to retrieve it, her thoughts drifted and within seconds she had forgotten all about the nightmare and her provocative question.

• • •

Zef cracked open one eye. He was lying on his side, his shoulder and hip crushed against the hard bench that served as a bed in the holding cell at the Linden Valley police station. His head was pounding and his mouth and throat felt raw, like he'd stuffed a handful of sand into both cheeks and swallowed.

He'd managed hardly any sleep since being processed the night before. He had no idea what the hell was happening. Other than informing him that he was being held on suspicion of drug trafficking, Signy's psycho cop buddy had been tight-lipped, flinging him into this cell and slamming the door without a single word of explanation.

It was obviously a set-up, but there was nothing he could do about it until the big cop made his intentions clear. Zef groaned and sat up, stretching his back and running his tongue over his teeth. He scratched at the fine whiskers sprouting on his chin.

From somewhere down the line of holding cells he heard some asshole cry out in his sleep, setting off a chorus of groans and sighs from the other human cattle. Zef paced the cell, the paper slippers he'd been given offering little protection against the unnatural chill of the concrete floor. He glanced at his wrist before remembering that Dalton had confiscated his knockoff Rolex as well as his phone. Since there were no windows in the cinder block walls, he had no idea what time it was. Breakfast in the joint usually arrived around six a.m., so he figured it must be earlier than that.

Signy had filled him in on her dust-up with the cop's wife-beating son, and the threats that Dalton had made in the park. She'd really stepped in it this time, and his luck being the bottomless pit of shit that it was, it looked like she was bringing him down with her.

He kicked half-heartedly at the heavy iron door but only succeeded in stubbing his toe. He dropped onto the hard bench and let his head fall into his hands, the muscles in his jaw working furiously. He was sure the cop had something up his sleeve, some plan for using Signy's sense of loyalty against her.

Signy had always been there for him. No matter how hard he'd made it for her over the years, he knew she was only a phone call away if he needed her. Resting his chin in his hand, he remembered the first time she'd come to his rescue.

Almost sixteen, he'd been transferred to the Shepherds' after screwing up at his previous foster home. It wasn't his first fuck-up and he knew it wouldn't be his last. He didn't know why, but it seemed he revelled in destroying any hope that was offered him.

That day, he'd climbed the rickety ladder to the loft of the Shepherds' barn and burrowed between stacked bales of hay until he was invisible to the prying eyes of the other kids. The air was redolent with the sweet fragrance of alfalfa, and he'd sighed deeply.

In the last shithole he'd been dumped, the reek of overflowing garbage cans stacked outside his window had regularly seeped into the room he shared with an acne-riddled sixteen-year-old motherfucker. He'd been forced to fight more than once when the asshole had sneered at him and accused him of crapping his pants.

In the loft he'd reached into the back pocket of his jeans and removed an expertly rolled joint that he lit with a flick of his ever present Bic. He inhaled the pungent smoke, holding it in his lungs until he felt a glow of relaxation spread through his chest. He'd need a hit or three if he was going to read the letter he'd received from his mother in the mail that morning. She'd never win a Mother of the Year award, that was for sure, but she was all he had.

She'd just completed three months in rehab and he was hoping that just this once a miracle had happened. He'd sent a letter to the halfway house where she was staying a few weeks ago, pleading with her to let him come live with her. And now her reply was burning a hole in his pocket.

After one last look around the dusty confines of the loft to make sure that no bratty kids were spying on him, he slipped the letter out of his pocket and ripped it open.

It did not take long before her apologetic tone and whining excuses provided ample proof that no staggering breakthrough had occurred. In fact, she hadn't changed at all. Spidery letters ran in shaky lines across the page, and he figured she was probably stoned when she wrote it. The words were the same too. *Sorry, baby. Soon. Hang in there. Blah . . . blah . . . blah.*

Zef crumpled the letter in his fist and flung it onto the floor, not bothering to read the final few lines. He'd seen enough to know exactly how his future would play out, and it wasn't pretty. He was a fucking loser, doomed to be cast out of one dump after another by dirtbags even worse than he was, and nobody cared one way or the other.

Tears welled and he swiped angrily at his eyes. A tide of grief and resentment overwhelmed him, and he could no more resist the inexorable advance of self-pity than a sand dune could hold back the surging ocean.

He flung himself face down between two bales of sweet alfalfa, one cheek pressed into the rough wood floor, and wept with childish abandon. He wept for himself and for his pitiful mother, but mostly he lamented what might have been. He cried until he had no tears left.

Spent, he pushed himself to his hands and knees, his abdominal muscles weak from the effort, and, looking over his shoulder, came face to face with the blond chick from the bedroom beside his.

The letter from his mother hung from the fingers of one of her hands. It had been smoothed out, and he understood by the look of pity on her face that she'd read it. He flew to his feet and rushed toward her, fists balled.

She hadn't run away as he'd expected but had stepped toward him, placing both hands on his chest. Caught by surprise, he stared down at her and had been even more startled by the shining gleam of moisture in her eyes.

She stood on tiptoe then and kissed his mouth, gently, barely brushing her lips against his. He stood frozen, until she'd reached both arms around him. The heat of her flesh against his had been a revelation.

He wound his hand around her thick blond plait and pulled her head back, exploring her eyes with his own. He was not the type of guy to analyze his own feelings, but the heady mixture of the compassion and desire he discovered in those dazzling blue eyes broke through any reservations.

He seized her then, grasping at her as though she were a lifeline. Ripping off her clothes, he dragged her down to the floor and covered her body with his own, devouring her mouth, her face, her breasts, every inch that he could take.

And when he heard the hiss of pain as he entered her and knew that he was her first, he had pounded out all his rage and all his pain into her willing body, while her unblinking eyes stared up at him in absolution.

She'd given herself to him that day, and she'd given up so much for him since. And what had he offered in return? Nothing but fuck-ups, misery, and heartbreak. And now this fucking psycho was probably going to use him to lure Signy into a trap.

He sprang to his feet and, pacing the confines of the tiny cell, drove his fist into the open palm of his other hand. There was no fucking way he was going to let her down, no matter what that psycho cop tried to throw at him. Not a fucking chance.

Chapter

31

By the time Signy stepped out of the cramped motel bathroom, a towel wrapped around her head, Elena was up and dressed. She was sitting on the bed, watching the news on TV.

"Good morning," Signy said.

Elena glanced over and Signy could see a shaft of sunlight pinpointing the girl's heart like the beam of a sniper's rifle. Signy nodded toward the TV. "Anything new?"

Elena shook her head. "They played the same story as last night. They still want to talk to me regarding Mr. Zhang's—" She covered her mouth with her hand, as if physically holding back the word might make Mr. Zhang's murder seem less real.

"It'll take time," Signy said, feeling the need to say something to fill the dreadful moment.

"Sure," said Elena, returning her eyes to the TV.

Signy threw on a pair of shorts and a T-shirt and slipped into her sandals. Outside, she could hear the growl of a motorcycle revving and a one-sided discussion on breakfast options as a couple strolled past their door.

"Are you hungry?" said Elena, switching off the TV and grabbing her small case.

"Hold on," Signy said, nodding her head toward the case. "Do you remember some kind of box that your mother kept at Mr. Chan's?"

Clutching the case to her chest, Elena stared at Signy. "Sure. He gave it to me after she died."

"Did you open it?"

"Of course. As a matter of fact, I have it with me."

"With you?" said Signy, her voice rising with surprise.

Elena nodded her head. "It's just an old photo album. Family pictures. I've been through them a million times."

"Let's see it. We need all the help we can get."

Elena tossed her case onto the bed. In seconds she had the old photo album lying on the bed between them.

Signy examined the plain, navy blue cover. It was constructed of extra thick cardboard; strips of black tape had been neatly applied to the edges to prevent wear. It was bound by several brown leather stitches to a series of black felt pages, nothing out of the ordinary. Signy's foster mother had kept several old albums just like this one inside the big cabinet at the foot of the stairs. Sarah Shepherd was a big believer in family tradition, and Signy had pored through the books, secretly wishing that even one of the sepia-toned people captured within their heavy pages could have belonged to her.

She lifted the album in one hand, surprised by the heft.

Elena lifted the cover and allowed it to fall open. On the first page a series of Cyrillic letters had been inscribed across the black felt with a white pencil. Elena ran her fingers over the words.

"What does it say?" Signy asked.

"For my darling daughter on the occasion of your marriage. May you create lovely memories. All my love, Mother."

"Your grandmother?"

Elena nodded.

"Do you remember her?"

Elena angled her head to one side. "When I think of her, I picture a dour woman in black, silent as a ghost. I'm not sure if that is a real memory or just a dream. She was killed just before we emigrated to Canada, so I would have just turned four."

"It was a robbery, wasn't it?"

Elena nodded. "It was horrible. She was killed in broad daylight for a few pieces of jewellery. I think it was the reason my parents decided to get out of Russia."

"God, I'm sorry," Signy said, shaking her head.

Over the next several minutes they flipped through the pages, taking care not to damage the aging paper. Scenes of domestic bliss leapt out at them. Elena's parents, taken before she was born, their faces unlined and carefree. Scenes at their beach house on the Black Sea, Elena's father posing in a skin-tight bathing suit, one arm cocked to show off his muscles, his eyes laughing at the camera. A heartbreaking series of shots of Elena's mother, her eyes brimming with young love.

About halfway through the book, Elena arrived, a squalling redheaded bundle of joy. A few notations scrawled in the margins attested to her great height, perfect weight, and even the exact date on which she took her first step. That picture was particularly sweet: Elena, her chubby legs barely holding her upright, arms outstretched, a look of sheer joy on her face as she toddled toward her mother.

"I think I remember this day," said Elena. She was looking at a picture of herself perched on a swing, at the apogee of its arc, her legs stretched out in front of her, her knuckles white on the chains. "My dad took this picture. See my mother over here?" She indicated a small figure in the background, standing just in front of a tall, thin man. "She was so frightened that I would fall. She kept shouting at my father to get me down."

"Did he?"

Elena shook her head. "He loved it when I took chances." She frowned, then turned the page. "At least he used to. Before we moved."

"Something changed after you came to Canada?"

"I really don't know for sure. I was so young. Like I said, it was just impressions. In Moscow, I remember my life felt carefree and full of laughter."

"And in Canada?"

"Not so much," said Elena, flipping another page. She peered at the one little photo sitting squarely in the middle of the page. "Look at this one."

Signy leaned over her shoulder and squinted at the picture. She could see Elena, half smothered in a bulky coat that fell almost to her ankles, the thick fur collar turned up high around her chin. A matching fur hat sat at a jaunty angle over one eye. The little girl was sandwiched between her parents, who were equally bundled up. All three were grinning at the camera. "You were so cute."

Elena smiled.

"Who's this?" Signy asked, pointing at the figure of the same skeletal man, standing just behind the trio, his face half turned from the camera.

"A bodyguard, I expect," Elena answered.

"Really?"

"Everyone had them," Elena said, flipping the pages. She pointed out the same figure in several more photos. "How much do you know about Russian history?"

Signy rocked a hand back and forth, palm down. "Let's just say I skipped that lecture."

"You know about the fall of Communism?"

Signy held her hands in front of her as if gripping a podium, and said, in the commanding tone of Ronald Reagan, "Mr. Gorbachev! Tear down that wall."

Elena chuckled. "What people don't understand is that as awful as it was, the Communist regime brought stability to the country. The crime rate was much lower than it is today. But after the wall fell, things spiraled out of control. In fact, during that period the country was often compared to the Wild West in the United States. A complete free-for-all." She touched the photo of the unknown man. "So, if your family had any money at all, you tended to hire protection."

Signy turned the final page. Centred in the middle of the page, a picture of Elena, holding her mother's hand and peering through a shop window. Behind them and to the left, a short, stocky figure, his eyes obscured by a dark fedora, hovered protectively, one hand on the little girl's shoulder. "Like this one?" Signy asked, pointing at the figure.

Elena glanced down at the picture, then frowned, hunching closer to the tiny, cracked photo.

"What is it?"

Elena didn't answer, only continued to stare at the picture.

"Elena?"

"It's probably nothing," Elena said, finally.

"Come on. What do you see?"

Elena looked up from the page. "Seriously, I'm sure it's nothing. I can't really see his face and he's much younger, of course, but he sort of looks like the man who came to my apartment."

Signy bent back over the photo, staring at the blurry figure, his great coat hanging on his shoulders like the skin of a bear.

"I'm probably just imagining it."

"Maybe," said Signy, running her finger over the man's face, "but if you're right, why would one of your parents' former bodyguards be coming after you? And why now?"

"Like I said," Elena said, shutting the book with a snap, "I'm probably just imagining things."

"Probably," said Signy, fishing in her purse for her cellphone, "but give me two seconds. I'll text this to Grace, and then let's get cracking. I want to make Sault Ste. Marie by tonight." Signy turned on the phone, disconcerted by the little red star that indicated she had an incoming text message. Grace had said she'd communicate only if absolutely necessary.

She clicked on the icon, expecting to see Grace's name at the top of the list, but was taken aback when she saw an unfamiliar number. She almost ignored it, figuring it would be an unsolicited advertisement or a spam message. On the off chance it might be Grace texting from another number, she opened it. As she scanned the terse message, her breath caught in her throat.

Mark Saunders, aka Zephyr, arrested for possession with the intent to traffic outside the residence of Signy Shepherd at 7 p.m. last night. No charges—yet.

Signy bit her bottom lip in an effort to hold back a shout of outrage. Dalton was using Zef as leverage against her. She reread the message several more times, but Dalton was savvy. There was nothing incriminating in the content of the message, nothing a judge and jury would find amiss. She knew exactly what he was telling her. Either she arranged the return of his daughter-in-law and grandchildren or Zef would be charged with trafficking.

Dalton almost certainly knew, as she did, that Zef was one trafficking bust away from a long stretch in federal prison. That was the bait he was using to lure her in. Her hands curled into fists. Dalton also knew there was nothing she could do to return his daughter-in-law and grandchildren.

He would demand something else for Zef's release, and she had a pretty good idea what that might be. She remembered the feel of his oily tongue inside her mouth. She shuddered. Dalton had just upped the ante, and she had very few cards left to play.

After a second, she sent Dalton an equally terse acknowledgement before typing out a second message for Grace.

When she looked up, Elena was standing near the door, her bag over her shoulder.

"Drive-through at Tim Hortons before we hit the road?" she asked the girl, the fake smile that was splitting her cheeks actually causing her pain.

"Sounds good."

Signy pulled a ball cap down over Elena's eyes. "Can you wait for me in the car? I'm just going to drop the key in the lobby." Waiting until Elena made it safely to the car, she walked briskly over to the lobby. When she pulled open the door, a middle-aged woman with dark circles under her eyes was manning the counter, the girl from the night before nowhere to be seen.

Signy dropped the key on the glass counter and turned to go. She had one hand on the door before she turned back. "Excuse me?"

The woman glanced up with a tired smile.

"This is none of my business, and I hope you don't mind, but do you know the young lady who was on duty last night?"

The woman sat up straight. "Why? What has she done?"

Signy heard the catch in the woman's voice and held up her hands. "Nothing, she hasn't done anything. It's just that I was a little worried about her last night."

The woman's jaw clenched.

Signy nodded. "I just thought you should know. I really don't mean to butt in, but I thought she might need help."

The woman shook her head. "She swore up and down she was clean, but I guess I already knew." She smiled wanly. "Thanks for the heads-up."

"Sorry again," said Signy, backing out the door, her face burning. She turned and hustled to the car.

Chapter

32

Sitting in a McDonald's parking lot, the Tracker watched the road. He shifted uncomfortably, chafing at the delay. The two women had left Winnipeg more than a half hour ago. He was watching their progress on his computer, and with every mile they burned up, he felt more anxious.

Before disclosing the location of the two women to Volkov, the Tracker had insisted that he be allowed to take the blond driver for his own purposes. Caught up with his own worries, the Russian had agreed, provided that nothing complicated the retrieval of the redhead. The Tracker had offered the necessary assurances and to that end was waiting to coordinate with the man Volkov had tasked with picking up Elena Morozov.

He'd been instructed to watch for a tall man in a blue ball cap, driving a black Crown Victoria. He scanned the road again. No sign of him yet. He sipped at his coffee, running scenarios through his head on how he might arrange a plausible interaction with Signy Shepherd in the middle of Elena Morozov's abduction without raising her antennae. He smiled wryly. Nothing brilliant was coming to mind, although he wasn't too worried. He'd think of something. Deception was his forte.

He winced as a memory of his mother flashed in his mind. He'd been sitting in her ample lap, winding his small hand through her long, black hair. He'd felt warm and loved, secure in the knowledge that no matter what he did, she would never abandon him.

She had been a good mother, teaching him everything he needed to know of the people and their ways. He'd treasured the hours they'd spent in their hogan, heads bent together as she elaborated on the healing properties of this or that bundle of dried herbs, or taught him how to spice up the corn, squash, and beans that were the primary ingredients of their simple diet.

Still, despite her unconditional love for him, he'd not hesitated to deceive her whenever it served his purposes. He recalled the time he'd poked his head inside the hogan after a day spent exploring the caves out behind Red Rock Butte. She'd been sitting on a wooden chair, examining her shoes, while a white man in a black suit asked her if she knew that her ten-year-old son had not been to school in over six months.

He'd almost run off then, back to the security of the harsh desert sky, but, captured by the thrill of hearing the tale of his own prowess, had eavesdropped as the man recounted how the boy had hacked into the Tuba City district school computer files, successfully generating all the documents necessary to withdraw his name from the system.

He'd watched, the corners of his eyes crinkling in silent amusement, as his mother rose and shuffled over to the battered wooden cupboard that hung on the wall over his tiny blue desk. She'd removed a handful of tests and assignments, most of them sporting a bright red *A* in the upper-right corner, then flipping through the pile, she selected a legitimate-looking report card, which she offered to the man.

He examined the paper, then shook his head sadly. Alex studied his mother's eyes as she realized that every piece of paper she held in her hand, every record she'd accepted from her son with an exclamation of joy, was no more than a passable forgery. He'd expected to feel a sense of triumph but instead was left with a metallic taste in his mouth, as though he'd swallowed a handful of pennies.

His mother had flicked her eyes at him then. She'd known that he'd been hiding just outside the door. The bitter taste in his mouth grew more profound and he found himself running, fleeing out into the savage beauty of the desert, where the rules were simple and he was invisible.

He crushed the paper coffee cup and shoved it into a plastic bag he'd set up for garbage. Being forced to live in a car for days on end didn't mean one had to behave like an animal. His mother had also taught him the importance of cleanliness.

He looked out the window and sighed. The consequences of his stunt with the Tuba City school records had been life-changing. Not long after the incident with the white man in the black suit, he'd returned home to find another man sitting opposite his mother.

This man had been different. Sitting quietly in the straight-backed chair, he'd seemed at first glance to be nothing more than a shadow. With his average build and unremarkable face, his black hair cut conservatively, and his trousers and button-down shirt those of the *bilagáana*, the Navajo term for white people, he would easily disappear in a crowd. But when young Alex had reluctantly entered the hogan, the man had glanced over, and the sight of his eyes, as deep and unfathomable as black holes, had sent a shiver down Alex's back.

"This is Uncle," his mother had said, as she'd pushed him toward the stranger. "He will teach you what you need to know." He remembered pressing back against her, unwilling to move any closer to the ominous stranger. Ignoring his obvious distress, his mother had propelled him forward until he was standing directly in front of the strange man.

Steeling himself, he'd looked into the impenetrable eyes. So this was Uncle, his mother's brother, the one that the children at school had claimed in hushed tones was a skinwalker. Fast, agile, and impossible to catch, skinwalkers, so the legend went, could change into animal form, wreaking havoc on their hapless human victims.

Uncle's black eyes had pierced his, and Alex felt the tortilla he'd had for breakfast turn to acid in his stomach. Uncle had turned then and moved silently toward the door. After a final glance at his mother, Alex had followed, knowing he had no choice.

The Tracker shook his head, erasing the disturbing memory before allowing his thoughts to wander back to Signy Shepherd. The image of her lit like a fierce Nordic queen under the amber glow of the street lamp burned in his head. Memories of Uncle aside, he didn't care about consequences or collateral damage. Not anymore.

Sitting up straight, he noticed the black Crown Vic pulling into the parking lot. He grabbed his bag of equipment, then exited his SUV and walked toward Volkov's man, his rising excitement masked by his stony blue eyes.

Chapter

33

The sun was high in the sky by the time Signy and Elena pulled out of a diner in Dryden, a small northern Ontario city two hours east of the Ontario/Manitoba border. They'd decided to have a quick lunch before tackling the most difficult part of the drive, a three hundred kilometre marathon on a flat stretch of highway that bisected the boreal forest of northern Ontario.

The Trans-Canada highway offered two ways through this section of the province. The more scenic was an L-shaped route that ran south to the American border before taking a sharp turn to the east and heading straight on to Thunder Bay. Tourists tended to choose this option.

The second route, a frost-damaged two-lane highway that cut a diagonal path through a never-ending wilderness of pine, spruce, fir, and scrubby black willow trees, was preferred by truckers and other hard-core travellers.

Signy remembered reading the story of a trucker, desperate to relieve his bladder, who had pulled to the side of the road and stepped only a few metres into the bush. When he'd turned around to walk back, the configuration of the gnarled and twisted trees in front of him appeared identical to those behind him and he was no longer certain which route led back to the safety of his truck.

When he looked up, the dark green branches wove together to form a dense, coniferous canopy, leaving him unable to orient himself by the sun. Within seconds he was lost. Luckily, he'd had the presence of mind to sit down and wait rather than attempt a blind trek through the undergrowth. A passing RCMP cruiser, noting the deserted truck, its engine idling, had called it in, and a few hours later, the trucker, cold, ravaged by mosquito bites, and more than a little embarrassed, had been rescued.

Signy had weighed the pros and cons of both routes and had settled on the northern option. She'd rather battle boredom than risk having Elena recognized by an observant tourist. With luck, they'd be in Thunder Bay in less than three hours, and from there it was only a few more hours before they stopped for the night.

The turnoff to the south was in sight when the shimmy in the steering wheel she'd been feeling through the palms of her hands for the past half hour worsened. "Damn," she said, louder than she'd intended.

Elena jumped in her seat, then craned her neck to look over her shoulder. "What's wrong?"

Signy smiled. "No worries. I think we picked up a stone or something when we drove through that fresh gravel a while back."

"Is that bad?" Elena asked.

"Not if I can clear the debris. There's a service station just down there," she said, pointing down the road that travelled south to the American border. Along with the majority of the other vehicles around her, she steered the Ford south, then made a quick turn into the gas station. Avoiding the row of pumps and a cluster of cars parked in front of the busy restaurant, she pulled to a stop near the back of the lot.

"Stay here," she said, then jumped out of the car. A quick inspection of the front tires revealed no discernible problem, nor was the left rear tire showing signs of damage. However, when she moved around to the right rear tire, the obstruction was obvious. A large stone had lodged between the tire and the hubcap, unbalancing the wheel.

She gave the thumbs-up to Elena, who was watching her progress in the side-view mirror. She poked at the stone with her finger but it was wedged tight. "Can you pop the trunk?" she called to Elena. A second later the trunk clicked open. Wiping the road dust from her knees, she found what she was looking for under the spare tire.

Squatting back down, she gave the stone a hard whack with the sharp end of the tire iron and was relieved when she felt it begin to give way. One more hit, she guessed, and the stone would pop free. With a flick of her wrist she tried to dislodge the offending stone. She missed by a mile. The wrench bounced off the tire and kept going, banging off the edge of the wheel well.

"Shit," she said, squatting down to peer at the impact point, hoping she hadn't scratched the paint. How would that look?

Her first solo job and she manages to damage the rental car. Nor was she sure that Maitland would cover the expense. She gritted her teeth. Her salary was tight enough as it was. She didn't need to add an overpriced paint job into the mix.

Bending lower to inspect an obvious ding in the paint, she caught sight of something clearly foreign, tucked high up in the wheel well. She got down on her hands and knees and squinted up into the darkness above the tire. There was a small disk, about the size of a dime, clinging to the metal. She reached her hand up and picked at it with a fingernail. It took some doing—the magnet holding it in place was powerful—but eventually it dropped into the palm of her hand.

She looked down at it, a worried crease forming between her eyes. It looked harmless, no more than a fraction of an ounce of flat metal, but the sight of a tiny antenna protruding from the centre of one side erased any doubts. It was a tracking device, and it was about as harmless as a nuclear bomb.

She scrambled to her feet, her head whipping from side to side. Scanning every corner of the service station, she could see nothing out of the ordinary. Nor could she feel anyone watching. Not surprising, she guessed. The purpose of a tracking device was to keep tabs on the quarry from afar. Whoever was following was doing so from a distance.

The small disk felt hot in her hand, and she almost tossed it into the scrubby grass near the rear of the car. Instead, she looked over at the row of cars parked at the restaurant. Chances were most of them were headed south on the tourist route.

Waving at Elena to stay put, she hustled across the lot over to the line of cars sitting at the restaurant. She scanned the row of licence plates before settling on a Lexus that hailed from Minnesota.

She knelt before the rear bumper and slipped the tracking device up under the rim, grunting with relief when she felt the magnet catch and the disk flew from her fingers. She stayed down a second or two longer, pretending to fiddle with the clasp on her sandal, then stood, took a final look around, and walked normally back to the car.

Bending down, she retrieved the tire iron and with a couple of quick thrusts removed the lucky little stone from the tire, then tossed the tool into the trunk and slammed the lid. After hopping back into the car, she smacked a fist on the steering wheel, then gave the key a vicious twist.

"What's wrong?" Elena asked her eyes wide.

Signy took a deep breath, willing herself to calm down. Finding the tracking device had been a stroke of luck and she needed all her wits about her if she was to take advantage of this small gift. Screaming out of the lot at a hundred miles per hour would not help. She twisted to face Elena. "Somewhere between Thelma's and our last pit stop, we picked up a tail."

"A what?"

Signy put the car into gear and backed, sedately, out of her spot. "I found a tracking device under the car. Someone has been watching us."

"Oh my God," said Elena, craning her neck to look over her shoulder.

"Probably not too close. With the tracker, they could be some distance behind us and still know exactly where we are. I think they've been biding their time."

"For what?" Elena asked. She stared at Signy for several seconds, then seemed to put two and two together. "Oh God," she groaned into her hands, "they're going to try and take me."

"Hey," said Signy, flashing a tight grin, "the asshole is about to take a wrong turn. With luck, he'll be halfway to the border before he realizes his mistake." She waited for a break in the steady traffic heading south before turning north. When she reached the fork in the road, she swung east, the long ribbon of highway stretching out in front of them as far as they could see, an impenetrable wall of green on both sides, hemming them in.

Signy hit the accelerator.

• • •

A tall man in a blue ball cap, his hand resting lightly on the nozzle of the gas pump, watched the two women exit the service station. He had prepaid at the pump and waited patiently while the large tank on his late-model Crown Victoria was replenished. When the pump clunked to a halt, he replaced the nozzle, then waited for the machine to print his receipt.

He was in no rush. He knew this territory like the back of his hand. The women had nowhere to hide and it would only take seconds for him to slide up behind them. He could afford to bide his time.

As he climbed back into the Crown Vic, he smiled to himself. He'd seen the blond driver discover the tracking device, then rush across the lot and attach it to another vehicle. The Tracker was going to be furious when he realized he'd been thrown off the trail by a little snip of a girl.

He turned the key, put the car in gear, and eased out to the road. Not that he was going to enlighten the arrogant asshole. He didn't care for the man's attitude. They'd met that morning in the McDonald's parking lot. The Tracker had passed on all the details he'd need in order to capture the redhead but had gone overboard reminding him that the blonde was not to be touched.

It had taken a considerable act of will not to take out his Glock and pop the son of a bitch, but Volkov's instructions had been clear: bring in the redhead and let the Tracker have the blonde. Still, it had rankled to have to put up with a lecture from a kid who was still loading his diapers the first time he'd put a bullet in a man's brain.

He swung the car north, then flicked on his right turn signal. When he hit the fork, he followed the cracked pavement east and was gratified to see the pale green Ford far in the distance. They were too far ahead to notice him in their rear-view mirror, but not so far ahead that with one tap of the accelerator he couldn't be right up their tailpipe when the time was right.

He smiled to himself. The Tracker's pleasure aside, Volkov had been clear. The redhead was the priority. He was to hand over the blonde only if doing so did not compromise his main target in any way. He glanced in his rear-view mirror. In the next few minutes the Tracker would be embarking on the scenic tour and with each passing minute would move farther and farther away from his precious blond bimbo.

He glanced at the digital clock on the dashboard. It would take about an hour before they reached the spot he'd chosen for the takedown. By then, the Tracker would be halfway to the US.

He rolled down the window and whipped the military-grade, hand-held radio the Tracker had given him that morning onto the side of the road.

It had been a bullshit plan anyway, squawking radios, tracking devices, secret codes. What a load of crap. Simple was always better. Watch, follow, and take. No fuss, no muss, as easy as shooting fish in a barrel. Too bad the cocky little shit wouldn't be around to see a real pro at work.

The man stared into the distance, his dark eyes focused on his target, his heart beat slow and steady. He stuck a cigarette in his mouth, lighting it with a match he scratched on the stubble at the side of his jaw. He inhaled deeply, at home in the toxic cloud.

Chapter

34

During the time Signy and Elena had stopped for lunch in Dryden, the Tracker had waited at a roadside pullout, ten kilometres west of town, taking the opportunity to do some research on the disconcerting blond driver.

Her given name was unusual, and within seconds of plugging the combination into the Canadian 411 database, he had her full name and address. Staring at the name on the screen, he rubbed his chin in anticipation, feeling like a kid in a candy shop.

This was always the best part, the covert forays into the life of another person, discovering the intimate details of their daily existence—the secrets, the lies, their hopes and dreams.

More often than not, the information he uncovered in this initial investigation immediately disqualified a potential candidate. If the girl had older siblings, or a twin, she would not do.

If she had two loving parents with whom she maintained a close relationship, she would be discarded. If she was a natural redhead or had been born with black hair, if she was too old or too young, or most critically, if her eyes were not the perfect shade of stormy blue, then he knew he had miscalculated and the girl would be scratched from his list.

It took several minutes for him to hack into the relevant Canadian government database. Keying in the name Signy Shepherd, he stared at the screen, holding his breath while he waited for the details to emerge. If he were a superstitious man, he would have crossed his fingers.

A few seconds later, he let out the breath with a relieved sigh. Signy Shepherd was in the system. She had been born December 19, 1986, although a quick scan of the birth certificate revealed an unusual detail. Typically, a birth certificate was issued no more than a few months after the birth of the child. Signy Shepherd's had not been issued until twelve years after her birth. He felt the pulse in the hollow of his neck quicken.

He tapped a few more keys and was able to bring up the original application. His heart flipped in his chest like a hooked fish. The spaces where the name of mother and father should have been were blank. Even more promising was the fact that the form was missing much of the other detail that was typically necessary for a complete birth certificate application. Place of birth and hospital name were both missing.

However, it was when he scanned to the bottom of the form and read the explanatory note that he actually stopped breathing. The note had been signed by Marion Entwhistle, a social worker with the Children's Aid Society of Toronto.

Female child, approximately 30 months of age, abandoned, City of Toronto, by persons unknown. Placed into foster care December 19, 1986. Application made before the courts in January 1996 by David and Sarah Shepherd to bestow the name Signy Gabriel Shepherd on said female child. Application granted January 27, 1996. See supporting documentation, attached.

A young child, female with blond hair and blue eyes, abandoned in the city of Toronto in 1986, placed in the foster care system but never formally adopted. A birth certificate issued in the name chosen for her by her foster parents issued in 1996, twelve years after her birth.

Resisting the urge to shout with excitement, he forced himself to sit back and think. The very idea that the little blond driver might be the girl he'd been seeking set his nerve endings abuzz. Fiery bursts of adrenaline blasted through his body and his mind raced.

He needed more information. He would do a search of newspaper articles and Children's Aid Society records from the time period. That should tell him something. He glanced over at the small window in the right corner where he was monitoring the girl's movements. The little red blip was still stationary. He had time.

He tapped a fingernail against his teeth, wondering where to start, then decided that it made the most sense to begin at the beginning. She'd been placed into the foster system December 1986, so he started by googling local newspapers, choosing the one that seemed to have the most sensational coverage.

Hunched over the keyboard, he followed the links into the

news archives. In the search box he tapped in the keywords *1986* and *Signy Shepherd*. A split second later a message appeared stating that no records matched his search criteria.

Focus, he thought, shaking his head. She had been given the name Signy Shepherd by her foster parents years after she'd been found. He erased the name and replaced it with the search criteria *abandoned* and *child*, then tried again.

The screen lit up immediately with an array of articles about a small girl abandoned in December of 1986. He chose the earliest entry, dated December 19, 1986.

BABY DISCOVERED IN DUMPSTER

A female child, estimated to be between two and three years old, was found yesterday afternoon inside a Dumpster in an alley off Yonge Street just south of the Eaton Centre.

Margaret Pierce, 24, a University of Toronto student, made the grim discovery.

Yonge Street? Shuddering, he recalled that it was a picture of that iconic street that had brought on his first panic attack. He bit his lip and continued reading.

"She's only a baby," said Ms. Pierce. "I just can't imagine who could do such a horrible thing." Ms. Pierce went on to say it was a miracle that she had even noticed the tiny blond-haired girl, noting that it had been quite dark in the alley.

"A Christmas miracle," said Ms. Pierce. "I just hope they find her family." Police are not saying at this time if they have discovered the identity of the child or how she came to be in the Dumpster, saying only that their investigation is on-going. In the meantime the baby is said to be in good health and is being cared for by the Children's Aid Society.

The Tracker jabbed at the keys, barely noticing that his hands were shaking. A second article, dated December 20, 1986, and titled "Do You Know the Bin Baby?" was accompanied by a two-inch-square photo of a small girl. His finger hovered over the key for a moment before he clicked on the photo, enlarging it severalfold.

He gasped out loud as the image of a stern-faced waif, maybe two or three years old and wearing a white T-shirt adorned with a bright yellow smiley face, jumped out at him. She had a bright spot of pink on each round cheek and a heart-shaped mouth turned down at the corners. He felt the hair on the back of his neck prickle.

The child had blond hair that was so light as to be almost white, and it curled about her round face in untamed waves. She might have been described as angelic had her features not been twisted into an expression of furious defiance.

He leaned in and examined the photo more closely. The photographer had captured the child with her eyes wide open, but it was the unique nature of those eyes that set his heart pounding inside his chest, hammering against his rib cage with such force that he had to take a few deep breaths to calm the palpitations. Savage eyes that flared both blue and grey.

Placing a hand over his pounding heart, he thought he might finally be glimpsing a light at the end of the tunnel.

He sat back and wiped a thin sheen of sweat from his upper lip, then glanced at the red blip in the upper-right corner of the screen. He cursed out loud. She was on the move.

He snapped the MacBook shut and cranked the engine. From the corner of his eye, he watched the blip stop briefly. Gassing up, he surmised.

He forced himself to ease up on the accelerator. Signy Shepherd was proving to be one of the strongest candidates he had ever encountered, but it would not do to let his excitement cloud his judgment. There was little to be gained in tipping his hand too early. He needed to stay close enough to be there when Volkov's man made his move, but far enough behind that he didn't frighten off his quarry.

It was a dance he knew well. One hand loose on the wheel, he flicked his eyes to the screen. He had been correct about the fill-up; the blip was once again on the move. They'd taken the southern route, exactly as he'd predicted.

About fifteen minutes behind the two women, he reached the fork in the road. Hot on their trail, he steered the black SUV south toward the American border, confident that by the time he was finished with her, Signy Shepherd would have given up all her secrets.

•   •   •

Grace hung up the phone in her office and sat back, her eyes scanning the ceiling. She could hardly process the news she'd just received from Maitland. Had she and Maitland made a terrible error in sending Signy out on her own?

Overhead, a cheery whistle heralded the arrival of the miniature train that had so delighted the Dalton girls. Had it only been two days since the little family had been spirited out east?

Running her hands through her bushy hair, Grace watched the cherry red engine steam into the room, followed by a series of brightly painted cars. Unlike the Dalton girls, Grace did not find her fears calmed by the little train chugging around the perimeter of her office.

Maitland had passed on the news in her typical fashion, terse and to the point. She'd finally been able to track down an old acquaintance at the villa in France where he'd been spending the summer. A former lieutenant general in the Canadian spy agency, CSIS, the man had insider knowledge of Leonid Volkov's life in Russia. Maitland had hoped to find out whether there was any truth to the rumours that Volkov was involved in the Moscow serial murders, but what she had found out was even more troubling.

According to the former operative, Leonid Volkov had served as a sniper in the Soviet Army, with over fifty accredited kills to his name. When he was recruited by the KGB in 1959, he took his specialized skills with him, racking up an impressive number of hits.

What was most disturbing, however, was that there was some indication that Volkov had, over the years, also amassed a fortune as a gun for hire. Known as Leo the Lion in the underworld, it was said that for him the money was secondary, that it was the pleasure of the kill that truly drove his work.

The problem, the CSIS officer had informed Maitland, was that Volkov never left a trace of his presence at the crime scenes, not so much as the tiniest strand of DNA. The Americans, the British, the Israelis, even the Russians would lock him up for life if they could, but to date, there was absolutely nothing to connect him to any crime.

Grace unclipped her phone from the holster at her waist. She needed to warn Signy. She typed in a quick message, then waited for confirmation that it had been sent. Nothing. Just the little clock icon that indicated the message was on hold. Grace glanced at her watch. If Signy was on schedule, she was probably somewhere in the wilds of northern Ontario by now, well out of cellphone service range.

Shoving her chair back, Grace leapt to her feet. She couldn't leave Signy out there, all alone, facing a notorious assassin with nothing more than her wits and a few months of training under her belt. The time had come to send in reinforcements.

As she watched the little train steam into the tunnel and out of the room, its yellow caboose flashing a cheeky farewell, she picked up the phone. She knew of one asset that worked the northern routes. She dialed the number, her knee bobbing up and down as she waited for the line to engage.

Outside in the hallway, she heard a series of high shrieks, a sign the little train was picking up steam, and she jammed the phone against her ear in a futile attempt to drown out the sound of the warning signal.

The fine muscles at the back of her neck quivered as she listened to the line ring on the other end. She held her breath.

• • •

The Tracker hit the accelerator, burning up the last kilometre separating him from his target. The red blip hadn't moved in some time and he was becoming more and more convinced that they'd been beset by car trouble. It couldn't be Volkov's man making his move on Elena; the man had assured him he'd contact him on the radio at least a half hour in advance.

No, they must have a flat tire perhaps or an overheated engine. Theirs wouldn't be the first vehicle he'd seen stranded by the side of the road, steam billowing from under the open hood. It had to be a hundred degrees in the shade.

Just ahead, he saw a sign advertising a scenic overlook about a half kilometre ahead. He nodded his head, certain that his assumption had been correct. No way were they stopping to smell the roses; they must be in some sort of trouble.

He hummed tunelessly as he scanned the row of parked cars for the green Ford Focus, wondering how he might capitalize on their distress. He smiled. It never ceased to amaze him the way the gods of serendipity just couldn't resist lending him a helping hand now and then.

Not catching sight of his target from the road, he pulled into the overlook, allowing the SUV to roll slowly past the row of parked vehicles. The Ford was not there. Out on the grass berm, about a dozen sightseers took in the panoramic view of a picturesque lake. Neither woman was in the group.

His eyes returned to the parked cars. Perhaps he was suffering from some sort of hysterical blindness and the green Ford Focus was sitting right under his nose. He slowed to a crawl, checking out each car twice.

A flash of red in the corner of his eye caught his attention, and he sighed with relief. The blip was once again on the move. Their car must have been tucked somewhere out of sight.

Craning his neck, he looked over at the exit lane, where the Ford should have been waiting to rejoin the traffic heading south. He frowned. There was only one vehicle sitting there, and it wasn't the Ford. It was a Lexus carrying two older men. Definitely not Elena Morozov or Signy Shepherd from Linden Valley.

He stiffened in disbelief. Someone had switched his tracking device to another car. For the past twenty minutes he'd been following the wrong car. It had to have been Volkov's man. He must have made the switch while the girls had stopped for lunch, and there was only one reason he would have done so. He was planning to take out both women.

Tires screaming, he peeled out of the overlook, oblivious to the honking horns and glares as he cut off the southbound traffic and steered the SUV north. If he'd been sent on a wild goose chase to the south, then, he concluded grimly, the girls had almost certainly taken the northern route. He checked the clock on the dashboard, realizing with a horrible start that they had at least a forty-minute head start on him.

With his foot hard on the accelerator, the Tracker grabbed the two-way radio and depressed the send button with his thumb. "You son of a bitch," he shouted into the speaker. His only response was static-filled airwaves. He listened for almost a minute before he thought he could hear a chuckle building in the white noise. Furious, he flicked the off button, then gave the SUV even more gas, his blue eyes fixed on the road ahead.

Chapter

35

"Do you need to stop?" said Signy, glancing around dubiously. They were passing through the town of Ignace, the only community between Dryden, 115 kilometres behind them, and Thunder Bay, almost 250 kilometres ahead. As in most northern towns, the wide main drag was lined with squat, utilitarian buildings built to withstand the extreme storms and subzero temperatures of a Canadian winter.

Bleak at the best of times, the town appeared to be feeling the effects of the downturn in the logging industry. Almost every other storefront was closed up and shuttered, faded Going Out of Business signs tacked to interior windows. The sidewalks were cracked and void of people. Even a nearby park was deserted with the exception of an emaciated hound, lying on its side, panting in the shade of a stunted Jack pine.

"I could use a quick bathroom break," Elena said.

Signy turned into the lone gas station and used the opportunity to fill up. As the gasoline poured into the tank, she turned on her phone, hopeful that a recent government initiative to bring cell service to major northern centres had made it this far.

Shielding her eyes from the relentless sun, she peered down at the tiny screen, gratified to see two service bars appear. Not great, but good enough to send or receive a text message. If there were any messages waiting for her, it would be only a few seconds before they arrived.

She glanced over at the pump and willed it to work faster. She wasn't convinced that dumping the tracking device was going to fool anyone for long. Volkov must have hired a professional, maybe even more than one. She shuddered. He was former military; perhaps he was even following them himself.

When the tank was full, she checked her phone again. No messages. Peering closer, she saw that only one service bar was visible, weak at best. No point attempting a distress call to Grace. She was on her own.

Powering off the phone, she walked inside. She grabbed a couple of chocolate bars, a bag of chips, and four Cokes, then after paying for her purchase in cash, walked back to the car, taking a moment to scrape off the bugs that had splattered her windshield. As she swiped the squeegee back and forth, she considered the implications of the tracking device.

In Vancouver, Volkov had seemed in a hurry to get his hands on Elena, but now he seemed content to watch and wait. She'd told Elena that he was probably waiting for the right place, but in reality, a professional could easily pick up the girl whenever and wherever he pleased. Was Volkov waiting to see where Elena would go and, if so, why? Was he hoping she'd lead him to something, or someone?

Just as she tossed the squeegee back into its container, Elena reappeared, carrying a white plastic bag stuffed with more treats. The girl must believe, as she did, that chocolate is the solution to just about any problem. With the mountain of junk they'd acquired between them, solving the Volkov mystery should be a cakewalk. Signy smiled. If only it were that easy.

A few minutes later, as the safety of the gas bar receded behind them, Signy tore open a Kit Kat bar with her teeth and bit off a large chunk. The sugar seemed to be the boost she'd needed. She turned to Elena. "I have an idea, but you might not like it."

Elena fiddled with an unopened bag of chips in her lap. "Spit it out," she said. "I don't like any of this. One more hit isn't going to kill me."

"Okay, how about this? What if we assume the guy from your apartment is the same guy in the photo with you and your parents?"

"A long shot," said Elena, shrugging, "but okay, what if?"

"He could have been a family friend, a business acquaintance, or maybe even a bodyguard, right?"

"I guess," said Elena.

"Let's discount family friend. He was a lot older than your parents."

Elena nodded.

"So that leaves business partner or bodyguard. What did you say your father did when you lived in Russia?"

"He was a university professor."

"What did he teach?"

"Classic literature."

Signy tapped a finger on the steering wheel. "Which means we can probably discount the obvious."

"Which is?"

"That he was a mole for the United States or a spy for the KGB or spent his spare time smuggling enriched uranium out of the country, that sort of stuff."

Elena rolled her eyes. "The worst thing he could have done was bore you to death with a reading of *The Iliad* in the original Greek."

Signy grinned. "Which leaves bodyguard."

Elena nodded. "Could be, I guess."

"So, what if years later the dead guy in your apartment also emigrates to Canada and is hired by Volkov as protection. Then when you walk into Volkov's bar, the guy recognizes you."

"After almost twenty years? I doubt that."

Signy shook her head. "I don't know. You're a lot taller," she said, shooting Elena a wide grin, "but from what I saw of those cute baby pictures, you haven't changed that much."

Elena rolled her eyes. "Okay, but if he used to work for my parents, and he knew I was their daughter, then why would he try to abduct me?"

"My guess is that he has a new boss now, and I have a feeling that what Leonid Volkov wants, he gets."

Elena flicked her eyebrows skyward in agreement.

"Still, I agree there has to be some connection between

Volkov, your parents, and this guy." Signy looked over. "And here comes the hard part."

Elena sighed, then crooked her fingers in a "bring it on" gesture.

"Correct me if I'm wrong, but I don't think university professors were all that well paid in those days. And your mother was a housewife. Where did they get the money to pay for a bodyguard?"

Elena frowned.

"What if your father had found a way to supplement his income? You said yourself that Russia was like the Wild West after the fall of the Soviet Union. Everyone was in on some scam or another."

"Not my dad—"

Signy raised a hand. "Hear me out. The Line has found out that Volkov was a person of interest in a series of sexual assaults in the Moscow area going back decades. On top of that, there's a decent chance he's running a money-laundering scheme here in Canada. He was probably mixed up in a lot more, a real mob-type guy."

"Which has nothing to do with my dad," said Elena, a hint of outrage creeping into her tone.

"Right," said Signy, "but what if your father got mixed up with Volkov somehow? Maybe even on the periphery. Maybe he did something for Volkov to make a few extra bucks. Or maybe it was accidental. What if he found something out about the murders? What if he had something that could prove Volkov guilty?"

Elena snorted. "That is a lot of speculation."

"True, but—"

"And you're forgetting one thing."

"Which is?"

"I lived with my parents for seventeen years. Nobody knew them better than I did. There is not a chance in hell that my dad or my mom would ever get mixed up in anything illegal, not even by accident. It was the antithesis of everything they believed in."

They drove in silence for several minutes before Signy let her breath out with a sigh. "Maybe there is nothing more to the situation than an old man's crush."

Elena's mouth turned down in an expression of disgust.

"But I can't really believe that," Signy continued. "Two men dead? The tracking device? It just all seems too much."

"You're probably right," Elena agreed.

"Which brings us back to the fact that there has to be something connecting your parents to that man."

"Maybe," said Elena, "but underworld crime isn't it." Elena folded her arms over her chest and stared straight ahead.

"Hand me that bag of chips, will ya?" said Signy. "I need to concentrate."

Elena popped open the bag and stuffed a handful of chips into her mouth before handing the bag over. The two women chewed furiously, but neither could think of a reasonable alternative.

Chapter

36

"Look," Elena said, stabbing her index finger at the windshield.

Following Elena's excited pointing, Signy noticed movement on the side of the highway, about a hundred metres ahead. She slowed as a large black bear with a head the size of a snow shovel lumbered onto the road followed by two gambolling cubs. The sow swung her bulky head around and glared at them with sharp eyes.

"Oh my God," Elena said in a hushed tone, "they're so cute."

"Adorable," said Signy dryly, "as long as they don't come any closer."

"I hate to think of them wandering on the road like this," said Elena.

Signy nodded. "Apparently they get run over all the time."

Elena shook her head. "I'll bet the trains get them too," she said, glancing over at the set of train tracks that paralleled the highway. The tracks were visible now and then when the trees thinned around lakes and rocky outcroppings. On a couple of occasions they'd heard the roar of the mile-long freight trains that travelled the northern route.

Despite the danger, however, the threesome appeared in no great hurry to cross the highway, so Signy flicked on the four-way flashers and the two women sat enthralled as the cubs engaged in mock battle, rolling and tumbling with joyous abandon.

"Did you have brothers or sisters?" Elena asked.

"Too many," said Signy, rolling her eyes.

"I wish I'd had a sister," said Elena. She smiled shyly at Signy. "It's kind of nice having someone to talk to."

Signy snorted. "Be careful what you wish for. Siblings can be a real pain."

Returning their attention to the bear family, they watched the mother follow her playful cubs at a more sedate pace. It was almost a minute before they disappeared into the pines.

Signy glanced in the rear-view mirror. "Oops," she said, flicking off the four-ways and hitting the gas. During their brief sojourn, a vehicle had appeared behind them and was closing in.

Signy watched the speedometer, not easing off the accelerator until she hit 120 kilometres per hour.

Glancing over her shoulder, Elena let out a low whistle. "Whoa, he's coming fast."

Flicking her eyes to the mirror, Signy nodded. "Do you think it's a cop?"

Elena twisted in her seat and took a longer look at the sleek black car tearing up the distance between them. "No lights on the roof, but it could be an unmarked car. It's going fast enough. Maybe there's been an accident ahead?"

"Maybe," said Signy, easing off the gas. "I'll let him get by."

It took only seconds before the black Crown Victoria had roared up behind them, crowding their rear bumper. Signy eased the Focus toward the right shoulder, allowing the larger car plenty of room to pass. But instead of zooming past, the Crown Vic hovered behind them, the dark tint on its windshield making it impossible to see the driver.

"What's he doing?" Elena asked, her voice rising.

Signy glanced down at the speedometer. She was under the speed limit and dropping fast. "I don't know. Reach in the back and hand me that plastic bag, will you?"

Elena opened her mouth, then apparently thought the better of it, reached in back, and snagged the bag full of supplies Signy had purchased at the camping store. She heaved it into the front seat.

Flicking her eyes between the rear-view mirror and the road ahead, Signy grabbed the bag and jammed it down into the space between the driver and passenger seats.

Twisting round to stare at the huge car, inches from their rear bumper, Elena said, "Why doesn't he just go?"

"I don't think he has any intention of passing," Signy said, grimly.

"What should we do?" Elena asked. She was facing straight ahead, holding her hands up to the sides of her head like a set of blinkers, as though by blocking the sight of the ominous Crown Vic, she might make it magically disappear.

"We wait," said Signy, through her teeth.

As it turned out, they did not have to wait long. Less than a minute later, Signy watched in the rear-view mirror as the driver's side window on the Crown Vic slid down and a hand appeared, fixing a portable emergency light onto the roof of the black vehicle. Almost immediately the light began flashing the distinctive blue and red of a police vehicle.

"Shit," said Signy.

"Here he comes," said Elena, her voice a high squeak.

Watching the mirror, Signy had seen the same thing. The Crown Vic had pulled into the oncoming lane and was surging up beside them. Her hands tight on the wheel, Signy glanced over as he pulled alongside. She watched him raise his left hand and gesture at her to follow him. He must have hit the gas because suddenly he was in front of her, his right turn signal flashing.

"He wants us to pull over," said Elena.

"Listen," said Signy, as she turned on her signal and squeezed the brake, tailing the cruiser on to the narrow shoulder. "When I say go, I want you to open your door and roll out onto the ground. Stay flat until I tell you to get up."

"What?" Elena said, twisting in her seat to stare at Signy.

"Look," said Signy, indicating the Crown Vic with a tilt of her chin.

Elena flicked her eyes at the black car, then back to Signy. "What?"

"A real unmarked police car has the flashing lights in the grille, not some portable job that looks like something out of a Hollywood movie. And where's the antennae? There's usually a whole array of antennae on the roof of a cop car. And the wheels are all wrong. We should be able to see right through to the hub. That car has silver hubcaps."

Elena peered through the windshield at the back of the Crown Vic. It had turned off the highway onto a single-lane pullout that dipped briefly into the dense woods before winding its way back out to the highway about two hundred metres further along. "What are you doing? Don't go in there. It has to be a trap."

"I'm sure it is," said Signy, rolling in behind the Crown Vic. "But there's no way we can outrun him and there's nowhere to hide."

"Oh, God," said Elena, her voice hitching, as though she could not get enough air to form words.

"Just do as I say," said Signy, in a tone that brooked no further argument, and was gratified to see the girl wrap her right hand around the door handle.

Signy pulled to a halt behind the cop car and glanced around. It was the perfect site for an ambush. They were hemmed in by the Crown Vic in front and on both sides by an impenetrable barrier of gnarled spruce and pine trees.

"Oh God, oh God, oh God." Elena was mumbling the two words over and over like a mantra, her eyes squeezed shut.

Signy felt time slow as she watched the driver's door swing open. She watched a foot emerge, clad in a black leather sandal and wearing a white sock, and for one brief insane moment, she had an urge to laugh.

"Hail Mary, full of grace," whispered Elena. "The Lord is with thee—"

Not taking her eyes off the man, Signy probed with her left

hand until she found the power button that controlled the driver's window. As it slid down, she could hear the musical trickle of water from a nearby stream. High in the canopy, a raven chuckled.

"Blessed art thou, amongst women, and blessed is the fruit of thy womb, Jesus."

The man stood slowly, slapping road dust from the front of his navy windbreaker. The heat was intense and Signy knew the only reason the man could be wearing a jacket was to conceal a weapon, and when he bent sideways to slam the door, Signy saw the bulge of a handgun at his waist.

"Holy Mary, mother of God—"

As she watched the tall man turn toward them, Signy jammed her right hand into the plastic bag. The man held up his hand and began strolling toward their car, his face a smiling mask of innocence. She flinched at the ominous crunch of his heavy step on the loose gravel. Her right index finger brushed cold metal.

"Pray for us sinners—"

"Ready—" Signy whispered. She flicked the safety mechanism off the canister of bear spray she'd purchased at the camping and hunting supply store in Calgary, her right thumb poised over the trigger.

The man opened his mouth as if to call out a friendly greeting, but Signy could see his eyes, hard and blank, and watched the fingers on his right hand twitch down toward his waist.

"Now and at the hour of our death."

"Go!" Signy shouted. Elena did as instructed, shoving open her door with a wild cry, then flinging herself down onto the rocky gravel in a tumble of arms and legs.

Not taking her eyes from the stranger, Signy watched him turn briefly toward Elena, and in that tiny moment of distraction, she took her one and only chance. Slamming her door open, she rolled out of the car in a protective tuck, her thumb hovering over the trigger. Using the driver's door as cover, she raised the canister up to the open window. "Eat shit," she shouted, slamming her thumb down on the trigger.

She heard the man scream as the full force of the bear spray nailed him dead-on. She didn't let up even as she was rocked by an explosion of gunfire. She kept the canister steady in the open window as a barrage of bullets whizzed through the air around her head. She heard the rattle of the trees as the bullets sliced through the dense woods. She was relieved. He was firing high.

It was only after she heard nothing but choked moaning that she risked peeking out from behind the driver's door. The man lay curled in the fetal position, his face and body soaked with the toxic capsaicin mixture she'd used on Daryl Dalton, only at almost twice the concentration. He had his hands covering his eyes and was gasping for breath. At his side lay a Glock pistol, coated in the Day-Glo orange of the bear spray but menacing nonetheless.

Signy continued to fire the noxious spray as she ran directly into the cloud of orange gas that hung in the air. Squeezing her eyes shut, she kicked out blindly, gratified when she felt the toe of her right sandal connect with hard metal. She heard the gun skitter across the gravel, then into the thick undergrowth. The can sputtered to a halt.

Backing toward the car, she watched the man writhing in the centre of the cloud. She briefly contemplated disabling his car or stealing his keys but discounted this. She had no idea how long he would be immobilized.

She turned and flew back to the car, shouting at Elena to get in. Within seconds, Signy had backed the Ford out of the turnoff and the two women were screaming back on to the highway. "Hold on," said Signy, her eyes watering, the skin on her face and hands burning.

Elena twisted open a bottle of water and shoved it into Signy's hand.

Pouring the contents of the bottle over her face, Signy put the pedal to the metal, the little Ford's engine screeching in protest.

Chapter

37

Signy rolled down all the windows, the searing wind that whipped through the car clearing some of the toxic pepper spray from her hair and clothes. The bottle of water had helped but not nearly enough.

Squinting through streaming eyes, she searched the terrain ahead and found what she was looking for less than a minute later. Elena rocked inside her seat belt as Signy slammed on the brakes, fishtailing the car down a narrow gravel strip that led to a small pond.

Screeching to a halt, Signy had barely slammed the car into park before she wrenched the door open and staggered down a sandy embankment to the edge of the water. Not bothering to remove her shoes or clothes, she plunged into the shallow water, falling onto her knees and dunking her head underneath the surface.

She thrashed back and forth, frantically scrubbing at her burning skin. When she eventually came up for air, she was grateful to see Elena standing at the water's edge, a dry set of clothes in her arms.

She ran back up the embankment, water sluicing in sheets from her arms and legs. In seconds she had peeled off her soaked clothes, wadded them into a ball, and tossed them into the trees. She stepped into a dry sundress without removing her wet sandals, then, with a wave of her hand, raced Elena back to the car.

"Better?" asked Elena, a few minutes later when they were once again flying east on the Trans-Canada Highway.

Squeezing water that smelled of algae out of her hair with one hand, Signy asked, "Can you get my cellphone?" When Elena had the phone in her hand, Signy gave her Grace's number.

Elena powered up the phone and peered at the screen. "Still no service."

"Damn," said Signy, taking in the miles of unbroken forest that stretched out ahead of them. She briefly contemplated turning up one of the narrow forest roads that led off the highway and into the woods but quickly thought the better of it. If she was lucky enough to spot one, and if she was able to negotiate the dirt road without getting lost or stuck or creamed by a logging truck, there was no guarantee that her car didn't have a second tracking device hidden somewhere in the undercarriage. If that were the case, she and Elena would be little more than sitting ducks.

She touched the accelerator. Her fingers twitched on the wheel.

Oh dear, what can the matter be? Johnny's so long at the fair.

The car hit a section of broken pavement head-on, flew up into the air, and landed hard, bottoming out onto the hard top with a sickening crunch.

Elena braced her hands on the dashboard, her knuckles white.

Signy's eyes flashed to the rear-view mirror. The road behind was as empty as the black ribbon stretching out in front of them. She loathed running. She wished she'd killed him. She could have killed him. She should have killed him. Fire burned in her chest at the thought. She should have rammed her foot into his throat as he lay gasping on the ground.

She could almost hear the crunch of his hyoid bone and the hiss of his last breath. She would have loved to see the mini-explosions as the tiny blood vessels burst in his eyes, and the sight of a swollen, black tongue protruding from his mouth as he gasped for air. Hunched over the wheel, she bared her teeth, the tang of urine spilling onto the dirt as his bladder gave way as real as if he had just died in the seat beside her.

Oh dear, what can the matter be?

"He was going to kill us, wasn't he?" said Elena.
Signy blinked her eyes.

Johnny's so long at the fair.

The path ahead swam back into focus.

"What now?" Elena asked.

"We drive like hell," said Signy, the words thick in her throat, "and hope that we make it to Thunder Bay before he gets his shit together."

"Do you think he can?"

"What?" said Signy, still trying to blink away the feel of the man's stretched ligaments under her foot.

"Get his shit together?"

Signy nodded. "I could hear water flowing somewhere nearby. If the bear spray didn't blind him, and if he was able to get cleaned off, he'll be coming. It's only a matter of time."

"Oh, God," said Elena, twisting around to look over her shoulder. "Do you think he'll catch up to us?"

Signy answered by rocketing over another bump in the road, her foot nowhere near the brake.

They drove that way for another twenty minutes, the sun sinking lower into the western sky, until Signy finally had to crank the rear-view mirror down an inch to stop the reflected sunlight from blinding her.

"These damn trees go on forever." Elena's fingers twined around the door handle as though she might jump out at any moment.

"And we have another hour, at least, before we start to see civilization again," Signy said.

"We're not going to make it, are we?" said Elena.

Signy frowned. "That kind of talk is not helping."

Her hand still hovering over the door handle, Elena gulped back a terrified sob.

Signy glanced at Elena. For the most part, the girl had proved to have a level head on her shoulders. It was amazing how quickly two people got to know each other when they were trapped in a car together for days on end. Still, Signy had never been the type to share her personal business with anyone, let alone relative strangers. She tapped her fingers on the wheel. On the other hand, she thought, strange times make for strange bedfellows and a brief diversion might be just what the doctor ordered.

"How about we talk about something else?" said Signy.

"Like what?"

"Well, I've got myself into a bit of a situation," said Signy, "and I'm not sure what to do about it. But if I tell you about it, you have to promise not to say anything once we get to Linden Valley."

Signy's titillating request appeared to have the desired effect. "I'm all ears," Elena said with a tentative smile, before drawing herself upright.

Signy nodded, then for the next several minutes, she told Elena all about Constable Richard Dalton, the scene in the gazebo, and his threats against Zef. When she finally wound down, she glanced over. The girl was staring at her, open-mouthed.

"Seriously?" asked Elena, shaking her head. "I mean, how crazy is your life?"

Signy flashed a brief smile. "Never a dull moment, I guess."

Elena opened her mouth and started to form a word, then seemed to think the better of it. She shut her mouth and shook her head. After a moment she said, "So, that's what happened to your cheek?"

Signy touched a finger to the scrape on her cheek, then nodded. "My crazy life aside, what do you think, any ideas?"

Elena grinned. "Zef sounds pretty cool. How long have you been seeing him?"

Signy rolled her eyes. "I think you're missing the point."

Elena shook her head, the corners of her eyes crinkling. "Nope, I think I get it."

Signy reached up and twisted the mirror up, squinting as a flash of reflected sunlight sliced across her eyes. The road behind remained deserted. She snapped the mirror back down. "The cops can only keep him for twenty-four hours without charging him, although that could be stretched to ninety-six hours with special consideration from a judge."

"So his twenty-four hours are almost up?"

Signy nodded again. "I sent Dalton a text and told him when I'd be back in town, but unless he has a judge in his back pocket, I don't know how long he'll be able to hold off on laying a charge."

"Either that, or he lets your friend go," said Elena.

"Not a chance," Signy said, drumming her fingers on the steering wheel.

Elena puffed out her cheeks and nodded. "I doubt this is about getting his family back as much as it is about showing you who's top dog in town. It must have been risky planting that meth on your boyfriend."

Signy rolled her eyes. "And you are like a dog with a bone," she said, clucking her tongue. "Zef is not my boyfriend."

Elena laughed and for the next few minutes they talked about men, commiserating over Elena's lack of experience and playing a game of thrust and parry around the subject of Zef. Signy told Elena about Constable Ben Tran and his invitation to dinner but dismissed Elena's insistence that she give the cute young cop a chance. "When it comes down to it," said Signy, finally, "even if Ben Tran really wants to ask me out, I'd say no. I have enough excitement in my life."

"If he really wants to go out with you?" said Elena, shaking her head. "Are you kidding? It sounds like he was very interested."

"Like I said, he was probably just—"

Elena waved her hand dismissively. "Oh, please. Don't give me that good cop, bad cop thing. The guy obviously liked you. You should give him a call." She twisted in her seat and smiled at Signy. "What's life without a few risks, right?"

Signy smiled.

"Besides," Elena continued, "isn't it better to be in the driver's seat?"

Signy paused, then glanced over at Elena, her eyebrows raised. "You're right," she said.

Elena nodded. "I told you so."

"Not about Ben," said Signy dismissively.

Elena's eyebrows gathered together under her new bangs and she glanced at Signy in confusion.

Signy's eyes twinkled. "It is better to be in the driver's seat." She glanced in the rear-view mirror. "You just gave me an idea."

Elena listened intently as Signy hashed out a potential solution to her Dalton problem. For the next several minutes, the two women weighed the pros and cons, deliberated on the logistics, and debated probabilities, finally hashing out a plan that Elena conceded might work.

"It's risky," said Elena, "and you'll need to solve the problem of the equipment, find someone who has access to that kind of stuff and doesn't ask too many questions."

Signy thought of Officer Ben Tran. Her mouth twisting downward, she shook her head. She wasn't that naive. Regardless of Elena's confidence, Ben Tran's nice-guy routine had almost certainly been a ploy. Cute young cop knocks subject off guard so that bad cop can finish the job. Who was she trying to kid? Guys like Ben Tran weren't interested in girls like her. She was meant for the Zefs of the world.

Signy shook her head. "I'll figure it out."

Elena looked at her. "Thelma wasn't wrong, you know. Sometimes you have to ask for help."

Signy just smiled.

After a while, Elena said, "I wish I could be around to see how it all turns out."

Signy shook her head. "I'd much rather you were back in Vancouver by then." The sun had slipped a fraction closer to the horizon, and Signy twisted the rear-view mirror back into its correct position.

"Do you really think that that will happen?" Elena asked, a hopeful light sparking in her eyes.

Signy didn't answer, her attention fixed on the mirror, the smile dying on her lips.

"What is it?" Elena asked, her voice tight.

"We've got company," Signy said, hunkering down over the wheel and jamming her foot to the floor. The Focus responded, surging ahead until the speedometer inched up over 130 kilometres per hour, a tremendous feat for the little car. Unfortunately, it was not nearly enough to hold off the Crown Victoria barrelling up behind them as though they were hardly moving at all.

Chapter

38

Her knuckles white on the wheel, Signy scanned the road ahead, desperate for an escape route. Her heart sank. If anything, in the gloom of early-evening shadows, the forest felt even closer, crowding the edge of the highway on either side. With the Crown Vic less than a hundred metres behind and gaining fast, she felt like an animal being herded down a chute toward certain death.

She flicked her eyes in the mirror, trying to see around the Crown Vic, hoping to spot another vehicle. With the exception of their pursuer, the road was deserted and they'd seen no oncoming vehicles for some time.

They were alone in a vast wilderness with the Crown Vic almost upon them. The black vehicle filled the mirror, so close that Signy could make out the features of the driver. Hunched over the wheel, he was glaring at her through red, swollen eyes, his mouth hanging open, and she felt a momentary sense of sick satisfaction.

Tearing her eyes from the mirror, she concentrated on the road ahead. She could hear the roar of the engine as it struggled to keep up to her demands for more speed, the tires screaming on the superheated pavement. Insects exploded on her windshield, leaving behind blood-streaked smears, and she tasted sulphur on her tongue, as though in the glacial rock a fissure had opened straight down into hell.

Elena sat crouched in the seat beside her, her hands covering her face, a whispered prayer on her lips.

The speedometer crept toward 140 kilometres per hour, close to the maximum speed of the overtaxed engine, not that it mattered: she had nowhere to run. Fifty metres ahead, on the north side of the road, the Trans-Canada railroad line was visible high atop a scree-covered ridge, and on the south side, a glacial lake, black and deep. Their only way out was straight ahead, and the Crown Vic was now only inches behind.

"Brace yourself," she shouted, a split second before the Crown Vic slammed into their rear bumper. The car rocketed forward and she felt the muscles in her neck brace to keep her head from whipping forward into the windshield. Her arms strained to hold the wheel steady, as the car fishtailed one way, then the other, then back again.

Elena screamed, a drawn-out howl that almost drowned out the shrieking scrape of the detached rear bumper as it dragged along the roadway behind them, scattering sparks high into the air.

Signy checked the rear-view mirror. The Crown Vic was

coming in for another hit and she didn't think the Ford could withstand the impact. Best-case scenario, the car would spin wildly down the highway, tires shedding rubber, until they came to rest in the ditch, with nothing to do but wait for him to appear at the window and blow them away. Worst-case scenario, they'd hit the rock face head-on and be torn into a million pieces.

She had run out of options. She would have to try ditching in the lake. If they were lucky, they could exit the car and swim to the other side before he had a chance to pick them off. She wrenched the wheel to the right. "Hold on," she cried, just before the car flew off the edge of the embankment.

It seemed they were airborne for hours. Signy watched in wonder as a flock of geese skittered across the sparkling surface of the water, their wings flapping wildly. She felt strangely weightless, almost as though she were floating out of her body. She could hear a high-pitched scream emanating from Elena's throat, but it was muted, as if they were already underwater. She could smell algae and iron.

The car hit the water with a tremendous crash and she felt the impact drive up through her spine and into her skull. Her face slammed into the exploding airbag, and for one horrific second, she thought her eyes had popped out of their sockets.

The shriek of twisting metal, the shattering of glass as the windshield imploded, and a metallic death groan assaulted her ears, as water choked the life from the engine.

Signy sat frozen, staring in disbelief as a wall of water flooded through the smashed windshield. For several long moments she struggled to understand what had happened, why she felt so cold and why her legs felt trapped in concrete. It took several more seconds before her head cleared enough to realize that the front end of the car was sinking, the heavy engine dragging the car down under the surface.

She exploded into action, shoving the deflated airbags under the water before grasping for her seat belt clasp. She freed herself, then probed under the roiling surface for Elena's belt, spending precious seconds unhooking the girl's seat belt. The car was nose down, the empty space where the windshield had once been almost completely underwater.

"Go, go, go," she shouted at Elena, just before the water rushed up over her chin and into her mouth. Elena didn't move.

As the water covered her head, Signy opened her eyes, searching in the murky depths for Elena's body. Elena was not moving. She was frozen in place, her eyes squeezed shut.

Signy tucked her feet up under her, bracing them against the driver's seat, then reached over and clutched Elena under her right armpit. She pushed off from the seat, driving her body upward through the empty windshield, hauling Elena's inert body along with her.

Water rushed across her face as she drove upward, and she felt a momentary sense of triumph. She could see the surface, they were going to make it. Then everything stopped. They had jolted to a halt. Eyes wide, Signy searched the churning water, trying to find the obstruction. She happened upon the problem almost immediately. Elena's little bag had floated up from the back seat and had wedged between Elena and the open window.

Signy slammed the case with her fist, driving it through the window. She watched it shoot to the surface, then after one more heave of her legs, the two women followed, flying upward, toward the glare of sunlight overhead.

They broke the surface together, both of them gasping for air and flailing wildly. Elena's plastic case squirted up between them. The moulded edges were tightly sealed, and although the water would seep through eventually, for now it served as a useful flotation device. Elena grabbed hold of it, gratefully.

Treading water, Signy looked down, barely making out a green shimmer from far below. The Ford was spinning in lazy arcs, down and down into the murky depths, and it took only seconds before even that faint outline disappeared and they were alone.

Spitting a mouthful of ferric-tasting water out of her mouth, she spun in a circle, trying to orient herself. Elena was beside her, breathing well, her legs and arms working in tandem to keep her afloat. "Are you okay?" Signy asked.

Elena nodded.

"Can you swim?" Signy said.

Elena responded by pushing the case out in front of her and using it as a flutter board, scissoring her feet out behind her. She had pointed her head back toward the road and began picking up steam.

"Wait," said Signy, grabbing one of Elena's long feet.

Elena paused, twisting her head over her shoulder.

Signy pointed up to the embankment, where a pair of slashes marked the spot where their car had flown off the road and plunged into the ancient glacial lake. The Crown Vic had pulled onto the side of the road and the driver was standing on the embankment, watching the women, eyes flat, while his right hand snaked around behind his back.

Signy kicked out with her legs, twisting her body in a 360-degree circle. The lake was much larger than she'd thought, almost a kilometre long and just as wide. They were floating only twenty metres or so from where the man stood watching them. Even if they turned and started swimming away, she didn't think they'd make it to the other side. And then what?

There was only one solution. Turning to Elena she said, "Swim in that direction." She pointed over Elena's shoulder. The route would take Elena parallel to the road. "I'm going to head straight for him. Keep an eye out. When you see your chance, swim to the shore. Try to make it up on the highway. Someone will have seen the accident by then. There's no way he'll try anything with witnesses around."

"What about you?" Elena asked.

"I'll keep him busy," Signy said.

"No, please."

"I'll be all right," said Signy. She grinned at Elena, her long blond braid floating around her head like a golden water serpent. She swam out in front of Elena and grabbing a hold on the little case pointed it in the direction she wanted Elena to swim. "Go," she said. "When you see your chance, swim like hell." She turned her back and kicked off, leaving Elena in her wake.

She sneered up at the man. He fired back an amused look, then turned his attention to Elena. Signy glanced over, relieved to see the girl, gliding slowly away, paralleling the road. The man looked back at Signy and shook his head, as if admonishing her for her useless effort. In the distance she heard the rumble of an approaching train.

"Fuck you, dickhead," she called, kicking her feet hard

enough that she surged up out of the water. She flipped him the bird.

He laughed and took a step back. He lifted his arm and extended his hand palm up, crooking his fingers in a "come hither" gesture.

She had been hoping to goad him into the water even though she knew that, realistically, the chances of his relinquishing the high ground were zero. So be it. She gave a few quick pumps with her legs and sliced through the water toward him, stopping when she thought she had pushed her luck far enough.

She grinned up at him. He was in the same spot, just in front of his Crown Vic, standing on the edge of the road looking down at her.

"What's the matter, asshole?" she called up to him. "Can't swim?" She splashed the surface with her hands as though nothing more sinister was going on than a dip in the lake on a hot summer's day.

She saw his eyes move and she followed his glance. Elena was hovering in the water, about one hundred metres away but nearer the shore now. The train was getting closer, the air thrumming with the vibration of the wheels on the tracks.

"Hey, moron," Signy shouted, gratified to see him return his attention to her. "Not such a tough guy without your gun, eh?"

The man stared down at Signy, her attempt to goad him into an imprudent action having about as much impact as a feather might have on the rock wall behind him. She wasn't surprised. This was no Daryl Dalton. He glanced over at Elena, then brought his hand out from behind his back. Hanging loosely between his fingers was the Glock.

She turned to Elena. "Go," she shouted. "Swim!" Elena just stared at her stupidly. The train was almost upon them, the din of multiple engines and the screech of the wheels on the track drowning out her words.

Signy turned back to the man. His hand twitched and the barrel of the weapon jittered. She flipped onto her back and kicked wildly with her feet, her arms extended behind her in a powerful back crawl. She felt as though she were trying to swim through thick treacle.

She watched him take a step closer to the embankment, then another.

Signy pumped her arms, her eyes riveted to the man's hand. She could see the barrel of the gun begin to arc upward, and she redoubled her effort. He shouted something derisive, the words, thankfully, drowned out by the din of the train as it rumbled north of the highway.

Arms flailing, she knew there was nothing more she could do but watch her own death.

The man spread his legs in a classic shooter's stance.

The train blasted its horn, the sound deafening across the open water.

The man squinted through his swollen eyes and bared his teeth, his finger tight on the trigger.

Signy blinked, reflexively, waiting for the bite of the bullet as it tore through her flesh. When she opened her eyes a split second later, she gasped in disbelief. The spot where the shooter had stood was empty.

Instead, he was flying straight at her, his eyes wide with shock, a spray of blood arcing out behind him, splashed across the blue sky like a Jackson Pollock painting. An SUV had appeared out of nowhere and slammed into the man from behind, knocking him high into the air.

It seemed to take forever before the shooter splashed down almost in front of her in a heap of broken arms and legs. Backpedaling furiously, she watched the man pop back up. His body completed one lazy roll before it settled face down in the water. A second or two later, the body sank below the black surface, a torrent of bubbles the only evidence that he had ever been there at all.

She treaded water for several more seconds, watching the last few bubbles wink out of existence before remembering Elena. She spun in the water. Elena hadn't moved. She'd dragged herself up onto her waterproof case, her eyes fixed on the spot where the man had gone down, as though he might explode back to the surface at any moment.

"Hey," Signy called, smacking her palm down on the water, trying to draw Elena's attention.

Elena blinked twice, still stunned, but finally turned toward Signy's voice. They stared at each other for several seconds before turning in unison to look up at the SUV that had saved their lives. It had come to a halt on the gravel shoulder, its nose pointed directly at them. Signy could see a nasty dent on the front right corner and the right headlight was smashed. The sound of her own heavy breathing was loud in her ears.

A few seconds later when the driver's door swung open, a young man climbed out. Spotting the two women in the water, he scrambled over to the embankment. Signy kicked backwards and Elena followed suit. He took a moment to look at the spot where the body of the shooter had slipped under the surface, then turned to Signy and shouted something.

She put a hand over one ear and shook her head. She was unable to make out his words over the clack of iron wheels and the sigh of metal, as the eastbound freight train bumped and rolled over the uneven ground high above them.

He waved her in.

Signy glanced over at Elena. Floating on top of her case, the girl was treading water right beside her.

Elena shot Signy a questioning glance.

"I think we don't have much of a choice," said Signy. She turned back to the man. "Who are you?"

Cupping his hands around his mouth, he shouted back at her. "Grace sent me."

Signy felt a moment of pure relief. Grace had talked about the possibility of sending reinforcements. She waved a hand in acknowledgement and within seconds had joined Elena in a mad dash up the embankment.

A few moments later, Signy and Elena watched the road for vehicles while the young man lined up the Crown Vic, then set a heavy rock on the accelerator. When he jumped free, the car shot forward, ramping over the embankment and down into the water with a tremendous splash.

He stood at the top of the embankment, watching the Crown Vic settle below the surface before turning and walking back toward the two women.

Signy watched him approach. He was good-looking, in that boy-next-door kind of way she found uninteresting, obviously fit, with tousled hair that fell over his eyes a little too artfully for her tastes. But when he got close enough, she saw that his eyes were a pleasing shade of blue and she decided he looked familiar. It wouldn't surprise her if they'd crossed paths somewhere on the Line.

Elena shouted a warning. A line of traffic was heading slowly toward them, an oversized load on a flatbed truck at the head of the line, holding up the cluster of vehicles. That was why there had been no traffic to observe the drama that had just unfolded.

The trio jumped into the SUV and were back on the highway before the long line of traffic reached the spot where the two vehicles had plunged off the road and into the lake. It was unlikely anyone would spot either car so far below the inky surface, but Signy didn't want to stick around to find out.

The young man must have felt the same way because before long they were cruising east at least twenty kilometres over the speed limit. Elena was in the passenger seat, Signy sitting in the back, watching him in the rear-view mirror. "Grace sent you?" she asked.

He nodded, his eyes fixed on hers. "There's been a development," he said. His eyes flicked over to Elena and Signy read the message. Not in front of the girl. She nodded.

"How did you find us?" she asked.

"The GPS in your phone."

"But it was turned off," she said.

"Doesn't matter if it's on or off, it's still possible to track the satellite signal."

"Huh," said Signy, then shook her head. "Not that it matters now. My phone is at the bottom of the lake."

"Well," he said, "that's probably a good thing." He flicked his eyes to the rear-view mirror. "Volkov is getting way too close. I'm sure Grace will fill you in when you get to Linden Valley."

"I understand," said Signy, glancing at the back of Elena's head. The girl was unusually quiet.

"My name's Jay, by the way," he said. "Jay Hunter. I'm going to take you as far as Sault Ste. Marie. You were planning on stopping there tonight?"

Signy nodded.

"Good. I'll get you set up with everything you need."

"What then?" asked Elena, turning to look at him.

He offered her a reassuring smile. "You'll head out in the morning and be in Linden Valley by early afternoon."

"You won't be coming with us?" Elena asked.

He shook his head. "I have to get back home. My daughter has a ballet recital I can't miss."

"A ballet recital?" Elena repeated, as though the incongruousness of murder and a ballet recital was just too much to compute.

"Elena?" Signy said. "Are you okay?"

"That man—" she said. "He's dead, isn't he?"

Signy glanced in the mirror. Jay was looking back at her, his face grave. "Elena?" she said. "He was going to kill us."

"I know," she said, turning to look at Jay. "Thank you." She glanced back at Signy. "I just can't believe this is happening." Tears filled her eyes. "I want to go home."

Signy put a hand on Elena's shoulder. "There will be time for all that later. Right now, we have to concentrate on getting out of this in one piece. Can you do that for me?"

Elena stared at her for several seconds before nodding solemnly.

"Signy's right," said Jay. "Try not to focus on it. You're safe now. It's highly unlikely that Volkov could get another man here in time. You'll be at the shelter by tomorrow afternoon, and I'm sure Grace will have good news for you by then."

Signy smiled at him in the rear-view mirror. *Thanks*, she mouthed.

He flashed a brief smile, then returned his attention to the road ahead, his hands loose on the wheel.

Chapter

39

Grace climbed the steps to the veranda a little more heavily than she would have liked. Her evening walk with Chivas, usually a pleasant way to unwind, had been cut short by the lingering heat.

Slipping her key into the lock, she pushed open the door, the blast of chilled air a welcome respite. Even this long after sunset, the evening air was oppressively humid and the smoggy haze that had been hovering over most of Ontario burned her eyes.

Fitting her key onto the hook by the door, Grace felt an odd tingle on the back of her neck, as though a goose had crossed her grave. Why a goose crossing one's grave would be cause for alarm she had never understood, but here in this moment the expression felt right, tailor-made for this strange day.

The world seemed off-kilter. There had been an unusually large number of intakes processed at the shelter today. The heat was getting on everyone's nerves, and men who normally took out their frustrations in the gym or on each other were turning on their partners. Those who commonly used their women and children as punching bags were breaking out the gloves even more often as the unrelenting heat lay waste to any lingering inhibitions.

The dog snuffled around her feet, his nails clicking on the hardwood. The irregular tapping, usually a comforting announcement of the big dog's presence, sounded like rats skittering under the floorboards.

She ran the paper bag with the wrapping paper upstairs to the bedroom, then hurried back down to the living room, switching on lamps as she went, shaking her head at her silliness but glad for the light nonetheless. Flopping onto the couch, she gnawed at her fingernail and decided she would feel better once Signy was back safe and sound. She hadn't heard a word from her northern asset since she'd talked to him earlier. She could only hope he'd found the two women.

"I'm home." Kim burst through the door, her arms laden with greasy brown bags of Chinese takeout.

Grace jumped to her feet and rushed over to rescue one of the bags, its bottom threatening to give out. She placed a hand under the rapidly collapsing bag and scurried into the kitchen. "Good heavens. Are we having company?"

"Nope," replied Kim, dropping the two remaining bags onto the counter with a wet plop. "I couldn't decide, so I got one of everything."

"As long as you didn't forget dessert," said Grace, reaching up into a cupboard and removing two large dinner plates.

"As if," replied Kim, producing a litre of Ben & Jerry's Cherry Garcia with a flourish.

"A woman after my own heart," said Grace, giving Kim a peck on the cheek before relieving her of the tub of ice cream. She gave it an experimental squeeze with one hand. "Oops. Better get this in the freezer."

"How was your day?" asked Kim, her arm disappearing into one of the sacks. She fished out a tinfoil container, its cardboard lid slightly askew, fluorescent yellow sauce seeping from the edges.

"Brutal," Grace replied, as she tossed forks and knives onto the wooden harvest table. "The freaks are getting freakier, I swear."

"Same here, we were swamped. I think people have reached the boiling point, literally. It was punch first, talk later in the ER today." She flattened the empty bags and tossed them into the recycling bin. "We had the cops out at least five times today just to respond to fights that broke out in the waiting room."

Grace popped the cork from a crisp Chardonnay she had chilling in the fridge. Pouring two glasses, she set them on the table before taking a seat and picking up her fork. Spearing a plump chicken ball, then dipping it liberally into a shockingly red sweet-and-sour sauce, she pointed the dripping mess at Kim. "I hope you're being careful."

"Hey, point that thing somewhere else. It looks a little too much like work."

Grace laughed and popped the entire chicken ball in her mouth.

Kim rolled her eyes, then said, "On a more cheerful note, I'm off as of Tuesday for two whole days." She speared a chunk of green pepper. "You want to go to Toronto? Maybe take in a ball game or something?"

Grace, her mouth now full of noodles mumbled, "Love to. I'm more than ready for a break, but—" She pushed a chicken ball around her plate with her fork.

"But what?" said Kim, narrowing her eyes. "Wait, let me guess. Signy Shepherd isn't back yet?"

Grace nodded.

"When do you expect her?"

"Tomorrow afternoon."

"That works. The Jays are at home this week. I'm pretty sure there's a game Tuesday night. We could catch that."

"It's a date," said Grace.

Kim eyed her suspiciously. "Promise?"

Grace sketched an X shape over her heart with a finger. "Cross my heart and hope to die."

Kim stared at her for a moment, then stood, walked around the table, and squatted down beside Grace. "Don't even joke about stuff like that." She ran her palm over the keloid tissue that bisected Grace's quadriceps muscle. "I couldn't stand it if anything happened to you. Not again."

Although she wanted nothing more than to wrench Kim's hand away from the raised flesh, Grace willed herself to remain still.

"I'm serious."

"I heard you," said Grace, finally pulling away, "loud and clear."

Kim made a harrumphing noise in her throat. "If it would make you feel better, why not get her a police escort or whatever?"

Grace nodded, started to tell Kim about the northern asset, then changed her mind. Despite her need for a comforting shoulder, Maitland's World War II axiom still held. Loose lips sink ships. "I think she'll be okay," she said, eventually.

"Signy?" said Kim. "I have no doubt she'll pull in here, spitting vinegar, like always."

Grace laughed, then stabbed another chicken ball. "So tell me. How's your diminutive chief resident? Any new victims on the horizon?"

"Paul?" Kim narrowed her eyes briefly, then apparently decided to let Grace's inept subject change go unchallenged. She fell into a story about the latest sweet young thing to succumb to Dr. Paul Stafford's dubious charms, and before long they were enjoying a titillating gossip session.

When the meal was over and the dishes cleared away, Kim retrieved the carton of Cherry Garcia from the freezer and filled two large bowls to the brim. She walked back to the table and held out one of the bowls.

Grace stood, grabbed a bowl in each hand, then led the way up the stairs to the bedroom. "How about we take dessert upstairs?" she said, a wicked smile playing around her lips.

Kim laughed, swatting at Grace's bum as she bobbed up the stairs.

Her back to Kim, Grace let the smile die on her face. She was more worried about Signy than she would ever let on. The Line seemed to get riskier with every new case, and she was beginning to feel inadequate. She'd been working nonstop, following every lead Maitland had given her, but was still no closer to finding the connection between Elena and Volkov.

Jumpy and out of sorts, she pushed aside the thought that dogged her more often than she cared to admit. It was only a matter of time before her work on the Line caught up with her, and she could only hope that she didn't take Kim down with her.

Chapter

40

Signy awoke with a start. She was sitting in the back seat of Jay's SUV, her head wedged at an uncomfortable angle against the window. Her arm was half asleep, a fact she discovered in a painful way when she raised her hand to brush her hair from her face.

She'd been dreaming again about the man with the raisin eyes, echoes of the monster's mirthless laughter causing her heart to race even as she sat up, scraping the sleep from her eyes.

She looked out the window. They were idling outside the office of a chain motel and she could see Jay inside talking to the clerk. The parking lot was almost full but the windows were mostly dark. Beyond, a traffic light turned green, although there were few cars moving on the streets.

In the front seat she could hear Elena snoring lightly. "Hey," she said softly, tapping the girl on the shoulder.

Elena shrieked, shouted something guttural in Russian, and shot straight up in her seat, the seat belt catching her before she smashed her head on the roof of the car.

"Elena," Signy said, patting her on the shoulder, "wake up. We're here."

"What?" Elena looked around wildly, her eyes finally settling on Signy. "Where?"

"We're in Sault Ste. Marie. Jay's getting us a room."

Eyes wide, Elena stared at Signy a few more seconds before relaxing visibly. "What time is it?"

Signy shrugged, "Close to midnight, I think."

Elena yawned and rubbed her eyes.

The driver's door opened and Jay jumped in. He grinned at Elena. "Hello, again."

She touched her hair and smiled, shyly.

He looked over his shoulder at Signy. "Sorry about this, but they only had one room left. You guys okay with sharing?"

Neither Signy nor Elena complained, so he restarted the SUV and drove around the lot until he found an empty spot. After retrieving the luggage, the trio hurried across the lot, Jay and Signy flanking Elena in the unlikely case that a sharp-eyed insomniac happened to notice the distinctive-looking girl and ponder her resemblance to a wanted fugitive.

Once inside, Elena opened her small suitcase, hoping to salvage at least some of the contents.

"Damn," she said. Her psychology textbook was sitting in almost four inches of water that had seeped into the tight-fitting case during its dunking in the lake. The cover was pulpy, the pages warped. The photo album was soggy, as were her clothes. Thankfully, the bottle of shampoo appeared unscathed.

"Never mind," said Signy, holding up a Walmart bag. "All my stuff is at the bottom of that lake, so I picked us up a few things in Thunder Bay."

"God, I slept through that?"

"You've been out for hours."

Elena accepted an armful of new clothes and smiled gratefully. "Think I'll have a shower. I smell like fish." She walked over to the small bathroom and shut the door.

Signy waited until she heard the water running before she turned to face Jay. "Should we update Grace?"

He looked at his watch and shook his head. "It's almost one in the morning. Besides, I did tell her that we'd fly under the radar unless things really went south."

Signy nodded. "What was it you were going to tell me back at the lake? Have they discovered something new?"

"Nothing concrete, unfortunately, but everything Grace has found so far points to the fact that in addition to his legitimate businesses, Volkov almost certainly has underworld ties."

Signy sniffed. "Why am I not surprised?"

Jay flicked his eyebrows in agreement.

"Take a look at this," said Signy, pointing at the mysterious photo album. "Elena's mother kept this hidden for years and it only came into her possession after her mother's death. It looks like nothing more than some innocuous family pictures, but in one of them, her parents are standing with a man Elena thinks might be the one who tried to abduct her from her apartment."

"Can I see?"

Signy reached into the case and tried to pick up the album. "Damn," she said. The waterlogged cardboard cover slipped from her fingers. She scooped her hands under the pulpy mess and lifted it onto the bed. The black tape that had lined the edges of the cover had peeled off and lay like a curled snake underneath the wet pages.

Signy bent her head lower, peering closely at the damp mess.

Jay looked over her shoulder. "What?"

"Here," she nudged a finger into the decaying cardboard, releasing a puff of toxic-smelling fumes.

Holding a hand over his nose, Jay leaned in closer.

"I think there were two layers of cardboard making up the front cover, and there's something hidden between them." She extracted a slim packet, about the size of a manila envelope, from between the disintegrating layers. It was covered in opaque plastic, faded Cyrillic lettering scrawled across the surface.

Jay was staring down at the package, his eyes speculative.

"What do you think it means?" Signy asked.

"Check the back cover," he said in answer.

Signy flipped the album over, being careful not to rip the pages. Plastered between the soaked layers of the back cover was an identical packet. She held it up between her thumb and forefinger.

"Well," said Jay.

Signy nodded. "It looks like Elena's mother had a secret."

"What secret?" said Elena. She was standing behind them, dressed in shorts and a T-shirt, a towel wrapped around her wet hair.

Signy handed her the two wrapped packages. "These were hidden inside your mother's photo album. There's writing on one of them. Is it Russian?"

Frowning, Elena plopped down on the bed beside Signy, then ran a finger over the Cyrillic lettering. "This isn't my mother's handwriting."

"What does it say?" asked Jay, a little too eagerly.

She read and reread the words, a puzzled expression on her face, before saying them out loud. "Insurance policy."

"Insurance policy?" Signy echoed. "What the heck does that mean?"

Elena frowned.

"Whatever it is, the person who wrote it sure wanted it kept secret," Jay said. He glanced over at Elena. The girl was staring down at the two packages, lost in thought.

"Maybe you should open them," said Signy.

Elena flashed a sickly grin. "I'm not sure I want to know." Nevertheless, she picked up one of the slim packages and peeled back the seal. Tipping it upside down, she tapped gently on the bottom. Three photographs, loosely folded inside squares of waxed paper, fluttered to the bed.

Elena reached down and, slipping the waxed paper off the first picture, held it up to the light. It was a Polaroid shot of a smiling man and woman in their mid-twenties, the woman holding a rosy-cheeked baby in her arms, the infant's round head crowned with a strawberry fuzz of fine curls.

"Is that you?" asked Jay.

Elena smiled and ran a gentle finger over the frozen faces. "And this is my mother and father."

"There's some writing on the back," said Signy.

Elena flipped the photo over and translated the Cyrillic letters. "'Lilia, Piotr, and baby Anya—age eight months.'" A deep crease formed between Elena's eyes as she puzzled over the strange names.

"It does look like you," said Jay, peering over her shoulder. "Did you have a sister named Anya?"

Elena shook her head, then glanced back down at the photo. "That's me, for sure." She looked up at Signy.

"Open the next one," said Signy.

Elena slipped off the waxed wrapping, stared at the photo for a moment, then looked up at Signy, her face awash in puzzlement. "It's that same man again, the one from my apartment. I'm sure of it now." She held it up.

In the photo, Elena was running down the side of a gentle hillside, pudgy legs barely holding her upright, her signature red curls flying out behind her. At the bottom of the knoll, the same short, stocky man that Signy had seen standing beside Elena's parents waited with open arms, a happy grin splitting his wide, Slavic face.

"More writing," said Jay, pointing to the handwritten label on the back.

Elena flipped it over. "'Pavel Ivanovitch and Anya, Black Sea, 1992.' What does it mean?" she asked, her breath coming in short, choppy bursts.

Signy stared at her, baffled.

"Try this one," said Jay. He slipped the wrapping off, then handed it to Elena.

Before she even looked at it, Elena translated the inscription on the back. "'Anya with Grandpa Leo and Grandma Olga, Black Sea, 1992.'"

"Leo?" said Signy, with a catch in her throat.

Elena slowly turned the picture over and set it on the bed with the solemnity of a tarot card reader uncovering the death card. The photo showed a beaming man holding a toothless Elena to his chest, a dour woman, her eyes rimmed with dark circles, standing stiffly beside them.

"Leonid Volkov," gasped Elena. She looked up at Signy. "Grandpa Leo?"

"Holy shit," said Signy.

"Well," said Jay, under his breath, "that explains a lot."

• • •

They sat in stunned silence for several minutes. Finally Signy handed Elena the letter. "The answer has to be in here," she said.

Elena reluctantly accepted the envelope, then tipped it upside down. Two thick sheets of linen stationery spilled onto her lap. The words were written in English, the handwriting tiny but elegant. Taking a deep breath, Elena began to read the note out loud.

My dearest Elena,

What a very special young woman you have become. Your Papa and I are so proud of you. It pains me to know that if you are reading this, then Papa and I are no longer with you. I am so sorry, my dear, sweet girl.

Elena looked up, the pages dangling from her fingertips, her eyes bright with tears. "I can't believe this."

"Do you want me to read it?" Signy asked, her heart breaking for the poor kid.

Elena shook her head. "I'm okay. It's just—"

Signy nodded, encouragingly. "I know."

Taking a deep breath, Elena continued.

I had hoped never to burden you with this terrible secret, but if you are to stay safe, you must know the truth. Elena Morozov was not your birth name.

The words choked Elena's throat. She half stood, her eyes darting between Signy and Jay.

Signy held out her hand. "Let me," she said.

Elena looked down at the pages in her hand, then thrust them at Signy as though they might burst into flames.

Signy nodded, then ran her finger down the page. "Elena Morozov was not your birth name," she repeated.

Your true name is Anya, and you are the only grandchild of Leonid and Olga Volkov, my father and mother.

"Grandpa Leo," whispered Elena. "Unbelievable."

Three weeks after your grandmother was killed, I received a sealed package in the mail. Taped to the outside was a letter from a legal firm in Moscow informing me that my mother had asked that this package be sent to me in the event of her death. Appar-

ently, she had been frightened for some time that my father might arrange an unfortunate "accident." Inside, I found a letter and several photographs.

This is going to be difficult to hear, but in the letter your grandmother told me that our lovely apartment in Moscow, the dacha on the Black Sea, and everything else we owned had been purchased with money my father had earned as a murderer for hire. The photographs provide graphic evidence of that horrible fact.

Elena brought a hand to her throat.

"My God," said Signy.

"Murderer for hire?" Elena exclaimed. "Is she saying he's a hit man?" Her voice had taken on a slightly hysterical note.

Jay nodded once.

"I guess that explains why your family had bodyguards everywhere they went," said Signy dryly, "and how they could afford them."

"Volkov is a hit man," Elena repeated, incredulous. "That's why he's after me? He's crazy. I didn't even know I had this stuff."

Signy looked at her. "I doubt Volkov thought you knew about the photos. He must have recognized you when you walked into that bar. But you didn't recognize him, did you?"

"He was just an old man that looked like Santa Claus," Elena said. "I'd never seen him before."

"He probably did a background check on you," Signy continued. "He would have tracked down photos of your parents, driver's licences or health cards or whatever. That would have been the confirmation he needed."

"So, when he found out his daughter had died suddenly,"

interjected Jay, "he was betting that your mother had not yet told you about the pictures, that you would have been too young."

"Exactly," said Signy. "He thought that if he could befriend you, then he could find the pictures without your ever being the wiser."

"That's why he talked so much about life in Moscow and holidays on the Black Sea," said Elena. "He knew everything about my early life. He knew what to say to put me at ease."

"To him, you're family," said Jay. "If he could find a way to get the pictures without harming you, he would try."

"So when I asked him to leave me alone—?"

"He upped the ante. He sent this man," Signy flipped the back of the picture depicting the stocky man at the bottom of the hill, "Pavel Ivanovitch."

"Pavel," whispered Elena, glancing at the photo. "That's why he was nice to me." She looked up at the ceiling. "When he was in my apartment, he identified my mother in a picture hanging on the wall. At the time I thought he was asking a question. You know, like, is this your mother?"

"For him," interjected Jay, "it would have been the final proof that you were the little girl he remembered, Volkov's granddaughter."

"Stop saying that," said Elena, harshly.

"Try not to think about that right now," said Signy, flipping the photo upside down. She smoothed the pages of the letter on her lap and bent her head. "Let's see what else your mother says."

She told me that one day many years ago she entered his office (a room that I remember as strictly forbidden). She was hoping to discover the identity of his latest paramour when she stumbled upon the photographs.

She realized she had irrefutable evidence that could earn him the death penalty. She told him that she had hidden the photos and should anything happen to her, the pictures would be released to the authorities. They had always had a difficult relationship, but whether my father had her killed I will never know. What I do know is that he must have been frantic to find the pictures after she was gone.

I don't know why she had the pictures sent to me instead of the police. I like to think it was because she wanted to spare us the scandal, but it is more likely that she didn't want to give up her lifestyle.

Nevertheless, as soon as we saw them, your father and I knew we had to run. Neither of us was prepared to gamble your life for the sake of a nice apartment in Moscow or summers on the Black Sea. We changed our names, we started a new life, but not before leaving word with my father that we had the pictures. We told him that if he tried to find us, we would take them to the authorities.

I'm so very sorry, my darling.

Signy's voice faltered. Jay handed her a glass of water and she smiled at him gratefully before taking a sip.

I was never sure that Papa and I made the right decision. At the time my father was a high-ranking member of the KGB. Who knows what might have happened had we gone to the authorities? All I know for sure is that your safety was our first priority.

Please know that I love you, Papa loves you, and we will watch over you until the end of time.

Forever and ever,

Your loving Mother

An oppressive silence pervaded the room, making it hard to breathe. Signy refolded the thick linen sheets and slipped them back into the envelope. She felt her chest tighten as she watched fat tears plopping onto Elena's lap. She leaned in and murmured empty promises that everything would be all right.

Catching Signy's eye, Jay picked up the second plastic-covered package. With her arm still wrapped protectively around the weeping girl, Signy watched as Jay slit it open and removed the paper wrapping from the first of the pictures. The photo was black and white, and when Jay held it to the light, Signy watched his face harden.

Leaning over to take a look, Signy flinched at the image of a young woman with her throat slashed from ear to ear, the wound gaping open like an obscene grin. The woman's head was bent at an odd angle where gravity had pulled the almost-severed skull away from the spinal column.

Signy pressed Elena's face into her chest, hoping the girl would not look up as Jay proffered the next photo, this one of a middle-aged man slumped over on a dark street corner, a neat bullet hole piercing the back of his bald head, his face blown apart by a massive exit wound. From his position, it appeared he had been kneeling just prior to the fatal shot.

The next several photos captured similar images of men, women, and even one young child torn apart by bullets. After flashing them at Signy, Jay flicked them back onto the bed.

"Christ," he hissed, after sliding the cover off the next one. Holding the picture by its edges, he held it up to the light. In it, a young woman not much older than Elena had been laid out on top of a rumpled bed. She was naked, her abdomen slit open from breast bone to pubis. Long ropes of intestines had been torn from her body cavity and arranged in looping strings around her neck.

The photograph had been expertly lit, a macabre vision of light and shadows. The carefully constructed flip in the woman's hair, stiff with industrial-strength hairspray spoke to the fashion prevalent in the early 1960s. As if to confirm this fact, Jay snapped the photo upside down onto the bedside table. A name was written in a neat hand, along with the numbers 10/61. In the bottom right corner a stylized drawing of a lion, crafted from no more than two or three pen strokes, expertly captured the menacing stance of a predatory male.

"Looks like he signs his work," Jay said, whipping the picture back into the envelope with the others.

Signy sneered. "An assassin that treats murder as an art form. What a sick bastard."

Drumming his fingers on the table, Jay stared at the ceiling.

Signy was about to ask him what he was thinking when he jumped up, retrieved his bag from under the bed, and slipped out a laptop. Googling Volkov's name, he clicked on an entry, then spun the screen toward her.

"Every one of those death photos was artfully composed and well lit. The photographer took pride in his work, wouldn't you agree?"

Signy peered over Jay's shoulder. Taking up the full expanse of the screen was an art gallery poster advertising an upcoming showing of the black and white landscape photographs of the renowned artist Leonid Volkov. "I'd forgotten about that. Maitland mentioned she'd attended one of his shows. How did you know he was an artist?"

Ignoring the question, Jay scrolled down so Signy could see the bottom of the poster. "Check this out."

He was pointing out an identical copy of the stylized lion, scrawled casually beside Volkov's written signature, which ran across the bottom edge of the poster.

"I'll bet the handwriting will be Volkov's as well," she said.

Jay nodded grimly. "He must have suspected Elena had these pictures. That's why he's coming for her."

Elena drew a rasping breath.

Signy turned to her. "Let's try and get some sleep. As soon as we turn these pictures over to the authorities, it'll all be over. In fact, I wouldn't be surprised if you're safe at home within a day or two."

"Do you really think so?"

Signy nodded, giving the girl a squeeze. "Volkov is a dead man walking. He just doesn't know it yet."

Later, Signy would wake in the night, shuddering at her hubris. She would replay the events of the next twenty-four hours over and over in her head and would often pause at this moment, berating herself for making promises she couldn't keep.

Chapter

41

Leonid Volkov cracked open a fresh bottle of Stolichnaya Elit and poured a generous measure of the chilled vodka into a hand-cut crystal glass. He brought the glass to his nose and swirled the liquid in lazy circles, relishing the electric buzz as the vapour from the eighty-proof alcohol zapped his brain.

Imbibing a large sip, he shuddered as the pure vodka slid down his throat, then roared out loud as the sensation of icy cold transformed into a searing chemical burn halfway down his esophagus.

He pounded his chest with his fist before bringing the glass once more to his lips. There was nothing like flawless Russian vodka to get the cobwebs out, and he certainly needed a clear head.

His keen instincts rarely failed him and his sixth sense was thrumming like an electrical cable in a lightning storm. The man he had hired to pick up his granddaughter had failed to check in. Something was wrong.

Volkov emptied the glass. With a seasoned assassin up against two young girls, there was only one thing that could have gone wrong. He should never have agreed to the Tracker's request to keep the blond driver for himself. The oaf he'd sent to extract his sweet Anya had likely defied orders and made a play for the blonde. The Tracker had almost certainly retaliated.

He could only presume that the Tracker had prevailed in the inevitable showdown and his granddaughter was safe and still on her way to the shelter in Linden Valley. Otherwise, he would have heard from the other man by now.

Retribution would be forthcoming, but that was a pleasure for another day. Today he needed to do what he should have done from the first time he saw the girl. He needed to go after her himself.

As soon as the pictures were destroyed, all would be well in the charmed life of Leonid Volkov. Draining the vodka in two great swallows, he imagined the lovely young woman strolling beside him on the grounds of his estate, gazing at him in adoration as he swept his hand across the horizon and proclaimed that all she could see was hers for the taking.

Setting the glass down on the edge of his desk, he snatched up the phone. "Call the airport," he ordered. "Tell them to get the jet ready." He paused, listening to a hurried inquiry from the other end. "File a flight plan direct to Toronto, and Kazimir? Tell the pilot to hurry. I want to be there by morning."

Volkov took a last glance out the floor-to-ceiling windows of his office. The next time he stood on this spot admiring the sailboats dancing on the waves of English Bay, he'd have Anya in his arms and a song in his heart.

Chapter

42

Accepting the keys to Jay's SUV, Signy said, "Are you sure about this?"

"Keep it. If anyone asks about the front-end damage, tell them you hit a deer. I'll pick up another rental in town."

She held out her hand.

"Keep the kid safe," he said, holding her hand in his longer than necessary. "Don't take any chances."

"I hope you make the ballet recital."

He pulled her in for a brief hug. "I never forget family," he said.

"Maybe we'll run into each other again, Jay," she said. "Although I imagine Jay isn't your real name."

He smiled and shook his head.

She pulled open the motel room door. Amber light from an exterior bulb barely cut the predawn gloom. As she walked out to the car, Signy pressed a button on the key fob, releasing the door lock on the SUV with a loud chirrup. Several plump Canada geese grazing on a patch of wet grass expressed their irritation with a chorus of disgruntled honks and waggling tail feathers.

Elena followed, keeping a cautious eye on the agitated birds. After they'd climbed into the SUV, Signy turned the key, flipped on the windshield wipers against a misty drizzle, and backed out of the parking spot.

In the rear-view mirror she could see Jay watching them, his blond hair shining in the amber light.

• • •

"This is it," said Signy, as she steered into the Linden Valley shelter parking lot several hours later.

"I can't believe it," said Elena, glancing around the tiny backyard, her gaze resting on the row of industrial-sized garbage containers. A crack of thunder split the air.

"Looks like the weather is finally going to break," said Signy. "The guy on the radio said the whole area is under a tornado watch." As if to emphasize her words, one fat raindrop smacked the windshield with a loud plop. "Come on, let's get inside before it really starts coming down."

The two women scurried across the parking lot and into the front alcove of the shelter. Instructing Elena to look up into a camera that was mounted in one corner of the ceiling, Signy followed suit.

"Hi, it's Signy and I have Elena Morozov with me."

They waited several seconds while a staffer examined them via video feed not only to establish their identity but also to ensure that they were alone. Finally, the door clicked open, and the two women stepped inside.

The door had barely swung shut behind them when Signy saw Grace barrelling down the corridor toward them. Bracing herself, she was at least partially prepared when Grace slammed into her, enveloping her in a bone-crushing hug.

Signy inhaled the heady aroma of vanilla and cinnamon and felt her shoulders begin to relax. "Something smells good," she said into Grace's ample bosom.

Releasing Signy, Grace took a step back in order to brush the remnants of powdery white flour from the apron she had tied around her waist. "I needed to keep busy." She gave Signy a stern look. "You didn't return any of my texts."

"I lost my phone. I was hoping that the man you sent would have filled you in on everything."

"He found you, then?" asked Grace. Placing a hand over her chest, she heaved a relieved sigh. "I wasn't sure. Last time I heard from him, he was still trying to catch up to you."

"He caught up with us, all right, in spectacular fashion."

"It's been a bit of a whirlwind," Elena said shyly.

Grace whirled toward the girl. "Look at you," she said, clutching the young woman's hands in her own.

Elena looked down at the floor. "It's good to meet you. I'm so sorry to have caused so much trouble."

"Don't be silly," Grace said firmly.

"Listen, Grace," said Signy, "we found out what Volkov is up to. We found pictures and—"

Grace held up a hand. "As soon as I saw you pull in, I called Maitland. She asked us to hold off on the debriefing until she gets here." She took a step back and surveyed them critically. "Besides, you both look exhausted and hungry." She turned and marched back down the hall toward the kitchen. "Follow me," she said over her shoulder. "Food first, talk later."

Elena glanced at Signy, eyebrows raised.

Signy shook her head. "When Grace tells you to eat, you eat." She tucked her arm through Elena's and led her down the hallway. "Her motto says that there's nothing that a whackload of butter and cheese won't fix."

"And chocolate," called Grace. "Don't forget chocolate."

• • •

"Gimme that back, you little brat," cried a tousle-haired boy of about seven as he chased his younger brother around the kitchen table where Grace, Elena, and Signy sat pulling apart sticky cinnamon buns with their fingers.

"It's mine," the smaller boy shrieked, diving under the table, clutching a battered action figure. Bracing himself against Signy's chair, he kicked wildly at the probing hands of his older brother.

Outraged cries of protest erupted from under the table as the smaller boy managed to connect a solid kick to his brother's shin at the same time as the older boy ripped the now-headless toy from his sibling's fingers. Their furious howls had attracted quite a crowd, with four more small faces framed in the doorway delighting in the drama playing out underneath the table.

Grace bent down and dragged both boys out by their feet. Hauling them upright, she scolded, "Thomas? Jeffrey? I expect better from both of you. Give me that." She held out her hand and waited until Thomas reluctantly dropped the twisted action figure into her palm.

"You can have this back when you show me you know how to behave." She glanced over at the pint-sized audience watching avidly from the doorway. "There is nothing to see here, people. Move along."

As the crowd turned and began to shuffle back to the playroom, Grace relented and called out, "Who's up for a cinnamon bun?"

"*Meeeeee . . .*" shouted the young chorus.

"All right," said Grace, rising to her feet. "You guys head to the playroom and I'll be there in a minute."

The sound of pounding feet as the children ran down the hallway almost drowned out the rumble of thunder from outside.

Grace picked up a knife and began to hack a large slab of cinnamon buns into smaller hunks, sliding each onto a paper napkin.

"Looks like we have a full house," said Signy.

"Since last week," confirmed Grace, "six women, eleven children, and two babies."

"That's awful," said Elena, wiping syrupy sugar from her mouth with a napkin.

"We figure it must be the weather," said Grace. "This heat has been getting to everyone." She paused as a crack of thunder split the air. "Thank God, it's almost over."

"If we survive this storm," said Signy. "It sounds epic out there. When are you expecting Maitland?"

"Later this afternoon," Grace replied. "She had a few loose ends to tie up first, but we'll meet her at the office in a couple of hours."

Signy nodded. "Good. We should call her and ask her to bring in the RCMP or CSIS, or whatever."

"CSIS?" Grace repeated, glancing between Signy and Elena. "You'd better tell me what you found out."

Over the next several minutes Signy provided Grace with a brief summary of the letter that Elena's mother had left and described the damning photographs signed by Leonid Volkov. She decided to put off the story of their close call with the assassin. She knew the reaction would be over the top and she only wanted to go through that once.

Grace sat back and regarded Elena. "So, you're Volkov's—?"

"Granddaughter?" said Elena bitterly. "It would appear so."

"Good Lord," said Grace.

"I would use different language, but yes, it seems I am the long-lost grandchild of a Russian assassin." She looked at Grace, then turned her exotic green eyes on Signy.

Signy watched with dismay as Elena's face began to collapse, muscle by muscle, as though the gravitational pull of the earth had suddenly intensified. The corners of her mouth twitched and she blinked once, twice, then in rapid succession. She dipped her head and her bangs fell across her eyes.

Grace reached for a box of tissues sitting on the sideboard behind them. "It's okay, honey," she said, sliding the box across the table toward Elena.

Elena snorted, a harsh braying noise.

Signy and Grace glanced at each other.

Elena guffawed, another harsh explosion of sound. She raised a hand to her mouth. "I lived like a shut-in for most of my life because my mother was trying to hide from her father."

"Elena?" Signy said, reaching out a hand, trying to soothe the distraught girl.

Elena stared wide-eyed at Signy, her mouth twitching uncontrollably. A shudder ran through her shoulders, then she brought her other hand up to her mouth.

Signy could hear bursts of air escaping from between Elena's fingers as the girl started to heave with laughter. Signy smiled uncertainly at Grace.

Grace pushed her chair back and hauled herself up. "Delayed reaction," she said. "I have something in my office that will help."

"Not to mention"—Elena wheezed the words between gales of laughter—"that when he finally found me, he tried to have me killed, not once but twice."

Grace froze. "What do you mean, twice?"

Signy dropped her head into her hands.

Elena peered up at Grace, her eyes streaming with mirthless tears. "If it hadn't been for Jay Hunter, Signy and I would both be at the bottom of a lake in northern Ontario."

Grace's hair quivered on top of her head and her mouth hung open, which only seemed to increase Elena's merriment. The girl rocked back in her chair, hysterical laughter bubbling out of her throat.

"Signy?" Grace turned to Signy. "What the hell happened out there?"

"I was going to tell you." Signy held up her hands in surrender. "I just thought it better to wait until the meeting with Maitland. I knew you'd freak out."

"Freak out?" Grace glared at Signy.

Signy glanced around wildly. The posse of children had returned and was watching with great interest as the drama unfolded at the adult table. Signy nodded her head toward the young eavesdroppers. "It was nothing."

"Yup, it was nothing," said Elena, from between her fingers, her chest heaving. "Our car was driven into the water and we had to swim for our lives." She chortled. "And if Jay hadn't come along in the nick of time, well—let's just say Signy and I would be swimming with the fishes." She lay her head down on the table, rocked with hysteria.

Grace stared at Elena for several moments before turning her attention back to Signy. "Someone drove your car off the road and into the water?"

Signy folded her hands in her lap and nodded.

"And when were you going to tell me?" Grace asked.

"I was kind of hoping Jay might have mentioned it to you," said Signy.

"And who the *hell* is Jay?" Grace demanded.

Signy looked at her in confusion. "Jay Hunter? The man you sent to meet up with us?"

"I don't know any Jay Hunter," said Grace. "I sent a man named Ross. Ross MacDonald. We've used him several times."

Signy shrugged. "He as much as told me he wasn't using his real name. It must be the same guy."

"What did he look like?" Grace asked, her hands clutching the back of a kitchen chair.

"Average build, blond hair, blue eyes, maybe thirty years old," Signy answered.

"And good-looking, don't forget good-looking," Elena interjected, still giggling helplessly.

Signy shot Elena a fierce look. Glancing back at Grace, she saw with a sinking heart that Grace's face had drained of colour. "What is it?" she asked, already knowing the answer but hoping she was wrong.

"Ross MacDonald, our one and only asset in northern Ontario, is a logger by profession. He's six foot five inches tall, bald as a cue ball, and built like a bull moose."

"Are you sure?" said Signy.

"Of course I'm sure."

"Then who the hell is Jay Hunter?" Signy asked.

"I have absolutely no idea," Grace replied.

"And why did he kill the man that attacked us?" Signy said, her eyes wide.

"*Kill?*" Grace almost choked on the word.

Signy nodded. "Jay said you sent him to find us. He knew your name. I believed him. I didn't have any reason not to believe him. Elena's right. If it hadn't been for him, we'd both be dead."

"My God," said Grace. "He used my name?"

Signy nodded again. "I'm sorry, Grace. I didn't know."

Grace shook her head. "What the hell is going on?"

"He said he used my phone's GPS to track us down," said Signy.

Grace stared at her grimly. After a moment, she said, "I'm going to call Maitland. We'll meet her midway. We have to get

Elena out of here. If that Jay Hunter person knew how to find you and knew my name, then he probably knows a lot more."

Signy nodded. "Do you think he was hired by Volkov?"

"I think that it becomes more likely by the second."

"Son of a bitch," Signy hissed.

"I don't understand any of this," interjected Elena. "What are you saying? Jay Hunter saved our lives."

"Look, honey," said Grace, piling her hair on top of her head, "we don't have time to speculate. I don't know what this Jay Hunter person might be up to. All I do know for sure is that we have to get out of here. If they know about me, then they probably know that you're here at the shelter."

Signy thought about the six women, eleven children, and two babies. The longer Elena and the pictures were inside the shelter, the greater the danger for everyone else. She nodded at Grace, then stood up.

Grace called sharply for one of the shelter staff. A young woman, her long brown hair tied back in two pigtails, rushed into the kitchen, then skidded to a halt, startled by the grim faces staring at her.

"Alison, I need you to get everyone to the basement safe room. Lock yourselves inside."

"Grace?" Alison's eyes darted wildly, and Signy thought she looked more like a frightened thirteen-year-old than a paid employee.

"Please, Alison, honey," said Grace, moving over to place a hand on the girl's shoulder. "You can do this, just like we've practised."

"Right," said Alison, her eyes pleading. "What do I do?"

"Push the alarm. Once the police get here, you'll be fine."

Alison took a deep breath, then squared her shoulders and walked briskly from the room, already starting to gather up the scattered guests.

"Signy, get Elena moving and meet me at the front door. I have to call Maitland." She took a few steps toward her office, then turned back. "You said there were pictures?"

Signy nodded.

"Get them," Grace ordered, then turned and hustled off to call Maitland.

Less than three minutes later, Grace joined Elena and Signy in the alcove.

"We'll take my car," said Grace, pulling open the front door with some effort against the rising wind.

"What do we do if Volkov is out there?" asked Elena, her voice hoarse.

"Whatever we have to," said Grace without hesitation. Then she dashed into the driving rain.

Chapter

43

The Tracker pushed the new SUV he'd rented as fast as he dared. After a journey of almost three thousand miles, he was less than an hour away from his destination. Rain slashed at the windshield. Less than an hour from finding out the answer to the question that had been plaguing him for as long as he could remember.

Glancing down at the speedometer, he forced himself to lay off the gas. If he was going to find out the truth, he needed Signy Shepherd in one piece. He'd done all he could to ensure that she made it safely to Linden Valley. He pinched the bridge of his nose between his thumb and forefinger. He just wasn't sure it had been enough.

The foul little tune cranked up inside his head, jangling along in time to the thwack of the wiper blades. He knew the concept of failure was anathema to Leo the Lion. They were alike in that way. As much as he needed Signy, Volkov wanted the red-head. And Volkov would stop at nothing to get her.

The thought of Volkov getting anywhere near Signy Shepherd set off an instant physiological response. He felt his heart rise into his throat and his hands become slippery on the wheel. Volkov's plans had been thwarted at every turn, and by now he had likely figured out that the very man he had hired to track the girl had turned against him.

Catching sight of a service station just ahead, the Tracker screeched off the highway and slid to a halt in a far corner of the lot. He punched in Volkov's private number. He had to know how much Volkov knew and, more importantly, what he was planning.

The phone rang several times before the line was picked up. *"Da?"*

The Tracker recognized the gravelly voice of Volkov's security chief. "Put the old man on."

The thug let fly with a stream of Russian, and the Tracker had been around the Russian mob enough to recognize some of their more colourful profanities. Question answered. Volkov knew. Everything.

"Listen, Boris, or whatever your name is, be a good boy and go get your boss. Tell him it's about the girl."

"Go to hell, Tracker," the Russian said.

The Tracker squeezed the phone until it threatened to snap between his fingers.

"The boss has the girl." The man made a noise deep in his throat. "And that little stunt you pulled? I promise you, he won't rest until he's put you in the ground. You're a dead man, asshole."

"What do you mean, he has the girl?".

"She's probably in the air and on her way home by now, and that little blonde you wanted so badly? I'll bet he's torn her in half, just to teach you some manners."

"Listen," the Tracker said in a level tone. "You call him right now and you give him a message from me. You tell him I have his pictures."

"I don't take orders from you."

"You won't be taking orders from anyone if you don't do as I tell you. Volkov wants the pictures, and you tell him they will be going straight to the media if he so much as sneezes on the blonde."

"Go fuck yourself."

"Tell that psychopathic freak to come get me." The Tracker severed the connection.

He rested his head against the steering wheel. He stared blankly, his mind whirling, barely noticing the turbulent storm clouds roiling in the sky overhead.

Volkov was already in Linden Valley. His heart thudded dully in his chest as the disturbing strains of that infernal tune caused him to bring his hands to his ears. He checked the clock. There was no way Volkov had had time to take down the women. Not yet.

The Tracker swallowed heavily. Unless he'd been waiting for them when they arrived at the shelter. The song tinkled away mercilessly in his head and he blinked his eyes, trying to regain his focus. The message he'd left with Volkov's man had been a Hail Mary pass, at best. If Signy was still alive, she needed to get out of there immediately. He had no choice. He had to warn her.

Slamming his fist against the steering wheel, he snatched up the cellphone and punched in the number of the Linden Valley women's shelter. No answer. Hoping he'd misdialed, he tried again, taking care to punch in the numbers correctly. He waited. The phone rang and rang. After twenty rings he snapped the phone shut. He knew that phone lines at women's shelters were manned 24-7. If the line wasn't being picked up, then something was wrong.

Shoving the car into gear, he screamed out of the parking lot and back on to the highway, knowing in his heart that he was too late. Volkov's invasion had already begun.

•   •   •

Zef sat on the cold bench, pressed against the back wall, glaring at Dalton.

"Good news, sunshine," said Dalton, leaning against the cell door. "Just got a call from one of my boys patrolling out on Route Twelve. It looks like our mutual friend is back. He saw her cruising into town in a brand new SUV." He grinned at Zef. "Maybe she picked up a sugar daddy while she was away."

Zef muttered something unintelligible under his breath.

Ignoring the insult, Dalton pulled Zef's cellphone out of his pocket. "Now's your chance to walk out of here."

"Fuck you."

"Suit yourself," Dalton said, turning away.

"Wait," said Zef, shoving his hands into his pockets.

Dalton turned slowly back.

"What did you mean, walk out of here?"

The walkie-talkie on Dalton's belt squawked. He used a thumb to turn down the volume. He winked. "Sometimes investigations stall, evidence goes missing—"

"Evidence you planted," said Zef bitterly.

Dalton shook his head. "If I had a dime for every time one of you dickwads claimed you was set up, I'd be richer than God."

"Fuck." Zef slammed a fist into the wall.

Dalton looked at his watch. "You're running out of time, sunshine."

Zef leaned in, wrapping his fists around the steel bars. "What do you want with Signy?"

"Well, now," said Dalton, his tone friendly, "all I'm asking is that she shows me the proper respect."

Zef glared at him. "Ya? What kind of respect are we talking about?"

Dalton narrowed his eyes. "What you need to decide is whether you want to walk out of here a free man or spend the next twenty years in the can. And you got about thirty seconds to make up your mind."

Zef twisted his eyes from Dalton. His mouth felt foul and dirty, as though an infected abscess had burst while he slept. His hair was stiff with grease and he could feel his skin beginning to shrivel under the unnatural lights. In a nearby cell, a scuffle broke out, the sickening thud of a fist hitting bone and a scream, choked off.

Zef looked at Dalton.

The big cop turned his head toward the sound of the altercation, then shrugged and turned back.

"You promise not to hurt her?" Zef asked.

Dalton's smile widened. "I can't guarantee she'll be able to walk right for a few days, but nope, nothing permanent."

Zef inhaled sharply. Signy could handle herself. She'd always been a fighter. His gaze slid down to the floor. Signy would be all right. But he couldn't handle another stretch. No way. He wasn't meant to be caged. He'd go crazy. Signy would understand. He glanced briefly at Dalton. "What do you want me to do?"

Dalton grinned. "Smart boy," he said. He put the cellphone in the palm of his hand and held it out toward the bars. "All you gotta do is give her a time and a place. I'll handle the rest."

Zef glared at Dalton for almost a minute. He could feel tears prick behind his eyes. He could smell the bitter reek of his own sweat, and he wondered if this was what cowardice smelled like. The struggle down the hall had ended and all was quiet in the holding unit, as though every one of the hopeless inhabitants was paying close attention to this unholy transaction, as if by observing the downfall of someone lower than themselves, they might boost their own self-worth.

Finally, Zef's hand twitched and he reached out for the phone.

The radio hooked on Dalton's belt squawked out a message and, despite the low volume, both men could hear the urgency in the dispatcher's voice.

Dalton reached down and cranked the volume.

"All units, the silent alarm has been triggered at the women's shelter on West Street."

The excited voice of a patrol officer reported that his unit was less than two minutes away and would respond immediately. Another officer joined the conversation, declaring that he would provide backup, and the dispatcher concluded the exchange by reminding the responding officers to proceed with extreme caution.

"Well, well," said Dalton, slipping Zef's cellphone back into his pocket. "Looks like the lovely Ms. Shepherd couldn't wait ten minutes before she started stirring up trouble." He unhooked his radio and spoke briefly to the dispatcher. "Think I'll go join the party."

Zef exhaled, dropped his hand, and took a step back.

Dalton glanced at him. "Don't get too comfortable, sunshine."

Dalton ignored the stream of invectives as he marched out of the holding cells, the heavy steel door clanging shut behind him.

Chapter

44

"We have to turn around," said Grace, her knuckles white on the steering wheel. The rain, which had been heavy ten minutes ago as they left the shelter, was now slashing down in torrents. Sheets of water coursed over the windshield, the wipers fighting a useless battle against the deluge.

Wiping at the fogged interior of her window, Signy struggled to see the pavement ahead. A river rushed down the middle of the street, and they could see fountains of muddy water gushing from the sewer grates as the massive volume overloaded the town's infrastructure. Even through the closed windows they could smell the distinctive odour of raw sewage.

"We'll have to wait it out." Grace shouted in order to be heard over the howling wind and pounding rain. She pulled over to the side of the road and rolled down her window. Sticking her head out, she squinted through the rain, then swung the

Prius into an arcing U-turn and headed back toward the centre of town.

Grace was shivering by the time she pulled the Prius into the driveway. With chattering lips she rummaged through the piles of detritus that lay scattered in the back seat until she located a used plastic bag.

"This'll do," she said, thrusting the bag at Signy. "Don't let those pictures get wet again."

Nodding, Signy slipped the bag around the small bundle of photos she'd retrieved from Elena's bag, then tied the ends into a tight knot.

"As soon as we get inside, run them upstairs," instructed Grace. "I want them out of sight. Kim might be home already."

Signy clutched the bag to her chest.

"Ready?" yelled Grace, loud enough to be heard over the rain pounding on the roof of the car.

The three women dashed up the walkway, splashing through ankle-deep puddles. A searing bolt of lightning lit up the dark sky, and for an instant the image of Grace, her mouth open in a wide O of surprise, burned onto Signy's retinas. At almost the same instant, a booming crack of thunder split the air and the sound of Elena's high scream twisted away into the howling wind.

Grace fumbled with her keys but found the front door unlocked, and the women tumbled inside.

"Kim?" Grace called.

Signy was relieved when instead of Grace's bothersome partner they were greeted by one hundred and fifty pounds of charging dog. Chivas almost upended Grace as he slammed into her. Shivering, he wound his huge body around Grace.

"Hey, big fella," cried Grace, digging her hands into the ruff of his neck, stroking and pushing away at the same time. "Are you all alone?"

As if in answer, he whined, a thin, lonely howl, and bounded back down the hall toward the kitchen, his nails scratching the wood floor.

Watching him go, Signy slipped out of her sodden sandals and took the stairs two at a time.

Grace and Elena followed the dog into the kitchen, and Signy could hear Grace call out for Kim once again. Signy crept down the hallway in her bare feet and slipped into the master bedroom.

A king-sized four-poster bed covered in a creamy yellow duvet dominated the large room. One large bureau, its oak top littered with the detritus of everyday life, sat next to a set of shelves. The top two shelves were crammed with hard- and soft-covered books, while a row of mismatched photo albums lined the bottom shelf. On the bedside table, an old-fashioned rotary phone teetered precariously on a stack of magazines.

Signy walked quickly toward the walk-in closet and stepped inside. Even in the gloom, she could see the closet was a mess, clothes heaped on the floor in haphazard piles, shoes tossed willy-nilly. Not to mention that it smelled like a gym locker. Feeling uncomfortably like a peeping Tom, she groped along the wall for the light switch and flipped it on.

Nothing. Signy's mouth twisted downward. The storm was likely wreaking havoc with the power system. As she pushed the door wide open, the dim light from the bedroom invaded the gloomy confines of the closet just enough for her to see. She set the bag of photos onto an upper shelf and slid it as far back as she could reach.

From below she heard the tone of conversation change perceptibly, a note of anxiety evident in the raised voices. Signy turned to head back downstairs when she heard the distant sound of a third speaker, a deep, rumbling voice, unmistakably male.

Signy froze, trying to make sense of what she was hearing over the drumming rain. Tilting her head down, she tried to listen through the wooden floorboards but couldn't make out the specifics over the howl of the wind and the clatter of tree branches on the metal roof. It was obvious from the tone of the conversation, however, that some sort of confrontation was unfolding in the kitchen.

She padded quickly across the hall to the bathroom. Like many century homes, this one was fitted with extra-large heating vents through which sound travelled freely. She'd discovered the acoustic anomaly when she'd spent an uncomfortable few hours at a staff party Grace had hosted. She flushed slightly as she remembered pressing her ear to the vent in a paranoid attempt to catch her colleagues talking behind her back.

Kneeling, she tried to make out what was going on downstairs. As if by magic, the sounds from the kitchen floated up, reverberating through the aluminum ducts, unimpeded by the noise of the raging storm outside.

"What is his name?" asked the male voice, his tone low and reasonable.

"Go fuck yourself." Grace sounded furious.

Straining to hear, Signy heard the man let go with a rumbling chuckle. "Well," he said, "Go Fuck Yourself and I have been having a good time, haven't we, boy?"

Chivas's happy bark seemed to back up the man's statement.

"Stupid dog," Grace said.

"What do they say?" said the man. "You can't teach old dogs new tricks?"

Listening to the clatter of nails on the wooden floor, Signy could picture Chivas doing his happy dance for the unwelcome guest.

"We're two of a kind," said the man, and Signy pictured him patting Chivas into a quivering mass of joy, "just a couple of old dogs. The old tricks work just fine, eh boy?"

"What do you want?" Grace's voice seemed thin and barely under control.

"Why don't you put our old friend into the basement," said the man. "We wouldn't want him to get hurt."

Signy heard the scrape of a chair against the floor, a few choice words from Grace, then the sound of the basement door opening.

"Go on," commanded Grace, obviously having some difficulty getting the dog to comply, "go downstairs."

"Here," said the man. "They say that the way to an old dog's heart is through his stomach."

Signy imagined he must have tossed Grace a dog treat, because almost immediately she heard the telltale sounds of Chivas scrambling down the steps and the click of the basement door as Grace shut it behind him.

"What do you want?" Grace spoke again, her voice more controlled now.

There was a longer pause broken by the boom of thunder

from overhead. Signy cringed as the walls of the old house rattled under the barrage.

The dog howled, his plaintive cry echoing in the hollow confines of the dark basement. The hair on the back of Signy's neck rose in an automatic response.

"Come," said the man, "let's leave the dog alone. Perhaps he'll settle."

More scraping of chairs and Signy heard footsteps as the trio left the kitchen. She popped up and exited the bathroom, rushing out on silent feet back down the hallway.

From her vantage point at the top of the stairs, Signy was able to see the man herding the two women into the living room. Endowed with a glorious head of thick white hair, he might have been an aging matinee idol but for the silenced handgun he had pointed at Grace's back. She recognized him from his picture. It was Leonid Volkov himself.

Elena moved completely into the room and within a second was out of Signy's line of sight, while Grace chose to sit in a wingback chair that left her in full view of Signy, crouched at the top of the stairs.

"No heroics," he said to Grace, "and we'll all get through this nice and easy."

"Why are you doing this?" cried Elena, her voice high and squeaking.

Volkov swung his head away from Grace. "You remember now, don't you, little one?" He moved further into the room until he was no longer visible to Signy. "When I saw you walk into the restaurant this summer, I could hardly believe it." He dabbed at his eyes. "All the years we've missed."

There was a pause and Signy could imagine Elena sizing up the big Russian with her startling green eyes. Volkov and Elena murmured back and forth, too quiet now for Signy to pick up the thread of the conversation, and she was gratified when Grace used the lull to flick her eyes up toward where Signy sat hunkered down at the top of the stairs.

In a series of exaggerated hand gestures Signy communicated that she would phone for help. Grace closed her eyes in understanding and Signy retraced her steps to the bedroom, where she was unlikely to be overheard. It was only then that she remembered that her phone was lying at the bottom of the lake.

From down below the tone of the conversation changed. She could hear angry shouts from Grace, then a harsh reply from Volkov. From behind the basement door, Chivas howled and she felt the reverberations through the wall as the big dog flung himself against the strong wooden door.

She heard the crack of breaking glass, a cry of pain, and then someone screamed.

• • •

"Hey, Paul," said Kim, tossing a pair of blood-stained booties into the hazardous-waste bin, "I'm going to head out. I promised Grace we'd go down to the city tonight."

"In this weather?" asked Paul, popping open his locker. He shrugged out of his sodden raincoat and shook it violently. Rising onto his toes, he reached into his locker, just managing to slip his coat over a metal hook.

Watching him, Kim grinned. What Dr. Paul Stafford lacked in height, he easily compensated for in ego. She didn't mind, finding his unrestrained self-promotion refreshing. At least he was honest.

He grinned at Kim. "It might be the end of the world out there."

"It will be the end of my world if I don't get out of here soon."

Sliding off his Italian leather loafers, he dried them with a clean towel before placing them carefully onto the floor of his locker. "Things still tense at home?" He didn't look up as he worked at undoing his belt buckle.

"You could say that." She rolled her eyes, then reached into her locker and pulled a clean shirt down from the upper shelf. Reaching down, she unbuttoned her soiled white coat, then glanced briefly at Paul before continuing, "I may have been somewhat unreasonable lately."

"What?" he cried in mock horror. "You?"

"Shut up," she said, tossing her coat at him, laughing as it wrapped itself neatly around his face.

He whipped the coat back at her. She looked at him, her expression serious. "I don't know what to do."

He slipped on a fresh pair of green scrubs. "Apologize."

"For what?" She stood, one hip slung out and her arms crossed over her chest.

"Does it matter? Just look into her eyes and tell her you're sorry for everything."

"Works for you?"

"Like a charm, without fail." He nodded with satisfaction.

She examined him critically. "And how many times have you been married?"

He turned his back on her as he buttoned a fresh white coat over his scrubs. "Suit yourself," he sniffed, adjusting his tie into a neat Windsor knot.

She laughed and, walking over, clapped him on the shoulder.

He was about to reply when their pagers buzzed simultaneously.

"Shit," Kim said, as she examined the small screen.

Paul had already checked the urgent message, "Multiple injuries out on the highway. One fatality at the scene and several other casualties on their way in. Two critical and one vital signs absent." He glanced at Kim. "Sorry about that, kid. Grace will understand."

As Paul hurried from the room, Kim called after him, "I'll be right there."

"Sure," he said over his shoulder, "you've got thirty seconds."

Kim frowned at Paul's retreating back, then reached into her locker and picked up her phone. She rang Grace's cellphone but there was no answer. Strange: Grace never went anywhere without that damn thing strapped to her.

She tried the land line and her frown deepened as she realized that the busy signal on the other end was not the usual slow beeping but the rapid signal that indicates the line is down or the system is overloaded. The storm must be interfering with the line into the house.

As she turned to head back into the emergency department, she thought about the girl Signy was bringing in. Nightmare scenarios flooded her mind and she had to pause for a moment to catch her breath. I'm being stupid, she thought. The storm has brought down a phone line, that's all.

Still, it was Signy Shepherd. There was no counting how many ways she might have found to screw up. Kim punched in the nonemergency number for the Linden Valley Police.

"Hey, Sandy," she said to the woman who answered the line.

"Hi, Kim, is there something going down at Crazyville?"

"No, nothing like that. It's just that I tried to call Grace just now and I can't get through. Have you heard anything about the phone lines?"

"Nothing yet," replied Sandy, "but it wouldn't surprise me. It's unbelievable out there."

"So I've heard. The thing is, I can't reach her and I've got to stay here."

"That big accident out on Highway Twelve?"

"Yup, we've got multiple vics inbound. Listen, Sandy. Would you mind sending a car round if you have someone to spare, just to take a look?"

"Not a problem." Sandy paused, then continued. "You know we were called out to the shelter this afternoon? Someone pulled the silent alarm."

Kim's heart began to pound in her chest. "No, I didn't know that. Everybody okay?"

"Looks like it. Our guys are still there trying to sort things out. Grace is probably over there right now."

"Uh-huh, but just to be on the safe side, could you send that car out to the house?"

"You got it, sweetie," said Sandy, her tone soothing. "I'm

sure everything is all right. You take care and don't work too hard."

Paul popped his head in the door and held up one finger, the universal sign for emergency room personnel. Inbound patient, one minute out.

Slipping her phone into her pocket, Kim hurried after Paul, the wail of multiple sirens already starting to make her head pound.

Chapter

45

Signy left the bedroom and flew back down the hall on silent feet. When she reached the top of the stairs, she peered cautiously around the edge of the wall.

Grace was hunched in the wingback chair, a crystal vase shattered at her feet. Her hands twisted in her lap, her wrists manacled in a set of plastic handcuffs. Signy winced. She could see the sharp bands biting into Grace's flesh. The BlackBerry hooked to Grace's belt rang.

Volkov reached out, plucked the phone from its holster, and switched it off.

Grace let loose with another stream of obscenities but was cut off by Volkov's heavily accented voice.

Signy froze as the Russian came into view.

"I believe you have something that belongs to me," he said, his tone reasonable again.

"Who are you? I have no idea what you're talking about." Grace glared up at him.

"Let's not waste time, my dear. I'll take the pictures, then Elena and I will be on our way. No harm done."

Grace laughed in disbelief. "You must be joking."

"Unfortunately," he sighed in a theatrical fashion, "I've never been known for my sense of humour." He ran the tip of his gun along the length of Grace's leg.

She shrank back into the depths of the wingback chair.

"Grace?" From the other end of the room, Elena's voice sounded raw.

"Look, you've been given bad information. I have no idea what you're talking about."

He tapped the barrel of the silencer against one of her kneecaps. Grace winced.

Loosening his tie, Volkov eyed Grace from the bottom of her feet to the top of her tousle-haired head, allowing his eyes to linger on her ample bosom. "You're not bad-looking for an old lesbian," he said.

Grace grimaced and twisted her head away.

Volkov chuckled. "Perhaps what you need is an experienced man to show you the way."

"Go fuck yourself."

His eyes narrowed. "Enough," he said. "I know all about your little Underground Railroad. I've had a man watching my granddaughter since she left B.C."

Grace stared back, her eyes expressionless.

"Unlike you, Ms. Holder, I am not an amateur. You can play

games with your little runaway rescue team, but I have had enough."

At the top of the stairs, Signy tried to process his words. He had to be talking about Jay Hunter. She wished he were here right now so she could personally kill him.

"Unfortunately, the Tracker lost sight of the objective, and all for the sake of a little blond piece of fluff." He paused. "Where is she, by the way?"

Grace's genuine puzzlement must have shown in her eyes.

"Where is the blond driver?" His voice had taken on an ominous tone, as though he truly were tired of playing this game.

"The blond—?" said Grace. "Oh, you mean—Jennifer? She's a driver, nothing more. She dropped off Elena and left." Apparently, Grace had decided to give up the pretense of ignorance.

Volkov regarded her for several moments, then shook his head. "The Tracker left word that he has taken possession of the photographs, but I don't believe him. You seem a careful woman. I don't believe you would allow evidence to slip through your fingers."

Signy felt her hands curl into fists. The image of the little tracking device she'd found on her car popped into her head. What the hell was going on?

"Where is the blond girl?" Volkov asked again. He twisted round and glanced at the stairway. "And why does the Tracker want her so badly?"

Signy melted out of sight.

"Ms. Holder? Maybe we should just give him what he wants?"

Grace shot the girl a heated glance.

Volkov grinned at Grace. "My daughter was shrewd. When I found out that she was dead, I knew she would have made sure that Anya had the photographs." He turned to Elena. "If you tell me where they are, I promise you will not be harmed." His words were gentle and Signy watched as he flipped the gun in his hand, holding it by the silenced barrel as if to emphasize its neutered status. He set it down on the coffee table.

"You see, my dear?" He glanced over his shoulder at Grace before moving deeper into the room.

Signy ground her teeth in frustration. There was no way she could thunder down the stairs and disarm Volkov with her bare hands. Her taser and her canister of Mace were safely stowed back at her apartment.

A spark flashed in the corner of her eye. She blinked down the gloomy hallway. A beam of light was coming from inside the master bedroom and playing across the back wall of the hall. Inching along the wall, she made her way to the bedroom and peered inside. A light was definitely shining in through the window. She tiptoed over to the window and, cupping her hands over the sweating glass, peered outside.

As a flash of lightning illuminated the street, she was able to spot the clear outline of a Linden Valley police cruiser parked out front. The officer sitting in the driver's seat was using a powerful spotlight to examine the exterior of the house.

Giddy with relief, Signy slid open the bedroom window and waved. No response. Unable to cry out for risk of alerting Volkov, she pried out the screen and set it down on the bed.

Then, propping her hips on the windowsill, she heaved her upper body through the open space and began waving her arms over her head.

Just when she'd almost given up hope that the cop would spot her through the driving rain, a flash of lightning lit up the world. Bracing herself for the boom of thunder that would follow, she resisted the urge to pull herself back inside. Her efforts were rewarded when the beam of light swung back in her direction, found her, and froze on her face.

Squinting into the light, Signy made an L shape with her thumb and index finger, the universal sign of a gun, then pointed toward the living room window. The cop flashed the light twice in acknowledgement, then switched it off. She'd done it. Everything was going to be all right.

• • •

Sitting in his cruiser outside Grace Holder's house, Constable Richard Dalton grinned as he watched Signy Shepherd hanging out of the window. He held the spotlight on her for several seconds, enjoying her writhing movements. He let the light linger on her breasts. Her flimsy top was soaked through. He licked his lips. With his empty hand he stroked his crotch.

After leaving her boyfriend in the holding cells, he'd joined the crowd at the women's shelter to see what was going on. From the level of activity it looked like a full-scale invasion was in progress. With any luck, some justifiably pissed-off father had finally had the stones to take back what was his.

He'd slid his car to a halt, entered the fray, and chatted up one of the staff. It seemed that Shepherd, Grace Holder, and some other girl had taken off seconds before the silent alarm had been pulled.

He'd been wondering about the significance of that when the call came from dispatch for a drive-by at the Holder residence. He'd immediately volunteered. Maybe if he was lucky he'd catch Shepherd there.

He chuckled to himself as he saw her almost fall out the window trying to catch his attention. His smile died as he watched her send the message that someone was inside with a gun. He'd been so looking forward to partying with the lovely Ms. Shepherd, but it appeared that some other devil had beaten him to the punch.

He picked up the radio to call for backup. He stared at the house for several seconds, then set the radio back in its holder. He shrugged. There was never a shortage of willing meat in this town, and while his plan to snare this tasty morsel had been doable, it had not been without its risks. If he had to settle for someone else taking her out, then so be it. He certainly wasn't in the mood for a gun battle, or the days of paperwork that would inevitably follow.

"Dick? Are you out there?"

Dalton frowned and picked up the radio. "What is it, Sandy?"

"All clear at the Holder residence?"

With some regret, he flicked off the light. "Just left. All quiet," he said.

"Good. Listen, Dick? Lavalle wants you to come in."

Dalton bit his lip against an exasperated retort. He didn't need this shit. "Why?"

There was a long pause before the radio squawked again. "I'm sorry, Dick, but it's about Daryl. There's been some more trouble."

Dalton gripped the wheel, willing himself not to shout. He flashed a dark look at the window. Whatever mess his moronic son had caused, it was all Signy Shepherd's fault. He slipped his hand into his pants and adjusted his growing erection. He took a deep breath, then pressed the send button on the microphone. "Ten-four, Sandy. Tell Lavalle I'll be there in five minutes."

He put the cruiser in gear. He hoped Ms. Shepherd made it out of the Holder house in one piece. He was looking forward to showing her what happened to anyone stupid enough to fuck with Big Dick Dalton. With those happy thoughts swirling in his head, he took off into the night.

Chapter

46

Signy watched in disbelief as the cruiser rolled down the boulevard and out of sight, her teeth clenched against the fury that threatened to spill out in a howl of outrage. She looked down and, spying the concrete patio far below, knew she was just too high to risk jumping. Reluctantly, she allowed herself to drop back down inside the room.

Whirling back into the bedroom, she scanned the space for anything she might be able to use. Noting a roll of Scotch tape on the bed, she padded over, lifted a sheet of striped wrapping paper, and pounced on a pair of scissors she found underneath. Picking up the scissors, she hefted them in her hand before hooking them onto the back of her shorts.

Poking her head into the hallway, she listened hard. She could no longer hear the sound of voices coming from the living room. She hesitated. It had been several minutes since the last crack of thunder, and the sound of the rain on the roof no longer seemed quite as loud. With the storm passing, the unmistakable sounds of someone poking about on the upper floor would be much more difficult to conceal.

In addition, it was still silent downstairs, too silent. Reluctantly, she turned back toward the stairs, every sense quivering. She glided down the hall to the landing in her bare feet, trying to avoid any loose floorboards. Leaning into the wall, she eased around the corner and peeked down the stairs.

She could see Grace, still huddled in the wingback chair, her eyes trained on Volkov, who was standing at the front door, holding back the lace curtain that covered the glass window.

"He's gone," he said, turning to face Grace.

"They'll be back. You should get out of here while you still can."

"For once we are in agreement." Volkov released the curtain and it fluttered back into place. "Police are like locusts: at first you see one, maybe two, but soon they are swarming all over the place." His eyes narrowed and he fixed his gaze on Grace. "And that means your time is up, not mine."

Signy watched transfixed as he stepped toward Grace, kicking aside the pile of wet shoes the women had left by the door. He took another step, paused, then looked down.

Signy followed Volkov's gaze and saw that her own sodden sandals were jumbled in with Grace's and Elena's wet shoes. She glanced over at Grace and saw by the look of alarm in her wide eyes that she too had recognized the implications of the third pair of shoes.

"Hey!" Grace shouted. "You win."

Ignoring her, Volkov bent down and picked up one shoe from each of the three pairs.

"Did you hear me?" asked Grace, perched now on the edge of the wingback chair. "I said you win. You can have your damned pictures."

He examined a size-ten Birkenstock sandal and smiled at Grace. "Yours, I believe?" Sniffing, he dropped the sandal back into the pile. "No offence, lady, but it fits with your ghastly sense of style."

Holding the other two in front of his face, he compared them. "And this one, quite large for a woman's shoe, no?" He flipped it over. "No wear on the sole. Purchased on the run, perhaps? And quite chic, a perfect fit for my sweet granddaughter." He allowed the shoe to slip from his fingers.

"Look," said Grace, her tone pleading, "I'm sure we can work something out."

Signy eased back around the corner and out of sight.

"But this one?" he said, holding Signy's small sandal in front of his eyes. "Well, I think I can guess. The pretty little blond thing the Tracker wanted so badly."

Grace tried to rise but Volkov stopped her with a wave of his hand. "I'll bet her charming little foot would slip into this shoe perfectly." He dropped the sandal with a thud.

"Cinderella," Volkov called, looking down the hallway into the kitchen, then swivelling his head to look up the stairs. "Come out, come out, wherever you are."

Signy shrank back, hardly daring to breathe. Fucking Jay Hunter. Hearing the slap of Volkov's shoes on the hardwood floor as he took a few steps toward the kitchen, she risked a quick peek.

"I've seen your sick pictures, you fucking piece of shit," cried Grace, struggling to stand.

Volkov barely glanced at her, standing still now, his eyes half closed as though trying to sense Signy's presence.

He almost didn't notice as Grace flung herself forward out of the chair and lunged for the gun that he'd left so carelessly on the coffee table only a few feet from her shackled hands.

If she'd waited just a second or two longer as he moved further down the hall, he might have missed her frantic rush. The steady drone of rain on the tin roof might have masked the sound of her charge. She might have made it.

Instead, Volkov caught the flurry of movement from the corner of his eye.

Signy watched, frozen, her mind oddly detached from the reality of what she was witnessing. Volkov moved like a dancer, graceful and controlled, and for half a second she was blown away by the fluidity of his attack. Like Baryshnikov and Dracula fused into a perfect killing machine.

Grace was lying on her stomach across the coffee table, and Signy could just make out her manacled hand, clutching at the grip of Volkov's big gun. She was attempting to slide it between her palms in time to slip a finger into the trigger.

But Volkov was almost upon her and Signy knew with a dreadful certainty that Grace was hopelessly outmatched. Unable to move, she watched the scene below play out, one agonizing frame after the other, as though the rules of time and space no longer applied. She could see Grace's index finger, the ragged nail bitten to the quick, slide into the metal trigger ring.

She could hear a furious string of incomprehensible Russian as Volkov's arm sliced through the air like a scythe.

She watched in horror as Grace rolled over on her back, the grip of the gun between her palms, her finger firmly on the trigger.

"Run!" screamed Grace, her eyes darting toward the landing where Signy was hiding, even as she swung the barrel up. She squeezed the trigger.

• • •

Out on the flooded highway, the Tracker hauled on the steering wheel, sending his rental Ford Explorer into a wild spin. He'd almost missed the sign to Linden Valley. Struggling against the bucking vehicle, he fought to regain control. Shoulder muscles screaming, he managed to force the SUV back onto the road.

Heart pounding, he could hardly catch his breath. He was going to let her down. He knew it in his bones. The multicar pile-up he'd had to negotiate a few miles north of town had slowed him considerably. He slammed his fists against the wheel as the Explorer bore down on a compact car that had slowed to a crawl, its hazard lights flashing.

Jamming his foot on the accelerator, he swung out and around the smaller vehicle, not bothering to check for oncoming traffic. "Motherfucker!" he shouted, glad when the spray from his SUV drenched the smaller car, blinding the silver-haired driver.

He blinked against a sudden picture of Signy, face up in silent accusation, her blue-grey eyes fading to clay. Shouting incoherent words into empty space, he punched the side of his head with his fist. Catching sight of his own eyes in the rear-view mirror, wild and half crazy, he blinked again and remembered one of his uncle's most important lessons, "If you must panic, panic constructively."

Drawing in one ragged breath, then two, he forced his mind to cease its wild racing. Alone and in the open, Signy would have no hope against a predator like Leo the Lion, but if she'd made it to the shelter, she had a slim chance. Glancing at the glowing readout of the GPS, he noted with relief that he was less than a kilometre from the centre of town.

He tapped the accelerator, urging the Explorer to give him just a little more speed.

Chapter

47

A silenced handgun is good for many things, not the least of which is its ability to muffle the roar of the explosion that propels a bullet from the barrel—a significant factor if one does not wish to attract the attention of passersby. The bullet that Grace had just fired, although louder than Signy had expected, would have been inaudible to anyone outside the thick walls of the old house.

On the flip side, a major shortcoming of a silenced weapon is its inability to describe an arc with the same efficiency as the shorter barrel of a gun not equipped with sound-suppressing technology. Signy, inexplicably, found herself remembering these random details from the single firearms lesson she had received as a new recruit to the Line, just as Volkov knocked the gun from Grace's hand with a vicious chop.

Grace had been unable to swing the barrel fast enough, and the bullet had missed Volkov entirely.

Volkov shouted in triumph.

Signy felt paralyzed, as though every muscle in her body had turned to stone.

"*Run,*" Grace cried again, then chopped out with both feet, driving them into Volkov's gut.

Signy watched the big man double over, gasping for air, his back to her. She saw Grace grab for the gun.

"*Go,*" Grace screamed.

In the time it took to draw her next breath, Signy considered giving in to Grace's demand. She had time to make it to the bedroom and jump through the open window. Even if she broke both legs, she still had a decent chance of alerting the neighbours. At the very least, she could save herself. It was the prudent thing to do.

Instead, she flung herself down the stairs, riding the rail with her hands, her feet barely touching the ground until she thudded to a halt at the bottom. She knew Volkov had heard her. He heaved back up and turned to face her. She could see the gun in his hand.

In one fluid motion, she grabbed the scissors from her waistband, raised her hand over her head, and launched herself at him.

She saw the gun rise up between them. She was almost upon him when she saw a blur of flesh and the gun spit fire, once, twice, again.

She skittered to a halt, the scissors falling from her hand. She looked down at her chest, and then looked back up at Volkov.

He bared his teeth at her.

She brought her hands to her throat, searching for a hot gush of blood, but there was nothing there but her own smooth skin.

A high, keening wail rose from the other end of the room.

Volkov shoved past her and she heard a string of frenzied Russian, then the sickening crunch of steel on bone cut off Elena's ragged screams.

Grace?

Signy heard herself gasp, a great deep inhalation of air. She heard it rush through her mouth and down into her lungs, as if she were standing next to a roaring waterfall. She turned and saw Elena tumble from the couch, her scalp torn open, bright red blood spurting onto Grace's expensive Persian rug.

Grace?

Volkov glared at her, the bloodied handle of his pistol slick in his hand. He pointed the gun at her and his mouth moved but she couldn't hear what he said.

Arms hanging limply at her side, she lowered her eyes. She moved in slow motion, as though her mind needed time to catch up before having to face what she knew she would see.

Grace was lying twisted on the floor, exactly where she'd thrown herself moments before—directly in the path of the bullets that had been meant for Signy. Blood was spurting in regular bursts from a hole in her left side, just above her midsection. Another wound pierced her left shoulder and a third had torn into her hand. Her eyes closed, her breathing rapid, sweat beading on her forehead, her crazy Marge Simpson hair limp and lifeless.

Signy exhaled the breath she'd been holding, and as it spiralled away, she almost dropped to her knees. She jumped when she felt the barrel of the gun jab into the side of her neck. Life flooded back into her muscles.

"You see what happens when you play games, Cinderella?" Volkov whispered into her ear.

She felt a shudder run through her spine.

"Where are the pictures?"

She didn't answer.

Volkov tapped her skull with the barrel of the gun. "Wake up. Where are the pictures?"

"Upstairs," she whispered.

"Let's go." He brought the gun down and jammed it into the small of her back. "Move."

She complied, leading Volkov up the stairs and into Grace and Kim's bedroom. She paused.

"Where?" he asked.

She turned to the bookcase and pointed at the bottom shelf.

"Get them," he said, sticking her with the point of the gun.

She stumbled forward, then squatted down, the balls of her feet pressed into the floor. She wrapped her hands around the largest album she could find.

"In there?" he asked, leaning over her shoulder.

She felt the gun barrel slide down the small of her back. She nodded, then hefted the heavy album in her hands and hunched over it, forcing him to lean even further over her shoulder. She could no longer feel the gun touch her flesh.

"Open it," he said. "I want to be sure—"

Signy didn't give him the chance to finish the sentence. She

380

sprang up, using her legs to drive the entire weight of her body backwards into the big man. She felt him take a step back, off balance. She twirled in place, swinging the heavy book like a baseball bat.

She followed through with every ounce of strength she had, just like her foster father had taught her. She aimed for his head and felt a thrill of triumph as she heard the outer cover crack into the centre of his face.

He roared in pain and stumbled backwards.

Signy shoved past him and was almost out the door when she felt a hand grasp her T-shirt and drag her back. She jabbed backwards with her elbow and felt it connect with soft flesh.

Another bellow of rage and she was free. She made it to the hallway before he was on her again. He grabbed her from behind and she bent forward at the waist, forcing him down with her. And when she felt him start to haul her back in, she leapt off the floor, whipping her head back, feeling it slam off his forehead. He fell to one knee.

She turned to face him. He glared up at her. Despite a significant gash above his right eye, he seemed relatively unscathed. Worse, he was between her and the top of the staircase, cutting off her only escape route. She turned on her heel and raced down the hallway.

She could hear him clamber to his feet behind her. She was out of time. Just ahead, on the wall, she saw the outline of an old-fashioned laundry chute. They'd had one in the Shepherd farmhouse. She gripped the handle and pulled the door open.

Hiking her lower body into the open space, she experienced a moment's cold certainty that in the next second Volkov would catch her hanging half in and half out of the chute and break her neck.

She had managed to haul her entire body into the chute and was hanging by her fingers just as Volkov regained his feet. With a wild bellow, he lunged at her. She felt his fingertips brush the top of her head.

She let go.

• • • •

The Tracker approached the fresh-faced officer standing on the sidewalk outside the women's shelter. Pulling up a few seconds earlier, he'd been shocked at the level of police presence. At least five or six Linden Valley cruisers lined the street; another two sat abandoned, doors ajar, in the shelter's driveway.

Exiting his own vehicle, he'd tried not to run toward the flashing lights and chaotic squawking of police radios, relieved that the cops milling about were attentive but not tense. There was a casual air to the entire situation that would not be present if anything particularly serious had gone down. He dared to breathe.

"Hey there," he called to what had to be Linden Valley's newest recruit.

"Sir?" asked the young cop, his desire to be of assistance to a good citizen evident in the eager lilt of his voice.

"What's going on?" asked the Tracker, nodding toward the shelter. "My girlfriend's inside." He wiped rain from his eyes, moisture he hoped the cop might mistake for tears. "She's not answering her cell. Is everything okay?" He pretended to push past the young officer.

Placing a gentle but restraining hand on the Tracker's arm, the cop said, "You'll have to stay back, sir."

The Tracker took a step back, allowing the cop the pleasure of exercising his newfound power while at the same time indicating that he was indeed a compliant, honest citizen genuinely concerned about nothing more than his poor, trapped girlfriend.

"Is everyone okay in there?"

"I can assure you that everything is under control. Everyone inside is present and accounted for."

The Tracker took his first real breath of air since he'd tried to call Signy over an hour ago.

"The thing is," said the cop, unable to pass up the opportunity to share his inside knowledge, "something big is going down in there. The whole place is in lockdown. No personal calls in or out."

The Tracker allowed his jaw to drop open.

"I heard they called in the feds," continued the cop, lowering his voice to a whisper, "RCMP or CSIS or something like that."

"No shit!" Assuming the casual slouch and monosyllabic speech of an average Joe, the Tracker shoved his hands into his front pockets.

The boy nodded, importantly.

"But my girl's okay? You wouldn't bullshit me?"

The young cop shook his head. "No, sir. Like I said, everyone inside is in good shape."

Peering over the cop's shoulder, the Tracker caught a glimpse of the SUV he'd rented back in Calgary parked in back of the shelter. That crazy girl, she'd done it. She was inside and she was safe. And if she still had the pictures, then Leonid Volkov was doomed. It took some effort not to jump for joy in front of the boy.

"How long before they can leave?" the Tracker asked.

"I dunno about the women and children, but they tell me they're keeping the staff for some kind of debrief. I heard my sergeant talking about taking statements and all that, but they aren't going to do anything until the big boys get here." He removed his police-issue rain hat and shook it before replacing it on his head. "I wouldn't expect her for a few hours yet."

"Guess I might as well wait for her at home, then?" The Tracker looked uncertainly at the boy.

The young cop nodded.

"Thanks a lot, man," said the Tracker, reaching out to shake the cop's hand.

Back inside his Ford Explorer, the Tracker punched Signy's address into the GPS, then smiled. She lived only a few blocks away. He turned the key in the ignition and swung out onto the road. Signy was safe. If he was lucky, she would give him a second chance.

He relaxed into his seat and smiled. Things could be worse.

Chapter

48

Signy plummeted like a stone into a pile of soiled linens, landing on her backside with an unceremonious thump. Momentarily stunned, she took stock, running her mind over bones and muscles. A sharp ache in her left ankle burned and she twirled her foot in a wide circle, shaking it out. Although her coccyx had taken the impact of the fall and she'd felt the jolt all the way up her spine, for now she was just numb. If she managed to stay alive until tomorrow, she knew she was going to hurt like hell.

She lay back in the pile of sheets and towels, overcome by a wave of apathy. Volkov was two floors above and she was squandering the time she'd bought for herself, lying amid Grace's wrinkled sheets. She had to move.

She sat up and was instantly ambushed by the sloppy tongue of Chivas. Gasping, she shoved his massive face away, which only caused him to redouble his efforts, and with much huffing doggy laughter he mounted a full-on attack.

Snapped from her momentary stupor, she managed to get onto her hands and knees and crawl away from the linen pile. Sweeping her hands in front of her, she recoiled as her palms scraped the icy damp of the crumbling concrete floor. The dark was absolute, making the crunch of Volkov's heavy steps overhead seem even more ominous.

Where was she? More specifically, where was the stairway that led up to the kitchen? Calling up a mental blueprint of the house in her mind, she pictured the location of the laundry chute. It had been installed almost dead centre in the house, which meant she had fallen somewhere near the middle of the basement space.

She pushed Chivas away from her face. If she was in the middle and if she was facing east, that put the stairs somewhere off to her right. Good. She would find the staircase and use it to get up to the main level. From there it was only a few feet to the kitchen door that opened out onto the back garden. Not much of a plan, but it was all she had.

She crawled forward, tentative in the pitch black, while the dog continued his game of push and shove. She didn't risk hissing at him to leave her alone. The violent scene replayed in front of her eyes. She shuddered. Leo's attack had been almost preternatural. He'd moved with the same lightning speed as his namesake, and she wouldn't be surprised if his hearing proved just as acute.

She had to find the stairs. Scrambling forward on all fours in what she hoped was the right direction, she plowed heavily into a vertical support beam. Her head struck the sharp corner of the metal jack with full force and she reeled back, unable to stifle a cry of pain.

Reaching up, she felt blood, hot and slick, dripping freely from a gash over her right eye. Shit. She felt an unsettling shimmer of nausea and gulped a breath of dank underground air. Beside her, the dog whimpered and she felt the cold poke of his nose as he explored her wound.

"Cinderella?" The aluminum walls of the chute amplified his playful inquiry.

The dog growled.

Signy pressed herself up against the metal beam and stared blindly over her shoulder, wondering for one sickening moment if Volkov might follow her down through the chute. Not possible, she thought, the guy was the size of a horse. She resumed her rapid crawl toward the stairs.

"Leaving the party so soon?" called Volkov. He sounded so close that Signy thought she'd been wrong, that he'd somehow managed to squeeze himself down the chute and had landed right behind her.

The dog's growling deepened, and Signy imagined the wiry hair on his back and neck standing on end.

"Good boy," she said. "Kill the fucking bastard."

As though he had read her thoughts, the dog answered with a deep, rumbling snarl.

"I can hear you," Volkov whispered down the hollow chute.

"Come on," she said, clutching a wad of fur in her hand. "You want a treat?" Could dogs see in the dark? She wasn't sure, but she knew Chivas liked his Milk-Bones and she was pretty sure he'd know that they were stored in the kitchen. "Come on, let's go get a treat." The dog charged ahead, dragging her with him.

Signy could hear distorted titters wafting down the tube.

"I haven't had this much fun in years!"

She flinched. The man was demented.

"Ready or not," Volkov shouted in a creepy singsong, "here I come!"

If Volkov was trying to terrorize her, it was working. Her muscles turned to rubber and searing cramps gripped her bowels. She gasped for breath. It was too much. She couldn't do this. She wondered whether if she squeezed her eyes shut tightly enough, she might wake up and this would be nothing more than one of her crazy nightmares.

It was the sound of Volkov's heavy footsteps pounding overhead that broke the spell. This was no imaginary boogey monster with raisins for eyes, and she had no magical powers. She allowed the dog to drag her forward and was rewarded when she struck the bottom riser of the basement steps with the palm of her hand.

"Go," she whispered to the dog, shoving him in front of her. The dog scrambled to the top of the stairs as she groped for the handrail.

"Come out, come out, wherever you are!"

She could hear Volkov thumping down the stairs toward the main level.

Grasping the handrail, she gritted her teeth against the bleak scenarios playing out in her head and climbed the stairs after the dog.

Standing on the upper landing, she pressed her ear to the

door and listened. Volkov had reached the bottom of the stairs and was making the turn around the newel post, heading directly for her.

She bent down and growled into the dog's ear, "Get him, boy. Get him. *Kill!*"

She flung open the door and let loose the hound. Chivas charged the crazed Russian, now just a few feet away and moving fast. Volkov raised his arm, the long barrel of the silencer aimed at the dog.

Chivas leaped, one hundred and fifty pounds of pure muscle, aimed directly at Volkov's exposed throat.

As she scrambled on wobbly legs toward the back door, Signy couldn't help casting a quick glance over her shoulder. But instead of seeing Chivas, his muzzle dripping with blood, savaging Volkov's prone body, she watched the big dog place a massive paw on the Russian's shoulder and whine happily.

She stopped dead, wide-eyed in disbelief.

Grinning at her over the dog's broad shoulder, Volkov called out in high good humour, "Looks like old Go Fuck Yourself is living up to his name. Every man for himself, as they say."

"Bastard," she shouted, then whirled back toward the door.

Behind her Volkov wrestled with the dog, which seemed immensely entertained by Volkov's thrusts and parries. Signy heard a grunt and then what she presumed must be the gun clattering to the floor before the wrestling match concluded with a serious yelp of pain from the dog. The click of the dog's nails on the wood floor as it retreated back down the hallway was one of the saddest sounds she'd ever heard.

In one last desperate lunge she reached the back door and

gripped the handle. She had just managed to turn the knob when her head was slammed forward, thick fingers gouging into the back of her neck.

Volkov's hot breath seared the side of her face as he brought his mouth to her ear. "Where are my pictures?" He yanked her head back, exposing the soft flesh of her neck. She tasted blood as the cut above her eye continued to drip unabated into her gaping mouth and up her nose.

"What?" She croaked, as he dug his fingers even deeper into her throat.

"No more games, Cinder—"

That was as far as he got. Signy lifted her foot and drove it backwards into his kneecap. She was almost overwhelmed by a sickening sense of joy when she felt his patella give way with a satisfying crunch.

Roaring, Volkov loosened his grip for a split second, just enough time for her to wrench free. She spun to face him, driving her fist into the centre of his face. She meant to shatter the cartilage in his nose and drive it directly into his brain if she could. But his skull felt like it was made of concrete, and instead of the satisfying crack of his nose, all she felt was a searing pain in her knuckles. She gasped.

Sheets of scarlet spurted from Volkov's nostrils, adding to the gore running freely from the split in his eyebrow. He grinned, using his tongue to swipe at the blood, smearing his perfect white dentures.

With Volkov standing between her and the kitchen door, she turned and raced down the hallway, following the same path that Chivas had taken a few seconds before. Stretching out before her like a demented Salvador Dalí painting, the hallway seemed to grow longer with every step she took.

Behind her, she heard Volkov cough once, the splat of his blood as it hit the floor, and then he was up and moving. Understanding that she was seconds from death, she wondered for a brief instant how much it would hurt.

Her fingers brushed the handle of the front door and she cried out in triumph. Once outside she could easily outrun an unarmed old man with a dislocated knee.

She yanked the door open, and just as she felt the cooling touch of rain on her face, her head was wrenched back so hard she thought her neck might break. Volkov had her braid in his fist. Tripping over her feet, she fell backwards, her head smacking against the hardwood floor with a sickening thud, sparks flashing before her eyes.

She tried to raise her arms, but in one blinding move he straddled her body with his. She bucked beneath him but it was as though an elephant were crushing her chest. She struggled to breathe.

As her vision blurred, she was still able to make out his shock of white hair looming over her and the dreadful spray of scarlet that dripped from his nostrils with every ragged exhalation.

"Looks like the clock just tolled midnight, Cinderella." The words were garbled, as blood pooled in his sinuses and filled his mouth. He wrapped the meaty fingers of one hand around her throat and squeezed. With the other he scrabbled in his back pocket.

She felt the delicate cartilage in her throat begin to crack under the pressure. He released his hold for a split second, and as she gulped in one breath of air, the world exploded in a blinding flash of light. She shut her eyes tight, but the image of his leering face was burnt onto the insides of her retinas.

He had taken her picture. The sick fuck was holding a camera in front of her face. She wrenched her head to one side, sinking her teeth into his arm. He grunted in pain but did not reel back as she had hoped. Instead, he pressed down again on her throat, and again she felt the world begin to recede.

She opened her eyes wide, trying to hang on to the light. She could feel the rain slashing across her face and into her gaping mouth. She could hear him panting and smell the ferric odour of his blood splattering on her face. Then a black cloud overwhelmed her, and her fight was done.

Chapter

49

Slipping into Signy's apartment, the Tracker wrinkled his nose. Outside, the rain had abated somewhat, the steady drizzle splattering against the window panes almost comforting. Striding over to the window overlooking the street, he flung it wide. Something reeked.

Standing in place, he conducted a quick reconnaissance. He approved. The small space was uncluttered. No useless bric-a-brac, and the furniture was cheap but serviceable.

He smiled as he picked up a taser that had been discarded carelessly in the middle of the kitchen table. He'd bet money that she'd found the need to use it more than once. To be on the safe side, he tucked it high on a shelf in the tiny front-hall cupboard before resuming his investigation.

He walked over to a rickety bookshelf that barely supported two rows of hardcover volumes. He ran his hand over the spines, taking in the titles. *Girl, Interrupted; An Unquiet Mind; A Memoir of Moods and Madness; The Curious Incident of the Dog in the Night-Time.*

Okay, he thought, running his eyes over other titles, all of them covering similar material. She works with people who live with these issues, why wouldn't she be interested? Squatting, he tried to find any lighthearted romance or mystery fiction.

He shook his head. Not one book had been purchased merely for pleasure. She was driven, but then he'd known that already. He popped back up. What was that foul smell?

Walking into the galley kitchen, he pinpointed the source of the odour immediately. She'd forgotten to take out the garbage and it was leaking an oily liquid onto the floor. He rummaged about until he found a carton of green garbage bags and, using one, scooped up the sopping mess. After tying the bag with a double knot, he ran downstairs and tossed it in a bin beside the house.

Back inside, he flipped on the tap and, as he waited for the water to heat up, picked up a bottle of liquid dish soap, squeezing a generous dollop into the middle of the greasy pool on the floor. Using a dishtowel, he scrubbed up the spill, taking care not to leave any slippery residue.

After a thorough rinsing, he hung the dishtowel neatly over the oven door. Exploring the remaining few cupboards and drawers, he found nothing out of the ordinary. He leaned against the counter and shook his head. He was not sure what he was looking for.

Having exhausted the living room and the kitchen, he walked into the bedroom. Her taste was commendable. The space was austere. No homey photographs in colourful frames festooning the walls, no scented candles or dried flowers or, God forbid, stuffed animals. Like him, she did not seem to have strong attachments.

Fortunately, a lack of strong bonds did not necessarily imply a lack of intensity. He smiled, ruefully. Signy had certainly displayed plenty of passion, and in his experience passionate people rarely existed in a vacuum. No matter how austere their surroundings, they always kept something, a memento of a time and place that held meaning.

He checked the armoire first. Opening the heavy door, he came close to revising his opinion. Despite her uncluttered existence, she most certainly did not maintain an orderly closet. Blouses and jackets and bright cotton dresses swung haphazardly from mismatched hangers, and there was no semblance at all of an organizational system. He clucked his tongue.

A mountain of laundry had accumulated on the floor. He sniffed. It must have been ages since she'd last been to the laundromat. Backing away from the offensive closet, he bent down and examined the space under the bed. He'd often noticed women using plastic bins on wheels that slid under the bed for extra storage. Under Signy's bed, however, he found nothing more exciting than a couple of forlorn dust bunnies.

Sitting on the corner of the bed, he scanned the room again. The only other furniture was a flimsy bedside table on which sat a student lamp. It had no drawer, but on a shelf underneath the tabletop he found a dog-eared copy of *Calming the Emotional Storm*. A definite theme was developing in terms of her reading choices.

Having exhausted all possible hiding places, he reluctantly returned to the armoire and began to haul out the soiled clothing, tossing armfuls onto the floor behind him. When it was clear, he slid his hand along the floor of the cupboard and was rewarded with the discovery of a hand-carved box tucked in the back corner.

Hefting it in one hand, he examined the exterior. Judging by its soft red glow, he surmised it had been crafted from cherry wood and the fine workmanship along with her name etched on the lid suggested it had been created by a loving hand.

He felt his heart beat in his chest.

Opening the lid, the first thing he saw was a thin stack of photographs. He picked up the first picture and smiled. It showed Signy at age eight or nine, dressed in a baseball uniform and grinning at the camera. She had a bat slung over one shoulder and was sporting an impressive shiner.

In the next, she stood awkwardly, stuffed into a frothy pink nightmare of a dress, glowering at the camera. Beside her, a pimply boy in a blue dress suit holding a gaudy corsage squinted into the camera. Grade eight graduation perhaps?

Setting aside the rest of the pictures, he rummaged through the remaining contents. A battered red dog tag in the shape of a heart with the name Jingles carved onto the scratched surface. A dusty roach still wrapped in disintegrating rolling paper carefully stored in a twist of saran wrap. A rectangle of cardboard on which two rows of numbers suggested some long-ago scorecard, and judging by the final result, it appeared she'd beaten the pants off someone named Jilly Anderson.

But it was the flash of scarlet in the bottom corner of the box that stole his breath away. He stared in awe at a tangle of sturdy red ribbon undamaged after all these years. Picking it up with trembling fingers, he laid it across his wrist and knew his long search was finally at an end.

Chapter

50

"Signy, darling," Maitland said, "this has gone on long enough."

Cracking open one eye, Signy glared up at the wizened yet strangely beautiful face. "Leave me alone."

"I really can't do that, dear. The ambulance is here and we're almost ready to go."

Signy jerked up into a sitting position, causing her head to spin with such force that she crumpled backwards. "Grace?" she whispered. Her throat felt like it was on fire.

Maitland looked over her shoulder to where a mass of uniformed bodies were milling about. Signy could hear the beeping of medical equipment, the squeal of a gurney as it was cranked into position, and the urgency of strained voices barking out orders.

"Grace is in good hands, dear."

Signy was not reassured. Underneath her calm composure, Signy could hear the grating anxiety in Maitland's voice. She felt a squeezing pressure on her arm and looked down to see an automatic blood pressure cuff filling with air. She reached out blindly, trying to rip it off her arm.

"Don't touch," said Maitland, brushing her hand away. "The paramedic is monitoring your vitals."

Signy tried to swallow but ended up coughing instead.

Maitland held out a small cup of water.

"What?"

"Take a sip of water, dear. You've sustained a rather nasty injury to your throat."

Raising her head enough to allow Maitland to bring the cup to her mouth, she had a vivid flashback to Volkov's leering face as he straddled her body, his blood spraying onto her cheeks with each snorting breath and the brutality of his thick fingers digging into her flesh. Her eyes flew open and she attempted to struggle to her feet.

Placing a restraining hand on her shoulder, Maitland said slowly, so that she understood the full implications, "It's all right. Volkov is in custody." Slipping an arm under Signy's shoulders, she helped her to rise to a sitting position before offering the cup again.

Signy sipped the water, slowly at first, the inflamed tissues in her throat recoiling from the cool liquid. After several sips, however, the soothing effects of the water began to have an impact and she started to feel better. She risked speaking.

"Grace? Elena?"

Maitland stared back at her, eyes brimming with tears, and

was about to speak when two burly paramedics were upon them, hustling Maitland out of the way and lifting Signy onto a gurney.

Maitland held her hand as the paramedics manoeuvred the gurney through the front door, then down the walkway toward a waiting ambulance. A steady rain was still falling and one of the attendants held a sheet over her head, effectively blinding her, but the wail of a siren and the screeching of tires told her that another ambulance had just screamed away.

Maitland accompanied her during the short ride over to Linden Valley General, holding her hand and fussing as a paramedic busied himself with applying a butterfly bandage to the cut over her eye.

Signy turned to face the wall. Two ambulances had left before hers, one for Grace and one for Elena. Hers had gone last and with much less fanfare. She felt beads of sweat bloom on her forehead and thought she might vomit.

"Self-pity simply will not do, darling," said Maitland into her ear. "You are not to blame for Volkov's actions."

Ignoring Maitland's silly words, she focused instead on the paramedic who was currently inserting a large-bore needle into the back of her hand. She revelled in the searing pain as the needle penetrated her skin, tearing into a delicate vein. She was gratified by the dull ache that pulsed in her hand once he had taped the needle down, and the unpleasant sensation of cold liquid seeping into her arm.

Who was to blame if not her? She'd been too stupid to spot Volkov's tail until it was too late. She'd been naive as a schoolgirl accepting that lying bastard Jay Hunter at face value. And it had been her decision to race down those stairs instead of going for help. She should have known Grace would try something stupid. She might as well have pulled the trigger herself.

Then she did vomit, hot bile searing her throat as she heaved over and over, the muscles in her chest and abdomen wrenching with the effort. The paramedic had been ready with a kidney-shaped plastic pan and held it under her mouth until she was finished. Maitland stroked her hair and murmured sympathetic bullshit, which did nothing but make Signy want to curl even further into herself.

A sudden jolt sent waves of pain through her injured coccyx, signalling that the ambulance had arrived at the hospital. The back doors were thrown open and the two EMS workers had her extracted and jostling through to the emergency room within seconds. She could hear Maitland calling out encouragement from somewhere behind as her gurney was slammed feet first through a set of double doors and into the treatment area.

The paramedic who had treated her in the ambulance checked her blood pressure monitor one last time before wishing her luck. She watched him saunter over to the triage desk, where he gave a verbal summary to the nurse. She'd been left in the hallway presumably because the two trauma treatment rooms were already occupied.

Grace.

Elena.

Signy turned her face to the wall and squeezed her eyes shut but was unable to block out the jarring racket. The rubber-soled shoes of harried nurses squeaking on the linoleum as they hustled past, metal instruments clanging in steel trays, the relentless squawk of the intercom as specialist after specialist was paged to the ER.

Kim was there, just behind the curtain where Grace was being stabilized less than ten feet away. Signy tried not to listen to the break in Kim's voice as she pleaded with Grace to hang on, to please hang on. When Kim started to sob in harsh, rasping gasps, Signy slapped her hands over her ears and clamped her jaw until all she could hear was the grating sound of her teeth grinding against each other.

And then Grace was being wheeled down the corridor in a flurry of tubes, machines, and wires, to be loaded onto a helicopter waiting to fly her to the nearest Level I trauma centre. Signy knew that this was a trip reserved for the most critically injured patients.

She squeezed her eyes tighter and sent out a silent prayer. She had never believed in God or any other sort of higher power. She only trusted in herself, a faith that had been misplaced, it seemed. She asked whoever might be listening to please save her friend, Grace, who had done nothing wrong other than offer a stubborn girl a second chance.

Things quieted down after Grace was whisked away. Signy dared to remove her hands from her ears and was relieved to hear Elena's voice, clear and steady, in one of the nearby examining rooms. She felt one small section of her gut unclench. Elena was okay. At least that was something.

It was some time before she felt gentle hands turning her over, examining the wound above her eye, then wheeling her gurney into one of the treatment rooms. Soft voices murmured encouragements, but she barely flinched as a needle filled with anaesthetic was driven over and over again into the ragged wound.

She was relieved when a green cotton sheet was draped over

her eyes while a row of sutures was expertly tied by a short doctor with an efficient manner. For those few minutes, as she hid beneath the sheet, she could pretend that she was alone in her apartment, that none of this had happened, and that she had not been the cause of Grace's death.

Then it was over. She was given a tetanus shot, the IV was removed, and she was helped out into the waiting room, where Maitland rose to greet her.

"Darling," cried Maitland, grasping both of Signy's hands in her own. "How are you?"

Signy allowed Maitland to complete a critical examination of her various cuts and bruises.

Threading her arm through Signy's, Maitland said that she would provide an update on Grace and Elena but that first she needed a hot cup of tea and something to eat. She led Signy to a small coffee shop located on the south end of the grand atrium and sat her at a table before going over to the counter, where she selected a bowl of hot chicken soup, a whole wheat bun, and two giant chocolate chip cookies. Waving off her chauffeur hovering nearby, Maitland tottered back over to the table, balancing the entire order on one tray.

Signy knew she should stand and offer to help but she simply did not have the energy.

Placing the bowl of steaming soup in front of Signy, Maitland handed her the spoon. Signy stared dully at the bowl, her stomach doing backflips.

"Eat!" commanded Maitland in her most regal voice.

With no choice but to comply, Signy brought a spoonful to her lips, forcing herself to swallow. Not bad. In fact, the sensation of the hot chicken soup sliding down her sore throat was so pleasant that she took another spoonful, then another. Before long she had practically inhaled the entire bowl and was working on the bun. She could feel vitality return to her body, although her spirits were still mired far below rock bottom.

"Your colour is coming back," said Maitland.

Signy looked away.

Maitland picked up one of the giant cookies. "Would you look at the size of this thing?" Protestations aside, Maitland proceeded to bite off an enormous section with great gusto. She handed the second cookie to Signy.

"Are you feeling steadier?" Maitland asked, dabbing at her mouth with a paper napkin, brushing away crumbs.

Signy stared down at her cookie, then nodded.

"Then I'll fill you in," said Maitland, leaning forward. "It was quite the scene, I must say. When I arrived, Volkov had you pinned to the floor and was quite literally throttling the life out of you."

Signy poked at some crumbs that had fallen onto the table.

"Marshall was there. You remember Marshall?"

Signy nodded. She remembered the driver with the kind eyes.

"He was amazing." She flashed Signy a wide grin. "Suffice it to say that, Russian mobster or not, everyone understands the power of a double-barrelled shotgun."

"Where is Volkov now?"

"The RCMP took over from the local force. They arrested him and he's in their custody now." Maitland took another bite of cookie and chewed thoughtfully. "To be perfectly candid, dear, at times like these I wish Canada had its own Guantánamo Bay."

Signy twisted her mouth in the semblance of a smile.

"Oh, he's making all sorts of noise about his rights, miscarriage of justice, and what not, but I'm sure it's all for naught. They have him dead to rights on forcible confinement and attempted murder, and with the pictures you described, he will be a guest of the Canadian prison system for the rest of his life. In fact, it's possible that Russia will seek his extradition." She looked at Signy. "Speaking of those pictures, you do have them?"

Signy explained where she had hidden the package.

Maitland opened her purse, extracted her phone, then placed a quick call. She relayed Signy's information to the person on the other end of the line.

"How did you know where to find us?" Signy asked, after Maitland had disconnected.

"When you weren't at the meeting location, and with the horrible storm, I figured you'd had to turn back. I tried to call but couldn't get anyone on the phone, and that's when I began to get very worried."

"Volkov cut the lines," said Signy. "I tried to flag down a cop, but—"

Maitland nodded. "You did your best, dear. Everyone understands that."

Frowning, Signy picked at the bandage that covered the hole in the back of her hand left by the IV needle.

"That reminds me, I brought you a new phone." Maitland reached into her handbag and handed Signy a brand new Samsung. "All set and ready to go."

Signy accepted the phone, mutely.

"You know what happened next," Maitland continued.

"Once the RCMP moved in, they left a guard at the shelter in the event Volkov decided to make his move there, and I raced over to Grace's house hoping that the three of you were there taking shelter from the storm." She brushed a few remaining crumbs from the table. "The rest, as they say, is history."

Signy nodded, picking at the little bandage until she'd removed it completely. She wrapped it in a paper napkin and stuffed it into her empty bowl. "Will Elena be okay?" she asked, glancing up at Maitland.

"She's resting comfortably. She sustained a concussion and they will be keeping her overnight for observation, but all signs point to a complete recovery."

Signy closed her eyes with relief.

"I peeked in on her while they were stitching you up. I arranged to have Mrs. Zhang flown in to be with her. A lovely woman. Despite her recent loss, she was more than willing to help."

Signy flashed a tiny smile. "Elena will be so glad."

"She asked me to give you a message, Signy."

Twisting a piece of Cellophane between her fingers, Signy stared at the rain-slicked window, barely noticing the bright lights of the cars as they streaked past outside.

"She told me to tell you how thankful she is, that she will never forget what you did for her."

Turning back to face Maitland, Signy said, "Do you think I could go home now? I'm tired."

"Goodness," cried Maitland, rising slowly to her feet, "of course. You must be exhausted."

Signy glanced around uncertainly. "I don't have a ride."

"Don't be silly, dear, I'll take you home." She placed a hand on Signy's shoulder, then continued. "You wait here while I find Marshall."

Maitland walked back into the grand atrium, her high heels clicking on the tile floor.

Watching her go, Signy caught the eye of a young girl staring at her with undisguised horror. Looking down, Signy realized she was a mess. Her thin T-shirt was sprayed with Volkov's blood and plenty of her own besides. Half her forehead was swaddled in gauze bandaging, and with the circle of bruises around her neck she probably looked like a monster.

"*Cinderella . . .*"

She shivered as the taunting voice of Volkov rang in her ears. Turning away in order to avoid further trauma to the poor little girl, she found herself eye to eye with Kim Blackwater.

Signy gasped.

"May I sit?" asked Kim, not bothering to wait for an answer. She barely rested on the edge of the plastic seat. She was wearing civvies, having changed out of her hospital scrubs.

"Grace?" Signy asked, looking down at her shoes.

"Critical. She was medevaced to Sunnybrook."

Signy didn't raise her eyes.

"I'm on my way there now." Kim folded the raincoat she had slung over one arm. "Before I go, there's something I need to say to you."

Signy raised her eyes and looked directly at Grace's spiky-haired lover.

"Before you came into our lives," said Kim, "things were good. Grace was better, you know? On track."

Signy held Kim's dark gaze with her own, not allowing herself the relief of looking away.

"But then you showed up and she changed. She started making poor choices again, taking risks." Her eyes narrowed. "I think she needed to prove something. It didn't matter that I practically begged her to stop. Nothing I said mattered. I didn't matter. Only Signy damn Shepherd mattered, so much so that she invited hell on earth into our home."

Signy opened her mouth to protest, to explain that it was not Grace's fault, that she had been the one who had brought damnation down on all their heads.

"Can it," said Kim, her tone final. "Grace thinks you're a bloody hero, a fucking Viking warrior." She brought her face within inches of Signy's. "We know better, don't we?"

Forcing herself not to shy away, Signy stared into Kim's dark, flat eyes and felt her hands curl into fists.

Oh Dear, what can the matter be? Johnny's so long at the fair.

She dropped her eyes to the floor, relaxed her fingers, then nodded.

Kim rose and strode toward the front exit without another word or a backward glance.

Signy hadn't moved by the time Maitland returned a few minutes later, Marshall in tow. She allowed herself to be lifted gently to her feet and propelled out toward the front entrance, where Maitland's Rolls-Royce waited.

Chapter

51

Slumped on Signy's bed, the Tracker wound the red ribbon around his wrist. As he stared at the flash of scarlet draped across his pale flesh, his thoughts flashed back to that icy day, so many years ago, when everything had changed.

He'd never been able to remember the events as a concise whole. Instead, they swirled in his memory as a fractured mix of hazy images, sharp smells, and half-remembered sounds.

The hiss of his leather slippers as he skidded through his mother's blood, then coming to rest by her side, the bottom of his pyjamas soaked with gore.

He remembered the terrible smell, coppery and dank, like the inside of his piggy bank. And from somewhere far away, the sound of shrieking, high and keening, that only later he understood had been his own.

Fingering the ragged end of the red ribbon, the Tracker drew in a deep breath that did little to fill the empty space in his chest. Above all, he remembered his mother's eyes. Her startling blue eyes, soft and tender as she tucked him and his baby sister into bed each night, safe and warm. How those blue eyes had danced as she sang them to sleep with half-remembered songs.

But on that icy night, he had not been safe. He had not been warm. On the night that had changed everything, he sat beside his mother, soaked in her blood, holding her hand, and watched while her blue eyes slowly faded to clay. He stayed by her side even after he heard the monster return, heard him climb through the smashed window and call out his name. *Johnny? John? Son?*

Barely aware of the firm surface of Signy's bed underneath his legs, he closed his eyes. He remembered climbing a mountain of stairs, each riser higher than the last, and the angle too steep for his small legs. Still, he scrambled upward—the monster, yelling his name, only seconds behind. He had to save her.

He remembered reaching the top of the stairs at last, then running down the long hall to where she lay sleeping in her small bed. His breath coming so hard and so fast, he was sure he would die before he could reach her.

He remembered slamming the door behind him, the monster so close behind that he could feel fire on the back of his neck. Holding a hand over her tiny mouth as he tried to lift her from her bed. *Please, please, please, run with me*, he remembered begging, but compliance had not been in her nature.

Opening his eyes, the Tracker fingered the picture of Signy at eight, a triumphant grin splitting her face despite her swollen eye.

Staring sightlessly, he recalled the crack of splintering wood

410

as the monster crashed through her bedroom door, and the consuming sadness that overwhelmed him when he realized they had nowhere to go, that he had failed.

Face contorting, he turned his head away, remembering the tiny blue-eyed demon screaming, slashing, and tearing at the monster. His blond-haired demon sister ripping, shredding, and clawing to live.

Mostly he remembered himself, stricken, shamed, a coward in the face of her defiant courage. The unrelenting horror he lived with every day of his life.

He remembered the back of the monster's car, tied together with the pretty red ribbon. He remembered how it looked just like the scarlet of his mother's blood. Bound this way together for how long? Minutes? Hours? Days?

The monster's voice, low and flat: "Eat some fries, kids." And when the monster bared his sharp teeth, both of them had shoved spongy, cold potatoes down their throats until he thought they might choke.

Time passed as they huddled in the back seat of the big car, the leather seats icy against his pyjamas. Minutes? Hours? Days? He'd craned his neck and chanced a look outside. Above him, round black eyes glared down from the sky.

Sam the Record Man?

Sam I Am, his mother once read to him with her lively blue eyes.

Eat some fries, kids.

He remembered the lights. And he remembered the people, hundreds and thousands and millions of people, lining the sidewalks, peering down from office windows, driving in cars.

411

And so, the coward brother had taken one last chance. Shoving his hands into the pocket of his jacket, his fingers closed on the little pocket knife his father had given him on his sixth birthday. He rubbed the familiar smoothness of the pearl handle before springing open the knife with a practiced flick of his thumb.

Watching the monster in the rear-view mirror, he used the knife to sever the tie that bound him to his sister. Then, with a banshee scream for courage, he'd buried the little knife up to the hilt in the monster's shoulder. When the car screamed to a halt, the monster roaring furiously, he'd flown, dragging his demon sister behind him.

Inside his head his mother had screamed, *Save her, save her, save her.*

He remembered throwing her, hiding her, keeping her safe. Begging her to please, please, please be quiet.

And this one time, above all others, she had listened to him, and when the monster came, drumming death in the hollows of the alley, he'd let himself be taken.

Unwinding the ribbon from his wrist, he returned it to its place of honour at the bottom of the little cherrywood box. For the first time since that icy day in 1986 when everything had changed forever, he knew that his efforts had not been in vain.

He walked slowly through the apartment, turning off all the lights. As the darkness settled around him, he sat at the kitchen table and, for the first time since that fateful day, covered his face with his hands and wept.

Inside his head he heard his mother's sweet voice, and he remembered that it was she who sang the little tune that had been bothering him since he first saw Signy. His mother sang the little song at night while she held him close and waited for him to fall into a dreamless sleep.

It tinkled to life in his head, sweet and pretty, and he listened to it without fear, then rested his head in his hands, and let himself remember.

Oh dear, what can the matter be?
Oh dear, what can the matter be?
Oh dear, what can the matter be?
Johnny's so long at the fair.

• • •

"Would you like some company," asked Maitland, as the Rolls slid to a halt in front of Signy's apartment, "just until you fall asleep?"

Signy had spent the ride from the hospital keeled over in the back seat, her forehead pressed to the cool window. She opened her eyes and stared blankly for a second or two, then shook her head. "I'll be fine."

Maitland squeezed her knee with a surprisingly strong grip. "Please, get some rest. I'll pick you up in the morning and we'll go see Grace."

Signy fumbled for the door handle, but Marshall was already out and trotting around the front of the car. He held the door open for her as she stepped out.

"Marshall?" Signy looked up into the man's face. A keloid

scar ran from the centre of his left eyebrow down toward his ear. On another man it might have appeared menacing, but Marshall's eyes were calm and kind.

He dipped his chin.

"Thanks."

He smiled, then shut the door with a soft click.

"I mean it," she said, holding his gaze. "If there's ever anything . . ."

He grinned. "I'll hold you to that, Ms. Shepherd."

"You do that, and Marshall? Call me Signy. Please." She headed up the walkway, unmindful of the light rain, turning once to wave briefly as the Rolls pulled away. Sighing, she dragged her aching body up the stairs to her apartment.

Slipping the key into the front door lock, she remembered the last time she'd arrived home this battered and exhausted. It was after that horror show with Dalton the younger and his haunted little girls. She shut the door. It seemed like a hundred years ago now. She leaned back against the door, soaking in the lonely silence.

It didn't matter now what their names were. It was over. Grace's grand experiment had turned into an unmitigated disaster. She'd proved herself, all right, confirmed what everyone had known all along. Signy Shepherd, unable to curb her impulses, a one-woman catastrophe.

Maitland, Elena, Grace, all deluded. Kim Blackwater was the only one who saw her for what she was. Kim had been right on the money from the start. She was nothing but trouble. She needed to get out of Linden Valley, tonight preferably. Flee before she got anyone else injured, or killed.

Flipping on the light switch, she turned and hung her keys on the hook by the door. She wished Zef were there to hold her in his arms and tell her everything would be all right.

Sighing heavily, she turned back into the room. She froze. Jay Hunter was sitting at her kitchen table like he owned the place. She took a step back, clawing for the door handle.

His mouth dropped open as he took in the bandage on her face and the fresh bruises at her neck.

"What are you doing here?" she said, her voice a harsh squeak. "How did you get in here?"

"What happened?" he asked, his eyes scanning her battered face.

She touched her fingers to her throat. "Your boss happened."

"My God, I thought—" He shoved the chair back and made to stand.

"Stay there," she said, casting her eyes about the room. Where had she left her taser?

"I'm sorry. I never meant for that to happen," he said, resuming his seat. Then, as though he had read her thoughts, he said, "I wouldn't hurt you." He turned his hands palm up on the table.

She leaned against the kitchen counter and folded her arms in front of her chest, gazing down at him, her face impassive. "Why are you here, Jay?"

He opened his mouth to speak.

"Sorry, I forgot. Jay isn't your real name. What should I call you?" She snapped her fingers. "How about Judas?" She flashed him a humourless smile.

He sighed. "My name is not Jay. It's Alex. Alex Nakai." He

held her gaze. "Although even that isn't the whole truth. My biological mother named me Jonathan." A ghost of a smile crossed his face. "My sister used to call me Johnny."

She frowned. "What the hell are you doing in my apartment?"

Oh dear, what can the matter be? Johnny's so long at the fair.

"I told you I'd tell you my secret." He held his hands out, palms up. "My name is Alex Nakai, and I hunt people."

They locked eyes for several seconds before she broke the spell. Bending down, she rummaged about in a cupboard below the sink, producing a bottle of whisky. She raised an eyebrow and, when he nodded, grabbed two glasses, setting them both down on the table. She opened the bottle and poured a generous measure into each glass.

Signy drained her glass in one long swallow. "There was no ballet recital, I take it?"

He shook his head. "I grew up in the Painted Desert. Not far from the Grand Canyon. My mother is Dine. She was of the Bitter Water clan, and born for the Corn People clan. She adopted me when I was almost six years old; you would have been two and a half."

She raised an eyebrow at this, but he ignored her query, taking a sip of the sharp spirits.

"We lived in a hogan in the desert."

She stared at him dumbfounded, as though he was speaking gibberish.

"A hogan is a traditional eight-sided mud dwelling."

416

"What the fuck are you doing here?"

He held up a hand. "Please, let me finish."

She brought the glass to her lips, not taking her eyes from his. "You've got five minutes and then I'm calling the cops."

He nodded. "It was a happy childhood. I was free for the most part to spend my time exploring the desert, and my mother taught me how to live in harmony with the land."

She rolled her eyes. "How pastoral."

"It was good," he said, ignoring her sarcasm, "until my uncle—not my biological uncle, you understand, but my mother's brother—came back."

"Came back?"

"He was the one who brought me to Arizona in the first place. He was the one who gave me to my mother."

"What do you mean, gave you to your mother? I thought you said you were adopted."

"Not in the traditional sense. But I thought of her as my mother. I still do, although she's been gone for many years now." He looked down at his glass and stared into the smoky liquid. "Like I said, when I was ten, my uncle returned in order to commence my formal education. He was a hunter too."

"Like you." Her lip curled as though she'd tasted something foul.

Alex nodded. "He'd been hunting people long before you and I were born. He was an artist, really, and he taught me everything he knew. Once I'd learned all I could from him, I added to my knowledge, picking up skills that wouldn't have been possible in his day. He didn't have access to computers or GPS or cellphones."

"Or tracking devices?" Signy asked the question with a bite to her voice.

He raised his glass in a salute. "Or the ability to access sensitive databases, to track people down through their online records, to locate them using cellphones, satellite feeds, whatever. It's really quite simple. Most people have no idea what it takes to stay hidden."

"Volkov said someone had been following Elena all the way from Vancouver. Was that you?"

He nodded. "I used a listening device to confirm her presence at the shelter in Surrey and to determine where they were taking her. I was waiting when she arrived in Calgary."

"And it was you who put the tracking device on my car?"

He nodded again. "I almost lost you when the man Volkov sent to take you out switched it to another car."

"I did that," she said.

He slammed his glass down on the table, shook his head, then grinned.

"How did you know to use Grace Holder's name when you picked us up?" she asked, not returning his smile.

"I'd listened in on your cellphone conversation when you parked at the market."

"You can do that?"

He nodded. "It's simple, really. All you have to do is—"

Her face darkened even further as she stared at him. "I thought I recognized you. You were the guy in the SUV that pulled up across from us. God, I'm stupid."

"Don't be so hard on yourself," he said. "I've been doing this for years. I was twenty when I took up where my uncle left off."

"So you're a hit man? You kill people for money?" Signy said.

"I do not kill people." His eyes slid downward.

"You did a pretty good job with that man out by the lake."

"That was different," he said. "He was going to kill you."

"Don't forget Elena," she said, caustically.

"And Elena," he said. He slid his hands along the table, as if reaching out to her. "But I'm not a killer. I'm what's called a tracker. When a person disappears, I follow their trail until I find them."

"People like Elena?"

He nodded.

"Oh," she said, "well, then. Pardon me for my nasty accusations. You're obviously a saint. All you do is turn girls like Elena over to monsters like Volkov." She picked up the bottle and refilled her glass. "That's a relief."

"For what it's worth, many of the people I track deserve to be found."

She glared at him from beneath hooded eyes. "I wonder if you have any idea how insane you sound."

He sat up straighter. "You don't get to be the best at something by holding back, by second-guessing yourself. Self-doubts and sentiment have no place in people like you and me. You either commit one hundred percent or you fail."

"People like you and me? What do you know about me?"

"More than you know."

"Bullshit," she said, slamming her own glass down on the table. "Here's what I know about you. Elena is a young, innocent girl whose only sin was to be born into the wrong family, and yet you tracked her down like a dog, made sure a monster like Volkov knew where to find her, and then left her to the wolves."

"I tried—" he started, then looked into her eyes and apparently decided further elaboration was useless.

"And what about me, Alex?" she said. Her fingers brushed the bandage above her eye.

"I was wrong," he said. "I thought you were safe. I went to the shelter first. I saw the SUV. I thought you were inside."

"And Elena too, of course?" she said caustically.

He glanced away. "Yes, of course." He looked back at her. "Is she okay?"

"Nice of you to ask," she said bitterly, then added with a catch in her voice, "Elena will be fine, but Grace? She's not okay. She's the one who stood by me, by Elena. She's the one who paid the price for your deceit." She dug her nails into her palms. "For my mistake."

He waited for a moment while she gathered herself, then said, so quietly she could barely hear him, "I know all about mistakes. I made a huge mistake, a long time ago."

"Go tell it to a priest," she said, her hand digging into her pocket.

"It's why I'm here," he said, "why I needed to find you."

"Time's up," she said, pulling out her new cellphone.

"I'm here because of what happened twenty-three years ago, Christmastime."

"What are you talking about?" She stared at him.

"It was me," he said, staring down at the table.

She looked around, wildly, as though searching for an escape route. "You need to go," she said, her voice taking on a slightly hysterical note.

"It was me," he repeated. "I'm the one that dumped you in that alley."

The phone slipped from her fingers and bounced onto the floor. She didn't notice.

"Signy?" He shot to his feet.

She lurched backwards, turned, and bent over the sink, hot whisky coming back up her throat.

He took a step toward her. "Mom begged me to keep you safe, and I tried, I swear I tried, but I couldn't run fast enough."

"You're fucking with me," she cried into the sink. "Liar."

"I should have been able to stop him," he said. "I should have been able to keep you safe."

She felt cramps grip her bowels. "Shut up. Leave me alone."

"And then he had us both in his car. And I thought he was going to kill us."

She put her hands over her ears. "No."

"And we stopped at a red light. And I opened the door. And I grabbed you by the arm."

She vomited into the sink, the sight of hot soup mixed with sour booze making her heave all the more.

"And I ran."

"Stop," she said, wiping at her mouth with the back of her hand.

"There was an alley. It was pitch-black and freezing cold. And I could hear his feet pounding so close behind me. And all I could do was put you into that garbage bin and cover you up."

He reached out to her. "I threw you away," he said. His fingers touched her shoulder. "I didn't mean to. I'm sorry."

She whirled, and slapped his face as hard as she could.

Chapter

52

Signy stared at the ruddy imprint of her hand on Alex's cheek, the crack of her hand across his face echoing in the room like a thunderclap.

He opened his mouth, then closed it again, then raised a hand to his cheek, his eyes locked on hers.

The wall clock in the kitchen ticked away the seconds as they continued to gape at each other, shocked passengers in the aftermath of a train wreck.

Finally, he broke the silence. "Signy, I—"

Her phone rang.

They both looked down at the same time. The new phone that Maitland had given her was lying on the floor, ringing loudly.

She picked it up. "Hello?" she said, unsure whether her voice still worked.

"Ms. Shepherd? It's Detective Lavalle."

Signy's eyes flew open. She stared at the Tracker.

"I was speaking with Maitland. She gave me your number."

"I don't mean to be rude, Detective, but it's been a long day. Can this wait?"

"I'm afraid not."

The police detective paused for several seconds, forcing Signy to ask if she was still on the line. "It's about Constable Dalton," Lavalle said, finally.

Signy inhaled sharply. "Is Zef all right?"

"Excuse me?" Lavalle asked.

"Never mind," Signy said. "What about Dalton?"

"I thought it prudent to inform you that Daryl Dalton has been arrested."

"Really?" Signy smiled.

"He was caught trying to force his way into the house where Jennifer Dalton and her children have been staying."

"My God. Are they okay?"

Lavalle made an affirmative noise in her throat. "When the local police arrived, he was using a tire iron to smash his way through the front door."

Signy gasped, then noticed that Jay or Jonathan or Alex, or whatever his name was, was listening with great interest. She turned her back. "But they're out east. Why are you telling me?"

"Constable Dalton is not pleased."

"I see." Signy bit her lip. "Did he threaten me?"

"Unfortunately, Dalton isn't that stupid. After he'd calmed down, he was the voice of reason." Lavalle paused for a moment, then rushed on. "But I don't buy it, Ms. Shepherd. Dalton is extremely angry."

Signy glanced over her shoulder. The Tracker lifted his eyebrows in a silent question. She turned away.

"Frankly, I'd have you wear a wire, but there's no way I'd be able to get a warrant."

Signy scoffed. "Look, I appreciate your concern, Detective Lavalle, but I'm not afraid of Constable Dalton."

Lavalle sighed. "You still have my number?"

"I do," Signy replied, tersely.

"Please call immediately if you get wind of anything."

Signy's thumb hovered over the off button. "Detective Lavalle?"

"Yes?"

"Thanks." She hung up the phone and slipped it into her pocket. She remembered the feel of Dalton's tongue in her mouth and shuddered. Lavalle was right. There was no way Big Dick was going to let her off the hook for his son's fuck-up. He'd be coming for her and the only question was, How soon?

She spun around to face Jay or Jonathan or whatever he called himself. "I've got a problem and you're going to help me."

"Okay," he answered, without hesitation.

"Besides tracking devices and listening equipment, what other surveillance stuff do you have on you?" She listened while he outlined the array of devices he had in his SUV. She briefly explained the situation, outlined her plan, and asked if he thought it would work. He responded with a few pertinent questions, then suggested a couple of small modifications. She ran the new idea over in her head and, unable to see any major flaws, nodded. "Get it," she said.

When he returned a few minutes later, she accepted the MacBook Pro from his hands and set it on the table.

"Here," he said, holding up a pretty gemstone on a gold necklace.

"What is it?" she asked, holding the stone in the palm of her hand, admiring the bands of pink and red and gold.

"Sardonyx," he said. "Your birthstone, as a matter of fact."

She stared at it for several moments, unable to ask the question.

"August," he said, disconcerting her once again with his apparent ability to read her thoughts. "You were born in August."

Unable to speak, she nodded, then slipped the necklace over her head. After a moment, she looked at him and said, "Show me how it works."

• • •

Signy sat up and looked through the safety bars on her big-girl bed. Something had woken her. She turned her face to the closed door and listened. She heard the shouting then, plaintive and terrified. Mommy?

Oh dear, what can the matter be? Johnny's so long at the fair.

Then a thunderous crash and her eyes widened. Someone had forced their way through the front door. She could hear him calling out. *Johnny? John? Son?* She could hear screams, then the scramble of feet barely audible over the thumping of her own heartbeat.

She stopped breathing. What came next was always the same. The black-haired nightmare with eyes like raisins and skin the colour of the desert burst into her room, charging straight at her, silent as death.

This time, however, something had changed. The dream was different. Instead of the monster, a blond-haired boy, wild-eyed and covered in blood, scrambled into the room, slamming the door behind him.

His crazed terror frightened her, and digging her tiny feet into the mattress, she pushed herself as far away from the blood-soaked boy as she could.

He climbed the railing of her bed, grabbing at her arms, trying to drag her onto the floor. His lips were moving, pleading with her, but she couldn't understand his words. She slashed at him with her feet, then her hands, her fists raining down on his head and shoulders.

She heard the splinter of wood, and then the monster was in the doorway, his raisin eyes hard as he charged toward her. With one hand, he batted away the boy. With the other, he snatched her from her bed, lifting her high into the air. And as he carried her away, she knew what she always did, that she was going to die.

Clawing her way out of the dream, Signy sat up, her heart pounding. Drawing the covers around her waist, she fingered the necklace that Alex had given her.

The dream had been different this time. The little blond boy, covered in blood. She hadn't seen him before. She wondered what it meant, knowing the answer even as she swung her legs around the edge of the bed. If she didn't get up and wash her face, the dream would stay with her all night, and she would never get back to sleep.

She froze. Had she heard a noise? Still half asleep, she wasn't sure what was real and what might be a hangover from the dream. She turned her head to the bedroom door and listened hard. She was certain she could hear something, the unmistakable snick of the front door lock clicking open.

She held her breath. She heard the sound of a body colliding with her kitchen table and a stifled imprecation. There was no doubt now. Someone was inside her apartment.

She drew her legs under the sheets and forced herself to lean back against the pillow. She closed her eyes. She could hear the shuffle of footsteps on the wooden floor in the living room moving closer until they were just outside her bedroom door.

She felt rather than heard the whisper of the curtain as it brushed against the screen of her bedroom window, the slight disturbance in the air pressure evident even before the door creaked open. She could smell his rank male sweat as he moved into her room, and something else too—ammonia, bleach?

A gloved hand came down hard over her mouth and nose.

Her eyes flew open and she kicked out, wildly.

"Don't move," he said, squeezing his hand tighter.

Choking, she forced her body to go limp.

"If you scream, I'll cut you," he said, holding an eight-inch hunting knife to her throat. "Got that, sunshine?"

She nodded.

He had one knee on the bed, the other foot still on the ground. He peeled his hand from her mouth, then, using it to prop himself up, loomed over her. With his other hand, he dragged the point of the knife from her jaw to the crook of her neck. "I told you not to fuck with me."

"I didn't, I—"

He drew a gloved thumb over her mouth, forcing her lips apart, then shoving the thumb inside, probing the tender flesh. The leather tasted foul, and she gagged.

"You talk when I tell you," he whispered, touching the tip of the blade to her breast.

It was all she could do not to cry out. She nodded again.

"Good girl," he said, sliding his thumb from her mouth. He tweaked her nipple between his thumb and forefinger, then seized the entire breast in his fist, pumping it as though he were milking a cow.

She stared up at him, her mouth clamped shut.

"The meth I planted on your boyfriend is going to send him away for a long time." He looked into her eyes. "Nothing you can do about that now. You had your chance and you blew it."

"I told you. I couldn't do anything. I was—"

He hit her across the face with the back of his gloved hand. She cried out.

He sat up, one buttock propped on the edge of her bed. He pointed the knife at her face. "His time in the joint can be easy or it can be hard. Believe me, I can fix it so that his only way out of hell is to off himself." He used his free hand to unbuckle his belt. "I think he needs himself an advocate, someone to look out for his interests on the outside. You get what I'm saying?" He slid his belt from the loops and unzipped his fly. He reached inside and freed his thickening phallus.

Signy stared at him.

He grabbed her by the back of the head and moved her face forward until her mouth hovered over his erect penis. "This is what happens when you fuck with me," he said, shoving her head down further until her lips touched the rubbery tip.

Signy gagged, overwhelmed by the smell of urine and dried semen. The necklace Alex had given her dangled between them, spinning slowly on its gold chain. She wrenched her head back. "I tried," she said. "By the time I got back, they were gone."

She heard the creak of leather as he sat back and yanked her head up by the hair. "Bullshit," he said, sliding his pants down over his hips just enough that he was able to bring his leg over her body, straddling her chest. He clutched his penis in his hand, slammed her head back on the pillow, then jammed the head of his phallus between her lips, forcing her mouth open.

"Bite me, and I'll cut your heart out," he said.

Probing under the covers, she felt her fingers close over the taser she'd hidden before she went to bed. Yanking her head away from his body, she buried the business end of the taser deep in his scrotum.

Dalton's eyes flew open.

She watched a bead of seminal fluid slide slowly down the head of his penis, hang for an instant on a gossamer thread, then fall toward her chin.

The knife clattered to the floor. He looked down at her, his mouth open in a silent scream.

Signy pulled the trigger.

She felt the big muscles of his thighs contract, and he jerked upright, his head thrown back, every muscle in his face contorted in agony, his arms, rigid as wood, flung out to each side, a crucified man. An indescribable groaning shriek tore out of his open mouth but was cut short by his malfunctioning electrical system.

He teetered there above her, before toppling slowly backwards, a fallen tree crashing to earth. She noted with a detached fascination that his bulbous testicles had completely disappeared, sucked up into his body cavity, his swollen phallus dangling between his legs like a dying trout. Drool dribbled from the corner of his mouth. His eyes were wide open but she could tell he was barely conscious.

Half expecting this assault, she had gone to bed fully dressed in a pair of jeans and T-shirt. Extricating herself from beneath his inert body, she scrambled out of the bed, slid open the drawer on her bedside table, and slipped out the plastic handcuffs Alex had left for her. In seconds she had his hands and legs restrained.

She heard him groan once as she opened the closet door, where Alex's MacBook Pro sat open on the top shelf, the video feed still running. She picked it up and, tapping a few keys, reset the video back to when Dalton had first entered her room.

Then she stood beside the bed waiting for him to regain consciousness. He did so, surprisingly quickly. She grinned down at him as the realization dawned as to the reality of his situation. She watched him thrash uselessly for several moments, then picked up his big hunting knife and jabbed it into his bare buttock, drawing blood. "You'll talk when I tell you." She stabbed the point of the knife in deeper. "Got that, sunshine?"

He glared up at her.

She dug the blade in even deeper.

Gritting his teeth, he nodded.

"Good," she said, swinging the screen of the MacBook around so he could see the video. She held up the little necklace. "Wireless video," she said, and pressed play. She was suffused with a grim satisfaction as he watched the video and realized how big a hole he had dug for himself.

"You fucking bitch." Each word was uttered in a painful croak.

"Shut your mouth." She brought up her email account and punched in the address Alex had given her. She attached a copy of the video to the email. She brought the cursor over the send button. "I'm sending this to a friend of mine, a very dangerous friend. If anything happens to me, if I so much as stub my toe, my friend goes public with this video." She stared into his eyes. "And then he kills you. Nod if you understand."

He nodded.

Signy pushed the send button. "Good. And there's something else. If I ever hear that you or that freak son of yours so much as send an email to Jenny and the girls, I'll send the video to Detective Lavalle, the *Linden Valley Gazette*, and the *Toronto Star*. And that's just for starters, got it?"

"Listen, you psychotic bitch—"

She gave the knife a sharp twist and smiled when he shrieked. "Hold on, we're just getting started. You raped your son's wife; you tried to rape me. I doubt we're the only ones. If I ever get wind of you going near another woman, I'll send the video. If I ever hear that you've set anyone up like you did with

Zef, I'll send the video." She grinned at him, her eyes flat. "If I see you looking sideways at a stray dog, I'll send the video. Do you understand?"

He made an angry sound in the back of his throat but nodded.

"Good boy," she said, then grabbed him under one arm and hauled him to a sitting position. She held the knife to his belly. "Stand up. Slowly."

He got to his feet awkwardly, his ankles still bound with the plastic cuffs. She pulled his pants back up over his hips, grimacing with disgust. Then she brought the knife up under his chin. "One last thing," she said. "I've always wanted an insider on the police force." She narrowed her eyes. "Someone who'll help me out now and then, give me the head's up when something is going down, that sort of thing. Think you can handle that?"

"Fuck you," he said.

She shoved the point of the knife slowly into his neck, feeling the tough skin give under the pressure. A trickle of blood stained the blade. "What did you say?" she asked, shoving the knife in even further, the trickle of blood becoming a steady stream.

"Psycho bitch."

"I don't think you understand the situation here, Dick," she said, turning back to the computer. She opened up a new email and typed in Winnie Lavalle's address. Placing the cursor over the send button, she looked up at him and raised a brow.

"Don't," he said, followed a few seconds later by a barely audible, "I understand."

She held the cursor over the send button for a few more seconds before taking a step back. "Prove it," she said. "First thing in the morning you make sure Zef walks free."

"I don't know if that's even possible," he said.

She shrugged. "You'd better hope it is, Dick, because if he isn't out of that jail by tomorrow afternoon, then I send the video." She looked at him and, satisfied by what she saw, continued. "By the way, I'll be putting this on a flash drive and leaving it in a safety deposit box first thing in the morning. Same deal. Anything happens to me, that version will go up on YouTube. A cop admitting to fraud, then sexually assaulting a woman in her own bed? It will go viral within hours."

They glared at each other for several seconds, then Signy bent down and used the hunting knife to slice through the restraints at his ankles. She jabbed the tip of the knife into his back and marched him to her front door. He turned and held his bound hands up toward the knife.

Keeping the blade pointed at his chest, she shook her head, then opened the door. As he hobbled down the stairs, his hands clutching his groin, she called after him. "By the way, you should take a shower. You stink like shit."

Dalton froze.

Signy tightened her grip on the handle of the hunting knife.

Swivelling his neck, he turned his face up toward her.

She could see a fiery red blotch burning on each cheek and hear his laboured breathing echo in the hollow space. His buzz cut seemed to sizzle in the dim light, as though the jolt of electricity had fried right through to the roots of his hair. A wave of dreadful malignance almost knocked her off her feet as he fastened his bloodshot eyes on hers.

"Go away," she said, her attempt at bravado ringing false, even to her own ears.

In response, Constable Dalton peeled back his cracked lips and grinned. A tsunami of hatred washed over her, and she lost her footing, the shifting sands of her own courage sliding away from under her feet. She turned and fled back inside, slamming the door behind her.

Leaning against the door, her heart hammering inside her chest, she waited until she heard the faint click of the big door downstairs, then rushed over to the table where she'd left her wallet.

She frantically rummaged through the slots until she located the blue-on-white business card. Staring into space, she ran a finger over the embossed logo of the Linden Valley Police Force and the raised lettering that spelled out Winnifred Lavalle, Detective Sergeant.

She picked up the new phone, her thumb caressing the talk button. Walking over to the door, she checked the deadbolt, then dialed the number, and when Lavalle picked up, Signy began to speak. "This is Signy Shepherd speaking, and I'd like to make a formal complaint against Constable Richard Dalton."

Chapter

53

Two weeks later, Signy helped Grace out of the passenger seat of the Saturn. Grace leaned heavily on her arm as Signy helped her negotiate the stone path up to the veranda.

"Is Daryl Dalton back in Ontario yet?" Grace asked.

Signy nodded. "Winnie Lavalle told me that he got back last week. His bail conditions are extreme. He so much as sneezes and he'll be sent back to await trial in New Brunswick."

"Good," said Grace, "he deserves to rot." She glanced warily at Signy. "And the case against you?"

Signy shook her head. "Detective Lavalle said the Crown prosecutor ruled there were no grounds to proceed. They've determined my actions were justified."

"Ha," said Grace, punching a fist into the air, her crazy Marge Simpson hair jiggling wildly on top of her head. She clutched her abdomen and her smile died. "Any fallout from Constable Dalton? That man won't take kindly to any of this."

"He's been arrested. He's sitting in the Linden Valley lockup as we speak."

Grasping the banister, Grace heaved her way up the veranda stairs. When she reached the top, she stood for a moment, breathing heavily. "Really? No way!"

Signy nodded. "Sexual assault, forcible confinement, aggravated assault."

Grace grinned. "I'm so glad someone finally had the nerve to come forward. Do you know who it was?"

Signy nodded. "I'll tell you later. Let's get you settled first."

Once inside, Signy set about getting Grace comfortable in the living room. Grace had been in the hospital for the better part of two weeks, recovering from the gunshot wounds. The shoulder and hand wounds had required no more than some packing and a few stitches, but the bullet that had pierced her spleen had resulted in significant blood loss. She'd been lucky that no other major organs had been damaged.

It hadn't been an easy recovery. She'd picked up an infection while in hospital, and it had been touch and go for several days as her body struggled to cope with both the catastrophic injury and the invading bacteria.

In the end, she'd recovered well enough to be sent home but would need a visiting nurse who would attend to the IV antibiotics she'd need to endure for a few more weeks.

"I'm going to make us both a cup of tea, but first, I think there's someone who's dying to see you," said Signy, with a smile.

"I can't believe I'm home." Grace glanced around the living room. "Everything seems so different."

Following her gaze, Signy nodded. Everything was different, and not just the physical layout. As soon as the police had cleared the scene, professional cleaners had come and gone, scrubbing Grace and Elena's blood from the floor and walls. The wingback chair had been thrown out. The walls had been painted in a neutral shade of taupe that Grace could change later, if and when she was ready to bring some colour back into her life.

Signy glanced at Grace. Deep sadness had carved grooves around her mentor's eyes. "I'm sorry about Kim," Signy said, clasping her hands in front of her.

"I'll tell you what," said Grace, a little too brightly, "why don't you go find the welcoming committee."

"Yes, boss," said Signy. She walked into the kitchen, pausing to plug in the kettle before opening the door that led into the backyard.

Hearing the click of the latch, Chivas bounded from the back of the garden, where he'd been wreaking havoc in a bed of azaleas. He flung himself at Signy, pushing her bodily back inside, his front paws on her shoulders as he covered her face with wet doggy kisses.

"Get off, you stupid dog," she cried, shoving ineffectually against his joyful waggling mass. "Get down!"

Chivas leapt about her in merry circles, his massive head butting up against her waist. She bent over and grabbed the ruff of his neck in her fists. "I've missed you, boy." She giggled as he resumed his frantic tongue washing.

When he'd calmed somewhat, she pulled his face close to hers and whispered, "I haven't thanked you yet for saving my life." He grinned at her expectantly. "You might not have been Lassie"—his grin turned to huffing laughter—"but you kept him busy for a few crucial seconds." She pulled on his ears and threw her arms around his neck, nuzzling her face into his wiry fur.

"Well," she said, standing up, "guess who's home."

His ears pricked and he watched her eyes with intense expectation.

"Who's here? Who wants to say hello?" She sang the words, whipping the dog into a frenzy. "Grace!" she said, finally, clapping her hands. "Grace is home!"

Chivas barked once, turned a few circles, then following his nose, dashed down the hallway toward the living room.

Signy followed, the sound of his nails on the wooden floor sending a shiver down the back of her neck. By the time she turned the corner to the living room, Chivas was almost in Grace's lap, his hind end wiggling so hard that Signy thought he might knock over the coffee table.

She grabbed his collar and hauled him backwards. "Whoa, dog. Be gentle."

Grace was laughing for the first time since that horrible night. Holding her hands protectively over the ten-inch incision that bisected her abdomen, she looked up at Signy. "It's okay. Let him stay. He's good for the soul."

"That he is," she replied, slipping her fingers from his collar and letting him slather Grace with his sopping tongue. "Kettle's boiling. I'll go make some tea, then take your bag upstairs."

Grace nodded absently, her fingers entwined in the big dog's ruff.

As Signy puttered in the kitchen, she remembered she had to tell Grace about the call she'd had from Elena that morning. It would perk Grace up to know Elena was okay. The girl was changed, there was no doubt about that, but she'd been excited as she'd told Signy how she'd been able to start her studies on time.

They hadn't talked about Volkov except to confirm that he'd been denied bail and that the Russian government was seeking his extradition. A search warrant of his home had not turned up any further pictures, but in the darkroom in his office, they'd found a series of gruesome photos of the torture and murder of Mr. Zhang. There was little doubt Volkov would die of old age in a prison cell.

Elena had mentioned, sarcasm dripping from her voice, that despite her own talent with a camera she was going to find a new hobby, if and when she ever had spare time.

Placing a steaming mug of tea on a tray along with a linen napkin and a plate of cookies she'd brought in with the load of groceries earlier in the day, Signy wondered why Elena hadn't asked about Jay Hunter. Hopefully, the girl had decided not to waste her precious energy on useless anger. Wallowing in the past would only hurt her, especially when she had so much to look forward to.

Meanwhile, Signy tried to focus on the present. Using her knee to keep Chivas at bay, she passed Grace the warm mug and set the plate of cookies on the table beside her. "Sorry about the store-bought factor," she said, nodding at the mass-produced gingersnaps.

"Hey, anything that doesn't come lukewarm under a plastic lid is okay by me." Grace picked up a cookie and took a bite, although Signy thought her smile seemed forced.

"Okay, how about I run upstairs and put your things away. You want to watch some TV?" She picked up the remote.

"No. I'll just sit here for a while. Enjoy the peace and quiet." Grace sighed.

Signy leaned over and squeezed her hand. "She'll come back. She just needs some time."

Grace looked down at her lap. The dry ginger cookie crumbled between her fingers. Acutely aware of the tiny gold mine, Chivas buried his face in Grace's lap.

"Do you know where she's gone?" Signy asked.

"Oh, she's still in town. She found some temporary digs near the hospital."

"Well, that's something."

"I guess—" Grace shoved Chivas's head out of her lap, then brushed away the last few orts he'd missed. He snuffled at her feet.

Not knowing what else to do, Signy picked up Grace's suitcase and headed for the stairs.

Grace called after her, "What about the other man?"

Signy took a deep breath. Setting the case down, she turned back to Grace. "What other man?"

"Volkov's man," said Grace.

"Volkov's man?"

Grace peered at Signy through narrowed eyes. "You can't have forgotten. What was his name?"

Signy shook her head, smiling weakly. "No, of course not." She snapped her fingers. "Jay Hunter?"

Grace nodded.

"Right. Apparently, Volkov gave him up right away."

"Good. At least that Russian bastard was good for something," said Grace, digging her fingers into Chivas's thick fur. "Have they picked the guy up yet?"

Signy shook her head. "The only information Volkov had on him was a telephone number and that led nowhere. Apparently, the guy is some kind of tech wiz."

"Damn."

"I'm sure they'll find him sooner or later," said Signy, picking up the case. She flew up the stairs, eager to get away before Grace probed any deeper into the elusive Jay Hunter. The RCMP had questioned both her and Elena extensively about why Volkov's man had taken out the assassin and helped them elude capture. Neither woman had been able to provide a satisfactory explanation and, as far as she knew, that particular piece of the puzzle remained a mystery.

After putting Grace's clothes away into the half-empty closet and drawers, she'd prepared a lunch of canned chicken soup and bagged salad. Grace had laughed in genuine appreciation of Signy's attempt to improve upon the meagre meal by adding a sprig of parsley to the greasy golden liquid.

Signy's cheeks had flushed but she'd joined in the laughter, commenting that she was sure that when the next shift of helpers brought Grace's dinner that evening, it would be a feast fit for a queen. Grace opened her arms and Signy stepped willingly into the hug, taking care not to squeeze too tightly.

It was close to two o'clock before Signy rose to leave. Grace walked her slowly to the door, then paused for a moment. "We did the right thing," Grace said. "You know that, right?"

Signy looked into Grace's eyes and nodded.

"And no matter what, we still have the Line."

Signy smiled. "I'm good with that."

Another quick hug and a promise to return tomorrow, then Signy headed down the sidewalk and, after a final wave good-bye, began to jog the few kilometres back to her apartment, her body flowing smoothly in an easy, comfortable rhythm.

Chapter

54

The air was brisk. Linden Valley was enjoying the cooling trend that had settled over most of the province as summer transitioned into autumn. By the time she loped up to her house, Signy felt warm and relaxed, despite the chill that added a rosy glow to her cheeks.

Walking in place, she checked her pulse before bending forward at the waist to stretch out her left hamstring. What she'd said to Grace had been true. Despite her many flaws, she'd managed to save the girl. Not only that, she'd been instrumental in bringing a Russian assassin to justice and reining in a rogue cop.

She might not be perfect, she might make poor decisions. Kim Blackwater thought she was a walking disaster and maybe she was right, but Grace understood. It was who she was. It was what she did. And Signy was okay with that, for now.

Rising back up, she switched legs, giving her other hamstring a deep stretch, her thoughts flashing to Alex's words that night in her apartment. "You don't get to be the best at something by holding back, by second-guessing yourself. Self-doubts and sentiment have no place in people like you and me. You either commit one hundred percent or you fail."

Sitting across from him that night, she'd silently agreed. She'd known that was why she could never be the best at anything. She was riddled with self-doubts, with second guesses, with sentiment. Every time she took a leap of faith, every time she jumped into the unknown, it brought her an instant rush, a moment of glory.

But afterward, when the dust had settled, when the consequences came to call, she was assailed by what-ifs and self-judgments. She had thought that this inability to maintain a clean singularity of purpose was what held her back, the anchor that kept her mired in guilt.

But she'd been wrong, as flawed in her perceptions as Alex Nakai.

She'd realized it the first time she'd gone to visit Grace at the trauma centre. Sitting at Grace's bedside, looking at the tangle of tubes that wound in and out of her body, Signy finally understood Grace's little plaque. *Never Regret, Never Explain, Never Apologize.*

Grace had committed everything, in spite of her flaws and her self-doubts. Burdened by unrelenting pressure from the woman she loved, Grace still charged ahead. And best of all, she'd done it without looking back.

Signy realized, as she sat there listening to the beep of the machines, that she could be just like Grace, flawed and perfect at the same time. She was both, and she would have to learn to live with that. Nothing was black and white, and for the first time, that thought was immensely comforting.

She smiled as she headed up the walkway. Alex was the same, he just didn't know it. As a man who seemed to value logic and control above everything else, he'd lived his life trying to make right the one thing over which he'd had no control. He was awash in sentiment.

Stopping to check her mailbox, she was startled to find a thick, brown shipping envelope sticking out among the usual bills and junk mail. Her name and address had been scrawled in bold letters across the front but there was no return address. It had an electronic postage stamp so she was unable to discern its place of origin.

She climbed the stairs to her apartment holding the envelope cautiously between two shaking fingers. Placing it on the kitchen table, she poured herself a glass of wine and decided to check her phone messages before tackling the mysterious package.

"Hey babe, it's Zef. You gonna be in Toronto this weekend? I thought maybe we could hook up?"

Rolling her eyes, Signy slurped her wine, then listened to the next message. *"Signy? It's me again, Ben Tran? I know things have been hectic but I'm really looking forward to that dinner. You probably won't believe it but there's a great steak house downtown. Unless you're a vegetarian? If you're a vegan or something, we could eat veggie. I'm good with pretty much anything."* A long pause and then the message continued. *"Anyway—I hope you'll give me a call. Anytime. I'm around. Um—it's Ben here, Ben Tran."* Signy smiled.

Downing the remainder of the wine, she examined the envelope. It didn't appear to be shedding mysterious white powder, and there were no wires or fuses, so she picked it up and slit it open, in one bold stroke.

Spilling the contents onto the table, she examined the odd collection. A white business-sized envelope, a smaller package about two inches square that had been carefully wrapped in blue tissue paper, and a plain white business card.

Picking up the white envelope, she examined both sides. Scrawled across the front in the same handwriting as on the outer envelope were the words "I Owe You a Toothbrush." The tiny hairs on the back of her arms shivered.

She slit the envelope with the knife and extracted an official-looking report that had been prepared by a company called Advanced Genetic Technologies, Inc. Cursive lettering running under the company logo at the top of the page read "Specializing in Familial DNA Analysis for over Twenty-Five Years." The thick white paper shook in her hand.

She ran her eyes over the report only to find much of it consisted of an incomprehensible series of letters and numbers, but she sucked in her breath when down near the bottom she found the author's conclusions printed in bold.

Sample A (male) and Sample B (female) were compared to determine a Full Sibling Index. Thirteen genetic markers were tested. The likelihood ratio that Sample A and Sample B are full siblings is 322 indicating a STRONG probability that these two samples belong to full siblings—a male and female who had both maternal and paternal parentage in common.

The paper slid out of her hand and fluttered to the table. She looked up, dazzled by a beam of light shining in through the window, in which dust motes fizzed with shimmering phosphorescence.

Eyes shining, she picked up the small tissue-wrapped package and tore it open with trembling fingers. She gazed in awe at a faded red ribbon made of strong cotton. Smoothing the ribbon flat, she saw that one end still retained its sharp edge, while the other was jagged and torn.

Sliding her chair back so violently she almost knocked it over, she rushed into her bedroom and lifted from its hiding spot on the floor of her cupboard the cherrywood box that her foster father had carved for her on her tenth birthday.

Inside the box she stored only her most treasured keepsakes. Rummaging through the meagre contents, she located the tangled ball of red ribbon her foster parents had kept for her all those years. The ribbon that had been found tied around her wrist the night she'd been found alone and shivering inside that filthy Dumpster.

She walked back to the kitchen and with steady fingers smoothed years of knots and tangles from the ribbon until it lay as flat as its partner on the table. She slid the jagged ends together, unsurprised when they came together like two pieces of a puzzle.

Unable to wait a second longer, she flipped over the plain white business card and revealed a ten-digit phone number printed in fine gold letters. She ran her fingers over the numbers with its unfamiliar three-digit area code. Turning the card over again, she held it up to the light, but it was blank. That was all there was.

She sat at the table for almost an hour, rereading the DNA

report several times and wondering at the way the two tattered shreds of ribbon had reconnected to form a flawless whole.

Finally, she braided the two ribbons together and rewrapped them in the blue tissue paper before placing them back inside the cherrywood box. She tucked in the DNA report and the small business card with the gold-embossed phone number, then returned the box to its hiding spot.

Back in the living room she stood by the window. Lit up in a sparkling beam of light, she thought about the people out there. Normal people caught up in the everyday tasks of everyday life. Nice people in a nice town. She could get used to this.

Maybe.

She snatched up the keys to her Saturn. Grace had insisted she take a few weeks off. Remembering the touch of Zef's lips on hers, she shivered. Her first love, her touchstone. She could be in Toronto in a flash.

She flew down the stairs. Ben Tran had called at least ten times since she'd been back. She thought about his goofy messages and wondered whether he was really as nice as he seemed.

She climbed in the car, then slipped the key into the ignition. Then again, she'd always wanted to see the American Southwest. Where had Alex said he'd grown up? The Painted Desert? It sounded beautiful.

Smiling, she backed down the driveway, then let the car take her wherever it wanted to go.

Acknowledgements

I will be forever grateful to Phyllis Diller Stewart and Tanja Hillis Ormiston. The three of us embarked on a novel-writing marathon together, and together we surged across the finish line. I couldn't have done it without both of you. Yay for us!

Thanks also to the various teachers who made a difference in my life: Ms. Anderson, who made Shakespeare come alive; Graham Nancekivell, who taught me how to master the essay; Dorothea Helms, aka the Writing Fairy, who showed me that anything worth saying can be said in five hundred words or less; Sue Reynolds and James Dewar for their hard work and dedication in offering the excellent writing course A Novel Approach.

Special thanks to Don Oravec, who graciously agreed to critique *Blown Red*. I will never forget that magical moment when an enthusiastic Don told me I was a real writer.

Acknowledgements

A great big LYLY to Andrew, Sarah, and Abby, not only for their enthusiastic support but also for stepping up with a twenty-something perspective whenever I sent an emergency text. "What is a hipster-doofus word for *groovy*?" Thanks to my sisters, Lesslie and Terry, for their unwavering support and to my mother, Audrey, for being my loudest cheerleader.

An especially huge thank you to my wonderful readers: Rosaria, Craig and Nancy, Megan, Wendy, Phyllis, Tanja, Jan L., Marilyn, Linda, and to Janice and Dan and all my wonderful friends at York Support Services Network and elsewhere, who offered support along the way.

Thanks to Becky Toyne and Alison Clarke for their editing genius, and to Anne McDermid for helping me navigate the publishing world.

I would like to acknowledge the heroic women who live with serious mental illness, addictions, and/or abuse. Your courage never fails to take my breath away. In some small way, I hope that I was able to give you a voice.

Finally, to my husband, and Number One Reader, Steve, I offer my deepest love and gratitude. I couldn't have done it without you. I am so lucky.

About the Author

Susan Philpott holds a master's degree in both science and social work. Over the years, she worked as a hotel chambermaid, furniture salesperson, teaching assistant at the University of Guelph, zookeeper, and mental health social worker. The mother of three adult children, she lives the dream in the wilds of Ontario with her husband, Steve. She keeps a canister of bear spray handy, just in case.